M

Echo Tre

THE COLLEC
OF H

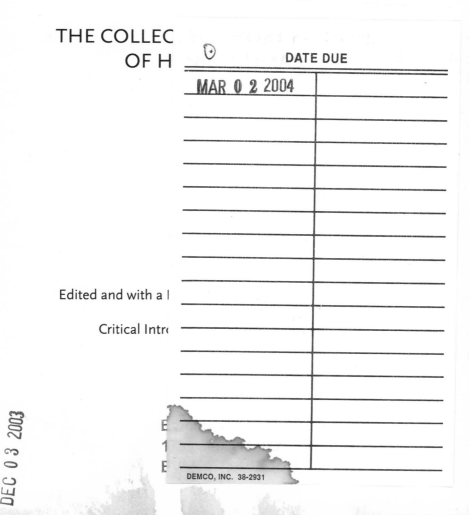

Edited and with a l

Critical Intr

LIBRARY OF CONGRESS CIP INFORMATION

Dumas, Henry, 1934–1968.
Echo tree : the collected short fiction of Henry Dumas / edited and with a
foreword by Eugene B. Redmond ; critical introduction by John S. Wright.
p. cm. — (Black arts movement series)
ISBN 1-56689-149-3 (alk. paper)
1. African Americans—Fiction 1. Redmond, Eugene. 11. Title. 111. Series.

PS3554.U43A6 2003
813'.54—DC21
2003055120

10 9 8 7 6 5 4 3 2 1
PRINTED IN CANADA

COFFEE HOUSE PRESS books are available to the trade through our
primary distributor, Consortium Book Sales & Distribution, 1045
Westgate Drive, Saint Paul, MN 55114. For personal orders,
catalogs, or other information, write to: Coffee House Press, 27
North Fourth Street, Suite 400, Minneapolis, MN 55401.

COFFEE HOUSE PRESS is a nonprofit literary publishing house.
Support from private foundations, corporate giving programs,
government programs, and generous individuals help make the
publication of our books possible. We gratefully acknowledge
their support in detail in the back of this book.

Acknowledgments for this book and the 1988 edition of *Goodbye, Sweetwater*
can be found at the back of this book.

In Memoriam for
DAVID HENRY DUMAS
(1958–1987)

Who Was Stamina.
Who Was Sweetsteel.
A Song Rendered Unto Us.
His Father's Witness.

&

MICHAEL HASSAN DUMAS
(1962–1994)

Whose accent was
Born on the wings
Of a country
His father loved

&

MARGARET WALKER ALEXANDER
(1915–1998)

GWENDOLYN BROOKS
(1917–2000)

RAYMOND R. PATTERSON
(1929–2001)

Pioneer-Navigators of the "Soular System,"

Advisory & Contributing Editors to Drumvoices Revue,

Trustees of the EBR Writers Club,

Contributors to a Special Henry Dumas (Double) Issue of
Black American Literature Forum *(Summer–Fall 1988)*

Shapers-Bearers of the Legacies Heralded & Extended by HD

THE COFFEE HOUSE PRESS
BLACK ARTS MOVEMENT SERIES

The postwar 1920s was the decade of the "New Negro" and the Jazz Age "Harlem Renaissance," or first Black Renaissance of literary, visual, and performing arts. In the 1960s and 70s Vietnam War era, counterpointing the white backlash against the civil rights movement and rising Black Power insurgencies of SNCC, CORE, and the Black Panthers, a self-proclaimed "New Breed" generation of black artists and intellectuals orchestrated what they called the Black Arts Movement.

This energetic and highly self-conscious Black Arts Movement accompanied and helped foster an explosion of urban black popular culture analogous in many ways to the cultural renaissance of the earlier era: Broadway shows and off-Broadway independent black theater; African inspired painting and sculpture and postmodern graphics; music-minded performance poetry and streetcorner "rapping"; avant-garde "free jazz" with consciously cultivated Afro-Asian references and mystical spirituality; independent and Hollywood-based black cinema riveted on street life and the politics of the urban ghettos; politico-religious sects and charismatic orators like Malcolm X and Stokely Carmichael; "soul music" performers such as Ray Charles, James Brown, Aretha Franklin—and a host of writers—who celebrated and critiqued it all from the vantage point of a newly articulated Third World conscious "Black Aesthetic."

Although most of the literary commentary on the movement emphasizes Black Arts poetry and drama, African American novelists too walked the walk. The transformations of black consciousness produced corollary changes in the forms, styles, techniques, and ethos of all the African American literary modes. The Coffee House Press Black Arts Movement Series is devoted to reprinting unavailable works of the period. In selecting the titles, the editorial panel of African American authors and scholars has employed no fixed guidelines. We have looked for works with distinctive voices, with historical value as windows on the literary and social world of the time, and with that subjective and impressionistic quality of "aliveness" that crosses boundaries of audience, era, and topicality. We have tried to choose work that is masterful, that deserves another chance and other audiences, and that will help us keep the windows to the future open.

Contents

INTRODUCTION TO HENRY DUMAS'S *Echo Tree*
BY JOHN S. WRIGHT

As best we know from circumstances that still remain unclear, on May 23, 1968, while seated unarmed in a Harlem subway station, a thirty-three year old father, husband, teacher, and emerging writer named Henry Dumas was confronted by a New York City Transit policeman who, in what may have been a case of mistaken identity or imagined provocation, summarily shot him dead. If, in the nationwide tumult that had followed the assassination of Martin Luther King, Jr. seven weeks earlier, such a death seemed journalistically uncompelling, the coming years would make it painfully clear that Henry Dumas's extraordinary artistic gifts and achievements make this particular loss tragically unique as well as compellingly ironic—given the extent to which his own posthumously published creative works infused mythic and ritual meaning into this American syndrome of deranged fatality.

Twenty years after his death, a 1988 special Henry Dumas issue of *Black American Literature Forum*, orchestrated by Eugene Redmond, his friend and literary executor, commemorated Dumas as a Black Arts Movement visionary and innovator of near sacred import. A cross-generational galaxy of writers that included Gwendolyn Brooks, Margaret Walker, Amiri Baraka, Toni Morrison, Jayne Cortez, Stephen Henderson, Pinkie Gordon Lane, Haki Madhubuti, E. Ethelbert Miller, Larry Neal, Arnold Rampersad, Ishmael Reed, Eleanor Traylor, and Quincy Troupe delivered a spectrum of homages that reveal the more precise ways in which, Redmond remarks, Dumas has come to be "idolized and emulated by a growing diasporean tribe of storytellers, critics, multiculturalists, Africanists, folklorists, mystics, students of the occult, linguists, songifiers, ethnomusicologists, and poets." [1] "A cult has grown up around Henry

Dumas—a very deserved cult," Morrison proclaimed in the course of welcoming ardent new proselytes such as Angela Davis, Melvin Van Peebles, John A. Williams; and she offered a devout rationale for their fervor: "he had completed work the quality and quantity of which are almost never achieved in several lifetimes. He was brilliant. He was magnetic, and he was an incredible artist."[2]

Henry Dumas had been born in Sweet Home, Arkansas on July 20, 1934, the son of Southern-born parents who, amidst the continuing northward migration of disaffected black fugitives from Dixie, transported him into the mid-1940s Harlem community. While it no longer had the allure of a Renaissance era "Negro Mecca," Harlem still offered prospects less manifestly threatening than those "down home." Dumas graduated from Harlem's Commerce High School in 1953, and attended City College briefly before marrying in 1955 and entering the Air Force, in which he served until 1957.[3] By then the father of two sons, he enrolled at Rutgers University, studying theology, etymology, sociology, and English while immersing himself increasingly in the civil rights movement and in the writers' groups and little magazines that were seedbeds for the emerging Black Arts Movement.

Black Arts advocate Larry Neal—another of the movement's guiding lights destined for premature demise—remembered meeting Dumas, then a virtual unknown, at Harlem's famous Liberation Bookstore in the mid-sixties, when Neal was still writing for *Liberator* magazine and had just begun assembling *Black Fire*—the manifesto anthology he and LeRoi Jones would publish in 1968.[4] Dumas had sent some manuscripts to *Liberator* for a short story contest that never materialized. But his querying Neal about the fate of his submissions served as the contact that would lead to the subsequent publication in *Black Fire* of three Dumas poems—"mosaic harlem," "knock on wood," and "cuttin down to size"—plus the riveting tale, "Fon." In the entry he supplied Jones and Neal for *Black Fire*'s list of contributors, Dumas offered the following capsule autobiography: "Born in Arkansas, came up to Harlem age of 10, Air Force and all that—spent a year in the great Arabian Peninsula—lived in New Jersey while attending Rutgers University. I am published in *Freedomways*, *Negro Digest*, *Umbra*, Hiram College *Poetry Review* and *Trace*. I have just finished my first novel which is long overdue. I am very much concerned about what is happening to my people and what we are doing with our precious tradition."[5]

Jones and Neal shared his concern and had designed *Black Fire* especially to showcase the talents and outlooks of emerging young black writers of the moment: the title they first proposed for the collection had been *Voices of the Black Nation*.[6] Cultural nationalism was at an apex; and Dumas's work debuted as part of *Black Fire*'s carefully orchestrated warrior uprising of "the wizards, the bards, the *babalawo*, the *sheikhs*, of Weusi Mchoro," who were engaged in the "conscious striving *(jihad)* of a nation coming back into focus."[7] Recently attracted to Maulana Ron Karenga's "Kawaida System," LeRoi Jones had renamed himself Ameer Baraka and, in a "self-consciously spiritual" phase, had become a Kawaida minister. The terms he employed to describe the young wordsmiths he anthologized served also to *invoke* their powers of magic, song, divination, theology, and ancestral blackness as weapons in a holy war for righteousness and justice. Weusi Mchoro—"the black scribes," in Kiswahili—was a phrase that reverberated in African American communities across the country at the time, as the tenets of Julius Nyerere's "African Socialism" and the allure of Afro-Arabic languages and literatures penetrated cultural nationalist theory and practice. In Baraka's, Neal's, and Dumas's Harlem three years earlier in 1965, a coalition of activist artists who called themselves Twentieth Century Creators had presciently adopted the new name, "Weusi"—"the Black Ones"—along with the corollary objectives of creating Black

Art for Black People, of developing a new iconography and visual vocabulary which, like those evolving in sister arts collectives such as Africobra, could help define and express a propulsively Black aesthetic.

More than any other work of fiction in *Black Fire,* Dumas's "Fon" demonstrated just how verbal analogues to the new iconography and visual vocabulary of Weusi Mchoro might operate. But the exhilarating "weirdness" and sense of the bizarre that seemed, in so many minds, to mark this and other fiction by Dumas somehow eluded the powers of decipherment within the Black Arts orbit at the time. From today's vantage point four decades later, it is easier to see that, beyond any sort of insular, self-referential "blackness," Dumas's revolutionary literary form and content bespeak an eclectic, hypermodern sensibility that fuses motifs of Pan-African ancestralism with the futuristic premises of science fiction and "crosshatched" fantasy tales, or with New Age political discourses familiar on the counter-cultural New Left. In the works published over the next two decades following his death, we find Dumas interlacing traditional Southern black folklore, legend, and myth with occult histories of the world and "instauration" themes linked in sixties "sidestream" fiction to utopian subversions promulgated by "Pariah Elites" or "Secret Masters." Elements of Gothic romance, the ghost story, biblical parable, the psychological thriller, and inner-space fiction blend with the naturalistic lynching story, the folkloric devil tale, local color reverie, or black nationalist apocalypse.

Today, re-reading the stories collected and arranged by Eugene Redmond in *Ark of Bones and Other Stories* (1970), *Rope of Wind* (1979), and then in *Goodbye, Sweetwater* (1988), it would be hard not to recognize the extent to which Dumas's conceptual breakthroughs to a new black literary sensibility were indeed facilitated by devices appropriated from the maturing international post-WWII literature of the fantastic, from supernatural fiction and "magical realism"—but, as Baraka noted, without being "euro-literary." Though critics before Tzvetan Todorov have conventionally associated the whole realm of "the fantastic" with political escapism, it is no less apparent that Dumas was resolutely putting the manifold devices of "the uncanny and the marvelous" to the service of black revolutionary moods of the time, which recognized, at least intuitively, that creating profound shifts in political structure is predicated on visions of alternate reality possible primarily through acts of artistic imagination.

Although "Ark of Bones," the opening story in this new collection, has become the most widely recognized single story by Dumas, it was "Fon" that first opened the window to his distinctive fictional world and style. So, to understand the patterns of action, character, imagery, and language in many of his works that have followed it into publication, we might approach "Fon" not so much in terms of its genre elements, as revisionary ghost story, or subverted lynching tale, or salvation parable—each of which it certainly incorporates—but as a more comprehensive cognitive and spiritual "giant step," to borrow a metaphor from John Coltrane, toward self-conscious mythopoesis. Behind much of the Black Arts Movement's strident literary nationalism, Larry Neal eventually concluded, lay a more quiet and contemplative but no less intense search for harmonious values, ontology, and self, a search that perceived Blackness as ultimately "embracing the Universal in man," and which employed the language of religious reform and the symbolism of ritual experience and spiritual transcendence.[8] Along with Baraka, Stanley Crouch, Paul Carter Harrison, Ishmael Reed, James Stewart, and Charles Fuller, Henry Dumas had become intrigued, Neal observed, with the aesthetic uses of African and African American cosmologies and mythological systems and their manifestations in music and the folk spirit.

By Neal's account, the Weusi Mchoro discovered Western precedents for their spiritual quest in such nineteenth century cultural nationalist endeavors as the European folk research of the Grimm Brothers and the Germanic mythology of Richard Wagner, in the Celtic Revival and Anglo-Irish Renaissance of Yeats, O'Casey, Synge, and Joyce, as well as in the American transcendentalist forays and local color folk experiments of Emerson, Whittier, Whitman, Bret Harte, Joel Chandler Harris, and Mark Twain. No less significantly, they discovered in the mid-century Francophone literature of Negritude and the 1950s and '60s postcolonial poetry, drama, and fiction of emerging Anglophone African and Caribbean writers, ways "to step out of the Western frame altogether." While Negritude poets like Leopold Senghor of Senegal and Aime Cesaire of Martinique had turned to the African oral tradition of the *dyelis,* or griots, for the canonical forms of a useable past, they still seemed to have symbiotic ties to the formal literature and philosophical systems of the West. Negritude, however, like the concepts of Black Power and the Black Aesthetic, remained a *defensive* frame, Neal conceded, shackled to the psychic resolution of cultural identity crises brought on by conflict with the West.[9]

This appeared to be less the case with the newer African writing that C.L.R. James spurred *Black Fire* contributors like Calvin Hernton to study: Chinua Achebe's *Things Fall Apart,* Ayi Kweh Armah's *The Beautyful Ones Are Not Yet Born,* Ngugi wa Thiongo's *Weep Not, Child,* Amos Tutuola's *The Palm-Wine Drinkard,* Ousmane Sembene's *God's Bits of Wood,* Camara Laye's *The Radiance of the King,* Cyprian Ekwensi's *Jagua Nana.*[10] As in classical African art and oral tradition, many of these works mixed realistic, mystical, and fantastic modes; and almost none were constituted so as to deliberately challenge or contradict the "reality" of mythological or religious or folkloric sources. Some of them, like *The Radiance of the King,* effected symbolic religious quests that fused fantastic animist beliefs imperceptibly with meditative koranic parables; while others, like *The Palm-Wine Drinkard* (1952) and Tutuola's even more extravagant *My Life in the Bush of Ghosts* (1954), presented examples of a modern African tradition of the fantastic not rooted in Euro-American myths and legends, and not preoccupied with the colonial or neocolonial Other. Though often filled with creatures and contexts beyond credulity, such works were not "fantasies" in the Western sense—they were not "invented" worlds, were not fairy tales or juveniles. But, like Western fabulation, magic realism, surrealism, and science fiction, they often employed myth to occupy the ontological space between the "weird" or "uncanny," on the one hand—stories where belief-defying events are overtly assigned a natural explanation—and, on the other hand, the "marvelous"—stories where events beyond credulity are clearly attributed to supernatural forces.[11]

Revealingly for the Black Arts Movement, the need to adapt or reinterpret classical African myths and legends led writers like Chinua Achebe to discover their own instructive affinities with Yeats and those mythopoetic attitudes of the Irish Renaissance that embraced interplay with supernatural creatures and the dead or the "living dead." For Henry Dumas and the Weusi Mchoro, as it had for the writers of the Celtic Revival, myth and folklore could provide a kind of "hygiene of the spirit," a means of seeing, of disciplined cognition and perception, that contravenes Cartesian science, capitalist materialism, and Anglo-Saxon abstraction.[12] The Irish Renaissance had revived the illuminist tradition of the eighteenth century Pagan Enlightenment and a theosophical cosmology saturated by hermeticist dream and symbol, together with the spiritual and political possibility of a Neoplatonic return to sources, to "the roots of the Trees of Knowledge and of Life"—as well as the possibility of recreating the Irish nation. Yeats believed, moreover, that mythology endows a race with its primordial unity, "marrying" it "to rock and hill," and rendering geography—"places of beauty or legendary associaton"—psychically and symbolically multivalent.[13] Clyde Taylor argues that, in an analogous way, Dumas became the first African American writer to burst through "the Veil" of nature, to master nature "as a subject for poetry on his way toward seizing an African conception of natural being" that takes as fundamental "black folks' reverence for fields, woods, and waters" and "our fabled love of coon-hunting, catfishing, our respect for root doctors."[14] Nature perceived as "an infinite order of balances, free of the sharp polarities of Western thought—good/evil, death/life, present/past"—merges in his world with a universe that is "relentlessly spiritual, never separated from a 'secular' order; and the deeper spirits frequently manifest themselves through the shallower spiritual texture of other living things—goats, birds, or blades of grass."[15]

Yeats had blended Celtic myths with a global potpourri in the course of fabricating his own private cosmology, which drew eclectically from his memberships in Madame Blavatsky's Theosophical Society and the hermeticist Order of the Golden Dawn, from intense study of Oriental religions, occult philosophies, magic, astrology, the Hebrew cabala, Neoplatonism, and the mystical "correspondences" of Blake and Swedenborg— alongside the revelations of spiritual masters communicated to him through his wife's automatic writing.[16] No single orienting tome akin to Yeats's outlandish and admittedly phantasmagoric *A Vision* would emerge from the Black Arts Movement. But Neal's brief compilation of "some sources for a poetic framework" capable of guiding the visionary explorations of Dumas and his peers included the following conceptual points of reference: first, Baraka's "seminal" ethnomusicological compass, *Blues People* (1963), whose "Herderian idea has had a profound impact on the recent generation of black writers"; next, Maya Deren's *Divine Horsemen: The Voodoo Gods of Haiti* (1953), which performed the feat, Joseph Campbell later declared, of delineating the Haitian religious tradition and its ritual choreography, "not anthropologically—as a 'relic of primeval ignorance and archaic speculation—but as an experienced and comprehended initiation into the mysteries of man's harmony within himself and with the cosmic process."[17]

Neal urged the Weusi Mchoro on to Cheikh Anta Diop's *The Cultural Unity of Black Africa* (1959), which had instigated the international "Afrocentric" revolt against European misinterpretations of African history, by debunking underlying theories of matriarchy and patriarchy propounded by J.J. Bachofen, Lewis Morgan, and Frederick Engels. Closer to home, W.E.B. Du Bois's *The World and Africa* (1947, 1965), reprinted two years after the world famous scholar's death in 1963, looked back from the "collapse of Europe" in World War II to "remind readers in this crisis of civilization, of how critical a part Africa has played in human history, past and present, and how impossible it is to forget this and rightly explain the present plight of mankind." [18] Janheinz Jahn's *Neo-African Literature: A History of Black Writing* (1968), followed up Jahn's earlier pioneering exploration in *Muntu* (1961) of Dogon, Yoruba, and Bantu cosmologies and aesthetics with a global analysis of Old and New World African languages and literatures that stressed continuities across space and time. Calvin Hernton, author of *Black Fire*'s essay on "Dynamite Growing Out of Their Skulls," recalls that reading *Muntu* "revealed a rich, 'hidden' landscape we had not recognized before. *The Palm-Wine Drinkard,* by Amos Tutuola, no longer appeared 'foreign', 'strange', or 'weird'; it was no longer thought to be some kind of African 'fairy tale'. We grasped the profound agency in black culture of song, dance, and rhythm." [19] To provide an offbeat complement to *Muntu,* and a Black Arts bridge back to the underground tradition of occultist scholarship, Neal proffered Godfrey Higgins's *Anacalypsis: an Attempt to Draw Aside the Veil of the Saitic Isis; or an Inquiry into the Origin of Languages, Nations, and Religions* (1829, 1965), the work of nineteenth century comparative Masonic mythography that broached a contra-Hellenist theory of the Afro-Asiatic origin of Graeco-Roman civilization in accord with what Martin Bernal, the author of the *Black Athena* series, today refers to as the Greeks' and Romans' own "ancient model" of their cultural origins and development.

In practice, this cluster of divinatory erudition constituted sources not only for a poetic framework, but for the edifice that would sustain prose fiction tales like "Fon" and Dumas's draft novel, *Jonoah and the Green Stone*, the intended trilogy he planned as an epic exploration of mid-twentieth century African American experience—and which he had initially named *Visible Man,* in generational counterpoint to Ralph Ellison's *Invisible Man.* But "Fon," in the much less than epic compass of a mere dozen pages, assimilates almost all of the loose Black Arts conceptual framework, along with an immersion in Islamic scripture, mythology, and language that had begun the year Dumas spent in the Arabian peninsula, and which eventually led to his being informally christened "Alhaji Samud."

"Fon" participates demonstably in Todorov's "literature of the fantastic"; but it is not "fantasy"—certainly not as escape or psychological safety valve. J.R.R. Tolkien argues that, even in that special form of the fantastic called fairy tales, what the reader experiences is not so much a flight *from* reality as a liberation *into* a wider reality; and C.S. Lewis makes the corollary assertion that "escape" in any case is a criticism of the reader rather than the work, and that escaping into *realistic* fiction is just as feasible psychologically.[20] Indeed "Fon" is very much about matters of the real world; but it conflates that world ambiguously with an alternate, transformational reality. As Todorov observes about the fantastic in general, "Fon" obliges the reader "to hesitate between a natural and a supernatural explanation of the events described" and at the same time to reject allegorical or "poetic" interpretations.[21] What begins as a seemingly familiar dirge of black victimization metamorphoses into a mysterious tale of avenging black ancestral spirits infiltrated or "astro-projected" into the framing structure of an otherwise naturalistic lynching story set at twilight on a back country road in Civil Rights era Mississippi. Its opening is both enigmatic and emblematic: "From the sky. A fragment of black rock about the size of a fist, sailing,

sailing. . . . CRAACK! The rear windshield breaks." Behind the windshield sits an archetypal Southern "cracker" named—ideographically, like so many Dumas characters—"Nillmon" (no man). He carries with him a triptych of cultural icons—a pistol, a half-bottle of whiskey, and a stick of dynamite—together with a murderous hatred of "niggers" that immediately targets the first black beings in sight—a group of children behind a billboard picture of "Uncle Sam saying *I Want You.*" Nillmon runs off in pursuit but loses sight of the children at the edge of a cotton field canebrake, where he instead confronts three inhabited shacks and the vague figure of an old granny on a porch, plus "the illusory tilt of a cross barely gleaming on top of a tiny wooden church far away." Defeated momentarily, he glances back to the roadside billboard, sees a gigantic black youth behind it on whom he can now turn his wrath and, at pistol point, forces him into the car, after first extorting the young man's name—"Fon," short for "Al*fon*so."

Uncertain from the youth's veiled responses whether Fon is arrogantly in need of a brutal "lesson" or merely a half-wit (the young giant carefully averts his eyes from the white man's), Nillmon summarily decides the former, that he "has a nigger that needs a thorough job"; and he drives home toward the white town to assemble a cohort of the like-minded. Along the way, Fon calmly tells the white man that he didn't break his window, that "nobody *threw* that rock," and that what he was doing behind the billboard was "teachin his brother to shoot his arrows." Nillmon subsequently becomes distracted at a roadside cattle-crossing by fond recollections of spilling black blood with impunity during his days as Sheriff Vacy's deputy, and Fon quietly slips out of the car and away from Nillmon's untender mercies. Silently cursing "all dead niggers," the brooding white vigilante continues on to town, where he recruits two eager co-conspirators. But the story Nillmon tells of seeing black folks at the canebrake shacks is disavowed by an old white man who warns him that the canebrake shacks are haunted, that "there ain't no niggers livin in them shacks," that none have since the days of a flood years earlier, when "the nigger woman put hoodoo on Vacy's papa."

Unbelieving and undeterred, Nillmon and his confederates drive back through the dark to the three shacks, torch the second, then head for the third, where they confront Fon on the porch, still unafraid, not far from an observing crowd of blacks over in front of the wooden church tower. The whites force Fon, once again, into Nillmon's car—but this time to a cheer from the black worshipers "such as the white men have never heard"—then take him back to the billboard where they prepare a lynching with dynamite and torches. Told again, at the point of death, to confess throwing the black stone, to divulge his brother's whereabouts, and then to pray before going to Hell, Fon instead repeats that the rock came from the sky, then defiantly declares that he is neither going to Hell nor in need of prayer—"prayer is for people who want help"—before advising the white men that his brother is in the trees somewhere. When one of the would-be lynchers slaps Fon as a last ugly preliminary, deadly arrows from unseen hands pierce in succession the necks of each white man; and Fon, revealed ambiguously as a possibly transmundane being on a salvific mission known only to the worshipers, stomps out the torches of the slain lynchers with his bare feet. The tale closes as he muses silently about the weakness of his adversaries and about the secret apocalyptic scourge with which he, his "brothers" in the canebrake church tower, and unnamed forces from the stars are patiently preparing to "set the whole earth on fire."

Here in "Fon," as in later stories like "Ark of Bones, " "Echo Tree," "Will the Circle Be Unbroken?," "Rope of Wind," "Rain God," and "The Metagenesis of Sunra," Dumas is engaged in the conscious fabrication, or re-fabrication of myths, an effort to "re-mythologize" human experience in reaction to the forces of dehumanization. This essentially mythopoetic attitude is rooted in the mental or spiritual state that impels certain artists to imagine "a metamorphosis of condition that allows them to free themselves from all controlling forces" and to live in a space and time that has become "reversible."[22] Dumas's *Black Fire* missive is designed to create a moment of enchantment for the reader that restores "the ineffable, the secret, the hidden, the sense of transcending the human condition and of returning to a primal language that enables us to experience an absolute freedom and mysterious beauty possible only outside the contingencies of ordinary life."[23] Disinclined to such transcendental hope, Nathaniel Hawthorne used Shakespeare's dour dictum in *King John* that "life is as tedious as a twice-told tale" to frame a collection of nineteenth century supernatural fictions in which the protagonists live in bondage to their nature and condition, and are "twice-told" in their conviction that nothing they do can release them from guilty reenactment of that which damned their ancestors—and will damn them as well.[24] In a decidedly antithetical way, Dumas employs the supernatural to foreground the existence of a horrifically oppressive legendary past in order to transform it into a story of liberation *from* bondage. Ghost stories and hauntings, Gillian Beer suggests, almost always have more to do with the *insurrection* than the *resurrection* of the dead; and in "Fon," the black dead that Nillmon curses are the generations of African ancestors—"four centuries of black eyes burning into four weak white men"—who are alive still animistically in nature as meteorites, sunbeams, moonlight, stars, and engaged in an insurrectionary struggle between sky gods and earth gods over human destiny.

Dumas's research in African and African American history, ethnography, and oral tradition had apparently led him—along with Baraka and many of the Black Arts intellects— to Melville Herskovits's *The Myth of the Negro Past* (1941), which mounted the first scientific case for widespread survival of specifically identifiable "Africanisms" in the New World, and from there to Herskovits's later cross-cultural analysis, *Dahomean Narrative* (1958), still the most authoritative study of religion, cosmology, and myth among the Fon peoples of present-day Benin.[25] The kingdom of the Fon has exercised greater fascination over Western minds than perhaps any other West African people.[26] From its remarkable seventeenth century genesis in the context of the expanding transatlantic slave trade, to the ceremonial complexities of its royal court and the warrior ethos of its vast army and fabled Amazon cohort, the Fon kingdom invited endless speculation about its religious continuities with ancient Egyptian solar theology and the pantheon of sky, earth, and thunder gods from which the worship of ancestral Vodu had first derived—and then had spread throughout the New World with the importation of vast numbers of Fon slaves. Fon sacred narratives all center on the cosmogonic myth that the universe was originally partitioned by the dualistic creator-god Mawu ("body divided"), typically female or androgynous—the eyes of the female aspect forming the moon, the eyes of the male aspect the sun.[27] As lunar-solar sky god, Mawu divided the realms of the universe among her offspring, the gods of the thunder and earth pantheons, and then retreated to the dominions of the stars, infinitely more populous than the relatively insignificant earth. The thunder god, Sogbo, represented iconographically by a ram-warrior painted red and armed with lightning, then quarreled relentlessly with the earth god, Agbe; and the cycle of earthly floods and droughts developed as a consequence of the ongoing cosmic conflagration.[28]

Dumas's tale is a "twice-told" version of Southern oral and literary lynching-burning rituals that in the re-telling is transformed mythopoetically into a modern reenactment of ancient Fon cosmological verities. As envisioned by Fon myth, in the primal struggle between good and evil, between sky gods and earth gods, human actors must regain their lost connections with the heavens to discover the god in themselves and to right the balance between cosmic drought and flood, between apocalyptic fire and the healing waters. They must build towers to the sky to re-establish communion with the divine. If so, heroes will again hold sway over heaven and earth, assuring that the culture they embody has heavenly sanction. Sublime or not, triumphant or not, they provide the promise of reunion with the messengers of heaven. So as a portent, a flaming stone falls from the sky—an analogue of the koranic *al-hajar al-aswad,* the Black Stone of the Ka'bah—and a hero emerges in its wake. In the course of events the flaming stone immolates in the face of evil, and from the bows of the thunder gods arrows ultimately rain down. At the beckoning of the sky pantheon, the hero has come out of a cosmic egg/omphalos to struggle with the Earth Devil/God for ascendancy. Accordingly, he makes a home in the sacred waters of the wilderness and establishes a community faithful to its heavenly ancestors and origins. A figure of priestly contemplation and inner calm, his secret strength is in his shadow, and as long as his secret remains safe, he plays the role of Savior God.[29]

So it is written in the book of destiny by Legba, the Fon divine trickster, the sacred linguist and transgressor of boundaries, the Vodu god of crossroads. And so in Dumas's re-mythologizing tale, "Alfonso's" name carries double meanings—mundane and spiritual—that identify the two planes of reality and ethical order in contention. Dumas incorporates Fon/Dahomean sacred narrative mythopoetically—as spiritual adventure that shares impossible experience in the form of *grace* which brings salvation and limitless freedom—rather than merely allegorically, as a fixed scheme of *ideas* in one-to-one secular correspondence. As literary artist Dumas's primary mythopoetic signatures are onomastic and metaphorical. The names of his solar hero and mundane antagonist connote their essential natures; and when the hero first appears—a silhouette descending from the heights, "almost liquid in his giant movements . . . swinging across a shaft of sunlight like an acrobat"—he bears the markings and colors and armaments of the High God, the "bands of fading light" that "make perfect angles and spears across his red shirt and black arms." Like the Fon thunder deity, the only child of Mawu, who in one telling of the myth is sent to earth to teach unseeing men the arts of living, Dumas's reincarnated spirit-warrior confronts a fallen world of human vice and victimization; and like the ancient Afro-Asiatic solar god whose side was pierced while on the sacrificial cross, and whose "Christian" worship the New World descendants of the Fon have sustained, Dumas's ebony avatar—pierced in the side by a lyncher's broken whiskey bottle—looks ultimately skyward for the coming of a New World Order. What Nillmon and his ilk ultimately face is not a force of earthly civil rights agitators descending from the above the Mason-Dixon line, but an apocalyptic instauration, a jihad, an interstellar visitation of spirit-warriors whose mere look contains disintegrative power beyond the merely human to withstand. But Dumas veils the transformational sacred mythos in the "ambiguous vision" of the fantastic until the story's denouement, in the wake of which the whole rich tapestry of his sacralizing signs becomes manifest.

Amiri Baraka and Larry Neal, years after publishing "Fon" in *Black Fire*, interpreted Dumas as an exponent of an "Afro-Surreal Expressionism" of which Zora Neale Hurston, Jean Toomer, and Toni Morrison were ostensibly the exemplary figures, and which had visual parallels in the painting of Jacob Lawrence, Vincent Smith, and Romare Bearden, and musical analogues in Duke Ellington, Thelonius Monk, John Coltrane, and Sun Ra. Two decades after *Black Fire*, Baraka reaffirmed that Dumas's power lay "in his skill at creating an entirely different world organically connected to this one," a "black mythological lyricism, strange yet *ethnically* familiar," a world comprised of fabulistic morality tales, "magical, resonating dream emotions and images; shifting ambiguous terror, mystery, implied revelation." [30] Dumas had become the agent of a New Blackness and a true art form—"not twenty 'Hate Whitey's' & a benediction of sweaty artificial flame, but actual black art, real ... and stunning."

Dumas's Afro-Surreal Expressionism was, Baraka asserted, a genuine embodiment of the Black Aesthetic—form and content—in its actual and contemporary lived life:

> MUSIC (drum—polyrhythm, percussive—song as laughter or tears), preacher and congregation, call and response, the frenzy! The *color* is the polyrhythm, refracted light! But this beauty and revelation have always existed in an historically material world. The African masks are shattered and cubed. Things float and fly. Darkness defines more than light. Even in the flow of plot, there are excursions and multi-layered ambiguities. As with Bearden, Dumas's is a world in which the broken glide by in search of the healing element, or are tragically oblivious to it.[31]

No antithesis with political praxis exists here, Baraka believes, since "the fact that [Dumas] was killed by Devils should continue to pull our coat, brains, heart to what is happening to us here in the Devil's land—and also what needs to happen. We can protect ourselves, our real selves, by protecting our artists (the formal expressive part of the race), only by *organizing*. By building large organizations based on nationalism."[32] Baraka grounds Afro-Surreal Expressionism in dialectical materialism, and attempts to ground Dumas in science as well as art, in the art and *science* of black liberation and the destruction of imperialism that becomes thereby scientifically predictable and "inherent in *nature*"—the nexus in which the tragedies and transformations of Dumas's fables so often take place.

Larry Neal retrospectively seconded Baraka's emphasis on Dumas's surreal mythological strangeness, and he glimpsed also Dumas's immersion in the cosmological mysteries of African American folklore. But Neal affirmed more specifically just how deeply Dumas had been influenced by the "occult and space science thing" in the music and theosophical mysticism of Sun Ra. A decade earlier, in an essay written when the Black Arts Movement seemed less in need of a post-mortem, Neal asserted that Henry Dumas, "more than any writer of the sixties, had effected a brilliant synthesis of Afro-American and African folk-and-myth ideas." [33] Dumas's importance "cannot be emphasized enough," he wrote; and Neal cited Dumas along with Ishmael Reed as a creator of literary works "which are uncompromising in their quest for Pan-African forms, yet refuse to sacrifice anything in the way of artistic integrity." [34] The New Blackness that Dumas and Reed were exploring presented the possibility of new forms of religious transcendence manifest in the NeoHoodoo Catechism that buttressed Reed's voodoo novels and poetry, as well as in the "analogous synthesis" that Dumas had erected from African American revisionings of biblical, vernacular, alchemical, and futuristic motifs gleaned from his own research and from his discipleship with Sun Ra.

"Like a lot of us," Neal recollected, Dumas "had been around Sun Ra in the Village"; and for Dumas, Neal suggested, the visionary musician, poet, prophet had been a very important force, "like a spiritual father." John Szwed, in his groundbreaking biography of Sun Ra, goes so far as to argue that Sun Ra was a "silent partner" in the Black Arts more generally, routinely present in Baraka's own historical allusions, "in the tone and pitch of his reading, in his sense of the importance of language, and in his consciousness of the possibilities of playing the spoken word against the written, unleashing the phonetics buried within the printed word." [35] Baraka acknowledges the debt in *Raise Race Rays Raze*, a book whose own titled homonymic reiterations evoke the symbolic heliolatry of Sun Ra's highly theatricalized and proselytic brand of Egyptology, and with it an ontological and historiographic Pan-African reorientation: "What Trane spoke of, speaks of, what [Sun] Ra means, where Pharaoh [Saunders] wd like to go, is clearly

another world. In (w)hich we are literally (and further) 'free'." [36]
Though Baraka had initially dubbed Sun Ra a "modernist
faddist" upon their first encounters during the early sixties,
extended exposure to Ra's strange conceptual universe led
Baraka to conclude that "Ra was so far out because he had the
true self-consciousness of the Afro American intellectual artist
revolutionary." So *Black Fire* had included eight poems by Sun
Ra—more than any other contributor.

For Ishmael Reed, the densely imagined cosmology
that undergirds Arkestra albums like *The Heliocentric Worlds of
Sun Ra* and *Cosmic Tones for Mental Therapy* could be read as an
extrapolatable "tone parallel"—to borrow the term Duke
Ellington applied to his Harlem Renaissance-inspired pro-
grammatic musical compositions—for the gnostic, syncretistic,
mystical historiography of Reed's hoodoo novel masterpiece,
Mumbo Jumbo, as well as for NeoHoodoo ritual poems like "I
Am a Cowboy in the Boat of Ra," which Szwed insists is Reed's
"most obvious point of contact with Sun Ra." The cosmic
metaphor of the Egyptian solar ark proved no less invigorating
for Henry Dumas, who fuses it with its biblical analogue to
singular effect in the gnostic tale, "Ark of Bones," which serves
as the titular lodestone for the posthumous first collection of
Dumas short fiction. Between 1965 and 1966, while employed as
a New York City social worker, Dumas communed devotedly
with Sun Ra: "of all the young black writers of the time, he was
closest to Sun Ra, and was inspired to draw on Egyptian and
West African mythological material, as well as Deep South
folksay and science fiction." [37] Dumas shared with Sun Ra the
"Afro-Baptist affinity for imagery of birds, eagles, the wind, and
other figures of escape, height, and majesty." He had been on his
way home from a rehearsal at Sun Ra's studio the day he was
killed; and when news of Dumas's death reached him, the
Arkestra leader raged unconsolably for days. [38]

Five years earlier, Dumas had written the liner notes for
Sun Ra's Arkestral experiment in "space music," *Cosmic Tones for*

Mental Therapy (recorded in 1963, issued 1967); and those notes proclaimed a seriocomic intergalactic instauration by the philosopher king of Afro-psychedelia, informing listeners in eye-winking breathlessness that:

THE QUASAR (QUASI-STELLAR OR STAR-LIKE) EMITTED RADIO WAVES REACHED OUR GALAXY AFTER 13 BILLION LIGHT YEARS. AND SUN RA, WHOSE MIND-WAVES ARE SYN-CHRONIZED TO NATURE WITH COORDINATED INTUITION, PRISMED THE VOICE OF THE QUASAR ON A COSMIC TONE PIANO AND THIS THUNDER IS LIKE SHOCK WAVES SHAKING AWAY THE STAGNATION OF LIFE IN THE MIND. WHEN YOU CAN MOVE IN A DIMENSION FASTER THAN LIGHT YOU SOLVE THE RIDDLE OF TIME AND YOUR MIND'S COSMOSIS COMPLETES THE EQUATION: LIFE EQUALS DEATH, FOR IN THE EXPANDING UNIVERSE THE INFINITE DESTROYS THE ILLUSION OF LIMITATIONS WHICH TRAP MAN TO THE PLANET EARTH. THE INFINITY OF CONTINUOUS AND ACCELERATING MOTION CHASES THE FLEEING GALAXY ANDROMEDA . . . THE MUSIC OF THIS FLIGHT ENERGIZES THE QUASAR AND SUN RA RECEIVES TONES FROM THAT QUASAR WHICH HAS BECOME PREGNANT WITH RADIATION AND THIS COMPLETES THE EQUATION: DEATH EQUALS LIFE IN A DYING UNIVERSE WHERE GALAXIES COLLIDE AND WHERE DEATH WEARS A MYSTERIOUS CROWN OF CONSTELLATIONS CALLED CREATION. TO HEAR THIS MUSIC IS TO HEAR THE SOLAR BAND OF REVE-LATION. THE TONES REVERBERATING HERE PASS THROUGH THE TIME SPECTRUM OF THE ARKESTRA'S MIND AND YOU SEE WITH EAR AND WITH EYE AND YOU BECOME THE METAGENESIS OF COSMIC ATOMS.[39]

In *The Ark and the Ankh*, the recently discovered interview tapes recorded by Dumas and Sun Ra in 1966, the bonds between the two artistic visionaries become even clearer. Myth and music emerge in their meditations as the dual agencies by which "spiritual rehabilitation and wisdom" can be communicated to a culture in crisis. Responding to Dumas's interrogations, Sun Ra presents himself as a seeker and as the oracular bridge from a "whole planet in trouble, in need of spiritual awakening," to another world where "nothing is impossible" and where "cosmic equations" hold the key to regaining the lost harmony originally given to humanity by the Creator. The Astro-Infinity music of his Arkestra, he proposes, is like himself a "force of nature" that speaks to transcendental goals in advance of earthly aspirations for freedom: "Astro-infinity music is beyond freedom. It is precision, discipline. It is not just freedom. It is coordination and sound interdependence. It is the design of another world."[40] The linking design to Dumas's quest for analogous literary means is perhaps best expressed in the words of a Nigerian reviewer he quotes to define Sun Ra's place in the New Music of the era: "This music is so complete in its awareness of and references to the American Negro experience that it corresponds 'to all the schools of the area of Negro musical heritage called jazz—going beyond the mainstream, past the New Wave and any other contemporary music played in America into a functional music that cultivates the sense of wonder, accustoms the mind to symbolic language, and restores 'myth' as an important and permanent part of culture."[41]

As such, Dumas's ties to what we might call the New Age "Astro-Africanity" of Sun Ra help distinguish his fictional world from the Euro-American surrealist orbit and from Latin American magical realism as well. Unlike most surrealists, Dumas only occasionally evinces manifest interest in Freudian psychological theories, dream imagery, or the ostensible "truths" of the unconscious. The surrealist abandonment of a consensual framing "reality," the deliberate randomness of its featured automatic writing, and the designedly irrational juxtaposition of realistic and fantastic phenomena that surrealist poets and painters have pursued, are not the primary techniques of estrangement that Dumas characteristically employs or that he saw modeled by extrapolation in the highly disciplined and precise "cosmic mathematics" of Sun Ra's arkestral soundings, nor in the fantastical tales flowing from the imaginations of contemporary African writers. Dumas's affinities with magic realism seem easier to divine. As in the fictions pouring after the 1940s from Alejo Carpentier, Jorge Luis Borges, and Gabriel García Márquez (though English translations of Márquez's work came too late to have been directly influential), in Henry Dumas's fiction the *terra firma* of the real world may indeed be "irradiated" with hallucinatory imagery, disjunctions of time and space, superpositions of the spirit world and the mundane. But that common-sense reality supplies the frame within or against which his narrations typically proceed. Magical realist techniques of re-interpreting reality have enabled writers from traditions rendered invisible in canonical histories and literature to reclaim lost cultural memories and to reinvigorate a sense of connectedness, security, and identity for themselves and their readers; and magical realist writers have not been averse to political engagement.[42] We still do not know enough, however, about Dumas's specific artistic influences to confirm direct magical realist influences, as we can by contrast for other Black Arts era writers like Toni Morrison or August Wilson.

But the clearest disjunction between Dumas's worldview and that of the Latin American originators of this movement may lie, once more, in his kinship with the Afro-psychedelic New Age astrophysics of the ancient astronaut of modern jazz, Sun Ra. One crucial aspect of Sun Ra's influence on Dumas seems to have been that Dumas was encouraged to adopt a metaphysics that was simultaneously more self-consciously "African"—on a temporal spectrum traceable from the ancient Egyptian to the modern Yoruba worlds—and yet more "scientific," as science has been redefined in the paradigm shift from Newtonian to quantum mechanics, and as it has in turn redefined the possibilities of literary and mythopoetic creation. Together with his liner notes for Sun Ra's *Cosmic Tones for Mental Therapy*, Dumas's cosmological fable, "The Metagenesis of Sunra," published here for the first time, unveils the playful metaphysics that undergirds Dumas's most distinctive ways of dramatizing character and the self. In this and his other more venturesome work, Dumas's intent seems determinedly at odds with the materialist realities and delineation of finite, sharply individuated "characters" that inhabit the nineteenth-century's Newtonian novelistic universe. Sun Ra's oracular worldview, shaped by the popular currents of Atomic Age "cosmic awareness" and post-World War II scientific discovery in astrophysics and genetic engineering, resonates to a quantum universe of boundlessness and metamorphosis for which the self is the most intimate and most mysterious metaphor. Accordingly, the fable of spiritual origins and development that Dumas spins around "the jazzman from outer space" models a narrative performance of what Sun Ra routinely referred to as "cosmo-drama." Appropriately, the concept of "metagenesis" that Dumas invokes to frame his own cosmo-dramatic homage originates in the polysyllabic discourse of modern evolutionary biology, where "metagenesis" is distinguished from "metamorphosis" by "that modification of parthenogenesis or alternate generation exhibited when an organism passes from the egg to the sexual form through a series of successively generated individuals differing from one another in form." Dumas grounds the fictional riff in a capsule narration of the "Terrible Child's"—Sun Ra's—hyperbolic myth-adventures among archetypalized Bluespeople, Redpeople, Yellowpeople, and Wofpeople as he journeys across the allegorical Kingdom of Ice. With elliptical aplomb, the fabulistic tongue-in-cheek paean to the free jazz cosmo-dramatist parodies the evolutionary mythopoetics of Madame Blavatsky's Theosophical Society—one of Sun Ra's oft-appropriated touchstones—and its gnostic rhetoric of "root races," Hyperborean Ages, karmic reincarnation, fifth-, sixth-, seventh-dimension exploration, and Egypto-Hindu-Sufi esotericism.

Afro-psychedelic influences notwithstanding, commentators trying to place Henry Dumas in the African American literary tradition have busily discovered antecedents for his distinctive voice and style in earlier Harlem Renaissance writers Jean Toomer, Langston Hughes, and Zora Neale Hurston, and in post-World War II figures James Baldwin, Ralph Ellison, Ernest Gaines, and Toni Morrison (who as a Random House editor shepherded the publication of his poetry collection, *Play Ebony Play Ivory*, and the short stories in *Ark of Bones*). But the strongest analogue to Dumas's unique synthesis of African American folk spirituality, Judaeo-Christian mythography, Afro-Eastern gnosticism, and modern post-Newtonian science may be in the world of spiritualized landscapes, polyethnic historical tracings, and psychic alchemy created by the prolific Caribbean novelist-critic, Wilson Harris. Beginning in 1960-63 with his *Guyana Quartet* novels—*Palace of the Peacock, The Far Journey of Oudin, The Whole Armour,* and *The Secret Laddder*—Harris became perhaps the premier Caribbean novelist of his generation by rejecting realism as blind to "the parallel universes of the Imagination," by developing a fictional method rooted in metaphorical transformations rather than in documentary-like reportage, and by fabricating an alchemistic historical perspective that draws the topographies of New World Arawak, Carib, Afro-Caribbean, Afro-Asian, and Euro-American mythologies into a luminous tapestry of "black holes," "quarks," and "neutrinos" visible only against the backdrop of what he calls "the womb of space." [43]

Wilson Harris was read enthusiastically in Black Arts literary circles; and like Harris, Henry Dumas employs the mind of science to expand the imaginative possibilities of his literary universe. But unlike Harris or his mentor Sun Ra, Dumas's own metagenesis was aborted by fate. The combinational and configurational principles behind the array of experimental fictions he created have been left incomplete or unarticulated; and as new pieces in the puzzle of his creative life and death have appeared, we are forced to rethink what we think we know about him and his work. Along with "The Metagenesis of Sunra," the prose creations appearing in this collection for the first time—"Scout," "Children of the Sun," "The Bewitching Bag," "The Man Who Could See Through Fog," "Riot or Revolt?," and "My Brother, My Brother"—conform in certain ways to what previous patterns in Dumas's work might lead us to expect; but in other instances they surprise. "Scout" is a fragmentary Kafkaesque fable of adolescent anxiety— sexual, filial, monetary—set in the unexpected world of Harlem boy scouts at parade time. Its story-within-a-story is related by interlinked first-person narrators so that it presents a quasi-surrealistic maze of parabolic encounters with dream-like figures—first a nubile young seductress and then a reminiscing scoutmaster—who turn the rote maxims of scouting into metaphysical riddles fielded quizzically by an ambivalent young tenderfoot. Briefest of the new offerings, "Children of the Sun" gives us a laconic rural sketch of an interracial group of boys confronting in disparate, uncertain ways the pain and terror of dying, during the awkward moments after having reluctantly killed a mad dog belonging to one of young friends. "The Bewitching Bag," appears to be what folklorists call a *Kunstmarchen*, a near-transcriptive literary retelling of an originally oral tale, in this case an instance of the rich lode of black Southern devil lore. In Dumas's rendering it combines conventional folkloric motifs about an escape-bound liaison between a man condemned to hell and the devil's infamous but disaffected daughter; and it features a Bunyanesque pilgrim's progress along allegorical Roads of Grace, Hope, Illumination, and Love & Respect, together with a repertoire of folk rhymes, chants, and songs interwoven within the frame narrative. "The Man Who Could See Through Fog" is a dryly comic, thoroughly modern but mundane story of machine-made human folly set on a Texas military post, as related by an ex-stable hand for the nearby rodeo who has become bored and bruised from working with animals, and who takes instead a job driving insect-fogging machinery better suited to asphyxiating humans than killing insects. Finally, "My Brother, My Brother" is a first-person tale of colonial Africa set in a decidedly unspecific geographic and ethnographic terrain: under threats of death to them and their families by mechanized invaders, two African tribesmen are forced to play a deadly "game" for the invaders' entertainment in which they are impelled by a mysterious, searing force-field toward a crocodile-infested river which they must cross before ultimately fighting to the death. Betrayed by his self-seeking companion, the storyteller must finally kill his spiritual brother in self-defense, then raise the titled lament for his lost soul-mate.

Among the works included here from earlier collections, the redoubtable "Ark of Bones" provides what is perhaps Henry Dumas's most startling fusion of conjure lore and biblical revelation, in a vernacular first-person narrative that converts the familiar conventions of the archetypal adolescent fishing adventure into an intensely symbolic confrontation between two antithetical communities of belief over how best to face a legacy of terror and spiritual assault. Like "Ark of Bones," "Echo Tree," the title story of this new cornucopia, is a parabolic, allegorical tale of gnosis—of ancient, secret wisdom and the deep need to transmit it from one generation to the next, from knower to novice, from believer to unbeliever. Both tales center around evanescent spiritual experiences shared by two young black men, one preternaturally a seer, the other less gifted metaphysically, less open to the invisible world of sacramental forces revealed by nature or by trans-historical visitation. These double-souled central experiences both entail the vexing, perennially painful problem of whether and how to create communion between the living and the spirits of the dead. "Ark of Bones" proposes one imaginative answer to that problem—a fantastical and macabre one, but somehow still rich with hope and consolation. "Echo Tree," drawing much more closely on the incantatory word-magic of children's fairy tales, and linked quite probably by its title to the cartoon fancies of Winnie the Pooh, proposes yet another. A modern "wonder tale" drenched in the oral rapture inspired by magical forces in the life-giving Southern landscape, "Echo Tree" nonetheless derives much of its narrative power from the larger-souled young chanter's repeated warnings to his mate that the latter's journey northward to the land of the dead has turned his own soul inanimate and unreachable.

Dumas gives his own deepest recurring fear and wonder symbolic form here, but in so doing makes it possible for us, in his wake, to share the warning signs and to seek our own healings. The reverberating question he troubled Sun Ra with prior to undertaking his own final fatal journey remains behind as well for us to remember him by as a seeker and a seer: "If the citizens of a necropolis are dead, how does one resurrect them? I mean . . . how are the souls called forth?"

John S. Wright
Minneapolis
August 26, 2003

1 Eugene Redmond, "The Ancient and Recent Voices within Henry Dumas," *Black American Literature Forum* [BALF], 22, (Summer 1988), 143.

2 Toni Morrison, "On Behalf of Henry Dumas," BALF, 22, 310-11.

3 Carolyn Mitchell, "Henry Dumas," *Dictionary of Literary Biography*, 41, (Detroit: Gale Research Co., 1985), 90.

4 Larry Neal, "Henry Dumas: Literary Landmark," BALF, 313.

5 Henry Dumas, in LeRoi Jones & Larry Neal, *Black Fire: An Anthology of Afro-American Writing* (New York: William Morrow & Co., 1968), 661.

6 Theodore Hudson, *From LeRoi Jones to Amiri Baraka: The Literary Works* (Durham, NC: Duke University Press, 1973), 37.

7 Ameer Baraka, Foreword, *Black Fire*, xvii.

8 Larry Neal, "The Black Contribution to American Letters: Part II, The Writer as Activist—1960 and After," in Mabel Smythe, ed., *The Black American Reference Book* (Englewood Cliffs, NJ: Prentice-Hall, Inc., 1976), 776.

9 Neal, 774.

10 Calvin Hernton, Introduction to Janheinz Jah, *Muntu: African Culture and the Western World* (New York: Grove Weidenfeld, 1990), xi.

11 John Clute & John Grant, eds., *The Encyclopedia of Fantasy* (New York: St. Martin's Press, 1997), 335.

12 "Myth in Twentieth-Century English Literature," in Yves Bonnefoy, compiler, *Mythologies*, 2 (Chicago: University of Chicago Press, 1991), 783.

13 "Myth in Twentieth-Century English Literature," 783.

14 Clyde Taylor, "Henry Dumas: Legacy of a Long-Breath Singer," BALF, 22, 356-7.

15 Clyde, Taylor, 357.

16 "Myth in Twentieth-Century English Literature," 783.

17 Joseph Campbell, Editor's Foreword to Maya Deren, *Divine Horsemen: The Living Gods of Haiti* (Kingston, NY: Documentext, 1983), xi.

18 W.E.B. DuBois, *The World and Africa* (Millwood, NY: Kraus-Thompson, 1976), xi.

19 Hernton, xxiii.

20 Quoted in Gary K. Wolfe, ed., *Critical Terms for Science Fiction and Fantasy* (New York: Greenwood Press, 1986), 31.

21 Tzvetan Todorov, *The Fantastic: A Structural Approach to a Literary Genre* (Cleveland: The Press of Case Western Reserve University, 1973), 33.

22 Max Bilen, "The Mythico-Poetic Attitude," in Pierre Brunel, *Companion to Literary Myths, Heroes and Archetypes* (London: Routledge Press, 1995), 862.

23 Max Bilen, 862-3.

24 *Encyclopedia of Fantasy*, 968.

25 Melville Herskovits, *The Myth of the Negro Past* (Boston: Beacon Press,

1958), and Melville and Francis S. Herskovits, *Dahomean Narrative: A Cross-Cultural Analysis* (Evanston: Northwestern University Press, 1958).

26 "Fon," in Richard Carlisle, ed., *The Illustrated Encyclopedia of Mankind*, 5, (New York: Marshall Cavendish, 1984), 631-33.

27 Harold Scheub, ed., *A Dictionary of African Mythology* (New York: Oxford University Press, 2000), 142.

28 Scheub, 224.

29 Scheub, 348.

30 Amiri Baraka, "Preface: The Works of Henry Dumas—A New Blackness," BALF, 22, 163. [a slightly amended version of Baraka's 1970 preface to Dumas's posthumous collection, *Poetry for My People* (Carbondale: Southern Illinois University Press.

31 Amiri Baraka, "Henry Dumas: Afro-Surreal Expressionist," BALF, 22, 165.

32 Baraka, "Preface: The Works of Henry Dumas . . . ," 163.

33 Larry Neal, "The Black Contribution to American Letters," 789.

34 Larry Neal, "The Black Contribution to American Letters," 788, 784.

35 John Szwed, *Space Is the Place: The Lives and Times of Sun Ra* (New York: Pantheon Books, 1997), 209.

36 Amiri Baraka, quoted in John Szwed, *Space Is the Place*, 210.

37 Szwed, 223.

38 Szwed, 223.

39 Henry Dumas, Liner Notes to Sun Ra, *Cosmic Tones for Mental Therapy*, reissued on CD, Evidence Music, ECD 22036, 1992.

40 Liner Notes to *The Ark and the Ankh: Sun Ra/Henry Dumas in Conversation, 1966*, CD, IKEF, IKEF 02, 2002, 4.

41 Liner Notes, *The Ark and the Ankh*, 3.

42 "Magic Realism," in Paul Schellinger, ed., *Encyclopedia of the Novel*, 2 (Chicago: Fitzroy Dearborn Publishers, 1998), 797.

43 Wilson Harris, *The Womb of Space: The Cross-Cultural Imagination* (Westport, CT: Greenwood Press, 1983), 28, 48.

Echo of a Dumas-Storied Arkansippi Conch/us/nest
(1934–1968 . . . 1968–2003)

Aba, I consecrate my bones.
Take my soul up and plant it again.
Your will shall be my hand.
When I strike you strike.
My eyes shall see only thee.
I shall set my brother free.
Aba, this bone is thy seal.
> —from "Ark of Bones"

Dear Ancient and New(est) Members of the Dumas *cult:*

Thirty-five years ago Henry Lee Dumas transitioned (from the *natural)* to the *spectacunatural*—thus entering the world that informs and configures so much of his writing and thought. In the intervening decades—which have filled more than half of my life—our "stories" have occasionally intertwined or over-lapped. *Possessed* of such layered complexity and collaboration, one easily gleans, even without an overt [drum-]voicing of the point, that there is more to this "fore"- and "aft"-word than meets the eye—or ear—literally and bi-dimensionally. Therefore, I shall not try to "strike through the mast"—or "mask"—but simply touch down on surfaces of the Soular System intermittently, much like a pebble might be scooted across a lake by one of HD's young characters in "Ark of Bones," "Echo Tree," "The Crossing," "Double Nigger" or "Rain God."
    Having known and yet "(k)not" known "Hank"—a.k.a. "Ankh" a.k.a. "Samud"—has been one of the distinguished joys

and inextinguishable plagues of my career as a poet, "accidental" academician, cultural worker, literary executor, and, now, elder. *Joy* because reading—and helping to tidy—HD's scrolls has been an experience of pure euphoric grit. *Plague* because the unclarified circumstances of his premature death—in 1968—still "ride" the memory; because his already brilliant oeuvre—defying category, catechism, and precedent—simultaneously holds inestimable promise; because his *legacy* challenges survivors to commit it to memory-fuel for the next leg of the race. And *career* because it, too, scripts us toward the past (and *pass),* helmed by HD's drum-rife blues odes, quite prophetic and therapeutic in their antiphonal/contrapuntal rejoinders to the anti-familistic and "commerce" motifs lacing so many psyches of the future . . .

> Now Sunra took his beautiful horn and aimed it toward the great mountain where dwelled the King of Ice and all his Woflords. And when the ebony horn grew into the third note this is what happened.
>
> All over the land, from north to south, the painted people—too hot to get near now—began to march. They did not follow any outward road or way, but . . . march[ed] toward the direction of the drum. For some time now, the Wofpeople had been trying to destroy the drum. . . . They bombed it, tried to set it afire, shot great guns at it. They even tried to round up all the painted people now, because they knew there was a connection between them and the drum's power. But the people were too hot to handle. The Kingdom of Ice began to thaw. And the heat was on. A helio heat.
>
> Suddenly the horn broke into full chorus and light came from it; and sweet sounds, deadly to the untrained ear; and the sounds penetrated and traveled and worked miracles.
>
> —from "The Metagenesis of Sunra"

"Ancient" and "recent"—and "ancestral" and "fresh"—echo the "Arkansippi" windage I've saddled to ride Dumas's multi-fabulous *ancestrails*. And few recent orbits, outside of Arkansas, Mississippi, and East Saint Louis (Illinois), have made me as aware of the def accuracy of his windage as Oberlin College (Ohio), whose African American Studies Department celebrated its thirtieth anniversary last April. Oberlin (circa 2003) created a riotous mixture of Dumas's life, death, and after- or neo-life: his river of drumscrolls flooding the banks of my memory before, during, and after I performed his famous poem "Ngoma."—fully blown with "familistic" call-and-response—the way he'd taught us to "reed" and "rite" it in East St. Louis. His "circle" continued "unbroken," yes, for Oberlin was the sanctuary to which I souljourned thirty-four years ago, in 1969, fifteen months after HD's death. At the time of his passing, our colleagueship was just ten months old: we were testy Black Arts Movement poets, expatriates from the nations of *Beat* and *Bohemia*, fresh-hewn aficionados of the "African Continuum," and teacher-counselors at Southern Illinois University's Experiment in Higher Education. Strategically, EHE also housed Madame Katherine Dunham's Performing Arts Training Center with its colorful-audible and popular seminars that complemented EHE's offerings: Caribbean dances, Afro-Cuban/Haitian drumming, Wolof and French languages, and martial arts including Brazilian *capoeira*. Some of our colleagues in EHE-PATC were actress-singer-dancer Camille Yarbrough, Cuban percussionist extraordinaire Rene Calvin, sociologist Joyce Ladner, World Saxophone Quartet co-founder Julius Hemphill, author Shelby Steele, and Senegalese master drummer Mor Thiam. Filmmaker Warrington Hudlin and poet-photographer Sherman Fowler are just two of Dumas's former students who later achieved great heights.

It was a time of enormous inter/national ferment—of the variety Dumas captures in scrolls like "Goodbye, Sweetwater," "Strike and Fade," "The Marchers," and "Riot or Revolt?"—and

EHE-PATC was at the center of the lower Midwest's version of that artistic-cultural vortex *cum* Black Arts Movement:

> The two organizations frequently presented concerts or performances during which Dumas joined other area literary artists and activists in choral readings. [These] collaborative *rituals* usually featured drum, dance, and woodwind ensembles. A serious student of Astro-ritual forms (as witnessed by his preoccupation with ancient fusion arts and philosophies, and . . . his profound love for Margaret Walker, James Brown, blues and gospel, John Coltrane, Sun Ra, and Malcolm X), Dumas was able to bring all of his "selves" into focus/play during those . . . happenings.(Redmond, *Black American Literature Forum*, Summer 1988, p. 152)

Although officially at Oberlin (1969) to teach, write, and conduct campus-community workshops, unofficially, I was immersed in its library of rare Afro-Americana and co-editing (with Hale Chatfield, HD's friend at Hiram College) Dumas's first posthumously published fiction and poetry: *Ark of Bones and Other Stories* and *Poetry for My People*. None other than Black Arts Oba Amiri Baraka and much-laureled poet Jay Wright provided the preface and introduction respectively for *Poetry*.

Across cultures, generations, and genders, seasoned and novice critics salivated over *Ark* and *Poetry*, released in 1970 by SIU Press (Carbondale)—in clothbound editions that sold out quickly—and in 1974 by Random House (in cloth and paperback). Under the RH imprint, I renamed the poetry *Play Ebony Play Ivory* to avoid readers' confusing it with Margaret Walker's pioneering 1942 volume, *For My People*. All nine of *Ark*'s stories were retained in the RH edition, beginning with "Ark of Bones" and ending with "Fon." Prior to the RH releases, however—and bearing trappings of the Black Arts

Movement—the "cult" segued and sashayed into Oberlin, the second posthumous "laboratory" (after East St. Louis) for the critical study of Dumas's stories and poems. Students like John "Bird" Brooks, Elaine Robinson, and Sherman Fowler (EHE); Avery Brooks, Cheryl Willis, and Michael Lythcott (Oberlin); and colleagues William Davis and (painter-Africanist) Oliver Jackson (who'd also left EHE for Oberlin) helped pace me through manuscripts and galleys en route to *Ark* and *Poetry*. Although he had placed poems and stories in litmags and collections (like *Umbra, Hiram Poetry Review, Negro Digest,* and *Black Fire),* HD did not "witness" publication of a full-length volume of his writings until after his death.

What Toni Morrison referred to as a "very deserved cult" (mid-1970s) and Jayne Cortez labeled "The Henry Dumas Movement" (mid-1980s) was launched during 1967–70 in East St. Louis and Oberlin. For it was in "East Boogie" that EHE administrators Donald Henderson and Edward Crosby proposed publication of HD's volumes to SIU Press; and at Oberlin that Dumas's manuscripts and proofs were poured over in classrooms and editors' work rooms. The "circle" was further empowered when, following the East St. Louis-Oberlin experience, two events proved fortuitous to the Dumas movement and helped establish the third "laboratory" for excavation of his literary genius: my relocation (from Oberlin) to California State University-Sacramento (1970) and the discovery of HD's then-out-of-print scrolls (1973) by Random House Senior Editor Morrison (during a visit to Quincy Troupe's New York apartment). Having met in the summer of 1969 at St. Louis's Lindenwood University, Troupe and I discovered that we both were headed to Ohio—he to Ohio University-Athens and I to Oberlin—as writers-in-residence. While in Ohio we visited each other regularly (commiserating also with Clevelanders Norman Jordan and Russell Atkins, and Wilberforce U's Calvin Hernton) and Troupe was privy to HD's original manuscripts and galleys prior to their SIU Press releases. Troupe would later publish Dumas's writings in his journal *Confrontation* and in *Giant Talk: An Anthology of Third World Writings,* which he co-edited with Rainer Schulte.

Sacramento became the launching pad for an almost decade-length collaboration—with Morrison and CSUS colleagues (and students/departments) like Marie Collins, Ted Hornback, Keith Jefferson, Oliver Jackson (who'd also relocated from Oberlin to CSUS), David Covin and Otis Scott of Pan-African Studies, Ronald Tibbs (another HD/EHE student), Maya Angelou, George Austin Jones, and Tommy Ellis—to produce and promote other HD fictions: *Jonoah and the Green Stone* (novel, 1976) and *Rope of Wind and Other Stories* (1979). The Sacramento/New York collaboration also led to the re-issuing of *Ark* and *Poetry* (*Ebony/Ivory*), for which Morrison shepherded New York-area celebrations. In September of 1974, for example, she sent out a letter from Random House announcing that:

> This will be a gathering for those who knew [Henry Dumas], for those who know his work, and for those who are being introduced to him. Already several people have agreed to come and read his work: Angela Davis will read, I will read, Jayne Cortez will read, Eugene Redmond will read—and Melvin Van Peebles, John Williams, and many, many others. . . .
>
> We are planning to have this commemorative book party at the Center for Inter-American Relations at 680 Park Avenue, New York City, from 6:00–9:00 P.M. on October 13. We will be calling together a number of artists and scholars to pay tribute to this extraordinary talent. We expect, of course, a large press representation, but I don't want our gathering to lose any of its beauty
> because of that.

Among "others" participating in the reading were vocal stylist Leon Thomas, June Jordan, Larry Neal, Baraka, Troupe, and Vertamae Grovesnor.

Upon the release of *Rope of Wind*, which contained twelve stories previously unpublished in book form, similar celebrations were held at Pegasus in New York and at numerous points in between the East and West Coasts. *Rope* further confirmed HD's promise and fed an appetite whetted by *Ark*. Consequently, a wider English-reading world began engaging Dumas (whom Baraka had called "an underground deity" in 1969) in homes, classrooms, workshops, prisons, Black Arts centers, and pulpits. At csus, HD's work became a central feature of the annual Third World Writers and Thinkers Symposium (1974-1982) and the Sons/Ancestors Players, founded by Paul Carter Harrison; and during the mid-to-late 1970s a Henry Dumas Creative Writers Workshop met at Sacramento's Women's Civic Center. Meanwhile, fewer than 100 miles away, in the San Francisco Bay Area, reception to HD's "ritings" was particularly powerful and sustained: numerous book celebrations (including an "Awushioo" at Mary Ann Pollar's Rainbow Sign) were held at and around uc Berkeley, sf State u, and community colleges, led by Clyde Taylor, Ishmael Reed, Cecil Brown, Joyce Carol Thomas, Maya Angelou, George Barlow, a Berkeley student named Terry McMillan, a relatively unknown Ntozake Shange, David Henderson, Margaret Wilkerson, and Adam David Miller, among others.

Between 1974 and 1979 HD's scrolls were staged, recited, entered in contests, filmed, put to music, and sung in Los Angeles (Inner City Cultural Center/Mafundi Institute), Chicago (Kuumba Theater/Culture Messengers Studio), nyc (Countee Colleen Library/Liberation Bookstore/Black Roots Festival), Baton Rouge (Southern u), Washington, dc (Howard u/Drum & Spear Bookstore), University of Wisconsin-Madison, University of Lagos-Nigeria, and the Afrika-Studi entrum at Leiden U (Holland). Dumas's story, "Thalia," won first prize in a 1976 *Black Scholar* magazine literary contest judged by James Baldwin and Joyce Ladner. That same year, during a party at Maya Angelou's Sonoma (CA) home (attended by scores of literati and culturati), Baldwin heaped praise on HD, calling him "important . . . important . . . very important." Also in 1976, Doubleday released my own *Drumvoices: The Mission of Afro-American Poetry*—which owed great "conceptual" debt to the Dumas-Dunham influence—and my native city, East St. Louis, named me its first poet laureate. PATC's drummers and dancers, and the words of HD, were centerpieces of the laureate appointment ceremony at Lincoln Park, attended by, among others, brother-poet-friend Troupe.

In East St. Louis—where many of Dumas's former students were (and are) teaching, doctoring, lawyering, and social working—he was/is read and recited widely. Simultaneously, SIU-East St. Louis and Kent State University (via its Pan-African Studies Department) established Henry Dumas Memorial Libraries; and Hiram College, where Hank had administered an Upward Bound Program before moving to East St. Louis, offered an Annual Henry Dumas Creative Writing Award through its *Poetry Review*.

Although his works were out of print for much of the 1980s, Dumas remained on the "screen" with "cult" members exchanging dog-eared copies of precious volumes and broadening the appreciation for his *vision* via lectures, written articles, and conferences. There was also an unsuccessful effort to have HD's "imagination" adapted to the commercial screen. Thanks to Morrison, his books, with letters of introduction and copies of reviews, were made available to Bill Cosby, Ossie Davis, Ruby Dee, and executives of major movie studios. While several more books of fiction appeared (*Ark, Jonoah*, and *Rope)*, it was not until 1988 that a collection of collections (*Goodbye, Sweewater*) came out from Thunder's Mouth Press. Previously un-anthologized stories, like "Rain God," "Thalia," and

"Goodbye, Sweetwater" were included along with excerpts from the novel *Jonoah*. Set off with titles from previous books, *Goodbye* retained eight stories from "Ark," nine of the twelve tales from *Rope*, and introduced readers to the three new stories listed above. Any online search engine will testify to the wonder-filled reception garnered by *Goodbye*. Whether it was Toni Morrison, Amiri Baraka, or Maya Angelou reading his fiction and poetry at SRO book parties; John O'Brien and Doris Grumbach reviewing him glowingly in the *Chicago Tribune* or *The New York Times;* or George Jones, Tommy Ellis, Keith Jefferson, and Ron Tibbs performing him in Sacramento or Cliff Top, West Virginia, the enormous power and genius of HD was celebrated. Also in 1988, I guest-edited a special HD issue of *Black American Literature Forum* (now *African American Review)* containing more than fifty critical essays, letters, interviews, and poems by Hank, Angelou, Russell Atkins, Arnold Rampersad, Cortez, Barlow, Troupe, Loretta Dumas (Dumas's widow), Jabari Asim, Vernon February, Shirley LeFlore, John A. Williams, Clyde Taylor, Margaret Walker Alexander, Fowler, Darlene Roy, Raymond Patterson, Herman Cromwell Gilbert, Michael Castro, Charles Wartts, Craig Werner, Eleanor Traylor, and Morrison. In 1989, Thunder's Mouth brought out *Knees of a Natural Man*, HD's selected poetry (combining the best of *Poetry* and *Play Ebony Play Ivory).*

Again, East St. Louis, this time via its public school district, came under the spell of HD's mythical/cyclical/biblical *badness*, purchasing several hundred copies of *Goodbye, Sweetwater* and BALF. Having returned to "East Boogie" from CSUS, I had become special assistant to the superintendent (of schools) for cultural and language arts (1985-1989). After the pattern of HD-oriented studies at EHE-PATC, Oberlin, CSUS, University of Wisconsin, Southern University-Baton Rouge, and elsewhere, I established an institute to train teachers and students in the exploration of HD's art and imagination. Hence, East St. Louis—coupled with Wayne State University in Detroit, where I was writer-in-residence from 1989–90—became the fourth "laboratory" for HD's art and ideas. Again his circle remained unbroken. Returning from a ten-year stay in Nigeria, HD's protégé Sherman Fowler became my assistant in the schools. During this same time, two peak events (aside from vigorous HD programming in the Midwest) were sparked by publication of *Goodbye* and BALF: an evening of readings by Cortez, Morrison, Troupe, and Xam Cartier at NY's Negro Ensemble Theatre; and a panel discussion-reading-dramatization at the Schomburg Center for Research in Black Culture. The Dumas Expo at the Schomburg, which, due to an historically huge turnout, had to be beamed by closed circuit into an overflow room, featured Baraka, Avery Brooks, Raymond Patterson, Darlene Roy, Taylor, and Troupe.

Coincident with, and interspersing, decades of editing and publishing Henry Dumas's poems and stories (in book form) has been the placing of his works in hundreds of newspapers (like *St. Louis Post-Dispatch, The Village Voice, Los Angeles Times,* and *East St. Louis Monitor),* journals and magazines (such as *African Voices, Fences, Drumvoices Revue, Literati Internazionale,* and *The Original Chicago Blues Annual)* and anthologies (from *Griefs of Joy: Anthology of Afro-American Poetry for Students* and *Dark Matter: A Century of Speculative Fiction from the African Diaspora* to *The Literature of the American South: A Norton Anthology).*

Now, happily and rewardingly, comes another incarnation of Henry Lee Dumas—*Echo Tree*—whose brilliant and occasionally baffling *arc* encompasses *Ark of Bones, Rope of Wind, Goodbye, Sweetwater,* and seven new tales including "Scout," "Children of the Sun," "The Man Who Could See Through Fog," "The Bewitching Bag," "My Brother, My Brother," "The Metagenesis of Sunra," and "Riot or Revolt?" (a late find). Whether he was bequeathing us a curse or blessing (and even in view of hints about how tales should be arranged in the maiden voyage of *Ark of Bones),* Dumas did not indicate an order or "flow" for most of these stories. So, during three-and-a-half decades of literary executorship, I have—in consultation with HD's notes, Loretta Dumas, members of the "cult," and related research—attempted to construct an "ark" worthy of the "arc" of building materials he left us. In the end, the "ark" of stories has been assembled from *seasoned* subjectivity. Since Dumas began his memorable souljourns in the South, it was appropriate to start building his "soulboat" there. Hence, Ark of Bones, the first section of *Echo Tree*, opens—and opens *with*—his South to North trek. His trajectory then tucks into its folds "The Crossing" and "Goodbye, Sweetwater" (which concluded its namesake 1988 collection of collections), two tales that mesh exquisitely with—and are sandwiched by—"A Boll of Roses" and "Double Nigger."

Jonoah and the Green Stone, the 1976 novel from which six sections were borrowed for *Goodbye, Sweetwater,* has been excised from *Echo Tree* and will be published later in its original form. The biggest rupture and re-alignment occurs in Rope of Wind with restoration of the twelve tales—published in the 1979 Random House tome—and the addition of four pieces including three new ones: "Scout," paired with "Harlem"; "Children of the Sun," paired with "Rope of Wind"; "The Man Who Could See Through Fog," paired rather tongue-in-cheekly with "Six Days Shall You Labor"; and "Thalia" (a holdover from the Goodbye section of *Goodbye),* paired with the equally mesmerizing and elusive "The Voice." Finally, The Metagenesis of Sunra subsumes what was the Goodbye section of the 1988 collection and completes this voyage of the "ark." HD's folkfeisty/funkfantasy, "Rain God," held over from Goodbye/*Goodbye,* s/witches off fabulously with the mystifying "The Bewitching Bag," the Afro-astro-pscyho-bi-dimensional thriller "My Brother, My Brother!" and the quantum-leaping "The Metagenesis of Sunra." And, finally-finally, were it not for the already alluded to "common pattern" of "late" finds (of works by deceased artists) there would be no "Riot or Revolt?"—a starkly-minted and marvelously layered urban scroll, reminiscent of "Strike and Fade" and "Harlem" . . . resonating like . . .

. . . an *Echo Tree*, which enters the Soular System behind the 2001 release of *The Ark and the Ankh: Sun Ra/Henry Dumas in Conversation* (a CD recorded in 1966 at Slug's Saloon, a jazz club on the lower east side of New York City). Just last night (June 22) we celebrated Katherine Dunham's ninety-fourth Birthday at the Katherine Dunham Museum and African Artisanal Village, sacred-ritual ground that Henry Dumas traversed frequently during his ten months in East St. Louis. As a bluesaic/mosaic, "The Metagenesis of Sunra" *intuits* and songifies a swath of *ancestrails* near the conclusion of *Echo Tree*, a scroll [re-]introducing to readers themes "ancient" and "recent." Morph and metaphor conspire a la genius and *continuum*. His Circle Remains Unbroken—like Headeye's, Probe's, Fon's, Sunra's, ours.

Welcome back to the "deserved cult," ancient-recent members; and make ready to navigate the Soular System for the first time, all you souljourneying maiden voyagers.

Eugene B. Redmond
June 23, 2003
East St. Louis, Illinois

Take This River!

We move up a spine of earth
That bridges the river and the canal.
And where a dying white fog, finger-like,
Floating off the bank, claws at the slope,
We stumble, and we laugh.
We slow beneath the moon's eye;
Near the shine of the river's blood face,
The canal's veil of underbrush sweats frost,
And this ancient watery scar retains
The motionless tears of men with troubled spirits.
For like the whole earth,
This land of mine is soaked. . . .

Shadows together,
We fall on the grass without a word.
We had run this far from the town.
We had taken the bony course, rocky and narrow,
He leading, I following.
Our breath streams into October
As the wind sucks our sweat and a leaf. . . .

"We have come a long long way, mahn."
He points over the river
Where it bends west, then east,
And leaves our sight.

"I guess we have," I pant. "I can hear
My angry muscles talking to my bones."
And we laugh.

The hood of night is coming.
Up the river, down the river
The sky and night kiss between the wind.

"You know," Ben says, "this is where
   I brought Evelyn. . . .
Look. We sat on that log
And watched a river egret
Till it flew away with the evening.

"But mahn, she is a funny girl, Aiee!
But she looks like me Jamaica woman. . . .
But she asks me all the questions, mahn.
I'm going to miss her mahn, Aiee!

"But I will . . . Evvie. Evvie I love you,
  But I do Evvie . . . Evvie . . . ," he says
And blows a kiss into the wind.
Broken shadows upon the canal
Form and blur, as leaves shudder again . . . again.

"Tell me this, Ben," I say.
"Do you love American girls?
 You know, do most Jamaicans
 Understand this country?"

  We almost laugh. Our sweat is gone.
  He whispers "Aiee" on a long low breath.

  And we turn full circle to the river,
  Our backs to the blind canal.

"But I'm not most Jamaicans. . . .
I'm only Ben, and tomorrow I'll be gone,
And . . . Evvie, I love you. . . .
Aiee! My woman, how can I love you?"

  Blurred images upon the river
  Flow together and we are there. . . .

"What did she ask you?" I say.
"Everything and nothing, maybe.
 But I couldn't tell her all."
We almost laugh. "'Cause I
Don't know it all, mahn.

"Look, see over there. . . .
We walked down from there
Where the park ends
And the canal begins
Where that red shale rock
Down the slope there . . . see?
Sits itself up like a figure,
We first touch our hands . . .
And up floats this log,
Not in the river
But in the canal there
And it's slimy and old
And I kick it back . . .
And mahn, she does too.
Then she asks me:
'Bennie, if I cry
When you leave would you
Remember me more?'
Aiee! She's a natural goddess!
And she asks me:
'Bennie, when you think of Jamaica
Can you picture me there?'
And while she's saying this,
She's reaching for the river
Current like she's feeling its pulse.
She asks me:
'Bennie, America means something to you?
Maybe our meeting, our love? has
Something to do with America,

Like the river? Do you know Bennie?'
Aiee, Aiee, mahn I tell you
She might make me marry . . .
Aiee! Evvie, Jamaica . . . moon!
And how can I say anything?
I tell her:
'Africa, somewhere is Africa.
Do you understand,' I say to her,
And she look at me with the moon,
And I hear the wind and the leaves
And we do not laugh . . .
We are so close now no wind between us . . .
I say to her:
'Evvie, I do not know America
Except maybe in my tears. . . .
Maybe when I look out from Jamaica
Sometimes, at the ocean water. . . .
Maybe then I know this country. . . .
But I know that we, we Evvie. . . .
I know that this river goes and goes.
She takes me to the ocean,
The mother of water
And then I am home.'
And she tells me she knows
By the silence in her eyes.
I reach our hands again down
And bathe them in the night current
And I say: 'Take this river, Evvie. . . .'
Aiee, wind around us, Aiee my God!
Only the night knows how we kiss."

He stands up.
A raincloud sailing upon a leaf, whirs
In the momentary embrace of our memories. . . .
"Let's run," I say, "and warm these bones."

But he trots a bit, then stops,
  Looking at his Jamaica sky.
"Let's run the long road west
  Down the river road," I say,
"And I'll tell you of my woman . . . Aiee."
  We laugh, but we stop.
  And then, up the spiny ridge
  We race through the trees
  Like spirited fingers of frosty air.
  We move toward some blurred
  Mechanical light edged like an egret
  And swallowed by the night.
  Into this land of mine.
  And the wind is cold, a prodding
  Finger at our backs.
  The still earth. Except for us.
  And from behind that ebon cloak,
  The moon observes. . . .
  And we do not laugh
  And we do not cry,
  And where the land slopes,
  We take the river. . . .
  But we do not stumble,
  We do not laugh,
  We do not cry,
  And we do not stop. . . .

Ark of Bones

Ark of Bones

Headeye, he was followin me. I knowed he was followin me. But I just kept goin, like I wasn't payin him no mind. Headeye, he never fish much, but I guess he knowed the river good as anybody. But he ain't know where the fishin was good. Thas why I knowed he was followin me. So I figured I better fake him out. I ain't want nobody with a mojo bone followin me. Thas why I was goin along downriver stead of up, where I knowed fishin was good. Headeye, he hard to fool. Like I said, he knowed the river good. One time I rode across to New Providence with him and his old man. His old man was drunk. Headeye, he took the raft on across. Me and him. His old man stayed in New Providence, but me and Headeye come back. Thas when I knowed how good of a river-rat he was.

Headeye, he o.k., cept when he get some kinda notion in that big head of his. Then he act crazy. Tryin to show off his age. He older'n me, but he little for his age. Some people say readin too many books will stunt your growth. Well, on Headeye, everthing is stunted cept his eyes and his head. When he get some crazy notion runnin through his head, then you can't get rid of him till you know what's on his mind. I knowed somethin was eatin on him, just like I knowed it was *him* followin *me*.

I kept close to the path less he think I was tryin to lose him. About a mile from my house I stopped and peed in the bushes, and then I got a chance to see how Headeye was movin along.

Headeye, he droop when he walk. They called him Headeye cause his eyes looked bigger'n his head when you looked at him sideways. Headeye bout the ugliest guy I ever run upon. But he was good-natured. Some people called him Eagle-Eye. He bout the smartest nigger in that raggedy school, too. But most time we called him Headeye. He was always findin things and bringin 'em to school, or to the cotton patch. One time he found a mojo bone and all the kids cept me went round talkin bout him puttin a curse on his old man. I ain't say nothin. It wont none of my business. But Headeye, he ain't got no devil in him. I found that out.

So, I'm kickin off the clay from my toes, but mostly I'm thinkin about how to find out what's on his mind. He's got this notion in his head about me hoggin the luck. So I'm fakin him out, lettin him droop behind me.

Pretty soon I break off the path and head for the river. I could tell I was far enough. The river was gettin ready to bend.

I come up on a snake twistin toward the water. I was gettin ready to bust that snake's head when a fox run across my path. Before I could turn my head back, a flock of birds hit the air pretty near scarin me half to death. When I got on down to the bank, I see somebody's cow lopin on the levee way down the river. Then to really upshell me, here come Headeye droopin long like he had ten tons of cotton on his back.

"Headeye, what you followin me for?" I was mad.

"Ain't nobody thinkin bout you," he said, still comin.

"What you followin long behind me for?"

"Ain't nobody followin you."

"The hell you ain't."

"I ain't followin you."

"Somebody's followin me, and I like to know who he is."

"Maybe somebody's followin me."

"What you mean?"

"Just what you think."

Headeye, he was getting smart on me. I give him one of my looks, meanin that he'd better watch his smartness round me, cause I'd have him down eatin dirt in a minute. But he act like he got a crazy notion.

"You come this far ahead me, you must be got a call from the spirit."

"What spirit?" I come to wonder if Headeye ain't got to workin his mojo too much.

"Come on."

"Wait." I grabbed his sleeve.

He took out a little sack and started pullin out something.

"You fishin or not?" I ask him.

"Yeah, but not for the same thing. You see this bone?" Headeye, he took out that mojo. I stepped back. I wasn't scared of no ole bone, but everybody'd been talkin bout Headeye and him gettin sanctified. But he never went to church. Only his mama went. His old man only went when he sober, and that be about once or twice a year.

So I look at that bone. "What kinda voodoo you work with that mojo?"

"This is a keybone to the culud man. Ain't but one in the whole world."

"And *you* got it?" I act like I ain't believe him. But I was testin him. I never rush upon a thing I don't know.

"We got it."

"We got?"

"It belongs to the people of God."

I ain't feel like the people of God, but I just let him talk on.

"Remember when Ezekiel was in the valley of dry bones?" I reckoned I did.

". . . And the hand of the Lord was upon me, and carried me out in the spirit to the valley of dry bones.

"And he said unto me, 'Son of man, can these bones live?' and I said unto him, 'Lord, thou knowest.'

"And he said unto me, 'Go and bind them together. Prophesy that I shall come and put flesh upon them from generations and from generations.'

"And the Lord said unto me, 'Son of man, these bones are the whole house of thy brothers, scattered to the islands. Behold, I shall bind up the bones and you shall prophesy the name.'"

Headeye, he stopped. I ain't say nothin. I never seen him so full of the spirit before. I held my tongue. I ain't know what to make of his notion.

He walked on pass me and loped on down to the river bank. This here old place was called Deadman's Landin because they found a dead man there one time. His body was so rotted and ate up by fish and craw dads that they couldn't tell whether he was white or black. Just a dead man.

Headeye went over to them long planks and logs leanin off in the water and begin to push them around like he was makin somethin.

"You was followin me." I was mad again.

Headeye acted like he was iggin me. He put his hands up to his eyes and looked far out over the water. I could barely make out the other side of the river. It was real wide right along there and take coupla hours by boat to cross it. Most I ever did was fish and swim. Headeye, he act like he iggin me. I began to bait my hook and go down the bank to where he was. I was mad enough to pop him side the head, but I shoulda been glad. I just wanted him to own up to the truth. I walked along the bank. That damn river was risin. It was lappin up over the planks of the landin and climbin up the bank.

Then the funniest thing happened. Headeye, he stopped movin and shovin on those planks and looks up at me. His pole is layin back under a willow tree like he wasn't goin to fish none. A lot of birds were still flyin over and I saw a bunch of wild hogs rovin along the levee. All of a sudden Headeye, he say:

"I ain't mean no harm what I said about you workin with the devil. I take it back."

It almost knocked me over. Me and Headeye was arguin a while back bout how many niggers there is in the Bible. Headeye, he know all about it, but I ain't give on to what I know. I looked sideways at him. I figured he was tryin to make up for followin me. But there was somethin funny goin on so I held my peace. I said 'huh-huh,' and I just kept on lookin at him.

Then he points out over the water and up in the sky wavin his hand all round like he was twirlin a lasso.

"You see them signs?"

I couldn't help but say 'yeah.'

"The Ark is comin."

"What Ark?"

"You'll see."

"Noah's Ark?"

"Just wait. You'll see."

And he went back to fixin up that landin. I come to see what he was doin pretty soon. And I had a notion to go down and pitch in. But I knowed Headeye. Sometimes he gets a notion in his big head and he act crazy behind it. Like the time in church when he told Rev. Jenkins that he heard people moanin out on the river. I remember that. Cause papa went with the men. Headeye, his old man was with them out in that boat. They thought it was somebody took sick and couldn't row ashore. But Headeye, he kept tellin them it was a lot of people, like a multitude.

Anyway, they ain't find nothin and Headeye, his daddy hauled off and smacked him side the head. I felt sorry for him and didn't laugh as much as the other kids did, though sometimes Headeye's notions get me mad too.

Then I come to see that maybe he wasn't followin me. The way he was actin I knowed he wasn't scared to be there at Deadman's Landin. I threw my line out and made like I was fishin, but I wasn't, cause I was steady watchin Headeye.

By and by the clouds started to get thick as clabber milk. A wind come up. And even though the little waves slappin the sides of the bank made the water jump around and dance, I could still tell that the river was risin. I looked at Headeye. He was wanderin off along the bank, wadin out in the shallows and leanin over like he was lookin for somethin.

I comest to think about what he said, that valley of bones. I comest to get some kinda crazy notion myself. There was a lot of signs, but they weren't nothin too special. If you're sharp-eyed you always seein somethin along the Mississippi.

I messed around and caught a couple of fish. Headeye, he was wadin out deeper in the Sippi, bout hip-deep now, standin still like he was listenin for somethin. I left my pole under a big rock to hold it down and went over to where he was.

"This ain't the place," I say to him.

Headeye, he ain't say nothin. I could hear the water come to talk a little. Only river people know how to talk to the river when it's mad. I watched the light on the waves way upstream where the old Sippi bend, and I could tell that she was movin faster. Risin. The shakin was fast and the wind had picked up. It was whippin up the canebrake and twirlin the willows and the swamp oak that drink themselves full along the bank.

I said it again, thinkin maybe Headeye would ask me where was the real place. But he ain't even listen.

"You come out here to fish or fool?" I asked him. But he waved his hand back at me to be quiet. I knew then that Headeye had some crazy notion in his big head and that was it. He'd be talkin about it for the next two weeks.

"Hey!" I hollered at him. "Eyehead, can't you see the river's on the rise? Let's shag outa here."

He ain't pay me no mind. I picked up a coupla sitcks and chunked them out near the place where he was standin just to make sure he ain't fall asleep right out there in the water. I ain't never knowed Headeye to fall asleep at a place, but bein as he is so damn crazy, I couldn't take the chance.

Just about that time I hear a funny noise. Headeye, he hear it too, cause he motioned to me to be still. He waded back to the bank and ran down to the broken down planks at Deadman's Landin. I followed him. A couple drops of rain smacked me in the face, and the wind, she was whippin up a sermon.

I heard a kind of moanin, like a lot of people. I figured it must be in the wind. Headeye, he is jumpin around like a perch with a hook in the gill. Then he find himself. He come to just stand alongside the planks. He is in the water about knee deep. The sound is steady not gettin any louder now, and not gettin any lower. The wind, she steady whippin up a sermon. By this time, it done got kinda dark, and me, well, I done got kinda scared.

Headeye, he's all right though. Pretty soon he call me.
"Fish-hound?"
"Yeah?"
"You better come on down here."
"What for? Man, can't you see it gettin ready to rise?"

He ain't say nothin. I can't see too much now cause the clouds done swole up so big and mighty that everything's gettin dark.

Then I sees it. I'm gettin ready to chunk another stick out at him, when I see this big thing movin in the far off, movin slow, down river, naw it was up river. Naw, it was just movin and standin still at the same time. The damnest thing I ever seed. It just about a damn boat, the biggest boat in the whole world. I looked up and what I took for clouds was sails. The wind was whippin up a sermon on them.

It was way out in the river, almost not touchin the water, just rockin there, rockin and waitin.

Headeye, I don't see him.

Then I look and I see a rowboat comin. Headeye, he done waded out about shoulder deep and he is wavin to me. I ain't know what to do. I guess he bout know that I was gettin ready to run, because he holler out. "Come on, Fish! Hurry! I wait for you."

I figured maybe we was dead or something and was gonna get the Glory Boat over the river and make it on into heaven. But I ain't say it out aloud. I was so scared I didn't know what I was doin. First thing I know I was side by side with Headeye, and a funny-lookin rowboat was drawin alongside of us. Two men, about as black as anybody black wants to be, was steady strokin with paddles. The rain had reached us and I could hear that moanin like a church full of people pourin out their hearts to Jesus in heaven.

All the time I was tryin not to let on how scared I was. Headeye, he ain't payin no mind to nothin cept that boat. Pretty soon it comest to rain hard. The two big black jokers rowin the boat ain't say nothin to us, and everytime I look at Headeye, he poppin his eyes out tryin to get a look at somethin far off. I couldn't see that far, so I had to look at what was close up. The muscles in those jokers' arms was movin back and forth every time they swung them oars around. It was a funny ride in that rowboat, because it didn't seem like we was in the water much. I took a chance and stuck my hand over to see, and when I did that they stopped rowin the boat and when I looked up we was drawin longside this here ark, and I tell you it was the biggest ark in the world.

I asked Headeye if it was Noah's Ark, and he tell me he didn't know either. Then I was scared.

They was tyin that rowboat to the side where some heavy ropes hung over. A long row of steps were cut in the side near where we got out, and the moanin sound was real loud now, and if it wasn't for the wind and rain beatin and whippin us up the steps, I'd swear the sound was comin from someplace inside the ark.

When Headeye got to the top of the steps I was still makin my way up. The two jokers were gone. On each step was a number, and I couldn't help lookin at them numbers. I don't know what number was on the first step, but by the time I took notice I was on 1608, and they went on like that right up to a number that made me pay attention: 1944. That was when I was born. When I got up to Headeye, he was standin on a number, 1977, and so I ain't pay the number any more mind.

If that ark was Noah's, then he left all the animals on shore because I ain't see none. I kept lookin around. All I could see was doors and cabins. While we was standin there takin in things, half scared to death, an old man come walkin toward us. He's dressed in skins and his hair is grey and very woolly. I figured he ain't never had a haircut all his life. But I didn't say nothin. He walks over to Headeye and that poor boy's eyes bout to pop out.

Well, I'm standin there and this old man is talkin to Headeye. With the wind blowin and the moanin, I couldn't make out what they was sayin. I got the feelin he didn't want me

to hear either, because he was leanin in on Headeye. If that old
fellow was Noah, then he wasn't like the Noah I'd seen in my
Sunday School picture cards. Naw, sir. This old guy was wearin
skins and sandals and he was black as Headeye and me, and he
had thick features like us, too. On them pictures Noah was
always white with a long beard hangin off his belly.

I looked around to see some more people, maybe Shem,
Ham and Japheh, or wives and the rest who was suppose to be on
the ark, but I ain't see nobody. Nothin but all them doors and
cabins. The ark is steady rockin like it is floatin on air. Pretty soon
Headeye come over to me. The old man was goin through one of
the cabin doors. Before he closed the door he turns around and
points at me and Headeye. Headeye, he don't see this, but I did.
Talkin about scared. I almost ran and jumped off that boat. If it
had been a regular boat, like somethin I could stomp my feet on,
then I guess I just woulda done it. But I held still.

"Fish-hound, you ready?" Headeye say to me.

"Yeah, I'm ready to get ashore." I meant it, too.

"Come on. You got this far. You scared?"

"Yeah, I'm scared. What kinda boat is this?"

"The Ark. I told you once."

I could tell now that the roarin was not all the wind and
voices. Some of it was engines. I could hear that chug-chug like
a paddle wheel whippin up the stern.

"When we gettin off here? You think I'm crazy like you?"
I asked him. I was mad. "You know what that old man did
behind your back?"

"Fish-hound, this is a soulboat."

I figured by now I best play long with Headeye. He got a
notion goin and there ain't nothin mess his head up more than a
notion. I stopped tryin to fake him out. I figured then maybe we
both was crazy. I ain't feel crazy, but I damn sure couldn't make
heads or tails of the situation. So I let it ride. When you hook a
fish, the best thing to do is just let him get a good hold, let him
swallow it. Specially a catfish. You don't go jerkin him up as soon

as you get a nibble. With a catfish you let him go. I figured I'd better let things go. Pretty soon, I figured I'd catch up with somethin. And I did.

Well, me and Headeye were kinda arguin, not loud, since you had to keep your voice down on a place like that ark out of respect. It was like that. Headeye, he tells me that when the cabin doors open we were suppose to go down the stairs. He said anybody on this boat could consider hisself *called.*

"Called to do what?" I asked him. I had to ask him, cause the only kinda callin I knew about was when somebody *hollered* at you or when the Lord *called* somebody to preach. I figured it out. Maybe the Lord had called him, but I knew dog well He wasn't *callin* me. I hardly ever went to church and when I did go it was only to play with the gals. I knowed I wasn't fit to whip up no flock of people with holiness. So when I asked him, called for what, I ain't have in my mind nothin I could be called for.

"You'll see," he said, and the next thing I know we was goin down steps into the belly of that ark. The moanin jumped up into my ears loud and I could smell somethin funny, like the burnin of sweet wood. The churnin of a paddle wheel filled up my ears and when Headeye stopped at the foot of the steps, I stopped too. What I saw I'll never forget as long as I live.

Bones. I saw bones. They were stacked all the way to the top of the ship. I looked around. The under side of the whole ark was nothin but a great bonehouse. I looked and saw crews of black men handlin in them bones. There was a crew of two or three under every cabin around that ark. Why, there must have been a million cabins. They were doin it very carefully, like they were holdin onto babies or somethin precious. Standin like a captain was the old man we had seen top deck. He was holdin a long piece of leather up to a fire that was burnin near the edge of an opening which showed outward to the water. He was readin that piece of leather.

On the other side of the fire, just at the edge of the ark, a crew of men was windin up a rope. They were chantin every time they pulled. I couldn't understand what they was sayin. It was a foreign talk, and I never learned any kind of foreign talk. In front of us was a fence so as to keep anybody comin down the steps from bargin right in. We just stood there. The old man knew we was there, but he was busy readin. Then he rolls up this long scroll and starts to walk in a crooked path through the bones laid out on the floor. It was like he was walkin frontwards, backwards, sidewards and every which a way. He was bein careful not to step on them bones. Headeye, he looked like he knew what was goin on, but when I see all this I just about popped my eyes out.

Just about the time I figure I done put things together, somethin happens. I bout come to figure them bones were the bones of dead animals and all the men wearin skin clothes, well, they was the skins of them animals, but just about time I think I got it figured out, one of the men haulin that rope up from the water starts to holler. They all stop and let him moan on and on.

I could make out a bit of what he was sayin, but like I said, I never was good at foreign talk.

Aba aba, al ham dilaba
aba aba, mtu brotha
aba aba, al ham dilaba
aba aba, bretha brotha
aba aba, djuka brotha
aba, aba, al ham dilaba

Then he stopped. The others begin to chant in the back of him, real low, and the old man, he stop where he was, unroll that scroll and read it, and then he holler out: "Nineteen hundred and twenty-three!" Then he close up the scroll and continue his comin towards me and Headeye. On his way he had to stop and do the same thing about four times. All along the side of the ark them great black men were haulin up bones from that river. It was the craziest thing I ever saw. I knowed then it wasn't no animal bones. I took a look at them and they was all laid out in different ways, all making some kind of body and there was big bones and little bones, parts of bones, chips, tid-bits, skulls, fingers and everything. I shut my mouth then. I knowed I was onto somethin. I had fished out somethin.

I comest to think about a sermon I heard about Ezekiel in the valley of dry bones. The old man was lookin at me now. He look like he was sizin me up.

Then he reach out and open the fence. Headeye, he walks through and the old man closes it. I keeps still. You best to let things run their course in a situation like this.

"Son, you are in the house of generations. Every African who lives in America has a part of his soul in this ark. God has called you, and I shall anoint you."

He raised the scroll over Headeye's head and began to squeeze like he was tryin to draw the wetness out. He closed his eyes and talked very low.

"Do you have your shield?"

Headeye, he then brings out this funny cloth I see him with, and puts it over his head and it flops all the way over his shoulder like a hood.

"Repeat after me," he said. I figured that old man must be some kind of minister because he was ordaining Headeye right there before my eyes. Everythin he say, Headeye, he sayin behind him.

Aba, I consecrate my bones.
Take my soul up and plant it again.
Your will shall be my hand.
When I strike you strike.
My eyes shall see only thee.
I shall set my brother free.
Aba, this bone is thy seal.

HENRY DUMAS

I'm steady watchin. The priest is holdin a scroll over his head and I see some oil fallin from it. It's black oil and it soaks into Headeye's shield and the shield turns dark green. Headeye ain't movin. Then the priest pulls it off.

"Do you have your witness?"

Headeye, he is tremblin. "Yes, my brother, Fish-hound."

The priest points at me then like he did before.

"With the eyes of your brother Fish-hound, so be it?" He was askin me. I nodded my head. Then he turns and walks away just like he come.

Headeye, he goes over to one of the fires, walkin through the bones like he been doin it all his life, and he holds the shield in till it catch fire. It don't burn with a flame, but with a smoke. He puts it down on a place which looks like an altar or somethin, and he sits in front of the smoke cross-legged, and I can hear him moanin. When the shield it all burnt up, Headeye takes out that little piece of mojo bone and rakes the ashes inside. Then he zig-walks over to me, opens up that fence and goes up the steps. I have to follow, and he ain't say nothin to me. He ain't have to then.

It was several days later that I see him again. We got back that night late, and everybody wanted to know where we was. People from town said the white folks had lynched a nigger and threw him in the river. I wasn't doin no talkin till I see Headeye. Thas why he picked me for his witness. I keep my word.

Then that evening, whilst I'm in the house with my ragged sisters and brothers and my old papa, here come Headeye. He had a funny look in his eye. I knowed some notion was whippin his head. He must've been runnin. He was out of breath.

"Fish-hound, broh, you know what?"

"Yeah," I said. Headeye, he know he could count on me to do my part, so I ain't mind showin him that I like to keep my feet on the ground. You can't never tell what you get yourself into by messin with mojo bones.

"I'm leavin." Headeye, he come up and stand on the porch. We got a no-count rabbit dog, named Heyboy, and when

Headeye come up on the porch Heyboy, he jump up and come sniffin at him.

"Git," I say to Heyboy, and he jump away like somebody kick him. We hadn't seen that dog in about a week. No tellin what kind of devilment he been into.

Headeye, he ain't say nothin. The dog, he stand up on the edge of the porch with his two front feet lookin at Headeye like he was goin to get a piece of bread chunked out at him. I watch all this and I see who been takin care that no-count dog.

"A dog ain't worth a mouth of bad wine if he can't hunt," I tell Headeye, but he is steppin off the porch.

"Broh, I come to tell you I'm leavin."

"We all be leavin if the Sippi keep risin," I say.

"Naw," he say.

Then he walk off. I come down off that porch.

"Man, you need another witness?" I had to say somethin.

Headeye, he droop when he walk. He turned around, but he ain't droopin.

"I'm goin, but someday I be back. You is my witness."

We shook hands and Headeye, he was gone, movin fast with that no-count dog runnin long side him.

He stopped once and waved. I got a notion when he did that. But I been keepin it to myself.

People been askin me where'd he go. But I only tell em a little somethin I learned in church. And I tell em bout Ezekiel in the valley of dry bones.

Sometimes they say, "Boy, you gone crazy?" and then sometimes they'd say, "Boy, you gonna be a preacher yet," or then they'd look at me and nod their heads as if they knew what I was talkin bout.

I never told em about the Ark and them bones. It would make no sense. They think me crazy for sure. Probably say I was gettin to be as crazy as Headeye, and then they'd turn around and ask me again:

"Boy, where you say Headeye went?"

HENRY DUMAS

Echo Tree

Two boys on a hill. Evening.

"Right there! That's the place!"

"How can you tell?"

"*Shhhh.* Be careful. Don't step where the roots is, not yet ... I know, cause we always come here together."

"These hills all look the same. How can you tell from last year?"

"You gonna get in trouble talkin like that. Don't you know that spirits talk, 'n they takes you places?"

"I don't believe about ..."

"Careful what you say. Better to say nothin than talk too loud."

"Did you and Leo always come this far?"

"That's right. Me 'n him."

The wind fans up a shape in the dust: around and around and over the hill. Out of the cavity of an uprooted tree, it blows up fingers that ride the wind off the hill down the valley and up toward the sun, a red tongue rolling down a blue-black throat. And the ear of the mountains listens. . . .

"Did Leo used to want to come up to New York?"

"He ain't thinkin bout you whilst you way up yonder."

"How come you say that? What's wrong with up there?"

"Leo's grandpa, *your'n too,* well he say up in the city messes you up."

"Aw, he's old."

"Makes no difference. He know. That's how come Leo know too."

"Leo is dead."

"So, I bet he never teach *you* bout this here echo tree."

"He was my brother."

"Makes no difference. He my friend more'n your brother."

"What're you talking about?"

"... 'n he taught me how to call ..."

"What you bring me up here for?"

"... how to use callin words for spirit-talk ..."

"What?"

"... *Swish-ka abas wish-ka. Saa saa aba saa saa.*"

"What's that?"

"Be quiet. I'm gettin ready ..."

The wind comes. Goes. Comes again. Across the sky, clouds gather in a ritual of color, where the blue-black, like muscles, seems to minister to the sides of the sun.

"Leo never talked that stuff."

"And he's dead now anyway, laughing at us."

"He *did* talk. He ain't all dead either. You get in trouble talkin like that."

"Why so?"

"Peep over there. See them little biddy trees? Well, if you want to know somethin then I tell you. One of them is another echo tree."

"Another?"

"Right there is where the first one died. And we dug it up and built a fire, and the smoke sailed out, *see?* Just like the dust."

"How can a tree grow all the way up here to us?"

"Cause it's the echo treee! Don't you know nothin?"

"If you don't believe in the echo tree and believe what it hears from the spirits and tells you in your ear, then you're in trouble."

"What trouble?"

"*Real* trouble! If you curse the echo tree, you turns into a bino."

"A what?"

"Can't say that word but oncet. You better start listenin."

"To what?"

"Quick! Let me look at you!" (He runs and examines the other boy's face.) "Aw, it's too late, too late. You's already beginnin to turn ..."

HENRY DUMAS

"What?"

"Hurry! Hurry, boy, and stand in the echo place. Where the tree is . . . Hurry up! You're turnin white . . .!"

"I . . . what?"

"*Shhhhhhhh.* Hold still. You be safe for a while there. Now I gotta tell you how to get outa trouble."

"Nothin's worse than a bino, nothin. A bino is anything or anybody that curse the echo tree and whichever spirit is restin there."

"I didn't curse."

"You got to be careful, I'm warnin you."

"But I didn't curse."

"You cursin right now . . . If you don't believe in the echo, if you don't believe what it say, 'n if you laughs, if you pee, or spits on the tree, it's all the same as cursin. Then you's finished."

"How come?"

"*Shhhhhhhh* . . . cause the spirit leave out your body, you pukes, you rolls on the ground, you turns stone white all over, your eyes, your hair. Even your blood, 'n it come out your skin, white like water."

"But I . . ."

"Bino! Then you's a bino."

"Albino?"

"Naw. That's different. If you let yourself to taint all the way till you's a bino, then you don't eat, you don't sleep, you can't feel nothin, you can't talk or nothin. You be like a dead dog with a belly full 'o maggots, and you thinks you livin . . ."

"I didn't really curse."

"Makes no difference."

"I . . ."

"*Shhhhhhhh.* See the sun yonder?"

"Umh-humh."

"Well, he's gatherin in all the words talked in the daylight. Next, them catcher-clouds churns 'em up into echoes. When the time is right, the echo tree will talk. Be still, cause

when the butt end of the sun sit down on them mountains, then
. . . *be still!* Then we can talk to Leo in the . . ."

"Leo is dead."

"Hush, man! Can't you see it's almost time? Iffen I'se you,
I ain't want to be no bino."

Shadows begin to fade into a tinted haze.

Red Oklahoma clay darkens.

Green stretches of Arkansas pine finger their way into the land.

White blotches of clouds edge into open sky, fading into
oblivion.

Orange filaments stream from the sun.

And blue-red-blue, green-blue, white-blue—all ink the sky.

Shadows become fingers of wind in the night.

Shadows take on shapes. They come to breathe.

And the blue-blue prevails across the heavens, and the weight
of the mood is as black as night. . . .

". . . *Swish-ka aba swish-ka.* Quick! Say the openin
words!"

"Er . . . *swish* . . ."

"Stop! *Saa saa aba saa saa!*"

"What're we saying?"

"Be still. I had to seal them off. You started too slow 'n
you cursed."

Silence.

"Shhhhhhhh. Now I have to make the call. Watch the
sun yonder."

(He stands behind the other boy and dances a strange
dance. He stops, but continues with his arms, and jerks his body
toward the valley and the sky.)

"Laeeeeeeeooooooo!"

The sound pierces the wind. It rides down into the valley, rolls
up Laelaelaeeeooo! toward the sun. It resounds like notes of thunder
made by children instead of gods. It comes back LaeLae-eee-ooo!

"What is . . .?"

"Shhhhhhhh. He's still talkin."

HENRY DUMAS

There is silence . . . the silence of an empty lung about to breathe in. Again the sounds vibrate and answer from the boy's throat. Again they travel and return as though wet, as though spoken. . . .

"I'm going."

"Shhhhhhhh."

Echoes come. Again and again and again.

"Is it talking to me too?"

"You're the tree. Be still and listen."

"I feel funny. I better go."

"Saa saa lae-ya saa saa." (And the echoes trail off. . . .)

"Do you think you really talked to somebody?"

"Hush. We gotta be quiet from now on till we gets home."

"Huh? Did you?"

Silence.

"Aw, you didn't talk to nobody but yourself!"

"I warned you oncet. Iffen you curse again, not even me and Leo put together, 'n your grandpa too, can save you from taintin."

"What am I doing?"

"Talkin too loud like you don't believe in nothin."

"I'm not doing anything."

"Don't move! You standin in the echo tree taintin it. Spirits be after you for good. Iffen you move now your soul leave your body."

"I don't believe you."

Silence.

"Then iffen, after I tells you what Leo said about you, and you still don't believe, you'll be a bino fore we gets down the hill."

(He points to the sun. He does a dance. He sings the magic words.)

"Step out of the tree!" (The other boy runs out of the cavity.) "Now you's safe for a while. I had to open for you to come out, and then seal 'em back before they reached out after you."

"I hear something."

Silence.

"Talkin spirit-talk, you gotta open everything and seal it too."

"What's that?"

"That's them spirits in the echo tree down there, 'n Leo is there with them."

"What is he saying?"

"He say you his brother, but iffen you don't get that hard city water out your gut, you liable to taint yourself."

"Taint?"

"Taintin is when you just feels tired, you don't want to do nothin, you can't laugh, and your breathin gets slow. You's on the way to bein a bino."

"Were you really talking?"

"With the spirits and Leo."

"Shucks, that kind of talk sounds like those tongue-speaking people who get on their knees in the dark in that sanctified church at home, a block around the corner."

"That's right."

"Leo teach you that stuff?"

"You just gotta know how to talk to the spirits. They teach you everything."

"How does it go again?"

"Can't tell you now whilst you laughin."

"I'm not laughing."

"Makes no difference. You is inside."

"Leo was my brother."

"You never stayed down here with us. You always lived up there."

"I don't care about it anyway . . . *Swisher Baba!*"

"Now! Oh now! Now you *is* in trouble."

"Shucks."

"You is marked for cursin whilst standin right in the echo tree. All of them heard you. Leo too. Ain't nothin you can do except . . . Ohhhh, boy, you is dead. You're worse than a bino now. Deep deep trouble."

"Nothing is happening to me."

"Just wait a few minutes."

Silence.

"Are you going to tell me about this echo tree?"

Silence.

"You won't tell me much. If I'm really in trouble . . ."

"I been splainin it all to you, but you got so much city taint in your blood, you be a bino fore you go back."

"I'm not scared."

"Oh no?"

"No."

"You'd better be."

The wind, the wind. All of a sudden it sweeps across the top of the hill like an invisible hand swirling off into the darkening sky. Whispers echo from the valley throat, and all motion becomes sound, words, forces.

"I hear something."

"*Shhhhhhhh.* Spirits done broke through. They comin."

"Where?"

"Here."

"I . . . don't."

"*Swish-ka aba swish-ka.* Let the seals bust open!"

A moanful resonance, a bluish sound, a wail off the lips of a wet night, sweeps over them . . . Shhwssssssss!

"I'm not cursing anymore! What is that?"

Shhhwsssss! The small valley seems to heave, and the sounds come from the earth and the red tip of its tongue. And then a harmonic churning swells up and up! and as the ink-clouds press in on the sun, a motion in the sky, a flash of lightning, a sudden shift of the cloud, churns up, and a speck of sunlight spits out to the Shhwssss! of the spirited air, and the ears of the boys hear and the sounds are voices—remade, impregnated—screaming out to the world. . . .

Wide-mouthed, one boy cannot speak now. He stands near the spot of the tree. He seems ready to run.

"Iffen you run, a spirit'll trip you up. Then you falls down and down, like you do when you dreams, and you never hit bottom till you is a bino, a foreverbino."

"Where is my brother? Leee!"

"Spirit got you now."

"Leeeeee!"

"Swish-ka aba, take the tainter,

"Swish-ka aba, count to three,

"Swish-ka aba, take the hainter,

"Saash-ka Lae, don't take me."

"Stop! Don't say it! I'm not cursing anymore!"

Silence.

"Please . . ."

"One . . ."

"Please . . ."

"Two . . ."

"I want to hear it too, please."

"Then seal 'em out. Seal 'em out!"

"I . . . er."

"Two 'n half."

"Saaaa . . ."

"Saa saa aba saa saa."

"Saa saa aba saa saa."

Two shapes on a hill. The sun has fallen down.

Two forms running the slope. And in the wind it is whispered to the ear of the hearer . . . The sun will rise tomorrow.

HENRY DUMAS

The Crossing

Wooden bridge—landmark. It hoods the narrow stream, poking out of the neck of the lake like an ear out of the past.

Two boys and a little girl: running down the road towards the crossing—giggling.

They stopped running.

"Hey, yawl," the bigger boy yelled. "Better keep up, else I run off and leave you on this side."

He zigzagged once in a while across the road, rubbing his rolled-up Sunday School lesson along a dilapidated fence that ended abruptly when the road sloped downward.

"You know what happen if we don't cross all three together?" He picked up a rock and threw at a bunch of blue jays squawking in the trees. "Talkin bridge talk a spell on you."

"Hey, Bubba," the shorter boy whispered. He was dressed in a faded pair of pants. From his back pocket a broken slingshot dragged the ground. Every once in a while he picked up a stone, examined it, and added it to a bulge in his pocket. He wore a dirty brown shirt with a worn collar, and the brown of his skin blended with his shirt.

"What?" asked Bubba.

"Wait for me!"

The little girl, her thin blue dress splitting slightly at the waist seam, skipped to keep up. Vaseline-shiny braids hugged her scalp in neat lines. She watched the birds more than the boys. Down the hill a mocking bird lit in the road just for a second, then flew away across the water.

"What you want?"

"Hey, look," he said, tucking in the slingshot and nodding toward the girl. "Let's do somethin."

"What?"

"Let's . . ." He pointed toward the bridge. "Let's throw Essie in the water."

It was a quiet area. The feeling one got was like the feeling that comes when one is standing beside a still pond staring at a school of hungry minnows. Here, where the rotting planks stretched over the life in the green water, distance broke through, and for a while, north and south and east and west filled the eye.

"Naw."

"Just for fun."

"What's the matter w' you, Jimmy Croon?"

The south end of the bridge gaped open like a mouth. Out of it the road leaped downward undulating into the low country like a tired tongue. The heat of the Louisiana summer pressed in upon the bridge, buckling it and sometimes making it squeak.

"Ah, you scared," taunted Jimmy.

"Naw, I said."

"Then watch this."

"You push my sister, Jimmy Croon, and I'll whale your head."

"Let's scare her."

"Naw. You must think she looks like Emmett Till."

"Who?"

"Emmett Till."

"Who dat?"

"Don't you know bout him? Whitefolks threw him in for good! They weren't playin either."

"What he do?"

"They lynched him, I'm tellin you!"

"What for?"

"For nothin, I guess. I don't . . ."

"Ah, he must've popped some white trash side the head with a rock."

"Naw."

"When they do it?"

"Before we was born, I guess."

HENRY DUMAS

"Where bouts? This same water?"

"Maybe. White man come up to him drops ole white sheet over his head. Then some more white mens, a thousand multitudes, all tote him off to a river, maybe right near here, and they all take a turn at whoppin that sheet with sticks."

"He holler?"

"Say he hollered so loud, they heard 'im yelpin all the way to New York."

"Ah, I don't b'lieve that. White trash'll cut your tongue out for hollerin too much."

"Know what?"

"What?"

"After that, they all kick the sheet over in the water and stand there for three days chuckin heavy rocks in."

"In the same spot where he hit the water?"

"Same spot."

Essie was approaching them.

"Come on," said Jimmy, "let's be quiet."

"Naw, boy. Told you once."

The other boy slowed. "Hey, Essie, come 'ere."

"Touch my sister and I whop your nappy head worse'n any whitefolks."

"Naw you won't."

"Try me."

They stared at each other for a moment.

"She too little to play like that."

"She big enough to meddle me, she big enough to meddle with."

"That ain't meddlin."

"Hey, Essie," Jimmy said as the little girl skipped up. "Me and your ole nappy headed brother gonna throw you in the water like they did Emmett Till."

Bubba was silent. He fell in line beside Essie.

"Touch me and Bubba hit you back," she said, cocking her head away from Jimmy who smirked and menaced her with an extended palm. She skipped out in front of the boys, the bow of her dress flopping loose with her bounce.

"Hey," said Jimmy, throwing his arm around the shoulder of Bubba, who pushed it off, "let's see if this ole bridge talk a spell on Essie when she go over."

Bubba pushed him off the road. Jimmy sprang back, elbowing Bubba in the side. They began to snicker. Jimmy broke away and ran toward the bridge saying, "Say goodbye to your sister," and pushed her off the road as Bubba, leaping after him, shouted, "If I catch you, you dead! Stay off the bridge, Essie!"

Jimmy laughed loudly and scampered onto the wooden planks. Essie whimpered and licked her lips. She halted a few feet away from the bridge.

The thin noon shadow of an oak sliced the front of the metal-braced rails and cut the planks, traveling at an angle until it fell off into the water below. The old bridge rested on log beams, many of which needed replacing. Several stumps slanted out of the water, marking where floods had raged by leaving memories in the form of wreckage.

Essie pouted near the edge now. She watched Jimmy, then leaned over to peer into the water. A water strider skated out of the way of a swarm of gnats, and a mocking bird's shadow glided across the hood of the bridge. A green frog, heaving its balloon sides from behind a clump of lake weeds, darted a tongue out and a bronze fly disappeared from a leaf.

Jimmy ran to the wooden rail, leaned over, turned, and beckoned to Essie as she began to back away from the bridge. Bubba leaped upon Jimmy. "What you doin, Jimmy Croon?"

"Don't mess with me, boy," said Jimmy.

"Ha! Who you?"

"Didn't know, did you? Well, I'm the Law."

"Ha! You mean the Lie."

"Okay, s'posin you was Emmett Till. What you do when somebody throw sheet over your head?"

　　　　　　　　　　　　　　　　　HENRY DUMAS

"Take my knife and cut right out of it."

"How come he ain't do it? How come somebody ain't help him?"

"Shucks, I told you. Whitefolks got him. And they get you too, tryin to scare somebody small as Essie."

"I ain't scared her yet." He punched Bubba sharply on the arm. They tussled, stirring up dust under the shed.

Essie stood entranced at the edge of the hood's shadow. A pebble, lodged between the planks, fell plop into the water. She jerked nervously and squeezed her Sunday School lesson.

"Bubba," she whispered.

"What?" he grunted, still scuffling with Jimmy.

"I'm scared."

Jimmy laughed, eluding Bubba's grasp for his neck.

"B'cause you little Miss Essie Till!"

"She ain't," grunted Bubba.

"I ain't."

"You is."

"She ain't." He succeeded in locking an arm around Jimmy's neck.

Suddenly Jimmy let out a long choking growl. He was pinned to the rail. Then, heaving his chest, he lunged outside the railing. Bubba's leg came half way through with him.

Essie hollered.

"You give?" shouted Bubba, still holding Jimmy's neck.

"Hey!" screamed Jimmy. They were falling.

Essie hollered again.

And suddenly they were pulling up together. Essie stood behind them at the other end of the rail and began watching the shadow of her little purse every time she swung it out over the rail. The shadow formed like a dart, a licking tongue on the rail and water below.

"Hey," shouted Bubba, "who's that down in the water?"

"You!" And Jimmy was upon him again.

"Emmett . . ." Bubba gagged. They were falling again.

"You give?"

"Naw," said Bubba.

Essie ran to them. "I'm gonna tell mama on yawl!" She looked at the shadows struggling on the water. They seemed to be drowning.

"You give?"

"Naw."

Jimmy's shirt hooked on a sharp splinter and ripped half off. They eased up a bit, but continued to hang dangerously over the side.

"You messed my shirt up," said Jimmy.

"You give?"

"Naw," said Jimmy. "Not till I put this shirt over somebody's head and feed her to the snakes."

"No!" cried Essie.

Bubba held him to the rail.

"How come you always scarin my sister?"

"She meddle me."

"Naw she don't, 'cept you meddle us first."

"Maybe I don't like her."

"Then leave her lone. You must be crazier'n a coon. If I don't like a body, I leaves 'em lone."

They were silent for a while. They stopped tussling.

"Ah, I's only foolin."

"You must be crazy, boy."

"You scared of this bridge?" asked Jimmy.

"Naw."

"Bet you is at night."

"Bet you is too."

"Mama told me this bridge growed up outa the water one time cause some white people drowned when they was crossin in a boat."

"Must've been real big then."

"Was. She said it was bigger than a river and deeper than a ocean. Had whales in it could swallow a thousand multitudes."

　　　　　　　　　　　　　　　　　　　　　　　　　　　　HENRY DUMAS

"Uncle Willy told me oncet this bridge built by some white people that did nothin but hung niggers. They never talked."

"What they do?"

"Just hunt you down."

"I know."

"Said they caught a swamp nigger once and burned him on a cross. Right here," and he pointed with his finger. "Right here bout where we standin."

"How the cross burn in the water?"

"Ain't no water here then. Long time fore you was ever born, fore me too, and you too, Essie. And then the swamp come lookin for its nigger cause the nigger was good to the swamp."

"How the swamp walk?"

"Didn't walk. Swim in with the water. See them mosses? They is the swamp. They hides things."

"Who got the swamp man?"

"Nobody knows. They put him on the cross and when it come just to burn, the swamp comes in ridin the river, and all them whitefolks, a thousand multitudes, was gone, and the nigger too. And when they heard bout it in town, they come and built a bridge over the water. They was scared too."

"Ah, I heard it different."

"Did you hear how it learn to talk spells on people?"

"Sure."

"How?"

"Ain't tellin you."

"How come?"

"What for you tryin to scare my sister?"

"Ain't scare her yet." He pointed at Essie. "Hey, Miss Essie Till. Wait till you feel them snakes tastin on your neck."

"Boy, you crazy," said Bubba. "Don't you know it was white trash killed Emmett Till."

Jimmy backed off, examining his shirt.

"Know it was," he said.

"So how we gonna act like them? Essie can't be no Emmett Till 'cause she ain't no boy, and we ain't no white folks, 'specially you, nappyhead."

"Know who you talkin to?" said Jimmy, climbing to sit on the rail.

"Jimmy the Coon," laughed Bubba. "Look." And they peered at their reflections in the water.

Three blue jays flew overhead. In a clearing across the bridge a mocking bird's trill pierced the summer heat. Essie, coming close to the boys, began to chant:

> Ole Jimmy Croono
> Nothin but a coono

Then suddenly she stopped. She leaped up into the air. Her feet came down stomp on the planks as she yelled, "Boo!" and skipped over the wood. The boys, flinching only a bit at her scare, never looked away from the water, Bubba saying, "We quit, Essie. Now don't cross too soon."

Jimmy, mouth open and eyes peering, watched the rings made by falling pebbles.

"How come they did it?" he asked.

Bubba scratched his head. "Don't rightly know. But pecker-woods did it same as they did that swamp nigger you told me about."

"You scared of white folks?"

"Naw. You?"

"You is."

"I ain't."

They watched the water for swimming things.

"Me neither," said Jimmy. "If I see one comin to get you and Essie, I fix my sling and knock his head off." He jerked out the sling and aimed a rock at Essie.

"Hey boy, what you doin?" shouted Bubba. "That rock touch my sister, you dead!"

"It's broke, see?" He let the rock fly.

"I don't care."

The rock sailed off weakly to the right, bouncing off the shed.

They moved off the bridge together—all three.

"I'se only foolin."

"Better be."

They pushed against each other—push and shove.

"How come you ain't go to church like other folks, Jimmy Croon?"

"Didn't have no shirt," smirked Jimmy," 'cause old nappy Bubbahead tore it."

"Quit lyin. You started it."

"Devil gonna get you," Essie chimed.

"Not me. Me 'n' the devil is friends. I'm sendin him out to hunt peckerwoods."

"Quit lyin," said Bubba. He drew out his Sunday School lesson and began hitting tossed pebbles.

"Hey, Jimmy."

"What?"

"What you doin?"

"Tendin my business."

"Betcha I can find that ole piece of inner tube in back of our yard."

"You makin yourself another sling?" asked Jimmy.

"Might. Feel like poppin one of them blue devils."

"Need to fix mine."

"Come on, let's go."

Essie was skipping far ahead of them.

"Hey Essie," Jimmy called. "We didn't throw you off the bridge, did we?" He put an arm around Bubba's shoulder.

"We didn't, did we?" Jimmy repeated.

Essie looked at Jimmy, then at Bubba. "He didn't push me in the water like they did before, did he, Bubba?"

Bubba looked across the marshes at a flock of birds. A mocking bird sang nearby.

"Huh?"

"He didn't, did he?"

"Naw."

They all were quiet for a second, moving away from the presences, the sounds, the memories. . . .

Bubba stopped.

"Listen," he whispered. "That old bridge talkin. Listen. Feel sorry for anybody cross it now."

They listened. A pebble plunked in the water, a fish splashed somewhere, perhaps the bridge squeaked faintly.

"Hush," said Bubba.

Looking over their shoulders, they stepped forward cautiously.

Suddenly they giggled, and broke into a fast run. . . .

Goodbye, Sweetwater

His arms flapping like a bird, Layton Bridges stood on the porch of the shack and listened to the distant whistle of the freight. Its long sustained peal told him that it was carrying a heavy load, maybe enough cars for the sun to set before the last one passed. He rolled up the frayed ends of his jeans above his bare legs so that the air could get to them. Sometimes after a long freight passed, all he could see was the shadow of the last car streaking across the fallen sun, plunging through the dusty evening, leaving behind only an echo and a hush of loneliness.

The little back country district of Sulfur Springs, Arkansas, sits upon a series of bauxite and sulfur layers. The mineral richness below the surface has transformed the once cotton and tobacco lands into little pocket mining communities, sticking like hardened sores beneath the white dust. A cement factory adds to the gray haze that has become the shroud over every village and rural town.

Holly Springs, where Layton lived, got its name because it has spring water untouched by chemical hardness. Most of the well water in the area was known for its hardness and the taste of sulfur, but this one district erupted now and then with fresh spring water. The spring played a hide-and-seek pattern, going underground and reappearing later.

The only source of soft water in Sulfur Springs was a tiny spring in the middle of a stretch of land closed off by the federal government. Located a mile south of the road near Layton's shack, this land was once part of a rich cotton plantation. Now it was broken up and leased to planters and corporations. The rural people, like Layton Bridges and his grandmother, thought of themselves as living on the edge of a great burnt-out plain, thirsty and bitter, cracking daily under the malice of men. Eventually the land would swallow them up. The big companies would move in and buy them out. Already Sulfur Springs was depopulated, as if overnight the earth had reclaimed or frightened away the people. Besides Layton and his grandmother there were five other families. None of them could claim any young people, except for the kids, too young to move out on their own.

Sixteen-year-old Layton went out into the bare yard where the chinaberry tree stood. The hot afternoon dust leaped up between his toes like fire. He put his arms out as if he were going to dive. Then he leaped, caught the limb of the chinaberry tree and swung himself up. The freight train, like a fleeing worm, crawled atop the horizon of distant trees and hills. It was about a mile away, and Layton wanted to get close to it now. He had believed that any day his mother would come for him or the man she had written about, her friend, Mr. Stubbs, would drive by and take him away. But he had been waiting long months now. He would leave soon, he knew, if he had to make a way himself. The only thing Layton could not reconcile with this joy of leaving Holly Springs was the gnawing feeling that his grandmother was not going. She did not want to go. She would shake her head and say, "Son, I reckon the Lord know best what your grandma gwine do. He been keepin me here on this land now since 'fore anything flyin in the sky 'cept the birds. . . . You go on wid your mama. You go to your mama up there in New York. Go on and finish school. Go in the army. Go to college. Get yourself some learnin. Take care of your mama. You do that and your grandma be happy." Layton always felt and trusted the deep faith and nobility in her voice.

Somehow his grandmother was bigger and stronger than the land. No matter how many factories they built nearby, or how many highways they proposed, or how many mines they dug, his grandmother's strength would last when the rest had crumbled to dust.

He climbed to the top of the tree. The freight still passed, its many-colored, many-shaped cars looking like the curious shapes of a puzzle.

HENRY DUMAS

Down the road Layton saw his grandmother coming. Beside her walked Mrs. Fields, who lived in the cabin with her ailing husband and his mother, Granny Lincoln. Nobody knew how old Granny Lincoln was except Granpa Fields. He claimed that his mother was born a slave and when she was a girl had seen Abraham Lincoln campaigning for the presidency. The two old women wore wide straw hats, which cast long boatlike shadows in front of them. Their aprons bulged with vegetables as they approached in the dust, an ancient silence walking beside them, a part of them, and yet, like them, a part of the land.

Leaning out from the tree with his feet firmly set in the notch where the limb sprung from the body of the tree, and holding to the neck of the tree with his left hand, Layton raised his right hand at the train. How many times had he waved at trains? If he could live as long as the number of times he had waved, he knew, without counting them, that he would live to be as old or older than Granny Lincoln. But there was something about waving at a freight train that seemed dry and meaningless. He lowered his hand. He had always waved at the swift passenger trains, and many times when he went across the river and sat by the tracks, people on the train would wave back. He never knew if the white faces waving at him would ever make the engineer stop the train for him. His brother had ridden on a train when he had gone off to Vietnam. But that was two years ago and his brother had been killed over there. They said he had been missing in action. He thought of himself in a few years riding on a train or maybe even an airplane and being a soldier somewhere. He would fight in his brother's place. He would save up all his money and come back to New York, give it all to his mother to help her. Yes, he would do all that and then he would buy a car, come back to Holly Springs and take his grandmother to Illinois where his uncle Joe lived. Uncle Joe had said that he wanted her to stay with him, but she had always refused.

Layton watched the last car on the freight. The hot white dust clung to the smooth hard surfaces of the tree like powder.

Long before the cement factory was built several miles down the road, Layton had fallen from the tree, but it had been because he was careless. Now with the dust from the trucks and cars and the factory, all the trees and shacks in Holly Springs took on the look of the blight. Granny Bridges called it the blight. It had come with the bauxite mines years before and now it had spread over the land like a creeping fever. A dry fever. One that made you sneeze, cough and choke. It killed the trees, the grass and gardens. There were certain vegetables that his grandmother could not grow anymore. Something about the land refused the seed, as if the land was sick, and didn't know any longer what its nature was.

Once he recalled, when Granny Lincoln was brought out to sun, some big trucks loaded with ores stopped in front of the house. The men had heard about some sweet water around somewhere in the area and wanted some. Granny Lincoln had wanted to know what the men were doing carrying away her yard, and when Granpa Fields tried to console her, she refused to listen. Finally she had taken consolation in the Bible, saying that all of those trucks and men were signs. She said it was written that in the latter days, Satan and his angels would come forth from the earth seeking whom they might devour.

He began to climb down, the deadly powder making his descent as treacherous as his ascent. He had seen no sign of life on the freight. He had only shaken white dust into the air. It was a three-o'clock afternoon sun, hot, direct, lapping at the wounded earth with a dry merciless tongue. Layton did not feel angry at the sun, not really. He had learned somewhere in school that the sun was the source of all power. It was the sun that made the gardens grow, made the fields of hay, and cotton, corn and sorghum. It was the sun that drew up the rain from the ocean and sent rain down to make things green. Yet he knew it was by some terrible agreement, something beyond his comprehension, that allowed the sun and the whitemen to weaken the land. It was the same feeling which took his joy away when he thought of his coming new life in New York. It was like waving at a freight train. Somewhere he felt betrayed. Perhaps he was betraying the land himself. He felt that it all was a part of a great conspiracy . . . with the sun in the center. He did not like to think of leaving her to the mercy of the heat and the dust. And yet . . .

The only thing that gave Layton any real consolation was the fact that his grandmother was indestructible. He watched her slow pace up the road, her blue apron bulging with vegetables she had gotten from Granny Fields. She would sit on the porch in the evenings and the white dust never settled on her. Sometimes, he would think, gwine live forever. . . .

The two old women entered the bald yard in front of the shack. Their heads were bent as if they were watching the direction of their shadows, but Layton felt instinctively that his grandmother knew that he was in the tree. She never had to look at things to recognize them. She knew because it was the same to her as her bones telling her it was going to rain.

Layton was about to swing down to the last limb above the ground when he turned his neck to get a last look at the horizon where the trains passed. The 6:00 P.M. passenger would be the next one on the line, and he imagined that in a few more days he himself would be on it or maybe riding in the car with Mr. Stubbs. They would cross the tracks in Mr. Stubb's car at the Sulfur Springs Greyhound station and he imagined telling Mr. Stubbs just what time the trains came by. . . . When he recognized the swirling dust as a car in the distance, he was already swinging down to the last limb. He never touched the ground, but swung, toes over head, back up onto the limb, grunting, his mouth open, his stomach flopping down on the limb. Upside down he saw the two figures climb wearily up on the porch. Mrs. Fields sat down in the rocking chair that was especially padded for her, and his grandmother rested in hers. He climbed back to the top. The car he saw had not taken the road which led to the cement plant. It was headed toward their house. He knew that no mistake could be made. There had been signs posted on the road for years. A screen of dust leaped from behind the car as it came like a racing beetle.

He almost blurted out the news of the car, but suddenly felt his throat dry up; in a careless movement of his foot, he slipped. . . .

Even the chinaberry tree, in its struggle with the land, had grown spiteful. It had not produced any berries in two years now, only a few scrawny pits that even the birds would not eat. He fell against the next limb, shaking the tree as if a wind had blown through. Before he caught himself he heard his grandmother's voice, calling him, warning him. He knew she had seen him fall, and in her voice, he could tell that she was saving him. His arms hooked the limb and he held it.

"Grandma," he said, swinging out of the tree and feeling grit in his throat, "yonder come somebody."

The old lady, as if she had known not only that someone was coming, but that her grandson would report it just that way, looked up from her lap where she was shelling green peas. "I reckon, your grandma and Mrs. Fields, 'bout to die of thirst, son."

By her voice he knew that the car was another betrayal. Yet there was no reason why it couldn't be Mr. Stubbs. The letter had said as soon as school was out and school had been out for weeks. He had not told Mr. Purdy at the cement plant that he was leaving, but he had told everybody else. No more night walking and night working. No more sleeping in the daytime and walking the dark roads at night with a flashlight. No more breathing the rock dust and chemicals, breathing them so much that you thought you were going to choke to death. No more looking in that cracked mirror at the plant and seeing a face covered with white dust, a black face underneath covered with a dry white fever. No more of the loneliness of walking to school and finding one less face there each day. . . .

Willy Strom, he gone off to Chicago with his brother. Maybelle Davis, she pregnant and gone to live with her cousin in Little Rock. Jesse Higgins, he left last night with Odell

Miller and Claude Sykes. They all goin to the Job Corps in New Jersey. Louise Watkins, she getting married to a guy some kin to the Lawrences. They goin to Los Angeles.

Layton walked across the yard and stood in front of his grandmother. "I get you some sweet water." He paused. "Grandma, who you reckon comin yonder?" He couldn't really believe that his mother's letters were also betrayals.

Sarah Bridges, her long silver hair tied neatly in a bun, stopped shelling peas and lifted her straw hat to her face to fan. The brim slapped a fly into her lap and Layton watched as the insect regained its wing power and buzzed off.

"Reckon it nothin but somebody lookin for somethin to get, son. Every empty truck and car or wagon come into Holly Springs nowadays, always roll out full. It the change of the seasons, son. You get old as I am and you learn when to see the change of the seasons."

Granny Fields, her black face shining in her perpetual silence, looked up from her lap of peas. Her short arms continued to work as the round peas fell from the shove of her thumb. The empty hulls fell with their brothers on the floor beside her ancient high-top leather shoes. After years of working in the earth, her shoes had taken on the color of the dirt.

"I hear your mama want you up there with her, boy," she said to Layton. She leaned out over the porch and spit a brown stream of snuff.

"Yes, mam," Layton said. Something began to ring in his head now, like a kind of church bell. He looked out over the flat land. He could not see the car now, but he picked the point in the distance where he knew it would come into view. "But I reckon if she don't, then I'm gwine go visit her and maybe work for the summer. . . . I might even go to school up there next year."

"You stay outa trouble, you hear. And mind your mama," said Granny Fields. She returned to her accustomed silence now, having gathered up all the forces of her intellect to deliver her familiar warning. Layton liked Granny Fields because she spoke only when she thought it necessary. Almost in his motion to go back into the shack there came the deep and respectful, "Yes, mam."

He went through the shack. On his bed he saw the dusty brown suitcase which he had put there every day since he got the word from his mother. Even if she didn't send for him, he was going to use that suitcase.

On the back porch he went to the earthen jug. It was the vessel which he had filled every one or two days since he could remember. He had gone with his mother when he was only a tiny boy, to fill it, and he had gone with Granny and Mr. Fields, and once with a man who Granny had told him was his own father. He couldn't remember his father because it was only that once that he had seen him.

His mother had gone off to get a job, and even though she sent money to his grandmother, Layton felt a kind of dryness, an emptiness, whenever he tried to imagine her living way up in New York. He wanted to go himself, and as he stirred the dipper around in the dark inside of the jug, he could hear the ringing of the train whistle, and the roar of sounds he knew he would have to learn to identify. New sounds. New smells. New sights. No more picking cotton. No more dragging the long sack of cotton over sunbaked fields of dusty stalks, kicking up the red dirt. No more choking on cement dust. No more squinting at the distant death-smoke which began early in the morning as a haze but which by afternoon had become a cloud, a cloud of white gray dust, catching the sun, and choking off the rain and smothering the land. He did not drink. He would have to go out to get some water. There was just about two dippers full left.

He could see the sulfur-water well half hidden by the clothes on the line between the shack and the well. He checked the two sulfur-water buckets at the far edge of the porch; they both were full. A yellowish scale clung to their insides. Layton dipped up some of the water with the dipper, held it in his mouth for a short while, rinsed his mouth as he had seen the old people do after dipping snuff, and then spat. The taste of the water was intensified because the sun had broken through cracks on the porch wall and heated the water. It was not for drinking anyway, only for washing.

He poured the water from each bucket into a large bent tin tub which leaned against the rear of the shack. His grandmother used it to wash and collect rainwater. He would fill both buckets with sweet water at the spring.

When he lifted his head, he could see the pillar of dust swirling like a miniature twister. He went to the earthen jug and poured the contents into one of the buckets. Then he went through the house and stood looking beyond the front porch, beyond the sound of his grandmother humming softly, beyond the almost silent flick of thumbs shelling peas, beyond the china-berry tree, obstinately clinging to the land, and beyond the edge of the young cotton, that Mr. Fields and he had planted and chopped, to the point where the car now appeared.

His grandmother lifted her head and squinted toward the road. Mrs. Fields in her silence lifted her head also, as if she had waited for the other woman to make the first indication that the car was drawing close enough to look at.

"Granny Fields, you want a dipperful now?" Layton asked, watching the scale from the bucket shine from its slakeness and wondering how it was that sulfur got into the water, and how was it that the sweet water managed to escape the sulfur.

"I can wait for the fresh, son," she said. A pea popped from a shell and rolled off the porch. Layton saw it disappear in the dust, and the neck of a chicken shot from under the porch and struck the pea. He knew his grandmother always waited for fresh water too.

He stepped off the porch around a feathered form of a chicken asleep in the sun, its wing fanned out in the dust as if it were taking a bath. His bare feet slapped the baked clay in a familiar rhythm.

He stepped in a hole, where as a small boy he had played with wooden blocks and tin cans nailed together by his brother for trucks, cars, tractors, airplanes, or anything they wanted them to be. They had played bauxite and coal mining, cement hauling, gold digging and war.

Who would go and get the sweet water from the spring? The trip was too long for any of them to walk. Old Mr. Fields could not walk that far every day for water. They would all have to drink sulfur water, and he knew that was a bad sign. He stood there, paused beside the house watching the rapid approach of the car now, prolonging his own thirst. When he heard his grandmother's call, he felt the same feeling when he slipped on the tree. She did not call him but once, softly, as if she knew he had not gone very far, as if she knew that he was watching the car from the side of the house.

He saw a tailspin of dust rise up and then fall forward over the car. It had stopped in the yard. A whiteman emerged from the dust, wiping his face with a handkerchief. Layton climbed up on the porch and watched the man. He was Yul Stencely who came now and then to collect money, and Granny Bridges always paid it without question, as if it were her duty. He knew that the money he made and the money his mother sometimes sent finally went into the whiteman's hands. He watched the man approach. Yul Stencely looked around the yard expectantly. Layton knew he was looking for a dog to rush out at him.

"How do, Mrs. Bridges," the whiteman spoke, mopping his blond head and then resetting the straw hat he wore back on it. He drew near the steps. Particles of dust floated and settled on the porch. "Mighty hot today."

"How do, Mr. Stencely." She had already put aside the peas in her lap. Now she brought out a paring knife and began to peel a large white potato. "Yes, 'tis hot."

The whiteman drew out a notebook from his bosom pocket. Layton watched him. The man did not once notice the presence of Granny Fields nor did he look at Layton.

Tall, thin and straight, he wore a coat that was too large. Layton looked closely but he could see no signs of sweat, although the man was constantly wiping his face. He would look at the dirty handkerchief, blow his breath into it as the cloth passed over his mouth and then look at his notebook with silent appraisal. He stepped into a tiny shaft of shade near Granny Bridges at the edge of the porch.

"Who told you I had anything for you this time, Mr. Stencely?" There was no real anger in her voice, but Layton could tell that there was a determination, a kind of defiance which always made him feel his grandmother was indestructible. She kept on peeling potatoes, without looking at the whiteman. He cleared his throat and continued his scrutiny of the notebook. Then he looked around the yard again.

"Well, Mrs. Bridges, aint no harm in comin. Is there? Sides, I reckon you owe me since the last time I was here. . . ." He paused. Layton studied the man. Granny was right. He had come like the rest. They come empty and leave full. Layton suddenly wanted to know the reason for this continued payment to the whiteman. Why was it that it was always Negroes who paid money to the whiteman? Yet he knew the answers, but asking the questions over again made him feel a fire rise up from his toes and churn away in his stomach. And the fire gave him direction. "Well, I reckon there aint no harm in comin, Mr. Stencely, and I reckon there aint no harm in me askin you to come again next month. I speck my daugher-in-law gwine send a bit of money . . ."

Layton set the bucket down. It made a noise. The whiteman turned and looked at it. Then he looked away around the house toward the well. Layton felt as if she had said something then to take away all the years of his faith in her strength. If his mother had sent some money, it would go to that man. . . . He knew that. But it just shouldn't. . . . Over and over now he heard the ring of the tin bucket on the ground. . . . The settling of the dust was millions of tiny bells.

The whiteman laughed. He couldn't go any further than the old woman would let him. He knew that they were poor, but that was not his fault. He collected from poor whites as well as poor blacks. He even had some Mexicans he collected from. He was hot and he needed a drink.

"Well, Mrs. Bridges, I tell you what I'm gonna do. You let me have a drink of your good well water and I'll be obliged to come agin when you able . . ."

Granny Bridges flipped a long curled potato peeling out into the yard where a chicken neck grabbed it and fled beneath the house.

"Layton, give Mr. Stencely a drink of water. . . ."

When she called his name, Layton was already in motion. He left the bucket with the two dippers of sweet water from the earthen jug and went to the back and to the sulfur-water well. He let the long aluminum cylinder down into the well shaft. The ringing of the rusty wheel which rode the chain up and down was a kind of music which Layton associated with dryness. The water from the well never really quenched your thirst. Only the spring water could quench your thirst. He felt the cylinder strike bottom, fill, and grow heavy. He coughed and began to pull. His muscles burned and the sun struck him through the hood of the well right in the face. He frowned, and his frowning made him hot. The whiteman would drink what he gave him. He would drink, but he would not lose his thirst. His stomach would swell and almost burst, but he would still be thirsty. Hours after drinking this water you would belch it and want to spit, but your tongue would be dry. Your throat would crack, and you would sweat.

He returned to the front porch with a bucket and a glass from the kitchen. He took the dipper from the sweet-water bucket and watched it sink in the freshly drawn sulfur water. Then he stood in the doorway, motionless. He expected the whiteman to reach and fill the glass and drink. He didn't hear his grandmother's voice calling him. He lifted the sweet water pail and stepped back into the doorway. . . .

"Layton."

The truth still rang in her voice. It halted him. He heard the slosh of the remaining bits of water in the pail against his bare leg. "Yes, mam?"

"Aint you got no manners?"

He returned to the doorway and saw his grandmother lifting the bucket of sulfur water and aiming it out to the yard.

She slung it. "This water aint fit to drink." Layton felt as if the water had been splashed in his face. A shiver went up his legs. He quickly looked at the whiteman, then set down his bucket.

"There be enough for one drink left," announced Granny Fields. She looked up at Layton as if she had suddenly come out of a cave after a long time.

Layton watched as the whiteman carefully drank two full glasses of water. Not one drop fell. He mopped his face again. "Mrs. Bridges, that's the sweetest water in Holly Springs. You sure you aint got a softener hidden out in that well somewhere?"

"The Lord provides." She was not receptive to flattery. She set the bucket down in front of Layton and then sat back down in her chair. Yul Stencely stepped into the sun. He looked at Layton. Their eyes met.

"That's your youngest grandchild," he stated rather than asked, without taking his eyes off Layton.

Layton came out on the porch, picked up the other bucket, walked off the porch in front of Yul and went around the side of the house slinging the two buckets violently. He did not hear what she said anymore. He passed the sulfur well, passed the old grassy area where their hog pen used to be. They could not afford to raise hogs anymore. They had a few chickens. Even dogs would not stay. Dogs would roam and die off, getting run over on the highway or killed by other dogs. Layton could hardly remember when he had a dog. It was his brother's dog that Yul Stencely had seen on his last visit, but that was months ago. His brother had gone off to Vietnam.

Layton felt funny thinking about that whiteman coming to get money when they didn't have any. The few pennies he made at the cement plant would not keep him away. He even began to wonder if his grandmother's sturdiness could keep the dust away any longer. His brother had gone. . . . And yet Layton knew that staying was like dying. He could not die. He would go off and take his chances. At least you had a chance. But staying here trying to finish school, by alternating it with chopping and picking cotton or with pit work at the plant, was sure death.

He pictured one day a whiteman coming after him. But it burned him inside to feel that. He had seen the fire in the eyes of the kids in Holly Springs last year in the marches and demonstrations. He would join in the voter drive, he would get out and work against the dryness.

He moved along a path toward the spring. It was a grassy path. When he reached the sign and the high fence which read GOVERNMENT PROPERTY KEEP OFF, he scanned the fence for a weeded spot, then broke over, throwing the two buckets over ahead of him. The spring lay a half mile within the boundary of the fence. He had to hurry.

When his grandmother threw out that water, it was like seeing her fall down in the dust on the road. No. He rebuked himself for a thought. Even the Bible . . . He didn't know much about the Bible. He could not quote it like she could. The Bible didn't hold that much interest for him. It was those preachers who always came looking for sweet water. He didn't want to distrust the Bible, but then he could not give it all of his trust. She did not really want him to leave and go North like she said; she wanted him to stay. There wasn't nobody around Holly Springs anymore. All gone. And his grandmother wanted him to be like Granny Lincoln and the rest of the old ones. The thought choked him. He reached the spring.

The cool clear water bubbled out of the little opening in the ground near an encirclement of trees. A slight depression in the ground marked the spot. The water flowed for a very short

HENRY DUMAS

distance and then disappeared again in the earth. His bare feet moved over little stone steps. The spurt of the water from the ground was about seven or eight inches. Layton drank.

Well, maybe she didn't really want him to stay, but then who would take care of her . . . after she couldn't do it herself? But he could not picture her ever reaching the point where she could not take care of herself. When all the rest were down, Granny would still be there.

He noticed that the spurt was thinner than it was yesterday. He wondered if anybody else besides the Negroes who lived near the spring had discovered it. It wouldn't be long before the government found out that it had sweet water on its plantation. By then the spring would disappear and come up again somewhere else.

Or maybe the spring was tired of feeding the sulfurous earth and was going to return to the deep darkness forever. Layton filled the buckets and drank again. . . . When he bent over he felt his head spin as if stars were falling on him. . . .

When he returned to the shack, the sun had gathered itself into a kind of orange brilliance and was aiming toward a line in the distance. Layton filled the earthen jug, letting the water fall to make bubbles like the sound of the spring. He took the women a bucket and a dipper. But before his grandmother drank she called him.

"Son, I reckon you see a lot of things in town and out at that plant that your granny don't see. I reckon you got a right to get mad like the young people these days. I'm all for that, but I aint for you gettin mad like a mad dog. You 'member when your brother's dog got the rabies, don't you, son?"

Layton nodded. He figured he knew what his grandmother was going to say. . . . But he could not run from it. Somehow he wanted to hear it even if it cooled him. The taste of the sweet water seemed to linger in the air. . . .

"A mad dog will bite anybody, son. It don't matter who it used to belong to. It even bite the man what raised it. A mad dog will bite its own mother, son. So I'm sayin, son, be mad but not like a mad dog. Be right first. Be truthful first. And when you get mad at somethin then you got all *that* to back you up. Don't spite that man cause he thirsty and white. That's wrong. Give 'em your best at all times. When you give 'em your best when you don't like him, he be the first to know it. God on your side then."

It never mattered whether he really agreed with Granny or not, because she seemed to be right. Mrs. Fields, in her silence, had only glanced at him, and he knew that she was backing up his grandmother. It was a conspiracy. It was a bond which he could not understand nor defeat, and nothing in his experience seemed full enough to satisfy him. His mother was not sending for him. She too was trapped. In the North she wasn't doing as good as she said. He had heard how that in cities up North they were having race riots and killing Negroes. Then what good was his trying to wait till she sent out Mr. Stubbs? There wasn't no man. His father was dead and that was it. He felt himself now ready to cast off the dreams and things people said. He would believe no one, and if he dreamed something, he would not believe it were true until *he* made it come true. . . . If he were going to leave soon, then it would be because he wanted to. Even if his mother sent a ticket, it would mean nothing unless he wanted to leave. His grandmother would not drink sulfur water unless she had to and he knew that as long as there was sweet water coming out of the ground, she would be strong. . . .

A long whistle broke the late evening heaviness, and Layton stopped packing his suitcase and went out to the bald yard. . . . If he climbed the tree to see the passenger train, he knew that he would not fall.

HENRY DUMAS

A Boll of Roses

A chilly wind reached under Layton Fields' collar and batted it against his neck. He snapped the collar up, stepped quickly in front of Floyd and picked up a rock. Aiming with one hand at the red horizon where the sun had fallen he hurled, "Umphh! How you know they comin tomorrow?" he asked Floyd.

"If they comin at all, they got to come tomorrow, cause sheriff say he gonna run all them out of town, them girls too."

"Can't run one of the colored ones out, cause she born down bout two miles from Greenville."

"If a white man run you outa his town and you a nigger, then you go, born there or not."

"They ain't comin then?"

"They got to come, if they comin at all."

"They can come and talk to me. I ain't scared of a few questions."

"They ain't got to do nothin. You ever see any poll takin people come and mess around with us niggers in a cotton patch before?"

"Ah, I know why you want them to come. Cause tomorrow the last day that professor be in Greenville. He leavin and takin all them students with him."

"Well, they might skip us."

"They might if they got any sense," said Floyd. He was a lean, tall boy, bent and humorless. He hunched as he walked.

When Layton heard that, he leaped forward and picked up another rock and hurled it toward the dark line that reached out from the land to the red haze. He was black, with quick, pulsing eyes. His nose, round and large, gathered directly in the center of his face and his constantly moving mouth was full and even. He was not as tall as Floyd, but more intense.

"Hey man, how much you say you pick today?" he asked.

"I told you once, man. Ain't you got no memory?"

"Yeah, but you say when you weighed up, them two girls was there askin questions?"

"Man, you crazy! That girl ain't thinkin about no cotton pickin nigger like you!"

"All right, Floyd Moss, watch who you messin with. I just asked you a simple question."

Floyd sucked his tongue and shook his head in controlled pity. He toned his voice as if a third person were listening, talking in a sing-song rhythm of semi-taunt.

"Yeah, this guy thinks so much of hisself, he think the United States government in love with him."

"How you get the government in with what they doin?"

"I bet the government sent that college professor down here with them girls and that uppity nigger to spy on what colored folks are really doin."

"Shucks," said Layton. "You the one crazy. I was listenin to them the other day, just before the truck took off and I could hear them from the road. That girl, all three of them were civil rights workers down in Louisiana last summer. They takin outa school now to help the professor get done with what he doin."

"Well, they best skip our field tomorrow, cause when they come to me I ain't answerin no questions about nothin."

"Well, I'll take your place, Floyd Moss. You ain't good for nothin no way but pickin cotton."

"Hell, they don't pay you anythang to ask you all that damn stuff, do they?"

"You know more bout it than me. I tell you they wouldn't have to pay me. That pretty Miss Stiles, she don't have to do anythang but look at me and . . ."

"You crazy, man. They ain't go no business astin questions without givin out some pay for it. That's law."

"What kinda questions they ask?"

"All kinds, but they tryin to find out if we gonna register and vote. My old papa he ain't vote, and he said niggers never vote in Haxfall County."

"Damn," said Layton, hitting his hand in his fist. "That little brown girl bout the prettiest thang I ever seen in a cotton field."

"Yeah, but you mess with that white gal and I know them crackers hear about it as fast as thunder follow lightnin. They come after you like a hound on rabbit tail."

"Man, ain't nobody thinkin about that white girl. But I tell you somethin, man. I think I'm gonna make it back to the field tomorrow, just to get her to ast me questions."

"Yeah. Your head messed up, nigger. I can see that."

Layton slapped his fist again. They were moving up a hill along the dirt road. Large granite rocks, gaping out of the ground like teeth, faded into the shadows. The two boys felt the wind pushing at their faces, and after a brief silence, both instinctively picked up their pace.

Layton Fields hadn't planned on going to the fields tomorrow, but all week there had been a lot of talk about the civil rights kids down there taking a poll. They actually picked cotton with the people. Layton had hoped that they would make the rounds to his field, but so far they hadn't made it. Now that tomorrow was their last day, he would have to miss school again. Besides he could use the three dollars. "Hot shank!" And he hit his fist, thinking about the girl.

When they reached the point where the road leveled off, Layton threw one last rock. He threw it over the house which sat some distance back off the road.

"Loose trigger, Layton Fields, you a crazy nigger. You be done busted a window out your own house."

"I ain't chunkin at my house, fool."

"What you chunkin for? Look like to me, you save that arm. Hard as I pick today, you don't see me runnin around in the dirt pickin up rocks and chunkin in the sky at nothin, do you?"

"How much cotton you pick today?"

"Told you once. Ninety-five."

"I beat you then. You work all day, pick ninety-five. I work from noon and pick sixty."

"How come you work from noon? You come all the way down in the field for nothin. That ain't no money—sixty."

"I got paid. Ha, ha! Don't worry bout that. Hap Kelly, he ask me help him unload that boll weevil killer. Then he ask me help him fix that cotton pickin machine. He say he pay me for hundred pounds if I pick fifty."

"So what you want me to do bout it?"

"Thought if you wanted a chance at some easy money . . ."

"Hell, I don't see nothin easy bout that. If some of that bug juice get on me, it eat a hole in me same as it do a damn boll weevil. Man, you must think I'm crazy. You sure want to see that old skinny girl a lot."

"She ain't skinny, man. I like to just talk with her once."

"Shucks, what a old cottonmouth scoun like you gonna say to a rich chick like that? I bet she one of the richest niggers in the United States."

"Ah man, shut up. She'll talk to me."

"Bout what? Bout what?"

Layton turned and faced the other boy as they approached an unkempt rose hedge. The thorny branches, dipping and blowing in the wind, leaned and flopped over a rotting fence-prop. The sky was still red, but evening had pushed away, and the fading of the shadows ushered in the night. From Layton Fields' house came the deep rhythmic pulse of gospel music. Two front windows, lit up on either side of the door, appeared like eyes.

Floyd laughed. "Bout what? Bout cotton and how much you pick and if you gonna vote when you get old enough, and do your mother and father vote?"

"She talk to me. Don't worry," he said, going around the rose hedge. He fell forward as if he were going to fall, caught himself on his left arm, spun around and sat down on the step of the porch.

Floyd looked at him from beyond the bush. Neither said anything. Floyd slowly came around the hedge and up the rock path where the remnants of an unkempt flower garden lay brown and dark.

"So you see me with Florence. Don't get mad."

Layton clenched his fist.

"Hell," said Floyd, "that black gal like you, but you just ig her. You mess with that city chick, 'n she gonna cut you down like a hoeblade cut a weed. She ain't studyin bout no young nigger like you, got mud all over his shoes and cotton in his mouth."

Layton stood up, stepped off, as Floyd approached the step. Layton headed around the house. One of the rose bushes struck his neck. "Ow!" He slung his hand at it as if striking a mosquito. He went around the side of the house. "Yeah, you'll see, Mr. Floyd Moss. She talk to me."

He wanted to get away. He didn't care if Floyd followed him in the house or not. He had to get away from him. It was dark now on the east side of the house. He could hear his mother working to the sound of radio music. His grandfather was still up the Lane with the Ryans. They were getting ready to kill hogs, and his grandfather was an old hand at that. Layton struck his fist. Lord, he had to go to the cotton patch tomorrow. She was the prettiest dark brown thang he ever seen from New York. And she talked so nice and pretty. He had never heard a voice sound so pretty. He had heard pretty singing, but never had he been conscious of the sound of the human voice. Not like that. She must be what angels sounded like.

He went around to the back of the house. Floyd was hollering at him. He didn't holler back. Floyd hollered several times. "You comin tomorrow? Hey! Layton Fields! You pickin tomorrow? Hey? Cotton or rocks?"

He went into the house. The screen door slammed *whack!*

"That you, Layton?" His mother's voice, mixing with the sound of the wind and hushed chill of the evening, followed the slamming of the door.

Layton stomped his feet free of dirt before he went into the kitchen. He replied with some vague, and reluctant, monosyllable that barely he could hear. He knew he would have to plan what he was going to say to Rosemarie Stiles. What was he going to do to get her to talk to him? After all, nobody had interviewed him yet. The gospel sound of the Five Blind Boys suddenly came up. He went though the kitchen door, feeling bits of dried mud crumple beneath his feet.

His mother was building a fire in the wood stove. She was a stout woman, brown-skinned, heavy boned, but with a delicately chiseled face. Her eyes swept over Layton as he stomped through the kitchen. The dull lamp seemed to waver in its brightness as the wind and the night approached and struck the old house. Shadows in the room hid in corners. Mrs. Fields reached behind the stove and brought out the last stick of wood. With one sure motion she fed it to the tongue of flame leaping from the large iron stove.

"Who that hollerin like a crazy man?"

"Floyd Moss," he said.

"Boy, I need some wood to cook yawl som'teat." She never stopped her motions. A rolled-up, wet newspaper lay on the window sill. A few flies buzzed near it. The smell of fish hit Layton as he passed by. He knew his mother would want something done. He was planning to go down to the Blue Goose Inn. He shoulda never come home. If he'd had some clothes, he'd been down to the Blue Goose before dark. If Rosemarie ever dropped in . . . and he knew she might, because Floyd had said that twice the civil rights people had stopped in. But Layton knew that it would be dangerous if that white girl ever came into the Blue Goose. But if Rosemarie came, nobody would pay it any mind, except him. . . . He thought again. . . . Knowing those crazy niggers down there, he knew they might try to mess with her. The thought made Layton clench.

"Boy, didn't you hear me talkin to you?"

He lit the lamp in his room. "Yes mam, I get it. But don't fix nothin for me. I'm eatin . . . in town."

"Better save them few pennies you make out there. I need some money now for groceries. What you talkin bout eatin out? Eatin out where?"

He knew she wouldn't understand.

"You better stay away from that place. All you do is waste your money."

Layton pulled out a suit his brother used to wear before he left home. It was an old-style suit, faded, torn, and unpressed. He tried not to listen to his mother. He shook the suit. Dust leaped from it like smoke. He threw the suit on the bed.

Another gospel song filled the house from the living room. His mother broke into a chorus.

"Didn't papa cut some wood?" Layton asked. He knew where the old man was, but he wanted her to know that somebody else could keep the place supplied with wood as well as he could. His grandfather was doing nothing all day. Why couldn't he take time out from messing with other folks' hogs and horses and cut more wood than a couple of sticks now and then?

"Eatin or not, you better get me some wood."

Layton marched out of the house. He didn't mind getting wood for her, but he was tired. At least he was sorry he ever came straight home. Maybe he should've stopped in town and put a down payment on one of those silk vests that he saw some guys wearing. Maybe he could get himself a shirt, an English collar, French cuffs, and all. . . . Then she would know him. . . . She talk to him then. . . .

He went out the front door. The sun had gone, but a faint red glow sifted upwards as if the hills were squeezing out the last bit of color. Layton paused for a second on the porch. He looked up the lane to see if his grandfather was hobbling along. A rooster crowed. Layton hurried to the woodpile in the back of the house. Suddenly he became conscious of the dying and the falling of things. He could hear in his head an echo and he could see where the echo was going without even taking his eyes off the axe and the echo was soft and pretty like a human voice and it flew like a bird flies across the sky, slow and fast but never too fast, and up and down in the wind and all he knew suddenly is that he felt real good and nobody could tell him different.

He raised the double edged axe and brought it down on an old oak log. The log had been taking a whacking since the beginning of the week. He struck the log, splitting it in one stroke with a grunt. Every time he heard his voice, something came alive and took him further and further away, and made him grasp at some notion, some vague connection of what to say to her. He wanted to laugh but he had to show Floyd and them ugly gals that he wasn't gonna pick cotton all his life. He didn't care what Floyd Moss said about Florence. That silly country gal couldn't do nothing for him except one thing. He picked up the wood and hurried to the house, kicking open the screen door and dumping the wood down in the kitchen wood box behind the stove. The screen door slammed behind him.

> Somethin's got a hold on me
> Yeah, yeah, yeah, yeah
> Somethin's got a hold on me
> Lord, I know somethin's got a hold on me.

Mrs. Fields had turned the radio up louder. Layton watched her sprinkle corn meal over six long gutted carp that lay on the table in a large platter. Hot grease boiled and popped in a black skillet on the stove in a rhythm all its own. Mrs. Fields, wearing an apron made from flour sacks, hummed and her voice held as much fire and conviction as the singers. Listening to her, Layton suddenly winced. He liked gospel but he didn't know how to like it when he was feeling good thinking about her. He felt ashamed. But something irritated him.

"Mama, you got to play that thing so loud?" He pretended his head hurt, knocking it a few times with the palm of his hand. "I can hear that thing all over the Lane."

Hardly before he had finished, his mother turned and faced him.

"Boy, what's ailin you?"

Layton knew that he had made a mistake. He felt a funny feeling rise inside him. He turned and was going out of the kitchen. It was a feeling he got, when, walking along the levee, he would come up on a bush or a pile of dirt and something would tell him 'look before you step,' but he wouldn't look, maybe just because he was in a hurry, but mostly because he was plain foolish, and every time he didn't look there would be a snake or a lizard there. Then he knew he had made a mistake, but it was too late because his foot was stepping there at that moment.

"Layton Fields, don't you hear me talkin to you?"

"Yes mam, I hear." He grabbed at the suit, flung its dusty shape back across the bed, and then sensing some wild terror running loose in the room and outside the house, he leaped off the bed toward the kitchen.

"Mama, I got to get some money."

She stood there, the dim light of the kitchen not hiding the troubled ridge that had marred her finely chiseled face. The sound of the Five Blind Boys rose again. . . .

I come to The Garden alone

"I gon quit and get me a job . . ."

His mother turned away, placing a mealed fish in the skillet as if she had not heard him. It was a familiar gesture and Layton, coming to the doorway, knew again that he had made the wrong step. But he did not care. Nobody knew how he felt about Rosemarie. He would quit school. He would pick no more cotton. He would get a job in Greenville or even go to Memphis, and he would make some money, some real money, not three or four dollars a day picking cotton. . . . That wasn't no money. He felt ashamed of staying out of school just to pick cotton. Not that he liked school, but to go to the cotton field. . . . He gathered himself to approach his mother.

The sound of the singing surged in the house. With the rhythm of the music going, he knew that he didn't have to follow up what he said. He could just let it ride, let what she had said ride, and put on a sweater and his good shoes and make it out of the house before his grandfather came in to eat. . . . He could do that and just go up to the Blue Goose, mess around outside there a while, and come back before it was too late.

He wouldn't go to school tomorrow either, and then maybe Monday he would start in and go the whole week. But it was Friday tomorrow. Only one day left in school.

He dug in a cardboard box stuffed with musty old clothes and pulled out a ragged green sweater. "Mama, I got to get me some money." The smell of fish rose to his nostrils. He wanted to get out of the house.

"Money ain't worth losin your soul over." She moved now with a hesitancy in her muscles. She knew the boy was troubled, and that he had been wanting money. But she also knew that he didn't know the value of an education. She wanted him to stay in school and someday go to college. And here he was thinking about quitting high school. She put the last fish in the hot grease.

"But Mama, I can't make no money pickin cotton, and Grandpa don't make none . . . I got to get somethin for you." He felt himself lying. He wasn't good at lying to her.

"I know you gettin so you want things, Layton, but fore your papa died I got down on my knees. Lord, I did. And I prayed that He see me through so my youngest finish school. My oldest got away from here without finishin, but I see that I want my youngest to finish. You be round here tonight and talk with them voter people."

"Aw, I'm gon finish school, but I first gots to get some money. We the poorest niggers . . ."

"Don't use that word in this house!" She faced Layton. He slipped the sweater over his head and noticed for the first time, the terrible strain in his mother's voice. Somehow, he wanted to reach and touch her. She was right about a lot of things, but he couldn't give in on this one thing. He knew how he felt. That was all. He was going by how he felt. Her dark brown face, pulled and drawn, seemed to plead with him.

"I don't want to hear no more of this talk, Layton. The Lord promise me what He gon do with my youngest. I ain't worryin . . . Money or no money, you gon finish. I ain't never seen Him failed yet . . . And if God can't fail, then He ain't gon let one of His children fail . . ."

With that she went to fixing plates on the table.

Layton turned to go, but he heard footsteps on the front porch, and the grunting and groaning of his grandfather. The old man knocked through the front door with his cane and then grunted about in the front. Layton thought about going out the back, but something had got a hold of him. He went back into his room, kicked the tiny stove with his foot, looked at his school book in the corner, looked at the dusty suit sprawled on the bed like a broken body. . . .

For a second, the terror that had raced about the room and outside in the yard came upon him in a sudden heave of hatred for his mother and his grandfather, for Floyd Moss, for the whiteman who had all the niggers picking cotton, for the world, for the whole world, for everybody, except. . . .

He went out the front, paying attention to his grandfather who had fallen wearily in his rocking chair and was puffing and blowing to catch his breath.

He frowned at Layton and Layton passed on through the door, closing it and looking at the darkness spitting out its stars. He walked outside around the house until a chill drove into him.

He wasn't chilly. He wasn't cold. He saw a star. He saw the moon, far over there, getting ready to jump there in the sky and take over from that head-whoopin sun. He looked at the faint profile of the bushes and the trees, bending, bowing, swaying, back and forth, dancing, a whole field of cotton in the night waiting for the morning, waiting for the morning. . . .

After supper he talked to his grandfather. He wanted to get over to the Blue Goose Inn, but he would wait and go tomorrow. Friday night was better anyway. Something held him to the house. He didn't know if it were fear, or what.

He got out his good shoes and began to clean them. He hadn't worn them in months, not since the big baptism back in July at Blue Goose Lake. He looked at the shoes. They were cheap, worn, and had been polished once or twice. That was one thing he'd have to do. Polish his shoes. Everybody in the city wore clean shoes. He knew that. Anytime you went anywhere outside of the damn country, people wore decent things. They never had mud on them. He could hear his grandfather now, complaining about the weather not being right for killing hogs. His mother was standing next to the radio now, where she had propped the ironing board. Layton could see her face, and there was something about the way she had told him he was her youngest. . . . Somethin about it. . . . Maybe he wouldn't go out to the Blue Goose. Maybe he'd stay home and think about what he was going to say to Rosemarie Stiles. . . .

Would she want to talk to an old cotton pickin nigger, like him, unless he had some clothes? Deep down he feared Floyd might be right. That girl was from the city, and she wouldn't pay him no mind. But he had to talk with her. After all, wasn't she supposed to interview all the people? He would find out exactly what questions she was asking and then he would find out all the answers, and when she came to him, he would be the smartest. He might even tell her that he would be down at the Blue Goose and if she wanted to hear more answers, then she could come down there. But she couldn't bring that white girl. He didn't want to be a part of them getting lynched or run out of town. He knew what he would do. With the $9 he had saved he would buy him a vest, a pair of dress shoes, a pair of gaberdine slacks, a silk white shirt, like he saw the guys wearin at the Blue Goose, a slim tie, a cuff-linked shirt, French style, and everything else. Nobody could tell him from the rest of the cats that had gone to the city and come back sharp. He knew what he would do. There wasn't nothing stopping him.

Layton took the great box of rags, dumped them out on his bed and began to ramble through them.

Before he came out of the room he heard the visitors' voices, at once strained and alien. And one of them he knew was not the voice of a colored person. He was seated on the floor, with piles of old clothes barricading him in. He had made three piles, taking items from the big heap on the bed with deliberate care.

". . . Mrs. Fields has offered any help she can give to get started . . ."

Layton knew that voice. It was Mrs. Hooper. Sometimes she picked cotton, but she had gotten old now and didn't go to the fields. The highway people gave her some money for making her move. Only now and then would she do any picking. Layton came and stood in the doorway. Only the young girl, Sheila Bauden, glanced his way when he appeared.

They had come to his house. He looked toward the door, then back to the old woman he knew so well. Mrs. Hooper was explaining the whole thing to his mother. The young white girl, relaxed and not at all nervous, listened and seemed to nod as Mrs. Hooper explained the project. Layton looked out the window. He could see no one else.

"It ain't just us who got youngsters who want to see this thang through, but everybody is behind it. At first I was like some of the rest. I didn't want to get into nothin I thought didn't mount to nothin. But this is gonna work. Like Rev. Tucker say, 'I know God got a hand in this thang.' We gonna set up the best school in the county."

"I said I would hep. Then I hep," said Mrs. Fields. "But somebody have to show me what to do."

The white girl began to explain something. Layton watched her. He tried to detect a patronizing attitude. He shivered at the thought that somebody from town knew she was out here in the woods in a poor nigger's house. What would they do? Layton fought the urge to leave the house. He wanted to ask them when the professor was going to leave. He wondered if the rest of the group were down the road, if they were interviewing, if Rosemarie Stiles were with them. Maybe they would come to the house when they finished down there.

He stepped back into the room and continued to sort the old clothes.

He could hear them talking. His mother was going to take part in a drive in which many kids, pre-school kids, were given some training. . . .

He listened to them. He had never heard Mrs. Hooper excited over anything done with or by whitefolks, but something had got a hold on her now. Layton looked at the young white girl Sheila. She was blondish, with greenish eyes, and wearing a light brown coat which covered her slacks.

They talked for half an hour. Layton's grandfather even nodded approvals and twice he rose up and grunted "Amen." He, too, caught the enthusiasm of Mrs. Hooper.

Mrs. Hooper took out some papers and passed them to Layton's mother.

Layton came out and stood near the door. The white girl, holding a stack of forms and papers under her arm, smiled, he thought. Her face was tiny and sharp. What she smiling at me for? But then, when he went past her he realized that he hadn't even caught her eye, and that what he thought was a smile was just a twist of her head. He wanted to ask them what they wanted out there. Suddenly he stood in the center of the room.

He paused to swallow. All eyes turned on him. He couldn't say what he wanted. His mouth worked rapidly now as he swallowed air. He was suspended in the room, held up by the quiet gaze of their eyes. He could feel them letting him down easy, but still he struggled. He had to get things out by himself. He knew how he felt.

He felt a sudden quivering inside. They told him he would be a part of a group of young people to meet at the church Sunday evening. The girl Sheila took his mother in the lamp light and showed her how to get people to fill out forms. But he went outside and stood on the porch. He thought he heard people down the road.

Layton felt himself breaking inside. "Yall gon be goin to the cotton field again?"

They had all stood up to go. Sheila turned to Layton. Layton didn't know how he had said what he said. He found his lips saying things that he didn't know he was going to say. Then, when he found that he had said it, he felt ashamed.

"Yes,"she said. "But just tomorrow."

"How come yall never come to Hap Kelly's field?"

"Tomorrow we hope to visit all the fields we missed."

"You know somethin? Is that other girl, is she gonna come tomorrow?"

"Who?"

"You know, that girl always be with you?"

"Rosemarie? Well, I think so."

Where she at now? Layton thought he said that but when he saw Mrs. Hooper nodding at his mother and saying good night, he knew it had been only air.

He stepped out into the night. Mrs. Hooper and Sheila B. left, walking out into the yard and past the flowers, the moon, and out into the road. Down the road the moon had taken up a spot as if to watch and shine on that spot. He wanted to follow them. But he knew what Mr. Hooper would say. They got into Mrs. Hooper's car, and the lights came on, and the car went on down the lane.

Layton Fields! Go with them! Fool! He walked out to the the edge of the garden. The headlights turned like searchlights pivoting through the night. They struck him. He jerked his hand instinctively and let it relax into a wave. Lifting his arm, he felt a sudden urge to run after the car, but instead he fell away from the light and watched the car dissapear down the lane. The moon held itself in the distance like a piece of ice, and he squinted at it, wondering if the moon were as strong as the sun. Which one could burn up the world? Which one could cool it off?

He clenched his fist. He walked a piece down the road trying to follow the disappearing tail lights. But he knew they weren't going to the Blue Goose. . . . But maybe they would in this moonlight and stop in to ask a few questions. He could see the one-wing blue bird flying nowhere in the broken neon light and he cold hear the loud shouts of beer-voiced field hands dancing because you had to shake the dust and the cotton off your back at night, after the sun under the moon. . . . You could smell the beer and frying fish on the road—

It was the wind which told Layton to return. He had slowed his pace, feeling the chill bite into his sweater and the moon shining on something else instead of him. He stumbled once on a rock. What was he doing out in the night?

He tore himself away from the urge to fly down the road . . . . And he wandered back toward the shack, whistling with gospel music. His mother's animated voice touched a great weight gathering up in his chest. He didn't know. The whole night swallowed him up.

He heard an owl once during the night and after the fire in the stove was built up, and the house settled, as it seemed, back into the earth, he found himself sprawled across the bed, covered and buried in the rags, like some ancient mummy or dead man. The smell of the rags angered him and he went to sleep, thinking about the smell of cotton.

He dreamed of a great streamlined train, a red streak, shaped like an arrow, zooming through the cotton patch, not following any kind of tracks but weaving and twisting in and out of the rows. It was like a giant red, black, orange, and green stinging worm. He himself was dressed in a fine silk suit, and all the world was bowing to him. He was king, the king of

HENRY DUMAS

something, but he didn't have any shoes on and he had to keep his beautiful robes down and spread out to cover his bare feet. Suddenly the train sounded. Light flashed from it and the wind whistled from the horn. Layton jerked, grunted. Then sitting bolt upright, his hand slapping his neck where he thought a worm was stinging him, he leaped out of bed. The sun was gathering up itself out the window. A faint line of dust rose from the rags when he leaped up. He hadn't changed clothes all night.

He could hear his mother humming in the kitchen. She was up early. The sound of her voice was like the waving of a fan over a fire which had smoldered all night, and then in the morning, when a piece of good, dry wood was lain on, it would catch and rise up. Layton knew she wanted him to go to school today. He walked out of the room, through where his grandfather sat, tying his shoes and spitting tobacco juice in a can beside his cot. He spoke softly to his grandfather, but the old man's eyes hung on him suspiciously. Layton opened the front door and the sun leaped in on the old man's cot.

"Better mind out and stay out that cotton field, boy. You got people come way down here to get poor colored folks to help themselves. And you a young man. Ain't many young people left that's go out an pick cotton all day."

Layton heard himself saying "Yes sir," but he was off the porch, into the sun, passing the garden, when the smell of cotton . . . then the rose garden, and then wet dew . . . the bowing of the dew laden bushes . . . and he hoped it would be his last day. He knew that they would come and he knew what he would say to her. He reached and pulled a rose stem, and it stuck him, and he thought of the worm dream, and off snapped the rose and he put it into his chest pocket.

He didn't care about eating breakfast. He wasn't hungry. Leaving the shack in the morning, especially this morning, made him feel as if he were leaving it for the last time. Never again would he live there. He would get a job, take his mother out, take the old man out, buy them a house, and he wouldn't never never work for the whiteman again. He ran along the road now, not looking back. If he heard her voice calling him, even if he heard the sound of the radio, he didn't know what he would do. But he would keep going.

He could see the road now. He ran a little faster. About this time the truck would be pulling along. It might already have gone on without him. They knew that sometimes he didn't go to the fields. Maybe Hap Kelly thought today that he wasn't going.

He wondered if old Floyd had come this way. The truck might have picked him up down by the Blue Goose. There was always a large crowd that waited there in the mornings, and then the truck would pick them up. But in the night it wouldn't go directly there, but would drop them off about a half mile away, along the Bottomsuck, and then go on to drop off the rest. But sometimes that whiteman wouldn't even drive the folks home. Layton recalled the time when he told all the pickers they'd have to walk home, or ride the best way they could, but he would make it up to them on the next day. And the people went along with that whiteman but that whiteman didn't do anything but the same thing the next day. Instead of making it up, he lied again and claimed that Negroes were trying to mess over him. He said the cotton was too wet to pick, and that he was paying less for it today than on dry days. There were seven or eight who quit pickin for him that very day. Hap Kelly was mean when he wanted to be, and that was most of the time.

Before Layton reached the road he heard the truck. He ran, but he could see that at the curve they wouldn't see him from the truck, and they would keep going.

He made a last effort to reach the bend before the truck passed the lane, but when he reached it he saw a cloud of dust. The truck had passed.

Layton ran out on the road. What did he look like running after a cotton truck? He threw up his hand, almost stopping, but seeing that people on the back were hollering for the truck to stop and the truck was slowing, he ran on. . . . He leaped up on the truck, and it lumbered back onto the road, grinding gears, and made the wide turn that took it into the delta flats. Layton stood for a while, looking over the cab of the truck. Old Lady Rusmaker pulled on his coat and coughed.

"Sit down, boy. You be standin all day. No use to do it on the truck."

They made room for him. The same people. Floyd was sitting near the front. Dust and the smell of weeds and cotton stalks filled Layton's nostrils. He sat down, squeezing himself in between Mrs. Jackson with her walking stick and the cab of the truck.

He looked at the people. Didn't they get tired of picking cotton and riding the truck? They were the same people. He knew that he would have to leave. He would get him a job. No more cotton. He would get him a job.

He looked at the faces. At the end of the truck was old man Jesse. He had picked cotton all his life. He had been a tenant farmer once, but now he picked with whoever was doing the hiring. Old man Jesse was stubborn, but Layton liked the way he sang. When old man Jesse sang, the whole field raised up a bit. Somehow the burden of the sack was lifted. Next to him was Sister Leah. She was a short black woman, with bad eyes. Years of cotton picking seemed to have even put a bend in her face. It drooped, even when she smiled, which was seldom.

The truck reached the downgrade. Everybody leaned forward a bit.

Two of the Parker children, both sitting next to Sister Leah, began coughing. They were two boys, no more than eleven years old. Layton looked at them. If there was anybody should be in school, it was them.

The truck rumbled on. Layton tried to look back through the dust. He knew that sometimes a car followed the cotton

ECHO TREE

pickers into the field. He knew that the interviewers rode with the truck sometimes, and sometimes they came in a car. He had seen them. He was going to ask Gladys Fisher, who was sitting with a silly grin on her face across from him, ask her if they were going to come to the field. But he held back. He better not say anything to her or Florence. Them two would be picking at him all day. He couldn't stand no ugly girls, but they all time found something to nag him about.

He loooked at Floyd, squeezed in between Mrs. Hattie Jones and Omelia Diggs. Layton wanted to laugh but he knew Mrs. Jackson next to him would detect it. She wouldn't hesitate to strike your feet with her cane. Layton never knew how she managed. She had been picking cotton since they invented cotton. He leaned out to try to catch Floyd's eye, and when he did, he saw Floyd laughing at him. Floyd was pointing at him and laughing. He drew back. What the hell you laughing at, nigger? He felt everybody looking at him. He felt a sharp prick in his chest. The rose was sticking out of his pocket. As he stuffed it back, he could hear them all snickering.

"Ain't nobody studyin yawl," he said, but his voice was drowned by the rumbling of the truck. He coughed, as if to challenge them. Even the Parker kids were laughing at him, but not because they knew what was going on. They were laughing because they saw the older kids laughing, and even *at* the older kids.

Layton could see that Floyd was really trapped in between the two fat women and they were slapping him back and forth as if he were a piece of dough ready to be rolled out and flattened for biscuits.

Layton wanted to laugh but Old Lady Rusmaker across from him was shaking her head watching everybody. She didn't like young people. Once in church she caught him and Floyd messing around, and sent them out of the church. Both of them got a whipping. He never forgot that and even though he spoke politely to her, said "yes mam" and "no mam," and all the right things, he never liked her. He rubbed his feet together. The truck picked up speed on a sandy stretch toward the levee.

"Boy, what your mama gonna do with them whitefolks and Mrs. Hooper?" asked Mrs. Jackson. She propped the cane up and leaned on it with one arm.

"I don't know."

"Heard they come out to your house last night."

"Yes mam."

"What your grandpa think?" Mrs. Jackson was always like that. She asked questions and got into people's business. Layton didn't mind telling her what he thought was going on because he knew it had to be good, since Mrs. Hooper was in it.

"He think it be good."

"You gettin mighty big yourself, now. You gwine get with them people, and let them send you back to school?"

"Yes mam."

"I picked cotton all my life, chopped, planted, cleared land, and I ain't got nothin to show for it. You younguns oughta get out of this field and get with them rights people. They got the Lord on their side."

Old Lady Rusmaker, sitting across from Layton, leaned her body over to hear. "What's that, Clara?"

Mrs. Jackson pointed the end of the cane at Layton's shoe. She jabbed it and held it on the toe.

"I say," she yelled, "these younguns gwine have to get out of the field and work with those gov'ment people. Colored folks' time is comin now. I just tellin this here boy to get with them people."

"Ain't it the truf," nodded Old Lady Rusmaker.

Layton was glad when the old women got into a conversation.

The truck rumbled slowly over a rutted road, and stopped in front of a dilapidated cotton gin—one of the old shacks that was now used to house a tractor and cotton pickers. Everybody got off.

The chill in the air was gone now. The sun had found its way up through the dust and dew. Layton leaped off the truck and looked around. The fields were empty. Their truck was the first. He wondered where the two big trucks were with the rest of Hap Kelly's pickers. He knew a lot of people on the other trucks too. He had to get out and choose a good row so he could be on the outside and when she would come along then he would be in a good spot. The cotton sacks were hauled off the truck. Another whiteman came out of the barn. He walked over to Hap Kelly and they talked briefly. He knew the other man, a narrow red-faced white man, named Fane, whose skin was so weathered that it looked like brown leather. To look at him you would think he was an Indian or a Negro, but then you would see the wrinkles and the shape of his nose, the blueness of his eyes and his matty hair. Layton pulled up a handful of grass and stood near them.

"There's that shale strip yonder and I want it picked clean first. It don't matter none after that who gets to the pecan trees. Yonder pass them trees is all from now till next week."

The man named Fane kept nodding his head and smoking on a cigarette. Layton didn't hear him say a word. It was all Hap Kelly. And Hap Kelly was keepin his eyes on Florence Meadows. Floyd had his sack and came over to Layton. Layton picked up a rock and threw it into the trees. The two white men moved off to the barn. The pickers gathered up their sacks and waited under a great live oak by the road.

"There he is," laughed Floyd, pointing at Layton. "There he is. Layton the Claytoe."

"Aw shut up. Didn't you see how that whiteman messin with Florence?"

"Yeah, I see. That gal old enough to take care herself. Funny you ain't say nothin about it till now." He laughed again at Layton.

Layton kicked some dirt toward Floyd. "Get away from me, fool, talkin that mess."

"Yeah, we all know what you got, boy. That city gal got your head messed up."

"Ain't nobody thinkin . . ."

"Or it must be that white gal. They tell me she and Mrs. Hooper come all over the Lane last night."

Layton didn't say anything. The rose in his chest pocket pricked him again. He wanted to take it and throw it at Floyd. What right had that overall-wearing nigger to make fun of him? What right had he even to see that flower? Layton wished he had kept his feelings to himself. He walked off. "Man, don't mess with me. I told you yesterday, I tell you today, if you mess with me . . ."

"You what?" He felt some dirt hitting him in the back. He turned. It was Floyd. He was standing beside the two girls, Florence and Gladys, and they were all watching him, laughing. The Parker kids even joined in.

"All right, yawl," Layton heard the whiteman's voice. The truck started up. "This here field is new." Fane pointed.

The day's work began. People listened briefly to Fane. Mrs. Jackson, as if she anticipated everything the man was saying, limped across the road, followed by old man Jesse, mumbling to himself. Fane kept talking as if he didn't see them.

Latyon moved to the outer edge of the circle. When the meeting broke Layton drug his sack across the road, clutching his stomach and wishing he had brought something for lunch. He would have to buy some lunch or beg. And he would not beg, and he could not buy. He was saving all his money for his clothes.

Approaching the cotton he hit an outside row. It was lower and the cotton was scrawny. There was something in the soil at that particular row which stunted the growth of the cotton. Layton swung his sack around, letting it drag comfortably from his right side. The first few bolls were tight and the cotton fought his fingers. He knew he was on a bad row.

For a long time he held his head down. When he finally looked up, everybody was ahead of him, except Mrs. Jackson, and she was about even. He had picked a clean row, but he was moving slow. Over the field he saw none of the interviewers.

When he was sure no one was looking, Layton took the crumbled flower from his pocket. He felt like slamming it down in the dirt and stomping on it. He squatted and examined the flower. He ought to spit on it. He ought to be in school. He knew what he was going to do. He was going to get a job. Hell, here he was. Maybe Floyd was right. So what if she did come today. She wouldn't look at him. He clenched the flower. Sweat began to rise out of his body. He ought to spit on it. He didn't have any clothes yet. Hell, he hadn't even went to town to look for any. What would she say to a dirty nigger in the cotton patch? He looked at the flower. Suddenly he had to stand up quickly. He felt himself giving way to a sudden urge to cry.

He put it back and went on picking.

Across the field he could make out Floyd. He had got himself a row next to Florence and they were laughing. He knew he didn't want to be next to them. He had gotten one next to Mrs. Jackson. Only trouble with her was that she was going to bother him about first one thing and then another. Picking *alongside* her was just the same as picking *for* her. The first time he ever got beside her he figured the best thing to do with her was to tell her to go and rest in the shade less she have a sun stroke, and he would take care of her sack and his too. It would be easier to do that than to have to put up with her noisiness and peskiness. Layton looked up ahead. Old man Jesse was just ahead of her. The next row over was the Parkers. They were ahead. One of the Parker boys would soon act as the water-boy. Between the two of them they could pick over a hundred pounds of cotton, and when the sack got too heavy for them Mrs. Parker would put all of the cotton in hers and the boys would go right on. They were a team. And nobody could outpick a team.

Sweat gleamed on his left arm. The morning had gone. The crew was working fast. They finished a couple of rows, going up, turning around, starting back, dragging their sacks. Old man Jesse had begun a slow hum that grew stronger and louder as he bent under the weight of the sack. Layton was in a row next to Gladys now, and Floyd was next to her. Mrs. Parker was next and then Old Lady Rusmaker. Over the fields cotton stretched beneath rises in the land as far as Layton could see. He wondered if people planted anything else in the world besides cotton. He swung at flies buzzing around him.

Suddenly he lifted his head. Way across the field he saw dust spreading out over the black edge of a car moving along just above the tops of the cotton. It wasn't going toward the field on the other side of the pecan trees. It was coming toward them. Like a wind striking the tops of cotton, an urgency swept over the pickers. They knew that the car was headed their way. Layton picked faster. Twice the rose worked itself out and fell on the ground. It was noontime. They had come. He picked faster, squinting his eyes at the movement of the dust.

The car stopped under the grove of pecan trees. Layton could make out several figures getting out. A truck pulled in behind the car. It was loaded with pickers. They were going to pick the other field.

"Boy, what you think you doin?" It was Mrs. Jackson. She had been watching him. Layton bent over, laid the sack down. "Yes mam," he said, and stepped over the next row and headed toward the trees.

"Boy, where you goin?" He kept going, saying "Yes mam. Yes mam."

That's what he had to say: Yes mam, yes mam. . . . Hell, what did old people have to come to the cotton patch for? Mrs. Jackson was crippled and she was always sitting up on somebody's truck, going to pick three dollars worth of cotton. She had helped her children all the way through school. Some of them sent her money. He couldn't figure what made her come back to the fields. If he had people sending him money, he would never come to a cotton field.

He saw Rosemarie Stiles now. People were crowded around her and the white girl, Sheila. The whiteman, driving the car, was talking to the pickers. He was the professor. Somebody had said he was working for the government. There was a young colored guy with the group. Layton approached from behind, coming into the shade of the grove on the field side. For all they knew, he might have been on that truck.

Layton brushed himself off, his pants, and shirt, trying to send the dust away.

He got in among the crowd. He could see her now again. She was laughing. Those niggers had her laughing. What could she be laughing at? Layton moved in. He asked the driver if they had any water. The man pointed to a tank on the back of the truck. He leaped over the tail gate. Rosemarie Stiles had her back to the truck. When Layton jumped up, Sheila, having seen him crossing the field, looked up at him.

Layton tried to remember everything in the world to say, but his throat was dry and filled with dust. He found a paper cup, filled it, and leaned against the high truck rails. Sheila looked at him again. He walked to the edge of the truck, and as if struck by some ireresistible urge, broke out all over in a big grin, reaching the cup of water down to the head of Rosemarie. Sheila saw the whole gesture, saw Layton and his eyes. He handed her the water and quickly got another. This one he reached to Rosemarie, and when he looked in her face he knew that he would never come to the cotton field again. He would go to school, get himself a job, maybe go on to college and . . .

"Thank you," Sheila said.

"Yes, thank you."

Layton was still smiling. But he did not feel as if he wanted to smile. He was just embarrassed. He had waited to talk to her and now he had a chance. . . . He leaned over the side of the truck and after swallowing a cup of water, he managed to feel his chest.

"I got to talk to you, about a job . . . Mrs. Hooper, she say I got to talk to you about that job."

"What job?" asked Rosemarie.

Layton felt himself slipping. He hoped the side of the truck would hide how he looked. "Mrs. Hooper gettin us jobs with the government."

More people dragged sacks and hollered, gathering around Sheila and Rosemarie.

"Mrs. Hooper is working with us."

"What's you think you writin in that book about us niggers?" Layton asked.

The girl continued writing and sat on the fender of the truck. "You must be Layton Fields," she said, after a long silence. She was filling out some forms, the same kind of forms that his mother had filled out the night before.

"That's right. What you think about it?" He clenched his hands, grinding his toes up into his shoes, digging his knees into the sides of the truck, letting the prick of the thorn sting him, and sting him, letting the sweat gather into a little dam and then leap into his eyes. . . .

He didn't know why he was doing it. He wanted to jump down and hit her and hug her. He couldn't figure out what made him get all messed up over a pretty brown gal. She wasn't pretty. Maybe to some people, but not to him. He let the thorn stick his chest, and he let the image of the figure of Old Lady Rusmaker coming across the field to gossip and stick her nose in business hang in his eyes. He did not look down at her. He still smiled, but it was not like a drink of water.

"Your mother has signed up for the pre-school course. She's going to make more money doing work in town than you will make here in the field."

Layton jumped off the truck and came around to face the girl.

"What you think you doin comin down here to mess with niggers? I bet this the first time you ever see a cotton field."

"Well, I certainly didn't come out here to talk with no dirty mouthed mannerless thing like you." She folded the last sheet of a form and went to the next one. Layton walked straight toward Old Lady Rusmaker slowly walking in the sun. When he got to the sun, he felt himself rise up, struck by the heat, and then rise up and trot and when he got to the first row of cotton, he leaped over it.

Floyd Moss saw him and hollered. He waved Floyd off, but circled in that direction. The sun was heavy on him. He liked the way it felt. He knew he was going to pick some cotton today. He was going to get that money, oh yeah, he was going to get it, and he was going to go to school. He might even buy him some clothes. That's right. He looked over his shoulder. All those Negroes picking cotton. He'd show them how to pick. Look at that black gal Florence over there. He ought to throw a rock at her. Laughing at him. Hell, he knew what he was going to do. When he got home . . . He thought of his mother's pinched face, the other night. A pain had knotted there so long that it was part of her look. He wanted to change that face. He wanted his mother to smile. He knew what he would do. He might even apologize to that gal. She was too old for him anyway. He picked up his sack, slung it over his shoulder, grunted *"Ummph,"* and dragged the weight of the sack. He saw his hands move, and he said, "move hands," and every time he said *move hands,* they moved, then he said *move once for my mama,* and he kept on picking, with the fields all under his power. There he was, and he said, "I'm gonna pick till it stick. I'm gonna finish this field so clean, people'll forget what cotton look like."

And he saw Florence coming toward him. He saw the Parker boys bring her water and she drank it and across the field, over the rows, Layton saw her, and he knew his mother wouldn't mind receiving a rose either.

Double Nigger

"Yeaah!" said Grease. ". . . and evah time I grunt, that damn peckerwood, he say to hisself, 'Damn if you ain't the workinest nigger I ever seed.'"

We laughed at Grease, but we won't payin him no mind. He was the onliest one who done taken his shoes off tryin to keep off that hot pike.

We was makin it back to New Hope, Grease, Blue, Fish and me. We had just got done with bustin up some road for a white man, helpin out his construction gang.

We was feelin good, headin back home with four dollars apiece. We'd all take out them bills evah mile or so, count 'em and match 'em up to see whose was the newest. They was the prettiest damn dollar bills we evah made. Totin rocks and stumps for that white man almost busted our natural backs.

"Shet up, nigger," Blue said to Grease. "Your mouth runnin like a stream." Blue was walkin along on the other side of the road even with me. We were fanned out a bit. Fish was ahead. Grease, he was behind him, jumpin off and on to the hot pike to cool his feet.

"Yeaah," I said. Put your shoes on. Ain't you got no civilization?"

"Yeaah!" said Grease, wavin his greens back at me and Blue. "He say, 'Niggah,' and yall know what it mean when a white man call a nigger a niggahhh, don't you?"

"Naw," said Blue. "What it mean?"

Old Grease, he half fell over laughin, but then he straightened up and posed hisself like he was a preacher givin us a lesson.

"Nigggahhh. That mean whatever you can do, it take *two* niggers to keep up with you. Then you a Double Nigger," and he fell to laughin again.

We moved on, payin Grease little mind, but glad he wasn't gettin tired. He funny sometime, but he nevah know when to stop clownin.

We come to a hill. The road turned around the hill. It was really hot. Your spit almost boil. We stopped under a shade tree. "I'm so damn thirsty," said Fish, "I could drink my own spit."

We all agreed.

"If yall come on," said Blue, "we be in Rock Hill less'n hour."

Grease said, "I bet that peckerwood there'll let us buy soda water with money look this pretty."

"Naw," said Fish, lookin over the hill. "I think we oughta cut yonder ways, hit the Creek and be home fore dark."

"Boy, you crazy!" shouted Grease. "Tired as my feet is, and full of snakes as that creek is . . ."

"What you say, Tate?" Fish asked me.

"All I want is one bucket of water now," I said.

"What bout you, Blue?"

"It don't matter one way t'other," he said. "We done come this far, we might as well walk the rest."

"Well, yall go ahead," said Grease, pretendin he wasn't payin us no mind. "I'll be drinkin soda water and snatchin on that black gal Lucille as soon as I gets to Rock Hill, and then I catch a bus or a ride with some niggers comin through."

"Yeah," said Blue, "you little squiggy nigger, and you get home tomorrow mornin too. Ain't no more bus comin through Rock Hill."

"Yes it is."

"Naw," said Fish.

"Yeah," I added. "If you do get home messin round down there, you have a rope around your neck. Ain't no colored people livin out here."

"The hell there ain't."

"Come on," said Fish. Blue and me broke off with Fish cross the field.

We knew that Greasemouth was only playin, but he had

worked over this way once with some white man sawin lumber. It was just before school started. I member, cause Grease ain't come to school hardly that whole year.

We climbed through the barbed wire fence settin way off the road. There was a creek over that way somewheres. If we went this way, it would cut off five miles, goin over the hills stead round them.

"Creek is yonder way," Blue said. We stood lookin over the area. We hadn't looked back to see if Grease was followin. We didn't much care. He had stopped laughin at us, and when we turned around, we didn't see him.

"Let that greasemouth nigger go," said Blue. "One of them razorback perckerwoods'll catch him sniffin round down over yonder and they'll saw that nigger's lips off."

"If the grease don't stop 'em," said Fish.

We laughed. We always had fun with Grease when he was with us or not. We called him Grease cause whenevah he ate anythang, he let the grease pile up in the corners of his mouth and all over, like he nevah chewed his food but just slide it down with grease and lard.

We all come together now, walkin down the slope, watchin for bulls, dogs, wild hogs, crazy peckerwoods, devils and anything that moved. We might be trespassin. After a while we got deep into the trees. All we saw was a few birds and a rabbit.

"As ugly as Grease is," said Fish, "them peckerwoods'll wind up sending for us and then they pay us to take that nigger outa their sight."

We doubled over laughin. I tripped on a rock and sat there, catchin up on my wind. Blue was just ahead of me. He walked under a shade tree. He was so black that everybody called him Blue. Fish, he wasn't too much lighter. He was about my complexion and they called him Fish cause he could stroke good. Natural fish, he was. They called me Tate cause my head shaped like a potato. I nevah could find no damn potato on my head, but they just keep callin me that anyway, and so I do like everybody else and tease ole crazy Greasemouth. Then I can stand them better teasin me. I stopped laughin and got up. I picked up a stick and thought about throwin it at Blue, but kept it and went runnin on down to catch up.

I don't recollect what I thought it was at first. But all of a goddamn sudden! there comes this wild-buck thang chargin at us from behind a bunch of trees, yellin.

Blue broke in front of me, screamin somethin I ain't nevah heard, and before all three of us knew anythang, ole Greasemouth was doubled over laughin at us.

Fish was the first to holler at him, cause Fish probably saw him fore any of us, and he wasn't taken aback by him jumpin out like that.

"Get up, boy. You ain't scared nobody but yourself," Fish said to Grease.

But he kept wallerin there on the ground, laughin.

"Scared all of you!" he hollered. He began rollin down the hill, still laughin.

"You shoulda seen that . . ." And he pointed at Blue, who was standin just shakin his head as if to signify on Grease for makin a fool out of hisself. But Blue was really scared a little bit. Me too, a little.

". . . that nigger get ready to run. Did yall see that?"

Blue swung his arm on a limb and chunked some leaves at Grease.

"Ah, get up, boy. As ugly as you is, the trees leanin over away from you."

Grease got up and kept on teasin us. We moved on now through the patches of trees and washed out ditches and holes. Grease had put on his shoes now and was way up front, call hisself singin.

Then he hauled off and stopped singin.

"Hey, yonder's a well!" We all ran over and looked where he was pointin.

"Ah, now damn!" said Blue. We stood there lookin.

"Told yall niggers live up here," Grease said.

It was a house sittin beside a busted-in barn and a old wellshed. About half an acre of shale dirt full of weeds was behind that house. Nothin grow on dirt like that but scorpions and mean peckerwoods.

"Dammit, Grease," hollered Fish, "you know it ain't no niggers livin there . . ."

"That's right, and I can't drink that damn house," said Blue.

"Hell," I said, "don't think a peckerwood mind givin four niggers some water."

"Who's gonna ask?" said Grease.

"You, nigger," said Fish. "Didn't you find the place?"

"Yall said I was ugly," he said, "and I don't want to scare nobody, as thirsty as I is."

"Just whoever do the askin, leave the gate open and watch for nigger-eatin dogs," I said.

As we moved toward the house, Blue said, "Ain't nobody liven there. Look, ain't no smoke in the chimney."

Nobody said nothin to that, but we didn't trust it for gettin us water. We moved in slow, waitin for a dog to smell us and start to barkin.

When we had come off the hill into a ditch that run up longside a little dirt road that run in front of the house, sure nough a damn dog caught scent of us, and come runnin. But it wasn't nothin to get scared of. That dog was a sissy-puppy, a fool dog, we called them. It was still a pup, but it was jumpin and switch-tailin round, lickin at strangers so fast it look like it was chasing its tail.

"Toe fleas got that damn dog," said Blue.

"Hey, get away, dog!" Grease stomped his feet. "Toe fleas got 'im itchin to beg." We headed for the well. "Up his ass and down his legs."

The place did look like nobody was home. We ran to the well. Fish hollered for somebody and then went round back. Me and Blue snatched that rope and let the well bucket down.

Grease was throwin sticks for the fool dog to run after. "Sic 'em," he was shoutin, "sic 'em!" But the dog liked us too much. She just wiggled her tail, lickin Greasemouth's feet.

"Look here!" said Grease. "I found somethin worse'n a nigger."

"What's that?" Fish said, comin back.

"A nigger's dog."

"Shet up, boy," Blue grunted. We were pullin up the bucket. The well was old, and the rope was so rotten it shot dust tween our fingers. One of the boards under us squeaked and then that sissy-puppy come up waggin its tail under our feet too.

"Peckerwoods live here," said Blue.

"Ain't nobody home, though," said Fish.

"Les drink and git," I said.

"I want to drink but that dog got to git," said Grease, and he kept tryin to sic that pup off.

Then we heard a loud crashin sound come from inside the well. Blue stopped pullin on the bucket. He leaned over. "I got it," I said.

"What's goin on?" asked Grease. "Hurry and get me some water."

I began pullin again. I could feel the ground shakin under me. The well was fallin, crashin in and givin away. But the bucket was almost up.

"Wait!" shouted Grease. "This is it. Blue, you right!"

I kept on pullin. "Right about what?" Blue asked.

Grease waved us all quiet and he began runnin around the well, lookin at it real close and pointin. Then he ran over near the house and began to study it. He looked dead serious. He almost tripped over a fruit jar, but he kicked it as if he knew it was there and didn't have to look.

He came back to us. I had the bucket up to the top. Grease began pointin at the well. "Don't drink this here maggot water, boys. I know I'm tellin you the truth."

"What's in here, Grease?" Blue asked.

"Look round here. Can't yall smell this place stinkin like a beaneater?"

"Hurry, yall," said Fish. "That nigger's lyin." But nobody was gettin ready to take the first drink.

"Naw, naw, Fish," Grease said. "It's somethin that woulda clear skipped my mind, cept for this here fool-dog. He was a pup then . . . Yall member back last year when I was workin for Tulsom Lumber?"

We ain't say nothin. I pulled the big dirty bucket up and sat it there. Cool water was shootin out the holes. I was gettin ready to plunge my mouth in when Grease said, "Go head, Tatehead. Your head swell up bigger'n a punkin, and when it bust you member my words. Go head."

We ain't say nothin. Then Blue asked him what he knew. He started tellin a long tale about how he was passin by with a white man who knew the peckerwoods that lived there. That's what he meant by Fish bein right, right that white people lived there, not colored. Fish walked off and spit. He nevah believed nothin Grease said.

When we looked in that bucket, we saw pieces of wood in there, dirt and a couple of dead bugs floatin around. Blue smelled it and frowned. I smelled it and Fish came over. The fool-dog was jumpin all over Fish now, and he was wavin it off.

"And here's the thang I couldn't help . . ." Grease lowered his voice. "That white man woulda killed me sure as hell is below high water if he find out what I done to his well. But it won't my fault."

"What happen?" asked Blue.

"It was night, see. That damn fool-dog's mama was a mean bitchhound, then. I was waitin in the truck for this here white man to come out. But he wouldn't come. It started gettin dark. I had to go bad. So I ain't want to bother nobody cause I knowed what he was up to in that house. There was a little ole skinny peckerwood gal in there. I was headin out past the well, see, and no sooner I got jumpin distance from the well, here come that fool-dog's mama towards me, growlin like she wanted some nigger leg. Hell, I ain't have no place to run. I jumped up on the well cover and I must've busted it then, cause it's gone now as yall can see, and jist bout time I got up, the bitchhound was snappin at me, mean as a peckerwood's dog want to be.

"I had to go bad, and that damn dog wouldn't let me down. And that sucker inside wouldn't get off that gal and come out, to help this nigger.

"So, brothers," he said, as if we woulda all done the same thing, "I had to crap in that man's well."

"Get this lyin nigger!" Fish shouted, and we all grabbed Grease. He started shakin his head, but I come right up to him with my fist drawed back, while Fish locked that devil's arms. Grease, he started tryin to shake us off. Blue got a hold on his legs and we started swingin that nigger all round.

"Hold him, yall!" I said, and we all was laughin, but we wanted to teach him a lesson.

"Go head, Tate," Fish said to me, "git your drink."

I cleared the dirt off the top of the water and got me some. That water was good.

Then I got a new hold on Grease who was still hollerin. "Come on now, can't yall take a tale?"

"Yeah, yours," Blue said.

After Blue and Fish got their drink, we drug Grease long towards the road. He was yellin. That damn sissy-dog got scared of us and started to bark, tuckin her tail under and peepin from under that raggedy house.

Before I left, I got that jar on the ground and filled it full of the dirtiest water on top, rot-wood and all. Then I stuck the jar in my back pocket and caught up with them niggers pushin ole Grease long. He kept up a natural plea with us, but we ain't listen to him. We act like we ain't even know him anymore.

"What we gonna do with this nigger, Tate?" Fish asked me.

"Make him eat a half sack of salt."

"What you say, Blue?"

"I tell you guys. That was the stinkiest water I evah tasted. I think we oughta let this nigger go back and drink a whole bucket full. If he let one drop fall, we tie his ass to the well and let the peckerwood find 'im there."

"That's too good," said Fish. "Les tie his mouth up. This nigger talks too much. Then les pour creek water over his head."

"Naw," I said. "Les lift him up by his big foot to the first low tree we come to and let that sissy-dog lick 'im till he slimes up from dog spit, and his mouth and eyelids stick shut."

All the time Grease was whinin. But we pulled and pushed him along. We got over a mile down the road. We was all sweatin with that squiggy nigger by now, and gettin tired of the game. We figured we was too far now for him to turn round and go back. So we turned him loose and soon as we did, that nigger broke out laughin at us again. He said that while we was tusslin with him he had picked our pockets, and had all that good money. He waved some bills in his hand. Damn, if that didn't get to us.

"Grease, you the lyinest nigger I evah met up with," said Fish, after drawin out his money and lookin at it. We did too, and was about to grab him again when we heard the sound of a truck comin up that dirt road.

We all got serious and pulled together. Round the corner came this beat-up truck with a skinny ole red-necked hillbilly bent over the wheel and a wide-eyed freckled faced gal sittin side him. The truck was goin so goddamn slow that I coulda read a whole chapter of God's Holy Bible by the time it passed us. But it didn't pass.

That peckerwood stopped it and called us over.

Fish stood where he was, but me, Blue and Grease come off the side of the ditch.

"You boys lookin for somethin?"

"Naw, sir," said Grease real fast. "We goin home."

"What you lookin fer around here?"

"We done two days work other side of Rock Hill," said

Grease. "We work for a white man named Mr. Nesbit. He paid us and said, 'That's it, boys,' so we goin back to Bainesville."

"You niggers lyin?"

"Naw, sir," said Blue. He looked back at Fish who was gettin mad, if he wasn't already. We coulda all beat that old man's ass, but if we did we'd have to leave the state. Even a poor white man like him could mess over niggers and niggers couldn't do a damn thing about it. Right then I wished Grease's tale hada been true.

"They puttin a cutoff out on the Memphis Highway," I said. "They know bout it in Rock Hill."

"How come you niggers ain't go round through Rock Hill like you ought to? I got a good mind to make yall go back the way you come. We don't allow no niggers over here."

We all just stood there. That young gal was steady twitchin and twitchin. We ain't look at her, but I could see her out of the corner of my eye, twitchin round in that seat like she sittin on a pile of rocks.

All of a sudden that old man hauled off and slapped her.

"Now keep still," he said.

Then he got up a shotgun.

"You niggers come long this road a far piece?"

Fish stood straight now and came towards us. I thought he was gonna say somethin, but Grease beat him to it.

"Naw, sir, we just come off that hill." He pointed. "We tryin to get to the creek, but I tole 'em we passed the creek and best keep on, since . . ."

"How come yall comin this away?"

"We thought we knowed the way cross these hills, but I reckon we got lost."

"How long yall come along this road?"

"We just got on it bout the time we hear a truck comin round the bend, and then it was you," said Grease.

"If I find you niggers lyin, and been in my house I'm gonna come back here and make buzzard meat outa your asses."

"Naw, sir, we ain't seen no house since we left the highway."

HENRY DUMAS

He raced the engine coupla times, then he turned and looked at me. "Nigger, what's that you got in your back pocket? Let me see."

I jerked my hand back there. I done forgot. Fish come over, but Grease beat him to the words. "That's mine," said Grease. I took out the jar of water.

"That's niggerwater for my feet," said Grease. "I got bad feet, and suffer with short wind."

"What you talkin about?" The old man looked like he mighta laughed then, but he didn't. He cocked his head.

"I fell out. Tate, he carryin the water for me." Grease rolled his eyes.

"I ain't never heard of a nigger fallin out," the old man said.

"Naw, sir, it ain't like you think. I was totin a rock weigh three times my size. I come near bustin myself."

The old man looked at each of us. We was all dressed dirty and sweat was pourin off us. He looked at the jar of water, then at Greasemouth, who was showin off how sick he was.

". . . wide open." Grease kinda motioned with his whole self to where he mighta busted hisself, but because that gal was sittin there, Greasemouth didn't point or say no more.

"All right, boy," said the old man. "Thas nough now." He turned to each of us.

"This nigger tellin the truth?"

We all said a loud "Yes Sir." Even Fish said it.

"All right. Yall niggers done missed the creek. You way off, and you better get hell outa my hills. Don't stop till yall hit thet highway. Now git!"

We moved off quickly. That old man still held that shotgun up in the air. He had braked the truck on the hill, but we never heard it no more, cause when we got round that bend we broke into the woods off the road, runnin fan-wise, cussin, movin down that road like we were four boats in a downriver. We didn't stop till Fish slowed and leaned up ginst a tree, puffin. . . .

"What the hell we runnin for?"

ECHO TREE

"Gimme my water," puffed Grease.

"What you talkin bout, your water?"

"All right, I'm goin back and tell that peckerwood yall busted into his house, stole his water and pissed and shit in his well."

"Yeah? And that white man shoot the first nigger he see, you first," I said.

Greasemouth must've been really thirsty then, because he was chokin. He was gaspin for breath.

I took out that jar of water and almost put my own mouth to it, but Grease was on it like a rat on cheese.

We all watched. We wanted some of that water so damn bad.

Then old Grease do somethin we ain't expect him to do. He saved back nough for each of us to have one swallow and then he twisted up his mouth. "I ought not to give you lyin niggers nothin."

"Go head, boy, and drink your water," said Fish, but he didn't mean it. Me and Blue took one swallow each.

Grease took that jar and gave it to Fish. "I knowed a Christian was livin in that devil heart of yours," he said, and he finished it.

We went on, pullin together, and not laughin anymore.

"You just watch," said Blue. "You just watch that nigger Greasy when he gits back. He gonna tell everybody how he did this here and did dat dere. You watch. He be done run a white man down, took his gun off him, whopped the white man's ass and then climbed upon the white man's well and shit in it just for devilment."

We were puffin a bit still, and everytime Blue took a step he puffed and dragged his words.

That fool old man wasn't comin after us. We knew that. We slowed down and Blue kept on teasin Greasy.

Fish was movin longside me now.

We laughed and kidded about what Blue was sayin.

Grease wasn't payin no mind to none of us. He kept movin long, puffin as much as any of us. Then he hauled off and stopped, scratched his head like a mosquito had stuck him one.

"Listen up, you niggers," Grease said. "I know the truth now. Goddammit, I know it."

We ain't paid too much attention to him, but we did slow down.

"I got it all right here." He touched his heart. "You see how that peckerwood jump at me when I tell him the truth. That was God Almighty truth what I told him. Bu that sucker, he ain't hear me, uh?" He grunted like Rev. Weams do when he windin himself up.

"The truth is the thing. May a dead dog draw red maggots as sure as you niggers hear me. I swear fore livin God, may cowshit stand up and walk, I swear. You niggers listenin? I swear, I ain't foolin round no more. No more lies for me. The truth for me!"

"Aw, you a damn lie," said Fish. "You a lie and don't know why. Shet up and come on."

"Yeaah," said Blue. "Double Niggaahh!!"

A Harlem Game

Mack and Jayjay stopped at the stoop and while Jayjay bounced the basketball around for practice, Mack slumped down on the concrete steps and fingered an iron spike jutting from the metal rail on the stoop. Up the street the block lights came on and the glow blended with the drugstore's orange-red neons. Mack looked up at the broken lamp in front of his stoop.

"Let's go to the show, Jay."

"I ain't got no money."

"Don't punk out. I can get some."

"You can't," said Jayjay, "You can't get nothin from them if they're playin cards."

"Don't punk out. If my old lady's got even a dollar, half of it's mine."

"Look, she just gave you fifty cents this mornin, didn't she?"

"So what? Come on, go with me upstairs again."

"No."

He watched Jayjay dribble the ball. Then he got up and his shadow formed on the sidewalk beside Jayjay.

"Look, she just gave you fifty cents this mornin, didn't you have enough to get in?"

"I don't know," said Jayjay. "It's gettin late and I got to take Frisky's ball back." He faced up the street as the ball slapped the sidewalk *pow pow pow pow* across Mack's shadow.

"Then wait two minutes. If I'm not back . . ." He turned and ran up the stairway. At the top a familiar odor came at him from the darkened hall. Beer cans sprawled near his door and a blood stain streaked the top step where somebody had been cut in a fight.

He hesitated for a minute against the knife-carved wood of his door, his sweaty hand gripping the handle. He leaned. The door opened. He moved in. He was panting.

Down the hallway in the kitchen he saw the back of the hunched figure in the usual position at the card table in the center of the kitchen floor.

He eased into the room. His sneakers made no noise but the loose floor boards gave his presence away.

The big man shifted his shoulders and poised himself as if he were listening for footsteps. But he didn't look at Mack. He continued to watch the woman, Lola, deal. Mack stood there panting. No one spoke.

Lola sat opposite Jim Davis. Mack glanced at her. She was pretty and Jim Davis was saying she was a queen of hearts.

Mack looked at his mother as she picked up her cards. She held them in her left hand and brought a can of beer to her mouth with her right. She glanced at him over the rim of the can. He hoped she would say something.

He looked at the pile of change in front of her. She was winning a lot. No one else had much except maybe Jim Davis and Lola. He sensed the vacant table in front of his father. He could feel the big man breathing like a bull. Jim Davis grunted and scratched his stubbled chin. Mack moved toward his mother.

The big man shifted himself in the seat.

"Punk," he said to Mack, "where you been all day? What you want now?"

Mack stood still. He saw a lone dime in front of his father. He opened his mouth to speak but only grunted something.

"How much bread you got?" the big man asked.

"I'm broke," Mack said. He looked at his mother. She was opening a can of beer. "I'm broke and I was sorta needin . . ."

"I didn't ask you what you needed," the big man said softly, staring at the center of the table.

Jim Davis wiggled his chair and hastily glanced at Mack. "Say kid, it would be good if you would lend your old man here some coins. He's been losin kinda heavy. We all been losin to your old lady here." He chuckled at Mack, but Mack didn't know whether to smile back or to say, yes, it would be good, or just to come right out and ask his mother for show fare.

He looked at her steadily but it was a long time before she looked at him.

"What you standin there for, Mackie?" she asked. Then she turned to her cards again.

"I . . ." He approached the table. "Jay and me want to make that last show. He's waitin for me downstairs."

The big man cleared his throat and raised a can to his mouth. There was a sound of gulping and the can was empty.

"Stop rubbin them things," Lola said to Jim Davis, who was scratching his chin.

Mack watched his mother. She smirked a couple of times as if deciding what to do. Then she plucked two quarters from her pile and jammed them into Mack's palm.

He felt like running. He turned toward the hall door.

"Punk, you forgettin somethin, ain't you?"

Mack paused.

"Don't you like potato chips?"

Mack wanted to say yes, but he didn't. He trembled and watched the fat arm flex on the table edge. The twist of muscles looked like twin ridges of metal stripping bent back to a rebound point.

Lola was frowning at Jim Davis. "Can't you stop that damn noise? It makes my flesh crawl."

Jim Davis said something about how rubbing his chin brought out the man in him and made him think fast. He wiggled his chair, snickering at the same time.

Mack glanced quickly at all of them and stepped off again. "I said somethin to you, punk."

Mack clenched his teeth. "Yeah, maybe I could use . . ."

"What about that wise kid, Jayjerk? He eats chips, don't he?"

"Guess so."

"Okay then," he said, looking at the cards dealt out by Mack's mother, "give 'im four more bits."

Mack looked at his mother. She hesitated and smacked her lips, making sounds of disgust with her tongue.

"How much is it to get in?" she asked.

Mack didn't know what to say. He just stood there. He tried to mumble something, but he caught a sudden movement of the arm on the table.

The big man stood up. His body pushed the tiny table and a can of beer fell. He laid his cards down and leaned slowly over the table. His body was like a steel beam bent by some force. It was ready to snap back when the force was released.

"What did I say give 'im?" He looked at the pile of coins in front of Mack's mother.

"This here's enough," Mack said, looking from face to face and holding two quarters out in his hand.

No one spoke. The sound of Lola blowing smoke over the table surface mixed with the sound of the big man breathing. That was all. Then Mack took two steps toward the hall. Lola smashed the butt.

"I thought I said somethin." The big arm flexed.

And Mack's mother, weakly shaking her head at her pile, pushed two more quarters to the edge of the table.

"Okay," she snapped, "but I want my money back."

It all happened so fast that Mack was still standing poised to retreat down the hall.

"Now, punk," the big man said, grinning, "you got nough coins, right?"

Mack said yes, and looked at the extra quarters.

"So looky here," his old man continued, "sposin I told you somethin." He grabbed Mack's wrist and jerked him to the edge of the table. He sat down and smiled at Mack.

Mack's mother said something about leaving the boy alone, but she was draining a can of beer and her words were swallowed.

"Like I was sayin," and he squeezed the wrist. Mack began to feel the sweat gathering up in him. "Like I was sayin, if you was playin a gamblin game here, see, like we all is, and your old lady over there just kept on winnin, see, and then I comes along with a pocket full of coins, what do you think I'd do?"

Mack's mother got up and went to the refrigerator where she began gathering and opening beer cans.

"Okay, son, what do you think would happen to me if I had bread like that and didn't want to lend you a few pieces?"

Mack frowned and took a deep breath.

"Well . . . I don't know, I don't know . . ." He felt tight inside and began to try to wrench his arm free.

"What the hell you mean?"

Jim Davis studied the cards after shuffling them; as he dealt he looked at the beer being opened.

Mack stopped struggling and clenched his teeth. He looked into his old man's eyes. But words wouldn't come.

"Son, son, son, son, don't you know that if I was to do that you'd haul off and knock the blue hell outa me, wouldn't you?"

Mack lowered his eyes. The big man gently tugged his arm for an answer. He glanced around at the others. They were busy and did not see him, and before he knew what he was doing he was putting three of the four quarters in front of the big man.

"Thank you, son. You're a smart punk. Now let me see." He pretended he was counting his money. "How about lendin me two bits?"

Mack frowned. He felt the lone quarter in his palm and wondered if he should try to break away and run. He looked at Lola lighting a cigarette. Jim Davis was rubbing his chin and Mack's mother was mumbling something about anybody wanting cheese with the beer. Her face was searching the refrigerator.

"But I . . ." He felt a squeeze and his wrist throbbed. He wanted to punch out at the big man or use a knife.

But he was alone. Looking at the arm digging into his wrist like a steel clamp, he tossed the last coin on the table. Lola's cigarette was jarred from the ashtray to the floor. "Maybe I'll lend you some show fare." He grabbed Mack's arm again and flicked a quarter into it.

Mack stared at the floor. "I ain't goin," he said.

"What the hell you mean?"

Mack stepped away from the table. "I ain't goin."

"Look here, punk, I don't want to hear none of that jive talk." He stood up again, hunching over Mack. "What did you want with that two bits in your hand?"

Mack took in a breath and gritted his teeth.

"Okay then, punk, let's get this all straight right now. Who did you just borrow a dollar from?"

Mack turned his head in the direction of his mother.

"You damn right. Now, who did you borrow that last quarter from?"

Mack looked at Jim Davis. Jim was dealing cards with a cigarette hanging so that the smoke made his left eye squint. Lola and Mack's mother were now talking about something.

"Who?"

"Maybe you," he gasped.

"What the hell you mean?"

"You, I guess."

"How much you owe all together? You heard your old lady say she wanted hers back, right?"

"But I ain't got . . ."

"Huh? Huh? Huh? Huh?" The big man leaned closer to Mack.

"Buck and a quarter." He stepped toward the hall.

"Now what you goin to do with what I lent you?"

"I was goin to the show."

"Then get the hell out of here. We're playin a game of

cards, can't you see?" He sat back down and hunched his shoulders. He gripped the sweaty coins in his hands, then slowly stacked them in a neat pile in front of him.

Mack went out the door and down the steps. Along the street the block lights made shadows of people. He did not see Jayjay.

He slumped to the stoop, wiping his face. Punk, punk, punk, punk. When he got bigger . . .

He stood up and touched the iron spike. He wanted to scream out and curse, but he didn't. He jerked the coin from his pocket and stared blankly at it. Then he slammed it down at the spike, which momentarily dug at the metal, then skidded off and gouged deep into his palm.

Blood spurted from the hole and he ran off up the street beside his shadow. And the neon light swallowed him up.

Will the Circle Be Unbroken?

At the edge of the spiral of musicians Probe sat crosslegged on a blue cloth, his soprano sax resting against his inner knee, his afro-horn linking his ankles like a bridge. The afro-horn was the newest axe to cut the deadwood of the world. But Probe, since his return from exile, had chosen only special times to reveal the new sound. There were more rumors about it than there were ears and souls that had heard the horn speak. Probe's dark full head tilted toward the vibrations of the music as if the ring of sound from the six wailing pieces was tightening, creating a spiraling circle.

The black audience, unaware at first of its collectiveness, had begun to move in a soundless rhythm as if it were the tiny twitchings of an embryo. The waiters in the club fell against the wall, shadows, dark pillars holding up the building and letting the free air purify the mind of the club.

The drums took an oblique. Magwa's hands, like the forked tongue of a dark snake, probed the skins, probed the whole belly of the coming circle. Beginning to close the circle, Haig's alto arc, rapid piano incisions, Billy's thin green flute arcs and tangents, Stace's examinations of his own trumpet discoveries, all fell separately, yet together, into a blanket which Mojohn had begun weaving on bass when the set began. The audience breathed, and Probe moved into the inner ranges of the sax.

Outside the Sound Barrier Club three white people were opening the door. Jan, a tenor sax case in his hand, had his game all planned. He had blown with Probe six years ago on the West Coast. He did not believe that there was anything to this new philosophy the musicians were talking about. He would talk to Probe personally. He had known many Negro musicians and theirs was no different from any other artist's struggles to be himself, including his own.

Things were happening so fast that there was no one who knew all directions at once. He did not mind Ron and Tasha coming along. They were two of the hippest ofays in town, and if anybody could break the circle of the Sound Club, it would be friends and old friends of friends.

Ron was bearded and scholarly. Thickset, shabbily dressed, but clean. He had tried to visit the Club before. But all of his attempts had been futile. He almost carried the result of one attempt to court. He could not understand why the cats would want to bury themselves in Harlem and close the doors to the outside world. Ron's articles and reviews had helped many black musicians, but of all of them, Probe Adams had benefited the most. Since his graduation from Yale, Ron had knocked around the music world; once he thought he wanted to sing blues. He had tried, but that was in college. The best compliment he ever got was from Mississippi John or Muddy Waters, one of the two, during a civil rights rally in Alabama. He had spontaneously leaped up during the rally and played from his soul. Muddy was in the audience, and later told Ron: "Boy, you keep that up, you gwine put me back on the plantation."

Ron was not fully satisfied that he had found the depth of the black man's psyche. In his book he had said this. Yet he knew that if he believed strongly enough, some of the old cats would break down. His sincerity was written all over his face. Holding Tasha's hand, he saw the door opening. . . .

Tasha was a shapely blonde who had dyed her hair black. It now matched her eyes. She was a Vassar girl and had once begun a biography of Oliver Fullerton. Excerpts had been published in *Down Beat* and she became noted as a critic and authority on the Fullerton movement. Fullerton's development as an important jazz trombonist had been interrupted soon after Tasha's article. No one knew why. Sometimes Tasha was afraid to think about it. If they had been married, she knew that Oliver would have been able to continue making it. But he had gotten strung out on H. Sometimes she believed her friends who said

HENRY DUMAS

Oliver was psychopathic. At least when he stopped beating her, she forgave him. And she did not believe it when he was really hooked. She still loved him. It was her own love, protected deep inside her, encased, her little black secret and her passport to the inner world that Oliver had died trying to enter. It would be only a matter of time. She would translate love into an honest appraisal of black music.

"I am sorry," the tall brown doorman said. "Sessions for Brothers and Sisters only."

"What's the matter, baby?" Jan leaned his head in and looked around as if wondering what the man was talking about.

"I said . . ."

"Man, if you can't recognize a Brother, you better let me have your job." He held up his case. "We're friends of Probe."

The man called for assistance. Quickly two men stepped out of the shadows. "What's the trouble, Brother?"

"These people say they're friends of the Probe."

"What people?" asked one of the men. He was neatly dressed, a clean shaven head, with large darting eyes. He looked past the three newcomers. There was a silence.

Finally, as if it were some supreme effort, he looked at the three. "I'm sorry, but for your own safety we cannot allow you."

"Man, what you talkin bout?" asked Jan, smiling quizzically. "Are you blockin Brothers now? I told him I am blood. We friends of the Probe."

The three men at the door went into a huddle. Carl, the doorman, was skeptical, but he had seen some bloods that were pretty light. He looked at this cat again, and as Kent and Rafael were debating whether or not to go get Probe's wife in the audience, he decided against the whole thing. He left the huddle and returned with a sign which said: "We cannot allow non-Brothers because of the danger involved with extensions."

Jan looked at the sign, and a smile crept across his face. In the street a cop was passing and leaned in. Carl motioned the cop in. He wanted a witness to this. He knew what might happen but he had never seen it.

Jan shook his head at the sign, turning to Ron and Tasha. He was about to explain that he had seen the same sign on the West Coast. It was incredible that all the spades believed this thing about the lethal vibrations from the new sound.

Carl was shoving the sign in their faces as the cop, a big, pimpled Irishman, moved through the group. "All right, break it up, break it up. You got people outside want to come in . . ."

Kent and Rafael, seeing Carl's decision and the potential belligerence of the whites, folded their hands, buddha-like. Carl stood with his back to the door now.

"Listen, officer, if these people go in, the responsibility is yours."

The Irish cop, not knowing whether he should get angry over what he figured was reverse discrimination, smirked and made a path for the three. He would not go far inside because he didn't think the sounds were worth listening to. If it wasn't Harlem he could see why these people would want to go in, but he had never seen anything worthwhile from niggers in Harlem.

"Don't worry. You got a license, don't you?"

"Let them go through," said Rafael suddenly. A peace seemed to gather over the faces of the three club members now. They folded their arms and went into the dark cavern which led to the music. In front of them walked the invaders. "See," said Jan, "if you press these cats, they'll cop out." They moved toward the music in an alien silence.

Probe was deep into a rear-action sax monologue. The whole circle now, like a bracelet of many colored lights, gyrated under Probe's wisdom. Probe was a thoughtful, full-headed black man with narrow eyes and a large nose. His lips swelled over the reed and each note fell into the circle like an acrobat on a tight rope stretched radially across the center of the universe.

He heard the whistle of the wind. Three ghosts, like chaff blown from a wasteland, clung to the wall. . . . He tightened the circle. Movement began from within it, shaking without breaking balance. He had to prepare the womb for the afro-horn. Its vibrations were beyond his mental frequencies unless he got deeper into motives. He sent out his call for motives. . . .

The blanket of the bass rippled and the fierce wind in all their minds blew the blanket back, and there sat the city of Samson. The white pillars imposing . . . but how easy it is to tear the building down with motives. Here they come. Probe, healed of his blindness, born anew of spirit, sealed his reed with pure air. *He moved to the edge of the circle, rested his sax, and lifted his axe. . . .*

There are only three afro-horns in the world. They were forged from a rare metal found only in Africa and South America. No one knows who forged the horns, but the general opinion among musicologists is that it was the Egyptians. One European museum guards an afro-horn. The other is supposed to be somewhere on the West Coast of Mexico, among a tribe of Indians. Probe grew into his from a black peddler who claimed to have traveled a thousand miles just to give it to his son. From that day on, Probe's sax handled like a child, a child waiting for itself to grow out of itself.

Inside the center of the gyrations is an atom stripped of time, black. The gathering of the hunters, deeper. Coming, laced in the energy of the sun. He is blowing. Magwa's hands. Reverence of skin. Under the single voices is the child of a woman, black. They are building back the wall, crumbling under the disturbance.

In the rear of the room, Jan did not hear the volt, nor did he see the mystery behind Probe's first statement on the afro-horn. He had closed his eyes, trying to capture or elude the panthers of the music, but he had no eyes. He did not feel Ron slump against him. Strands of Tasha's hair were matted on a button of Ron's jacket, but she did not move when he slumped. Something was hitting them like waves, like shock waves. . . .

Before his mind went black, Jan recalled the feeling when his father had beat him for playing "with a nigger!" and later he allowed the feeling to merge with his dislike of white people. When he fell, his case hit the floor and opened, revealing a shiny tenor saxophone that gleamed and vibrated in the freedom of freedom.

Ron's sleep had been quick, like the rush of post-hypnotic suggestions. He dropped her hand, slumped, felt the wall give (no, it was the air), and he fell forward across a table, his heart silent in respect for truer vibrations.

The musicians stood. The horn and Probe drew up the shadows now from the audience. A child climbed upon the chords of sound, growing out of the circle of the womb, searching with fingers and then with motive, and as the volume of the music increased—penetrating the thick callousness of the Irishman twirling his stick outside of black flesh—the musicians walked off, one by one, linked to Probe's respectful nod at each and his quiet pronouncement of their names. He mopped his face with a blue cloth.

"What's the matter here?"

"Step aside, folks!"

"These people are unconscious!"

"Look at their faces!"

"They're dead."

"Dead?"

"What happened?"

"Dead?"

"It's true then. It's true . . ."

Strike and Fade

The word was out. Cool it. We on the street, see. Me and Big Skin. We watch the cops. They watch us. People goin and comin. That fire truck still wrecked up side the buildin. Papers say we riot, but we didn't riot. We like the VC, the Viet Cong. We strike and fade. Me and Big Skin, we scoutin the street the next day to see how much we put down on them. Big Skin, he walkin ahead of me. He walkin light, easy, pawin. It daylight but you still got to walk easy on the street. Anytime the Mowhites might hit the block on rubber, then what we do? We be up tight for space, so we all eyes, all feet an easy. You got to do it.

We make it to Bone's place. Bone, he the only blood on the block got a business. Mowhite own the cleaners, the supermarket, the laundry, the tavern, the drugstore, and all the rest. Yeah. But after we burn out half them places, Mowhite he close down his stores for a week.

Our block occupied with cops and National Guard, but the Guard left yesterday. Man, they more cops on the street now than rats. We figure the best thing to do is to kill the cops first so we can get back to killin rats. They watch us. But they got nothin on Big Skin and me. Naw. We clean. They got Sammy, Momo, Walter and his sister too, Doris, Edie, and they even got Mr. Tomkins. He a school teacher. I had him once. He was a nice stud. Me and Big Skin make it to Bone's place. There a lot of guys inside.

We hang around. Listen to talk. I buy a coke. Big Skin take half. I hold my coke. Police cars pass outside. They like wolves, cruisin. We inside. Nobody mess with us. A cat name Duke, he talkin.

"You cats got to get more together with this thang. Look at the cats in Brooklyn, Chicago. Birmingham and Cleveland. Look at the cats in Oakland!"

A cat name Mace, he talkin. Mace just got out the Army. "Don't worry, man. It's comin." He point out the window. "This is raw oppression, baby. Look at them mf's. Raw oppression." Mace, he like to use them two words so he sayin them over and over again. He say them words all the time. It ain't funny cause they true. We all look out the window at the cops.

Bone, he behind the counter makin hamburgers. When he get too many orders he can't handle, then one of the cats come behind the counter and give him a hand. Me and Big Skin light up cigarettes. Big Skin pass them around. I take the last one. I squeeze the pack up so tight, my fingernails cut my hand. I like to make it tight. I throw that pack at the trash can. It bounce in and bounce back. But Duke, he catch it. He throw it in. Not too hard. It stay. He talkin.

"I mean, if every black man in this goddamn country would dedicate one half of a day next week to a boycott. Just don't go to work! Not a black pushin a thing for Charley. Hell, man, we tie it up. We still the backbone, man. We still got this white mf on our backs. What the hell we totin him around for?"

Mace, he talkin.

"Wait. No sooner we make another move, whitey be down on us like rats on warm cheese. It be raw oppression double over. Gestapo. Man, they forget about Hitler after the man come down on us."

Big Skin he talkin.

"They say that the cats in Harlem is gettin together so tight that the Muslims and Martin Luther King got their heads together."

Nobody say nothin. Couple cats laugh. We heard it before. Word been spreadin for all black men to get ready for war. Nobody believe it. But everybody want to. But it the same in Harlem as anywhere else.

Duke he talkin.

"An organized revolution is what the man can't stand. They say it's comin? Man, when it do I be the first to join. If I got to go I take some Chalk Whitey with me and mark him all over hell."

We listen a while. The cats all talkin. We just want to get what's happenin.

We split the scene. Duke, he split too.

We move down the block. It gettin evenin. We meet some cats comin.

We stop and talk. We meet them later on 33rd Street. They pawin like us.

Duke talkin.

"You cats see Tyro yet?"

We say naw. We heard he back in town, but we ain't seen him yet. Tyro was a Green Beret in Viet Nam. But he back. He got no legs and one arm. All the cats been makin it to his pad. They say he got a message for all the cats on the block.

Duke say he makin it to Tyro's now. We walk on. I kick some glass. We see a store that is burnt out. A cop is watchin us. We stakin easy, all eyes, all feet. A patrol car stop along side us. The gestapos leap out. I see a shotgun. We all freeze.

The Man is talkin.

"You niggers got one hour to get off the street." Then he change his mind. "Against the wall!" There is three of them. Down the street is more. They frisk us. We all clean. One jab the butt of a gun hard on my leg. It give me a cramp in the ball.

They cuss us and tell us to get off the street. We move on. Around the block. Down the street.

I'm limpin. I don't say nothin. I don't curse or nothin. Duke and Big Skin, they mad, cursin and sayin what they gonna do. Me, I'm hurtin too much. I'm lettin my heat go down into my soul. When it come up again, I won't be limpin.

We see some more cats pawin along the block. About fifty. We join. They headin to 33rd. Some cats got heats, some got molotovs. One cat got a sword.

Tyro on 30th Street. We go up. Three other cats come with us. We run up the steps. We pass an old man goin up. He grunt out our way. We say excuse. I'm the last up. The old man scared. We hear a siren outside. The shit done started already.

Tyro's sister open the door. I know her before I dropped out of school. She know me, but she iggin. All the cats move in. I close the door. "We come to see Tyro," I say. She chewin some food, and she wave with her hand. It mean, go on up front. I watch her walk. "You Tina?" She swallow her food. "Yeah. You come to see Tyro, he in there." She turned and went into a door and closed it. I followed the other cats up front. My ball still hurt.

There were six cats already in the room. Six more come in. Somebody pass around a butt. I scoot in a corner. So I am meetin Tyro. He known on the block for years. He used to be the leader of the old Black Unicorns. They broke up by the cops and social workers.

I look at Tyro. He a black stud with a long beard. He sittin in a wheel chair. He wearin fatigues like Fidel Castro. When we paw into the pad, Tyro he talkin.

". . . the Cong are masters at ambush. Learn this about them. When we fell back under fire, we fell into a pincher. They cross-fired us so fast that we didn't know what hit us. Out of sixty men, I was left. I believe they spared me so that I could come back and tell you. The cat that found me was hit himself, but he didn't seem to care. He looked me in my eye . . . for a long time. My legs were busted up from a grenade. This VC stood over my blood. I could tell he was thinkin about somethin. He raised the rifle. I kept lookin him in the eye. It was one of the few times my prayers been answered. The cat suddenly turned and ran off. He had shot several of my buddies already, but he let me go.

"All I can figure is that one day the chips are all comin down. America is gonna have to face the yellow race. Black and yellow might have to put their hands together and bring this thang off. You cats out in the street, learn to fade fast. Learn to strike hard, but don't be around in the explosion. If you don't organize you ain't nothin but a rioter, a looter. These jigs won't hesitate to shoot you.

HENRY DUMAS

"Naw. I ain't tellin you to get off the streets. I know like you know. Uncle means you no ultimate good, brothers. Take it for what it is worth. I'm layin it down like it is. I got it from the eagle's beak. That's the way he speak. Play thangs careful. Strike and fade, then strike again, quick. Get whitey outa our neighborhood. Keep women and children off the streets. Don't riot. Rebel. You cats got this message. Do what you got to do. Stick together and listen for the word to come down. Obey it."

When Tyro finish talkin, some cats get up and shake his hand. Others leave. Out in the street sirens are going. The doorbell rings. Everybody freeze. It some more cats. We all leave.

Down on the street, it like a battlefield. A fire in a store down the block. Cops see us. We fade. I hear shots. Then I know somethin.

The word is out. Burn, baby, burn. We on the scene. The brothers. Together. Cops and people goin and comin. Some people got good loot, some just hoofin it. A police cordon comin. We shadows on the wall. Lights comin towards us. We fade. Somebody struck them. The lights go out. I hear shots. I fall. Glass get my hands. The street on fire now. We yell. 33rd Street here we come! Got to get together!

We move out. Strikin. All feet. All soul. We the VC. You got to be. You got to be.

Fon

From the sky. A fragment of black rock about the size of a fist, sailing, sailing. . . . CRAACK! The rear windshield breaks.

Nilmon snaps his head to the rearview mirror, wheeling the car off the road.

"Goddammit!" He leaps from the car, leaving the door open. He examines the break, whirls around and scans the evening countryside with squinting eyes.

The distant mooing of cattle blends with the sharp yap of a dog.

And then he catches a movement.

Through the trees behind him—past a large billboard with the picture of Uncle Sam saying *I Want You*, over and down a rocky incline, toward a final rise at the top of the levee— Nillmon thinks he sees several pairs of legs scurrying away.

"Niggers!" He steps back to the car, leans across the seat, jerks open the glove compartment, snatches up a pistol lying between a half-bottle of whiskey and a stick of dynamite, and crosses the torn asphalt in four quick strides. Pieces of pavement scatter beneath his feet. The road is in disuse except for an occasional car and a few cattle crossings.

He runs toward a path by the billboard. As he loses sight of the point in the distance where he thinks the figures disappeared, he runs faster. He reaches the beams supporting the billboard. The area behind the sign is a large network of angled shafts and platforms. He follows the path, stooping his shoulders and grunting. He lurches through an opening, twisting his way from the entanglement of wooden beams. He curses. Then he slows his pace, realizing that he's chasing children.

He slips the pistol in his belt. He clears his throat and spits at the long edge of the billboard's fading shadow. Then he resumes his march up the hill.

　　　　　　　　　　　　　　　　　　HENRY DUMAS

He looks over the countryside. No niggers running. Across a thin stretch of young cotton three shacks lean back on their shadows, and the shadows, bending at every bank and growth of the land, poke at the muddy inlet of a Mississippi tributary. The only movements are the lazy wag of tattered clothes on the back porch of one shack, the minute shifts of what looks like chickens scratching in a bare yard, the illusory tilt of a cross barely gleaming on top of a tiny wooden church far away, and the fragmentary lines of black smoke climbing lazily but steadily higher and higher. Nillmon peers. He thinks he sees a figure rocking slowly back and forth on the porch of the third shack. Probably an old granny. A cowbell jangles in the distance, and from the shacks Nillmon thinks he hears an angry voice rise and fall amidst a scurry of noises, and then trail off in a series of loud whacks and screams. He tries to locate that shack. He is about to descend.

He smothers a strange impulse to laugh and spits down the incline, jerking his eyes toward the road, over the levee cotton and through the trees.

Then he snaps his neck back toward the road for a second look.

It is not the slow motion of the car door swinging to the uneven idle of the motor that catches his eye. Nor the slight movement of leaves and branches.

Somebody is watching him.

A silhouette sits at the back of the billboard. The slow dangle of a bare leg is the only motion. The mesh of beams looks like a web. The billboard is empty except for the lone figure.

"Goddammit!" He snatches out the pistol. "Git down!"

The shadows in the trees waver and merge like a field of tall reeds marching gently under the steady touch of the wind. Nillmon wipes his mouth with his sleeve.

"Nigger, can't you hear?"

The figure, almost liquid in his giant movements, begins a slow descent, swinging across a shaft of sunlight like an acrobat. He drops to the ground and stands. A muscular black youth. Bands of fading light make imperfect angles and spears across his red shirt and black arms.

"Who else is up there?"

"My brother."

Nillmon attempts to approach the figure. The youth is standing with the weight of his body on one leg. Nillmon stops in front of him and searches for signs of resistance. The youth holds his head level, but his eyes glare outward, always away from the eyes of the white man, as if they were protecting some secret. Nillmon searches the billboard and trees. The nigger is a half-wit.

"All right, move!"

The tall youth slides into motion on the path made by children. But he carefully steps around the beams, over a few rocks, and proceeds toward the road.

"Black boy, I'm goin to see you put every piece of that glass back in place."

Nillmon watches the rear of the figure moving down the path, and he feels a rush of blood to his head when he thinks of the bullet going right through the dark head.

"I didn't break it," the youth says without turning around or slowing his pace.

"Nigger, you in trouble," says Nillmon. They reach the car. The youth is looking straight ahead. "Aside from gettin your ass beat, and payin for that glass, you goin to jail. Git in."

The youth turns slowly—as if in some fearful trance— and is about to look squarely at the other man, but instead he rivets his eyes on the white man's neck.

"Boy, what's your name?" Nillmon asks.

Cowbells sound up the road. The youth shifts his weight, wets his lips, and looks off. Far, far down the road, cows gather at a fence and a voice yells, a dog barks, and then the cattle neck into the crossing, and some are mooing.

"Fon."

"Goddamnit, Fon what?"

HENRY DUMAS

The sun has almost fallen. The shadow of the car bounces nervously. Then it stops.

"Al*fon*so."

Nillmon squeezes the pistol butt. This boy ain't no halfwit. Nillmon knows he is going to break him now. The nigger is trying to act bad. Maybe he'd break him later. Maybe Gus and Ed would want a piece of him. He looks at the youth and he can't decide whether he is bad or not. He hates to see a fool-headed nigger get it. No fun in it. He sees a thin line of smoke coming from the back seat of his car. Sniffing and leaning, he sees that his back seat, where the black stone landed, is smoldering.

"Set fire to it, too, eh?" He moves toward Fon.

He swings his foot upward, aiming for Fon's rear. Seeming to anticipate the move, Fon, without moving his legs, twists his back and avoids the blow, which strikes the air.

"Nobody *threw* that rock from there," Fon says.

Nillmon, half-stunned, finding himself kicking the air when what he wanted to kick was so plain, wipes his mouth in a nervous sling of his arm, and while the sleeve is passing over his face he tries to see if he holds a pistol, feels himself squeezing it and emptying it. But he can't. It is all too easy. This Fon nigger ain't scared. He knows now he has a nigger that needs a thorough job. Nillmon smiles and spits on the gravel in front of Fon. "Git in."

Fon moves around the car, opens the door, and slowly gets in, closing his door carefully and firmly. Nillmon slams his and jerks the car forward. The car picks up speed. Nillmon grips the steering wheel until the blood is cut off from his hands. A thin line of smoke issues from the rear window.

"Yesss, nigger, think you can count them pieces of glass with the tip of your tongue?" Fon is silent. Nillmon relaxes his grip and looks at him from the corner of his eye. "What the hell you niggers doin up on that sign chunkin at cars anyway?"

A cattle crossing. The car, slowing, slowing . . .

"Teachin my brother how to shoot his arrows."

. . . and the car stops.

Nillmon feels himself lunging toward Fon, pushing him out of the car with his foot, and blasting his body till it swells and bleeds black blood like that Huntsville nigger they got last year. . . . He was deputy sheriff then. Hell, if he hadn't been implicated in that case he would still be on down there in Huntsville. That goddam Federal Agent even suggested that he and Gus lay low till things got under control. The nigger civil rights groups were kicking up so much dust that an honest white citizen in the state couldn't see straight half the time. But it wasn't like that up here in Columbia County. He lowers his foot on the gas and the noisy engine stirs the cattle.

Fon seems to watch the rising humps of the cattle. They pass in quick strides. A brown-skinned boy, about twelve, hollers and whistles and a dog is barking at the heels of a straying heifer.

"You teachin your brother how to chunk at white folks? How long do you expect your brother to live, actin on what you say?"

"I'll take care of him."

Nillmon feels himself laughing, but his anger rises over it. "You bout a bad nigger, ain't you?"

The straying cow, a large black and white with a swinging udder, turns and heads toward the car.

Nillmon spits out the window. The cows are mooing, their bells are banging.

"Hurry up, boy. Git them heifers outa my way!"

The stray cow lopes nervously back to the line, followed by the dog. Nillmon scans the field for the last cow. A hot wave seizes him, and he gives in to the urge to chuckle under his breath. He looks back at the broken glass on the rear seat. He does not see the rock now, only a haze of smoke in the car.

Suddenly, Fon, his movements like those of a mechanic testing a loose door handle, opens his door, slides out, closes the door firmly and quietly, and walks across the road toward the levee which bends around a clump of trees and past the billboard.

Nillmon, dazed by the sudden movement of the car, aims the pistol at the last cow, but the car rolls over a heap of cow manure and he submits to the urge to curse all dead niggers, but he doesn't say anything then. Through the rearview mirror he sees that the sun is gone and the levee is a thin line hiding the river inlet, and on the road a dog is chasing the car, and in the field the cows are mooing and their bells are banging.

Only shadows fall in front of him now. The shadows in the trees are going over the hill with the cattle, and he sees a light far ahead in the road.

Suddenly he slows the car, leaps out and looks over the countryside. "I shoulda taught that sombitch a lesson," he mutters to himself. When he puts the pistol back in the glove compartment, he brings out the bottle and takes a long drink.

After about three miles on the flat straight road, the light becomes a filling station. Nillmon runs in. An old man with one leg is wiping his hands on greasy rags. "And just whar you been last two weeks? Drunk?"

Nillmon harldy looks at the old man, but breaks through the door leading to the rear of the store which is part of a series of rooms. The top of the house looms in the back. "Where's Gus, Pop?" he asked the old man. "A nigger just about ready to git hisself gutted."

"What nigger?" Pop asks, throwing the rags in the corner. "What's his name?"

Nillmon moves toward the house as the old man hollers, "Gus! Get out here!"

Before Nillmon can ascend a long row of rickety wooden steps up to a screened porch, a figure appears in the screenless doorway. Girlish laughter rises and falls, and the figure, struggling with arms around his waist, yells, "What the hell you want?"

"It's me, Gus." Nillmon approaches.

"Who?"

"Goddammit, it's me." He doesn't advance anymore. "A nigger just bricked my car. I'm goin to get him."

As if Nillmon had spoken something he had been waiting for, Gus, a short wiry man of about thirty years, freezes. He pushes the retreating arms away from his body, tosses his left hand in the air as a signal, and begins a slow deliberate descent. Nillmon turns and walks past the old man.

"Call Sheriff Vacy."

"Where's this nigger?" Gus asks. His words are clear and precise.

"Out at Canebrake. . . . A nigger named Alfonso, a big black sucker."

The figure of a blonde girl stands now in the doorway at the top of the steps. She straightens out her clothing. Pop limps toward her. "I'm goin call Vacy," he mutters. "Gus, I'm callin Vacy, you hear?"

"Yeah," Nillmon hollers, "and tell him we're pickin up Ed Frickerson."

"Naw we ain't." Gus examines Nillmon's pistol. They both take drinks from the bottle and slam the doors.

"Where's the nigger at?" asks the old man, limping out with a bundle of oily rags. "I'm callin everybody."

"Canebrake . . . nigger name Alfonso . . ."

"Canebrake?"

"You comin?"

"There ain't no niggers livin in them shacks."

Gus looks at the bottle, clears his throat and takes a long swallow. He hands it to Nillmon who finishes it.

"There is now, and there's gonna be one less come sunup."

"Them Canebrake shacks is haunted, I'm tellin you. Niggers ain't live in them since the flood back in . . . you member, Gus?" the old man says, limping toward the car. Then he whispers, "The time the nigger woman put hoodoo on Vacy's papa . . ."

"Shut up, Pop!"

The old man mumbles.

Nillmon races the motor and jerks the cold car off in a cloud of dust. Down the road, just before they turn off, Nillmon flings his arm out the window and the bottle crashes on the road.

They pick up Ed Frickerson about ten miles later at a town cafe. They get another bottle and circle the town picking up two younger men. Then Nillmon aims the car down the road toward the levee. The faint red crown of the sun is the only thing left of day.

"Vacy's over in Huntsville," says Ed Frickerson. He is ruddy-faced, thick-necked, round-nosed, with a permanent smile wrinkling down his whiskered face.

"I'm the goddam deputy, ain't I, Gus?" says Nillmon, spitting out the window.

"I want to see the nigger that'll chunk a brick at a white man," says Gus. He has the pistol in his belt and is patting the stick of dynamite steadily in his left hand. "Gus wants to see that boy."

The car moves fast. The men pass the bottle around. Nillmon describes the last party he attended in Huntsville. They all listen, devouring with fear and a dark relish the exaggerated details that pour out of Nillmon. They all tremble inside as the cars turns off onto a dirt road along the levee. All except Gus.

Nillmon drives the car within a few feet of the first shack. The lights illuminate every weather-worn line in the warping boards.

"Alfonso!" Nillmon shouts, standing near the broken step.

There is a silence over the whole night.

The car stalls and cuts off. Gus jumps out of the car, walks up on the porch, pushes once, twice, on the rickety door which falls as if the light from the headlights had struck it. Dust travels across the plane of light like legions of insects. The shack is empty.

The car backs out and then spins out of its own dust. At the second shack they find the same thing. Nillmon snatches up the oily rags. The two younger men light them and hurl them in and under the shack.

"Where'd this nigger chunk that rock from?" asks Gus. He lights up a cigarette. The car races down the road.

Nillmon spits out the window. "Back up the road by that signboard." He feels his hands tighten around the steering wheel.

"Lights down the road," says Ed Frickerson.

"Hell, I know niggers live up here cause I saw about five or six herdin cows."

"What this nigger look like?"

"Like any nigger. Had a nasty tongue. I gotta get me some of him."

They reach the third shack. The outline of the second shack a quarter-mile down the road slowly rises in the flames that leap out of its windows. "Ain't that a crowd of niggers in front of that church yonder?" asks Ed Frickerson.

Nillmon does not look. The headlights of the car strike the doorway of the third shack. A figure stands illuminated there, his hands behind his back as if he is contemplating the situation. It is Fon.

"All right, boy!" shouts Nillmon. "I'm back to settle that business tween us."

Gus is out of the car, advancing toward Fon in rapid strides. He holds the pistol in his right hand and the empty bottle in the other. Fon steps off the steps before Gus reaches the shack, and heads toward Nillmon, who is now standing right in front of the headlights. Lighted rags fly through the night.

The other men surround Fon. All of a sudden a series of flashes comes from the area of the church. It practically blinds Nillmon. Gus aims the pistol at Fon's head. They shove Fon into the rear between the two younger men. Gus sits in front. Ed Frickerson, who is sitting behind Nillmon, has collected pieces of glass in an oily rag and tosses the mass in Fon's lap. The bright light continues to shine and the men instinctively turn away. Nillmon slows as he approaches the structure which seems like an old church. "What you niggers think you're doin out here?" Ed Frickerson asks Fon.

"Those are my brothers," says Fon.

"What I want to know," says Nillmon, "is who threw that rock."

"It came from the sky."

Gus whirls and strikes at Fon with the bottle, which breaks on the door frame and the glass falls in Fon's lap. "You *are* a smart nigger." He japs the bottle neck at Fon, and the sharp edges dig deeply into Fon's side.

Nillmon slows the car in front of a column of black people. They murmur and stare inside the car.

"Keep goin!" shouts Gus.

Suddenly they see Fon inside, and a cheer leaps up from them such as the white men have never heard. A sound of distance and presence, a shaking in the air which comes from that invisible song, that body of memory, ancient. A long sustained roar from the bottom of the land, rising, rising. . . .

"Move out!" shouts Gus.

The car jerks forward and the light from the church follows it far, far in the distance. . . .

The headlights strike the billboard. The sign is old and worn. They shove Fon from the car and push him beneath the wooden structure. The night crowds in around the sharp line of the car's headlights. They make torches with the rags.

"All right, nigger, git on your knees." Gus wraps his bloody fist in a rag.

Fon—slumped slightly, his right hand touching the ground lightly by his right knee—does not blink in the direct light of the headlights. Nor does he look in the faces of the men around him. They are lighting torches and threatening him. Only Nillmon speaks to him. Fon watches the trees and the long shadows of the beams.

"Boy, what you mean, that rock come from the sky? I thought you said your brother chucked it."

"My brother shoots only arrows."

"Goddammit, you gonna let your brother go, while you go to Hell?" asks Ed Frickerson.

"I'm not *goin* to Hell," says Fon.

Ed Frickerson stuffs the dynamite in Fon's rear pocket. Gus lights the last torch.

Nillmon seems confused. He eyes Fon. This nigger still ain't broke.

"Nigger, you mighty popular, eh? You know how to pray?"

"Prayer is for people who want help," says Fon.

A torch is pushed near Fon's feet.

"Where's your goddam brother now?"

Fon does not answer right away, but seems to watch the flickering of the shadows from the torches. High in the heavens now, a star comes into view from the clouds. A thin glow from a hidden moon peeps ominously from a horizon of clouds.

"My brother is in the trees somewhere, now."

Gus slaps Fon. One of the lights of the car goes out. Something has broken it. A puff of blue smoke sails away from the dying light. One of the torches falls, and Nillmon, standing next to Fon, thinks he hears a man's voice moan. "Gimme the pistol." Nillmon turns to see Gus—the pistol falling from his hand—stumbling, clutching an arrow which has completely pierced his neck. Suddenly the other light explodes, and the only light is the darting flame from the dying torches on the ground. Nillmon leaps to where he thinks he saw the pistol fall. . . .

But as he leaps he finds that he is falling, grabbing a sharp pain in his neck.

Silence.

In the distance a dog barks and Fon hears the faint sound of a cowbell. He clutches his side and walks deliberately over to each torch, stomps it out with bare feet. He thinks, *That was mighty close. But it is better this way. To have looked at them would have been too much. Four centuries of black eyes burning into four weak white men . . . would've set the whole earth on fire. Not yet,* he thinks, *not yet. . . .* He turns toward the levee where a light in the night reaches out to him and to the great distance between him

HENRY DUMAS

and the far blinking of the stars. The light from the church reaches out almost to him. They are expecting him back. . . . When the tower is finished . . . One more black stone. He will be able to see how to walk back. A fragment of the night, kicking, kicking, at the gnawing teeth of the earth.

Rope of Wind

The Marchers

In the dome the prisoner, alone in the silence of centuries, waited....

And all the people gathered together and began a trek across the land. From every corner of the land they came. Crossing the great rivers and mountains, they came on foot, in cars, buses, wagons, and some came IN THE SPIRIT FROM OUT OF THE PAST....

Their leaders stopped them at every crossroad and made speeches, reassuring them that to march against the white-domed city was sanctioned by God Himself. And the people believed. They went forth in processions, chanting, singing, and praying. Sometimes they laughed and shouted.

All the leaders were men of learning. They were men who believed that a law existed higher than the law of men. They believed that Justice was that law. They were men who believed that Freedom existed when men exercised restraint in doing that which they had the power to do, and courage in doing that which they had never done. In speaking to the people about these ideas, the leaders always spoke of Equality.

And the people believed. They marched gladly. Never in the history of the nation had so many people who felt oppressed gathered in a great multitude to express thier grievances.

In the dome the prisoner waited ... shackled to inertia by a great chain of years....

And the marchers grew in numbers. Work ceased. Factories puffed no smoke. The highways thronged. The past moved forward. And the great white dome in the great stone city became a hub to the troubled mind of a great nation traveling in a circle....

In the dome the silence was stirred by the sound of legions of feet marching. The rumble sifted through the years. The prisoner heard ... and waited....

Then the marchers descended upon the city. And when the sun was high in the midday, they gathered together and built a great platform. Their leaders came and stood upon it and made speeches, and the people cheered and roared.

In the dome, where webs floated in the semidarkness like legions of ghost clouds, where echoes from the outside sifted in the dome, the prisoner . . . stood up.

Outside the dome the marchers listened to their leaders:

TODAY IS THE DAY!

And the people cheered.

TODAY IS THE DAY WE WILL SET OUR SOULS FREE!

And the people roared.

TODAY—and the leader pointed to the dome shining in the noon sun like a giant pearl half-buried in the sands of the sea—TODAY WE WILL OPEN THE GREAT DOOR OF THIS NATION AND BRING OUT THE PAST!

And the people cheered.

NO ONE CAN STOP US NOW! NO ONE! WE HAVE SERVED IN THIS LAND FOR CENTURIES. WE HAVE SLAVED FOR THOSE WHO OPPRESS US. WE HAVE BEEN CHILDREN TO THEM! BUT TODAY WE SHOW THEM THAT WE ARE MEN!

And the people cheered.

IF THE DOME-MAKERS SEND THEIR GUARDS, THEIR SOLDIERS, AND THEIR DOGS UPON US, WE WILL NOT FEAR . . . NO. FOR WE MARCH IN PEACE. WE MARCH IN THE NAME OF *HIM* WHO SENT US, AND WE ARE NOT AFRAID. . . .

And the people knelt down and prayed.

JUSTICE WILL PREVAIL! FREEDOM WILL BE OURS! EQUALITY SHALL NOT BE TRODDEN DOWN!

Then another leader stood forth. He was very great amongst the people.

NOW . . . NOW IS THE TIME. TODAY . . . FREEDOM CAN WAIT NO LONGER. WE HAVE ACCEPTED TOKENS OF FREEDOM TOO LONG.

And the people cheered.

OUR FATHERS WERE BROUGHT HERE IN BONDAGE. AND WE HAVE FELT THE SAME YOKE LIKE BEASTS IN THE FIELDS. BUT WE WILL WAIT NO LONGER. WE HAVE LIVED IN A TOMB FOR YEARS, AND WHILE WE SUFFERED

WE SANG OUR SONGS AND FOUGHT AMONGST OURSELVES BECAUSE WE HAD HOPE. GOD GAVE US THAT MUCH STRENGTH TO GO ON. AND WITH THAT HOPE, WE SURVIVED, FOR WITHOUT A VISION, WITHOUT FAITH, A PEOPLE WILL PERISH.... LET US GIVE THANKS UNTO THE LORD....

And the people roared.

THE SUNSHINE OF A NEW DAY AND A NEW FRONTIER IS UPON US. RAISE YOUR HANDS, MY PEOPLE, AND STRIKE....

"Freedom Freedom Freedom!" echoed the people.

WE WILL REVIVE THE DEAD AND CONVICT THE LIVING!

"Justice! Equality!"

LISTEN, MY PEOPLE, AND REMEMBER THIS.... FOR WHEN YOU TREK BACK TO YOUR CITIES AND TOWNS, THE PRESSURES OF LIVING MIGHT MAKE YOU FORGET.

REMEMBER THIS: YOU HAVE SERVED IN THE FIELDS. YOU HAVE SERVED IN THE KITCHENS, IN THE WAREHOUSES AND THE FACTORIES. YOU HAVE SHED YOUR PRECIOUS BLOOD FOR THIS NATION, AND ALL THE TIME YOU COULD NOT EVEN ENTER THE FRONT DOOR OF THE HOUSE LIKE A MAN.... BUT TODAY, WE WILL KNOCK ON THE DOOR AND WITH THE ARM OF THE GREAT SPIRIT, WE WILL OPEN THE DOOR. WE WILL ENTER. WE WILL SIT DOWN AT THE FEAST TABLE, AND WE WILL REST AND NOURISH OURSELVES.

"Justice! Equality! Freedom!"

OUR BACKS AND OUR SWEAT HAVE BUILT THIS HOUSE.

"Yes, it's true!" roared the people.

THEN I FOR ONE THINK IT ALTOGETHER FITTING AND PROPER THAT WE LIVE IN THE HOUSE WE HELPED TO BUILD, NOT AS CHILDREN, NOT AS SERVANTS, NOT AS MAIDS, NOT AS COOKS, NOT AS BUTLERS, SHOESHINE BOYS, AND FLUNKIES! BUT MEN! THIS HOUSE IS OURS!

And the people applauded.

In the dome the words stung the prisoner. He stirred himself and took a step. But the weight of his chains shook him ... and he fell.

Outside, the cheers grew louder. The dome trembled. Specks of dust leaped up from centuries of rest and wandered like souls in limbo. Suddenly a passion seized the prisoner.

From the ground he came up slowly, as if he were a lost seed in a sunless cave, a seed that had sprouted into a pale limp stalk trying to suck a bit of precious sunlight into its impoverished leaves.

Riotous cheers heated the day. The sun stood high and hot. Soldiers came. Dissenters and extremists—organized sometimes and sometimes not—jeered at the leaders and threw stones at many of the marchers. More soldiers came. The police rode around in patrol wagons. People fainted. And the great city seethed while its troubles flashed around the world.

A ray of light shot through a sudden crack in the dome. The beam stabbed the prisoner, and he fell back, groaning and moaning as if he had been struck by a great hammer.

"I remember," he wept, "I remember."

Then the doors came crashing open. The people rushed in. And they trod upon sentiments, the truths, the lies, the myths, and the legends of the past in a frenzied rush to lay hold of Freedom. They cheered their leaders, and their leaders watched the movements of the soldiers and dissenters constantly. And no one knew who was to make the right move.

They lifted the prisoner, as if he were a flag, and carried him out of the dome, rejoicing as if a great battle had been won.

And when they carried him into the bright light of the noon sun, he felt a great pain in his eyes. He blinked, shook his head, moaned . . . for the intense light immediately blinded him.

And the people shouted, "Freedom, Justice, Equality!"

They put the prisoner on the platform and all the leaders gathered around for a ceremony. A hush descended like dust on a windless plain.

Shackled in his chains, the prisoner opened his mouth to speak.

"My eyes," he murmured. "If I could see . . . *see* this Freedom . . ."

The leaders all stood forth around him and hailed the people.

TODAY! TODAY! TODAY IS HISTORY!

HENRY DUMAS

"A drink, please," whispered the prisoner. "The heat . . . a drink . . ."

WE HAVE SET HIM FREE! GLORY TO GOD! THE LORD IS WITH US! LET US MARCH AS SOLDIERS OF THE GREAT SPIRIT! WE CAN SEE THE SPIRIT MOVING AMONGST US! WE CAN SEE! PRAISE GOD! OUR FREEDOM IS OUR SIGHT!

And the people cheered. The leader wrapped his arm around the prisoner, and the chains clanked and pinched the leader's arm.

LOOK! echoed the leader, OUR SOUL LIVES!

THAT WHICH WE THOUGHT WAS DEAD IS ALIVE! THAT WHICH WE THOUGHT WAS LOST HAS SURVIVED! And he raised his hand for silence. THE GREAT SPIRIT IS MOVING MIGHTILY AMONGST US. CAN YOU FEEL HIM?

The prisoner trembled. His lips hung open. "I want to see," he said. "Please, these chains . . . I want to walk . . . for I . . . remember . . . I remember when I had no chains . . ."

WE MARCH FOR OUR FREEDOM, boomed a leader. WE MARCH THAT OUR CHILDREN WILL NOT HAVE TO MARCH!

And the people roared like never before.

ALL OF US MUST BE FREE BEFORE ONE OF US IS FREE!

And the people applauded.

SO ENJOY YOUR FREEDOM! GIVE THANKS UNTO GOD, FOR WE HAVE WALKED BY FAITH, AND FAITH HAS GIVEN US LIGHT! WE HAVE PROVEN THAT WE CAN MARCH IN PEACE AND NOT IN VIOLENCE. FOR WHO AMONGST US TODAY DOES NOT KNOW THAT THE SPIRIT IS STRONGER THAN THE SWORD?

And the people sang and danced around the platform until all the leaders came down and joined them.

Beneath the sky the prisoner stood . . . alone . . . trembling, as if he were only a thin line of summer heat wavering in the noonday sun. His chains clanked and choked him.

Suddenly . . . as the people roared in a wild song of joy and freedom, the prisoner stared into the darkness of his sight, and except for the intense heat and the pain, he would have thought he was back in the dome. . . .

Then the platform creaked, broke in splinters, and tumbled to the ground. The people laughed merrily and followed their leaders up the streets of the city. Today was a great day. Freedom had come to them . . . at least for a while . . . and the marching of their feet was their song of freedom. . . .

The prisoner fell to the ground. The wreckage of the mob buried him, and the weight was like all the centuries linked together around his neck. The pounding of the marchers shook his flesh, and the heat of the day burned his thoughts away.

The sun beat down upon the great white dome. The sun beat down upon his head. And the dome was as white as ever before, and the prisoner was as black as night.

　　　　　　　　　　　　　　　　　　　　　　　　　　HENRY DUMAS

The Eagle the Dove and the Blackbird

An eagle once captured a young blackbird, and was about to slay him with the edge of his claw when he realized that in time the blackbird would grow fat with many feathers. So he cut off the wings of the blackbird, and after leading him to a great forest, he summoned his friend the dove to come. And when the dove came, the great eagle commanded him:

"Guard my treasure here. When he is unhappy, raise your voice like the mockingbird, and make him happy, lest he struggle and exert himself. When he is happy, lower your voice and wail plaintively, like you do always, that he may be pacified and forget his troubles."

And the eagle flew away to the heights of the mountains. The blackbird eyed his keeper with suspicion, and after the dove had showed himself only a bird of pale beauty, the blackbird saw how to free himself.

Whenever the dove thought it was time to induce the blackbird to act melancholy or joyous, the blackbird would pretend to do a dance, and all the time he was strengthening his wings.

Then one day the dove, having feasted off the seeds scratched up by the blackbird, grew tired and fell asleep, for he was very fat with feathers. And as he was falling asleep, the blackbird summoned all his strength and stole away into the forest. There he nursed his wounds.

When the dove awoke, he began to sing for the other to come and bring seeds. But the only bird left in that part of the forest was a laughing crow, who perched himself happily upon a nearby limb and mocked the dove.

Now the eagle, seeing this commotion from far off, became alarmed and swooped down from the heights. When he found the crow and the dove arguing and fussing over the seeds of the forest, he became fierce.

"Who is this sneak of a bird?" he asked the dove.

Not realizing his error, the dove said, "Why, he is your treasure, which I have guarded and held for you."

With this the eagle examined the crow.

"You have deceived me!" he shouted to the dove. "He is only a common thief of the fields."

And upon saying this, the eagle slew them both. And the blackbird lifted his wings above the trees and a great wind carried him away.

Scout

"Before I got off the bus I thought something was wrong. But when I tried to get back on, I knew that this . . . this *guy* was chasing me, *and me alone.*"

"Maybe he thought he recognized you," I said to the Scoutmaster.

"No, no," he whispered, "I recognized him then as only a street hoodlum, and I knew he didn't know me. Besides I had on my scout uniform," and he paused when a sound of coughing came through the door which hung darkly at the top of a studio-type elevation about three steps high. And he continued, "If there were any scouts in Harlem they were either too poor to have uniforms or too wise to wear them, especially on the day of the Parade." I looked back at the Scoutmaster. His graying hair looked like cotton mixed with bits of coal. We were sitting in his living room. The sound of music and laughter sifted in from the streets of Harlem below. The city was celebrating. The Parade was over. Now the parties were beginning.

"No," he went on. "He seemed to know me. He knew me better than I knew myself." He paused and lit a cigarette. "I was young then. My mother . . . we all were living on what was then called Sugar Hill."

"Yes," I said, "I remember Sugar Hill."

"Yes, over 20 years ago now. Nothing but project housing there now, and one dirty factory."

"Harlem has changed," I said.

"Toward progress," and he paused, sighed, ". . . the progress of death."

I looked out the window. People laughed and cheered. They moved like slow cross-currents in a river. Cars honked. Taxis screeched amidst the fever of singing, cursing and shouting. Indistinct sounds played over the dominant ones like subtle melodies from some invisible haven. By listening carefully I could make out faint patterns of sound. The familiar *clang clang* of a beer can sounded on a metal fire escape across the street or down the block, and before he spoke again, we looked quickly at each other—waiting for the familiar clanging of the tin to ring again from the concrete sidewalk below. We were still waiting when he went on.

"I was just a kid then, of course." And he leaned from his chair and looked past me out the window. "Sometimes on a clear night you can see that spire from Holy Pilgrim Temple there on Sugar Hill." He grinned quickly. "Light from down *here,*" and he leaned back sighing, "shines up there and sometimes the old spire can be seen all over the city."

A low coughing and a soft rustle sifted through the room from behind the door again.

"Yes," I said, "I know that spot."

"No, no, I mean a *lot* of lights. You're talking about a spotlight. It wasn't. It's the reflection from the Valley and I guess it is the paint or something on that spire. There's too much smoke and haze out tonight. I remember Sugar Hill when that spire would reflect the light from down here like a mirror," and he waved his hand in a gesture, pointing toward the neon haze over Harlem.

I put my head out the window. The dampness and the smells were returning in the August heat like the perfume of some temptress. It hugged my whole face and I saw over the rooftops of the city a dazzle of lights—flashing like some festive costume, swaying on threads of smoke like the excited gown of a woman. And above the roar of the great city of earth, over the concrete body of building and lights, the fog spread out, clinging like a river of cloth.

"Well, I was just a kid as I said," he went on, glancing quickly toward the room in one of his unconscious sweeps. "And you know, the Parade hasn't changed really."

"What do you mean?" I asked, for the Parade *had* changed. At least with each new arrival of peasants the Parade was revitalized. The old-timers relived the past and tried to recapture it.

"The *people* haven't changed," he said. "Deep inside they are the same. Okay, so the rules are changed. Today we watch television, tomorrow it will watch us." He smiled. "Automation, you know."

"Of course I don't have to worry anymore like I did that day when I realized that this . . . this guy . . . or this . . ." and he paused to chuckle, but he chuckled a meaningful laugh unmellowed and unsweetened by a smile, ". . . this *scout* was chasing me across the city for . . ."

Footsteps—as if someone were walking slowly in a circle—sounded and then a faint cough punctuated the interruption.

How many times had he told this story, and relived it?

". . . Well, I was just a kid then, a kid with too much money to know what to do with. And it was hot then too. The sun hit the bricks early that morning too, just like today, and all the snobs on the Hill were getting up to get out of Harlem. The Parade was a constant embarrassment to many of them, just like now—and I said the people haven't changed—and believe me, you'd been surprised to see so many families leaving with picnic baskets or suitcases, all trying to get away from the heathen celebration of the low classes, who were only celebrating the day of Emancipation. Of course my mother wasn't going to leave. My father was away, out of town, on business, so I was always told, and to keep me well adjusted, she gave me thirty dollars for my birthday and said, 'You're learning how to spend money, but you'll have to learn how to spend it wisely.' The next morning, also the day of the Parade, I found an envelope on my dresser signed in her hand: *From Mom and Dad.*

"It was Saturday, and with the money I thought I'd catch the subway and go down to Scout Headquarters and buy some decent equipment. I rushed into mother's room where she was fixing her hair and gave her a big hug. I could tell she liked it by the way she chastised me for not knocking at her door. I had always knocked before.

"Then we got in an argument. My mother had funny ideas about how I should dress. You know. Lots of women are like that. She wanted me to wear the new suit I had gotten for Easter. Just to go downtown to 34th Street and buy scouting gear, it was necessary to look like a businessman! She always liked to show off the fact that we were 'upper class.' I used to hear her and my father talking about how utterly degrading most 'Neegroes' dressed. How poor and sickening 'they' looked. I paid little attention to these enlightenments even though they were affecting me and creating the personality cloak that I would have to wear myself. Anyway I couldn't always be too sure that we were 'upper class.' Nor was I sure of what 'upper class' Negroes were supposed to be like.

"I refused to wear my suit. I wanted to be a scout then not a model, you know. She respected my stubbornness, and gave in slightly. But she wouldn't give in completely. She said quite definitely that I couldn't wear the sneakers that I was wearing then, or the dungarees, and I, picturing how silly I might look walking down amongst a street of clean white people who for certain would be keeping their eyes on me to see how I behaved, suddenly said, 'I'll wear my uniform. Is it clean?' But I knew it was because I had been looking at it in my drawer every day. It was my father's old scout uniform which he had worn only a couple of times. He hadn't done much scouting when he was young. The uniform was highly faded but otherwise fairly new.

"And so I dashed to get going. The morning was still young and I got on the phone, called up another patrol leader, my friend Vince, told him about the cash, and invited him to go along. But he expressed neither desire nor hope of going on a hike. The whole summer in the city had drugged him. In fact he wasn't coming to the next meeting. Our troop wasn't very interested in scouting anyway. We all knew it but hated to admit it. The Scoutmaster seldom showed for the meetings. I didn't really care about Vince not going along. He started telling me that he was going to watch the Parade. I laughed at this and all but called the Parade a monkey dance.

"'Well,' he said, 'some of the best people come to see the Parade.'

"'So what?' I said, '*seeing* it and *being* in it are two different things.'

"'Well, I'm going to *see* it.'

"'Yeah, but when you *see* it, you'll *join* it.'

"'Is that why you're not going?' he asked.

"We argued briefly. Then he hung up. I readied to leave, putting all my scout medals on and shining my shoes. Since I had to go past Vince's house to get to the subway I told him I'd meet him near the church and we'd walk to the subway together. He was leaving in about fifteen minutes. I would get on the subway and Vince would go on down into the Valley to fool around before the Parade.

"And now here's the strange part," he said taking a sip from his glass of lemonade and sweeping his eyes around the room. One light shone in the living room, and shadows stood bold around the wall. But there was a tiny light coming from that other door. Once, at the clink of the ice in his glass, I thought I saw a shadow move, but it was only a moth which had probably crawled under the bottom edge of the raised window while I wasn't looking. It fluttered near the lamp, spun, darted here and there, bashed into the lamp, shot off at an angle like a comet and landed in a vase hanging on the wall. A drop of water splattered on the Scoutmaster's head. Apparently he didn't even feel it. But he *seemed* to be aware of what was going on. The green vines from the vase hung down near his head. I looked up. A tiny struggle raged above his head. He continued to talk, and soon I heard a cough, and when I looked again—at the same time getting up, mainly out of nervous excitement—the moth was soaked, shuddering in spasms of death. Inside the transparent vase the tiny roots were strangling it.

ECHO TREE

". . . . Just at that time, who should come visiting but Mr. Vancourier who lived on the top floor. He came down once or twice a week, usually to gossip. He had a daughter who was very strange . . . and that day, I learned just how strange she really was. I seldom saw the daughter. As a matter of fact I had never seen her except on a picture that Mr. Vancourier once brought down. He was a photographer or at least he did it for a hobby, and he often showed my mother and father (when he was home) a lot of his work. His wife had died, and he took care of the daughter, who was out of school and who apparently never went out. From this one faded picture she looked incredibly beautiful. It was a full-length shot of her in a bathing suit poised on a diving board. Anyway I was so preoccupied with myself and hobbies and scouting that the thought of girls was only vaguely coming to life.

"But I didn't have time to listen to him. Before I left I had to take precautions about so much money. Mother had given me freedom I thought, and I was almost giddy. I looked at my scout knife and thought about carrying it along for protection. After hesitating, I left it. A good scout doesn't need a knife, I thought. I put all but five singles in my right shoe, an old trick I learned at school with lunch money.

"I went out the door and was about to go down the stairs when I heard a voice calling from high above. I paid it little attention because my mind was on the trip. I looked at my uniform and tried to assure myself that I was looking very out-standing. In fact I figured that perhaps Vince would be so envious that he'd go back home and get his old uniform and we would go downtown together after all.

"I never got down the stairs.

"The voice called again. It was a woman's voice. I looked up. I couldn't see her, but I could make out a vague shadow on the top floor.

"'You there, little man?'

"I felt her calling me.

HENRY DUMAS

"'Are you looking for my father?'

"It dawned on me who she was. 'No,' I said and made an effort to go on, listening for her, but . . .'" and he paused as a roar from the streets came blasting through the window. An ensemble from the Parade was marching by, some beating drums, others marching in costumes on the sidewalk and staggering between parked cars. Somebody exploded a firecracker.

". . . but she didn't speak for a while. I continued and suddenly a flash of light seemed to come from up there and when I turned to look I was blinded and I stumbled, waiting. I waited for my sight to come back. When it did I saw nothing but the stairs. As I poised there about to leap down the stairs, it came again:

"'Come up here *scout.*'

"I tried to force my legs to run down the steps but something in her voice was calling me and as I walked down a couple of steps, I knew that I would turn around and go up to her. I was afraid. But I was curious. Panic was creeping into me. When I did turn around and run up, I felt as if something were pulling me by my neckerchief.

"She called me scout as if she were a scoutmaster.

"The door stood ajar when I got there and something, some feeling made me look around to see if she were hiding behind the stairs but she wasn't and I went on in the door, sensing that I was entering some new world. It was dark when I stepped inside. The door closed by itself. I was conscious of an oppressive mood—like the mood of a funeral but *not* quite like one. It was sort of like that feeling I got once when I passed by a church in the Valley and the people were having a funeral, but I didn't realize it until I saw the casket being brought out of the church and a few women screamed. Otherwise the funeral was as joyous as the Parade. Before my eyes could focus, before the reality of the light coming from another door came to me, before I even realized that I had made the stumbling run up the steps, I heard the voice again.

"'Come here scout.'

"Reaching out of the room like a giant rope, a flood of light grasped for my neck. I moved toward it. I loosened my neckerchief. And then I was in the room.

"'Is my father downstairs with your mother again?'

"I stood in the doorway. What I saw I'll never forget. And her question was ringing in my ears. Light. A huge lamp. It stood over a large table. On the table were patterns, cloth, scissors, needles, tapes, several disengaged arms and legs from manikins which seemed to inhabit the whole room. Brilliant colors flashed from heaps of cloth stacked in the corners. I found myself nodding . . . slowly . . . and a glint from a large pair of scissors caught my eye, and I said 'Yes' almost inaudibly because all I saw were two eyes looking at me from behind a large partition.

"'You are Herall, correct?' she asked me.

"'Yes,' I said. My courage lifted. 'I don't know you. How do you know . . . ?'

"'O what kind of scout are you? Haven't you ever heard my father talk about Glorias?'

"'No,' I said realizing that I had never heard him speak about her and had never known her name. 'Do you go to school?' I asked, sensing I was asking the wrong thing.

"And then her eyes disappeared and she came slowly out from the partition and she was naked.

"Then something grabbed me, something inside of me, and her bronze body hung in my memory—blinding me—and I felt a stir in my stomach roll down into my loins and I turned my head and moved to the door, and when I did, it closed.

"'So you're the little scout downstairs,' she said. 'Well scout, when you grow up you can look at me, but if you stand there like a baby, I'll run you out of here like I would any ten-derfoot.'

"I turned and looked at the table. She had begun to work, measuring, modeling, cutting, and sewing. 'I have to go,' I said.

"'What do you think I called you for?' she asked, not looking at me.

"'I don't know,' I said looking at the sudden curve of her thighs. Her face was like none I had ever seen. She looked nothing like that distant photo. Her body was full, firm and so perfect that I was speechless.

"'Do you know who I am?' she asked.

"I was dumbfounded. I leaned against the door.

"'If you want to go, go,' she said and looked at me, and I saw strange illuminations in her eyes like the far off twinkle from the stars and felt the urge to reach for the handle of the door, but I didn't. She seemed to be aware of my hesitation and spoke very softly.

"'For a scout, you have not done much scouting.'

"I felt as though she were looking right through me. How had she known that?

"*Who is this girl?* I was thinking," he went on. "*Doesn't her father know that she's running around in the apartment . . . ?* and she stood up and went to a red curtain which covered the east wall, and while I was standing there shaking inside—and beginning to shake on the outside—she began to pull a long sash and I felt that I was trapped. I had never been that close to a woman before and I was in a foreign land with no means of communication except what my feelings told me.

"'Come here tenderfoot,' she whispered.

"I struggled. 'What are you doing?'

"'I have to go and buy some equipment.'

"A bright light leaped in from behind the wall and bathed her so that for a second she seemed to disappear.

"'A friend is waiting for me,' I said blinking, groping, and wondering if she were going to touch me, and praying that I wouldn't stumble and fall into her.

"'A scout buying equipment? What for?'

"'We have to have it, knives, and packs and blankets and . . .'

"'What is the scout motto?' she asked, her voice sounding far off. The light seemed cold, not warm as sunlight is supposed to be. Perhaps I was chilled inside. I don't know yet why it felt cold.

"I began—sheepishly—to quote the scout *oath* by mistake and she let me finish.

"'Now what is the scout *motto?*'

"I choked. 'Be Prepared.'

"'Are you?' and she turned and looked at me. Her face was enchanting, purely a haven of beauty and mystery. She seemed to come closer to me in every breath she spoke. I felt she was handling me, and trying to guide me somewhere. I began to fear more what she was doing than seduction. It is a constant question that baffles me. How was I being seduced and by whom?

"'Well I'm trying to get prepared for . . .'

"'What is a scout?' she injected.

"The light seemed to be going out. Perhaps a cloud was sailing over the sun. She closed the huge red curtains and fell into the shadow of one of her half-dressed manikins, from where she watched me and began rubbing her body with some exotic sweet smelling oil, a green oil in a yellow bottle.

"I attempted an explanation, got confused and remained staring blindly into her deep eyes where things leaped out at me.

"'I gotta go . . . ,' I said. But I never moved.

"'Do you know that I am a scout?'

"I didn't know what she meant. She didn't look like a girl scout to me. 'I'm a Scoutmaker for the Parade.'

"'What?' I peered around the room which was surprisingly tidy. A scout knife lay on her table. I saw uniforms of all sorts, costumes of every sort and every conceivable color and shoes and hats, scarves, and . . . she was a designer! of some kind.

"'How can a woman be a boy scout,' I asked, sensing my chance to counter her. 'Your father never said you were a scout.'

"And she smiled for the first time and I knew she was older, much older than I had thought, but her age was more in her manner, in her perceptiveness, in her experience, tone, audacity and wisdom than in her form, for she was no more than eighteen or nineteen.

"'My father? He is not my real father,' she said.

"'Stop kidding me,' I said fearfully.

"'Come here scout,' she said and reclined on a large bed in the shadows.

"I mumbled and went forward, looking at her body as if it were the first meal for a starving man too hungry and too weak to eat.

"'I want to tell you something,' she whispered.

"I stood trembling beside the green bed and avoided her gaze by watching the lighted table top where all her tools lay out.

"'A scout is a man who searches new pathways, and a marker of pathways for others; a scout is *always* prepared unless he's only a tenderfoot. Be an eagle scout and see the world far off.'

"I nodded, sensing that she might be some kind of den mother after all.

"'Now you're still a cub scout.'

"I resented that and I moved away from the bed, but her hand was pulling my neckerchief.

"'A true scout would have learned about me the first day we moved into this apartment.' She was trying to pull me onto the bed. Truly I was a kid, a cub, as she well knew, only fourteen.

"'Your father is a cub, your mother is a cub and all who live *downstairs* have a lot to learn about scouting. Life is a trail.' And she took off my neckerchief. 'You have no right to wear this uniform until you've proven *to yourself* that you deserve it. Take it off.'

"I stood up. What was she doing? I felt myself under a spell of some kind. It was getting strangely darker in the room. A panicky feeling raced through me like a wild horse. I began to mumble and protest. I felt that she was trying to take something from me. My money was sweaty in my hand but my right shoe was still safe as a bank.

"'Do you see my room?' she suddenly asked as if it were a timed question.

"I looked again. Doors led off from each wall, including the curtained one. 'This is a big place, bigger than you'll know. Do you know what work is done here?'

ECHO TREE

"I shook my head—staring at the workshop ablaze suddenly with colors as the lamp brightened.

"'Herall?' And she spoke with a voice I never heard again. She lay beneath the covers, seeming to go further and further away. She seized my hand.

"'Who told you my name?' I asked.

"'I'm a better scout than you, true?' I was ashamed.

"'But you're older than me,' I countered.

"'Who told you my age?' she asked, pulling my hand.

"And before I knew it I was on my knees beside the bed and my hands were being pulled over her body and it felt like nothing I've ever known and my hands were exploring—at first guided by her—then eagerly, searching the wet mountains of her breast and I was beginning to . . . die or something and she said:

"'Get up scout. Go. Go to your friend. He must be tired of waiting for you. And take this,' and she led my hand to her breast. Warm liquid flowed over my fingers. Then she fell away, leaving me panting on my knees and torn inside, and before I knew it I was going and she was a voice again.

"'Go Herall to the streets, go to the world and learn to be a scout, but do not wear that uniform until you are a scout to yourself. Then you will come to hunt for me. You will find me someday. When you return from the Parade you mustn't ask about me. I will be gone. Go scout, for other scouts await you.'

"I was plunged into darkness as I left the apartment and I didn't stop stumbling until I was on the streets and it seemed that no time had been lost. What seemed at first like an intolerably long time now seemed only as if I had paused on the steps.

"I decided to run back up and see if Mr. Vancourier was still showing my mother photos. It began to dawn on me that not only was his . . . daughter? strange, but so was he. He was always showing you something as if he were trying to see your reaction. All his photos were costumes and clothing of some kind. I remember once he tried to interest my dad in a suit, a red suit. Imagine. He must have been crazy. What was going on

HENRY DUMAS

with him and mother? Well I knew mother could take care of herself. . . .

"But as I ran through the streets, a thought came: If he anticipates danger, a brave scout remains to face it. Perhaps Mr. Vancourier would try to do something to mother. *Of course not!* And I went on to search for Vince. What a fool I was.

"My sense of time was upside down. The sun was up high. It was noon and the people were out. Everybody was going somewhere.

"When I reached Vince's block, I was running and sometimes walking fast. I felt oddly conspicuous in my uniform and I knew that in my haste I would pass up chances to do a good deed, a thing I thought about every day, but seldom accomplished unless I pretended the errands and chores for mother were good deeds. I didn't feel like a scout anymore. A policeman began watching me. I came to the corner near the Holy Pilgrim Temple and stood for traffic. The policeman's blue uniform caught the sunlight and his buttons flashed in my eyes. His uniform was blue like my neckerchief. He looked like a cub scout. I began to cross the street—deciding that maybe Vince was just down the hill at the subway station on Convent Avenue. The Temple spire! The glaze from it!

"I was crossing Convent and a Parade ensemble passed in several cars. When I peered through the windows I thought I saw *her!* And when the car whizzed past, a lance of light from the spire burned my eye. I stumbled down the hill not realizing that I was going deeper and deeper into the Valley where everybody was getting ready for the Parade. Yet perhaps I did realize something for Glorias' words suddenly rang inside me and I began to tremble: the policeman was following me. . . . I turned around. He was coming and I drew near the subway. And not seeing Vince right away I turned around to look for him. And when I looked the cop was gone. I felt panicky, not because he was there or not there but because he was making me fear going into the Valley. Vince had probably gone on down and was playing around with some girls and some guys he knew. I wished I wasn't going downtown. I heard the subway roar down the tunnel, felt hot air rush through the grates, bring up a stench and a piece of green candy wrapper which floated near my feet and then away away, down the hill like a toy butterfly. I lost it in a clump of trees that ringed the church.

"I began looking for Vince and in several minutes I was in the heart of Harlem on Seventh Avenue. The people crowded the streets as if it were a national holiday or feast day."

He paused again.

"It was like that today," I said.

He nodded abstractly, peering again toward the Hill.

"Sugar Hill," he laughed, but no smile followed the sound. "Did you ever wonder why they called it Sugar Hill?"

"Yes," I said, "But I never found out, really. Perhaps because those who moved *there* were able to buy sugar during the rationing of the War years."

"Perhaps, perhaps," he went on, seeming to accept my explanation only as a person accepts as a hope, the *picture* of a mountain spring when he is traveling on a long journey and is thirsty and dusty. "But for me the reason, *my reason*, my discovery, began to come that day.

"I was standing in a crowd near a bus stop at 144th Street and Seventh when it suddenly dawned on me that my neckerchief was in my pocket, flapping the sides of my pants. When I had left that room, it had been in my hands . . .

"And when I reached for it, I thought I saw Vince coming down from the hill of 144th Street, but the figure—seeming to lope—mingled in the crowd and was gone.

"I pulled out the neckerchief and Glorias filled my head. Her scent was there, fragrant beyond words. In wrapping the dampness around my neck as a scout does—with the V shaped in the back and the two equal legs on my chest—I felt my hands guiding the damp blotch to my tongue and the taste was *honey running sweet honey sugar nice good* and I blinked, was blind for a

HENRY DUMAS

second as a bus' headlights caught the sun in a glint, and for some reason I decided right then to take the bus.

"The crowds pushed me on. I was intoxicated with something. I was an unfit scout. I felt ashamed. I couldn't uphold a decent image then. I wanted to take off my uniform. And as I was about to get on the doubledecker bus I saw a pair of eyes from the crowd, a pair of reddish eyes and a narrow hungry face, a red-black face, pointed as if the wind had chiseled it. The eyes were coming at me—it seemed—through the crowd down the street at the foot of the hill. My safety was on the bus. I got on quickly, wondering why I had not brought my scout knife, or borrowed Glorias'. But I felt ashamed for such thoughts. The bus jerked off and I climbed the steps to the top deck where I always liked to ride whenever I rode the great buses. There were two seats to the rear, one toward the east where the sidewalk was and one toward the other half of the street.

"The taste of something thrilled my tongue and I wanted to be as close as possible to the Parade. I sat to the east and looked out past an old man who was trying to read a strange looking newspaper, a tract of some kind.

"There were a lot of photographs—it seemed—of crowds of people marching and parading with floats and banners. I saw one picture of a man with his hand in the air. I assumed he was preaching, but when the old man turned the page I saw the same man being buried; he had been shot.

"I was startled as the bus stopped with a jerk. My head snapped and a scent of Glorias fanned me and I felt ashamed. It was disgraceful for a boy scout to have allowed that episode to happen—and then come and sit next to an old man who was dressed almost like a preacher."

Then the Scoutmaster pointed with his finger. "See. There's that light from the Valley shining up there on that old spire, see?" I leaned and I saw. But it was vague, like a dream. I nodded.

"Well," he continued, "the bus went down Seventh Avenue, weaving slowly, through the gathering Paraders like a beetle amongst ants.

"And when the old man closed his paper and glanced disapprovingly at me, I shuddered, twitched and was thrown out of my seat by either a jerk of the bus or the knee of the man, or by both—I'll never know—and when I stood up, I was thrown back to the rear of the bus by the bus' start, and I fell into the vacant back seat where I looked out the window, and when I did, colors flashed from the crowd like a dream. I was knocked down for what I saw. Running behind the bus on the sidewalk—eyes glued to mine—was the same figure, and he was trying to get on the bus, I thought then, but as I watched, I knew that he wasn't running after the *bus,* but after someone on the bus . . . *me.*

"But I pushed the thought aside. Yet I heard Glorias' words echoing and sighing: *Other scouts await you on the hills of the scoutmaker and after you meet one, come and see me. You cannot now, for you are only a cub. Take off your mask.*

"And at every stop I glanced back through the window and I saw him, running like a pacer, his red shirt flying. His lope was steady, determined and frightening.

"Who was he? He did resemble Vince a bit but he was a stranger. Or was he? *Other scouts await you. Go to them and they will meet you halfway. . . .* What was she doing to me? Panic trampled me.

"I leaped from the seat, weaved my way up the aisle— *must get off the bus, I was thinking.*

"The bus stopped and noise filtered in to me from the Paraders gathering in the streets. We were at 110th Street where Central Park begins. The bus was going to turn after it started again, and I wanted to get off—to take the subway, to do something—for this guy was definitely following the bus and he was running after it as if it were nothing, as if it took no effort. I could see him in my mind, see him—red eyed—staring up at me from the Valley streets as if I were a mirror and he was primping himself. I fought through the crowd and several remarks resounded from people I rudely brushed against, but I went on, and was *off!*

"I stood at the rear door panting and the old man bumped into me. He was departing behind me.

"But once upon the street, the sun—and the people, the loudness, the fervor that settled upon me as if the whole of Harlem was seething, the fervor—riding on currents of hot air—choked me and I coughed and felt my neckerchief fly in my mouth.

"I stood upon the street jerking my head in fearful circles while the old man, brushing past me, said something—I am not sure: '*Going to the Parade young man?*'"—and then I saw *him* again, this guy, loping, coming, gaining, running through the crowd like an arrow, and I whirled to reboard the bus, which was closing its doors, and I leaped toward the front—knocking desperately—but my leg was the only thing that got in, and the bus jerked, stopped, hissed, opened. . . .

"I never got on.

"The V of my neckerchief tightened. I was pulled backwards. The bus driver even seemed to understand more than I. He closed the doors as the bus was moving off.

"I'd never been more frightened in my life. I thought I was dreaming. I tried to yell and when I spun around I was staring into his eyes.

"He yanked me back from the bus, wrestling with me. I swung at him frantically and knocked his arms away, and I guess we looked like two birds in a pool of water—seeming to scuffle, but bathing together. I broke away and flew toward the park, not wanting to believe that the guy was really chasing me. . . .

"Who was he? I looked for a policeman, and a shame—more dreadful than anything—overtook me and froze my insides even while I ran.

"I puffed up a hill above the lake. A couple of kids were fishing in the lake for the great gold fish that were seldom caught and seldom bit a hook.

"I stopped at the crest. My insides burned. The bus was out of sight on another avenue. But down through the trees, running along the edge of the lake, weaving in and around the shrubs like a snake, the guy was coming. . . .

"I had a little time to think. What was all this about? What kind of game was this? Perhaps there were reasons for him running after me. What were they? And why was I running? I had done nothing wrong. I had never mingled with the gangs in the streets. I knew about the gangs in the Valley. I figured he was a member of one. He looked ragged and lean. But he didn't really know me. Or did he? I decided it would be better to face this guy alone than run from him anymore and I watched him approach me, still running the same pace. He was coming up the hill. I hollered at him, 'What do you want with me?'

"And a smile, then a chuckle, a quick jerking laugh exploded in the air, subsided and slid away into a flow of giggles, and all the time his eyes were pinning mine. Panic seized me. I felt in my pocket for the scout knife I knew was not there. But he was lunging toward me. I reached for an imaginary something, a weapon, but he was upon me and we fell down, my right shoe coming off in a flash. My arms flailed away at him, but seemed to miss or slide off him. Then my neckerchief was pulled tight. I gagged, coughed, kicked and suddenly he was gone, running down the hill and both my shoes were sprawled away from me, and as I loosened the neckerchief, the thought hit me: my money! *In my shoe!* I felt in my pocket: nothing! and I stumbled down the hill, trying to yell at the disappearing figure. I was afraid, stunned, choking tears—and my shoe was *empty!* and I ran down the hill, screaming. *How had he known where my money was?*

"But you know the curious thing is that people didn't seem to pay me much attention. I saw a squad car, which seemed to slow when I waved, but then sped off as soon as I drew near enough to catch the eye of the driver. The guy was getting away. My other shoe was off and I ran on, trying not to lose sight of

HENRY DUMAS

him. Fear was driving me more than the scout instinct. . . . fear of losing some part of myself, fear of losing something I couldn't even define.

"Before we got out of the vicinity of the park, the other stopped, turned and seemed to be scouting the area for something he had lost. I stopped running but began shouting wildly at him, cursing and almost pleading. He paid no attention.

"I ran to him and flung myself at him. He was a boy about my size but perhaps a few years older. Scars marked his black and pointed face. I grunted and wrestled him, demanding that he give me my money back. He didn't attack me, but fell away, rolling with my blows. And he said that he didn't have it, and I looked at him unbelievingly, and resumed again, when suddenly he turned on me with a ferocious intensity. But his blows were all aimed at my clothing and before I knew it, I was wearing a shredded uniform. My medals scattered to the wind, dirt clogged my mouth, grass stains and bruises burned my skin, and I blinked: my shirt lay torn nearby, my neckerchief was gone, and the other loped back along the side of the lake in the same manner he had approached.

"But even though I felt defeated, I wasn't completely sure about it all, and I got up, washed in the lake where the two kids were still fishing. I stared at them. They looked at me. Why hadn't they heard us fighting? Why were they just sitting there not paying any attention to me? While wetting my feet in the lake, I asked one of the boys had he seen me fighting the thief. He said he had. I was stunned. 'Well, why didn't you call the cops . . . ?' The other boy pointed over his shoulder to a squad car parked right where I had just wrestled the guy. And the same look shot out at me from the same cop.

"Then I got a shock. The two boys suddenly got up and prepared to leave—as if the presence of the cops was annoying—I don't know—and when they did, the cop, as he skidded the car forward, yelled: 'Why ain't you kids at the

Parade?' And the two boys responded as they trotted away: 'Where do you think we're goin' now anyway?'

"And they all were gone. I felt as if I were dreaming. And to this day I am not sure. Sometimes I relive that experience as if it were happening over and over again inside me right now. But it could have been a dream, a nightmare, except for the last part ..."

The Scoutmaster took a long drink, licked his tongue out and sighed. The sound of footsteps came again from the room, then ceased at a faint snipping noise like scissors. High up in the sky we saw the moon for the first time, and the Scoutmaster— leaning far out into the night air and taking deep breaths—began again, as the beat of drums and roar of voices and the blast of a band and the rhythm of bells rose. . . .

"Well, I guess we'd better get on over there before the troop gets too hungry and begins without us."

"Yes. . . ." I said, and when he stood up, I did too, waiting to hear the rest of the tale.

But he didn't speak for a long time afterwards . . . until we were well in the streets. He only grunted a few times or coughed as we put the packs on our backs, gathered all of our miscellaneous gear, and went out of the house down into the streets. We were certainly dressed like rugged mountaineers or pioneer scouts, life scouts or something. My pack must have weighed a hundred pounds. We walked through the streets, stopping to taste or buy sweet fruit from the night peddlers. They would probably be the last group in before the sun came up the next day.

We passed a decorated platform where a guy was haranguing a crowd of Paraders. The Scoutmaster stopped.

" . . . and just what I'm saying? What I'm saying? The rich man got the money, storekeepers got the dime, while the niggers ain't got nothing but time. Is that my answer, huh? My friends, it is beyond that. Beyond economics. Beyond race. Beyond even religion. Listen. It takes time to teach yourself. It takes time to break the chain inside us. We waste too much of our time on foolishness. Now whose fault is that? Why I'd be a damn fool if I

HENRY DUMAS

was a farmer and saw a weasel come sneaking into my chicken coop, and I stood there and grinned talking about 'Now ain't that a cute weasel, must be hungry, but I know he is harmless.' Why I'd be a damned fool if I was too lazy to get my shotgun and blast that blood sucker to hell and back. Now ain't that right?"

And the crowd roared, but the speaker wasn't impressed; he went on, waving them to quiet down.

"Now you Paraders pay attention. Listen. This thing is beyond everything you ever thought it was. Now listen. I'm your friend. You can trust me. I got out the bed this morning with a pain in my stomach. Now that pain has moved to my heart, my head, and my soul." And he pointed to each, stretching his arms to the wind when he said soul. "You are with me. I am with you. We are together. We are one. Now what has happened to you people has happened to me too. There ain't one of you in the audience," and he pointed, "that ain't woke up some days so sick of trouble that the pains of your stomach doing like this," and he rubbed his hands together fiercely, "becoming all the same." He paused.

"See those men there!" he pointed at us, but looked at the Scoutmaster. "Well, they know. Am I right, brothers? Am I right? Listen. When Jesus—and I use the name of Jesus because so many of you out there know who I'm talkin' about," and the crowd murmured and swayed, "when Jesus was in trouble, who did *He* pray to? Huh? Jesus was in trouble and He had to pray! Who did He pray to? What did He say? Listen, I'm telling you . . . Our Father, *our* Father! Huh? Hear me!

"The spirit of Jesus had to ask guidance from someone who knew the way. Is that right, brothers? If you don't know the way and you're in trouble then you got to come to somebody who has traveled that road, not only that, but somebody who is a master at following ways and making ways. When one of their tenderfoot scouts gets into deep water and he's about to go down, then the master swimmer, the lifeguard, is right there with the arm of strength. Is that right or is that wrong?" And the crowd stirred. And he asked again, "I say, is that *right* or is that wrong?" And the crowd was roaring before he finished.

We were leaving, for we had only paused for a few minutes. We had to get to the Hillhouse before 10 P.M. because the troop was expecting me to bring the Scoutmaster in after delaying him for a surprise birthday party, which he knew about—scouts have to know those things—and after the party we would take a bus out of the city to ride all night into the mountains where we would hike for several miles in the morning to a crest on the mountain, a way station, and then we would proceed on up to our destination. . . .

"Now you take that Scoutmaster brother going there . . . ! He knows what I'm talking about. If a man knows where he's going, and he's guidin' himself, then he's a free man. If a man is free, he is alone, yet among free men, loneliness is a bond. . . . Right or wrong? If a man is free, he is independent in thought, in deed, in action and choice, my friends.

"Listen. I don't know much about boy scouting, but I know that a scout, a real scout knows the way. He's a pacemaker and a pacesetter and he's a free man. He makes the garment to fit right, he prepares you for traveling, he's your light, your word and your meat when you're hungry because he's closer than a brother, closer than I am to you." He pointed out into the audience. "Closer than this," and he clasped his arms around himself, "so close that you don't really know him until you *know yourself.* Now am I right or am I wrong?" And then he paused. . . .

"When you sing in the Parade, you sing to what? Now tell me, eh? You sing loud and strong and you carry on as if this were your last day to live. Listen. You sing to the day of your birth. Sing *your* freedom before you sing of someone else's of long ago. Sing yours first and then others will sing with you. Am I right or wrong. . . . ?"

And the voice died away as we moved down the street through the crowds. The Scoutmaster didn't say anything until we were climbing the hill toward the meeting place. We could see the light from the spire. The night was hot, but the haze was lifting. The city was beginning to rest from the fast pace of the Parade. We bent our backs and took the hill.

"I heard the same speech that night long ago," said the Scoutmaster in almost a whisper. "Afterwards we all went to a big hall. They dressed me, fed me, and I met . . . Vince there, and I joined the Parade."

And as a honking car passed, he said something else. But even though I was not sure of exactly what it was, I did not ask him to repeat it, for perhaps I knew. Maybe I would have thought and done the same things. What it sounded like was: *and her too* but I wasn't certain, for we neared the church and a sign announced the title of tomorrow's sermon: Where is God? And I began to wonder about that sign.

Then an insect fluttered near us, darted, dashed and was gone, flying away toward the earthly lights of the city, beyond which the eye of the moon blinked a strange flame of cold light down upon the spire. And we went on.

Harlem

Prologue: Harlem Square

Micheval's bookstore, guarding the northeast like an outpost for over thirty years, has been an important intellectual meeting place for Africans, Nationalists, Reformers, Muslims, and various dissenters. Some people call it Harlem Square. Almost every weekday evening a small crowd will gather to listen to the haranguing of one of a half-dozen speakers who stand on small platforms or ladders. On weekends the crowd has to be watched by the police. Harlem Square is then in some ways the pulse and the barometer of the community. You can tell the mood of the people by visiting Harlem Square. Of course, over the past ten years the mood of Harlem has been the same, and one doesn't have to visit the square to ascertain what it is. . . . Many Harlemites feel that they are living in hell.

The Lenox Avenue subway shot through its tunnel, shaking the tracks and debris. A hot blast of air leaped from the subway cavity, as if the train had screamed. The train roared into the station, stopped, recharged itself, and waited. Harold Kane, sitting with his head down and his eyes closed, suddenly looked up, peered through the standing people, and pushed his way off the train. Just as Harold was half out, the doors began to close. His leg caught; the train hissed, the doors reopened and Harold stumbled off the train. He looked around, went through the turnstile, and slowly made his way up the steps, brushing often against people, as ants do in a moving line.

Harold was tall and muscular. He looked older than twenty-two. As he came up out of the subway and onto the street, the sunless haze over Harlem showed his skin to be dark but tinged with redness, as if the blood were going to suddenly break through. His eyes were very large and watered a lot, and even though he moved along the street in a glide, a slow, aimless flow, there was a latent quickness about his walk. At the corner, he did not wait for the light as did some other pedestrians, but weaved behind a passing car, around another, alongside another, and then with his head held dreamlike he stepped upon the sidewalk on the other side of the street. There he stood beside a fire hydrant and looked up at the skeletal ruins of the Islamic Temple.

High over the ruins a flock of pigeons circled, arcing off, and then swooping up again, playing in the wind. Harold squinted closely at the building. A man came and stood by him. They both looked up. People passed. A woman stopped at the corner newsstand and bought a paper. The man was young and neatly dressed. He looked at Harold, who continued to examine the wreckage without acknowledging the other.

"Well, Broh," the young man finally said, "I see you anxious to know when the mosque will be rebuilt." Harold rubbed the fire hydrant with his right hand. He looked at the bundle of newspapers under the young man's arms. "Paper?" The young Brother was handing him one. Harold paid for it and tucked it under his arm. The other moved away and began to hustle off the papers to passers-by. The wreckage was strewn all over the sidewalk—bits of burnt wood, debris, and broken glass. The police had erected a barricade around the burnt-out stores. There were several beside the temple, which stood right in the center. On one side was a beauty parlor, dress shop, bakery, and a drugstore. On the other was a tavern, barber-shop, poolroom, and pawnshop. All these had been completely burned down. But the temple was the hardest hit. A bomb had leveled the walls and pillars. Harold watched the scene with a curious familiarity. While the young Brother was selling papers, he kept a close eye on Harold. Soon he and another Brother had their heads together. They had seen him gazing every day now for the last week. At a certain time Harold emerged from the subway like a man in a trance, and stared at the wreckage for a long time. His expression, twisted up with some concealed misery, kept the astute young Brothers from questioning him. They expected him, any day now, to break out in tears.

A bus roared past. Harold leaned his head against the newsstand. He slowly brought his right hand around and touched the top as if he were feeling for something very small. Then he looked at his smudged fingers. He put his head down on his arms again. For ten minutes he leaned up against the rear of the newwstand, not moving except for the shaking and shuddering of his body like spasms of pain. The subway roared beneath him. The street was loud and noisy. People darted here and there. Many stood and looked at him. Most of them thought that he was about to vomit. Perhaps he was. But the heaving of his body was far deeper than his stomach. Suddenly he raised his head and walked off toward Seventh Avenue and Harlem Square.

A group of kids was running toward Harold, and behind them was a man in an apron waving a stick. People stopped to look. There were shouts, but the kids soon dissappeared, zipping across the street in the middle of traffic. Several cars screeched to a halt. In front of a record store where the music was pouring onto the street like syrup, four teen-age girls and two boys were dancing, and one of the boys was beating out a rhythm on the showcase window with his fist. Harold moved through the crowd. An elderly woman dressed in a long cloak and with a big gold cross around her neck was weaving through the throng, handing out pamphlets. She put one in Harold's hands, but he put it in his pocket automatically, without even looking. A siren sounded blocks away, and a few people ran off in the direction of the siren. A wino was stopping people up the block near Seventh Avenue. He was holding out his hand and leaning forward. When he came to Harold he assumed a different posture, straightening himself up a bit and wiping the dribble from his mouth with his sleeve. Instead of holding his hand out to Harold, he grabbed him by the elbow.

Harold was dressed in a worn suit coat and a pair of khaki pants. His blue sport shirt had sweat and dirt stains overlapping

HENRY DUMAS

the collar, and his shoes were runover and unshined. The beggar appeared no better off, but he looked Harold over carefully and probably surmised, *Here comes a good one.* "Please sir," he said—a slight affectation slurring his words—"could you help me get a sandwich?" He showed his hand. "I just need a dime . . ." He was pulling on Harold's coat. Harold dug into his pocket, brought out the newspaper, searched around, brought out cigarettes, then a quarter, and gave it to the man without looking at him. The man, speechless for a split second, thanked him in a low voice and backed off, inspecting the quarter, squeezing it, and then looking around the crowd. He looked as if he were trying to find out who saw him. Then he moved on down the street and began to beg again, adopting the same pose he had taken before he had tapped Harold.

A cop stood in the midst of a group of young toughs across the street. Another cop was crossing the street to them, holding his hand up to stop traffic. The cop on the sidewalk was tongue-lashing the toughs, who taunted him loudly and then scattered. Later, the two cops stood waving them away. The toughs, moving through the crowd, suddenly began to run, and a bottle crashed against the sidewalk. The cops took off, chasing them. They all disappeared around the corner of Lenox Avenue. Harold went on toward Seventh.

At Harlem Square the crowds were gathering. Traffic moved slowly, and all along Seventh Avenue people were sitting on boxes, in chairs, on rails, on the ramp in the middle of the avenue, and even on the roofs. High over the city heads sprouted, leaning over the roofs, making it look as if the building was boiling over. And the street received the crowds, who found that the heat and the boredom were too much to fight alone in the musty roach-ruled tenements. Men, women, children, old and young, poured into the streets. Gangs perched on roofs like vultures waiting for something to happen below. A small parade ensemble made loud music in one block, and the music carried up and down the avenue. Conga drums, timbals, cowbells, guitars, gourds, and flutes harmonized raucously and shook the streets. Even small children were infected by the strange malady of hate and boredom. They had formed little squadrons, and went about with sticks and toy rifles, pistols and cap guns, firing and ambushing unseen enemies. They often aimed at the targets on the roofs, and they ducked down into the basements or into alleyways behind garbage cans for protection and concealment.

Harold stood across from the bookstore. At the corner was Goodman's Jewelry Store, with its huge multicolored diamond flashing on and off overhead. Harold looked up at it, squinting his eyes. He rubbed his head and leaned back against the wall. Closing his eyes briefly, he wavered on his feet. Then he crossed the street with the green light amidst a crowd of people who moved along like ants on a march. When Harold reached the other side he stood by a fire hydrant and watched the sojourn of the American flag as it moved from the door of the bookstore to the center of a crowd standing around a platform under the diamond.

Elder Dawud was preparing to deliver his evening message to the people. He walked behind a man carrying the flag. Another man was setting up a ladder for the Elder, and every once in a while somebody shouted a greeting at Elder Dawud. The people knew him. He was one of the many sidewalk prophets who—more than once—had indirectly caused the people to react in concert over some issue of concern to Harlemites. He was a short, dark man, about forty years old, but his thinness gave him the appearance of youth. He was clean-shaven, but his hair—thick and woolly on the sides, but balding on top—stuck out from the sides of his head. After carefully cleaning his spectacles, he folded some papers, put them in his small brief case, and handed the case to one of his aides. They stood around the ladder like a cordon. He shook hands with several people, looked at his watch, and mounted the ladder. When the people saw him, a hush flowed over them. The only noise was the whine of the siren in the distance, the honk and flow of traffic, and the unidentified roar that emerged from all of the streets of Harlem.

Harold Kane began to cough. He bent over, holding his sides, and coughed into the gutter.

"Many of you out there . . ." began Elder Dawud, his voice slow and liquid, as if it were being oiled for something. From his throat came a slight rattle, and it gave the impression of motion and force. ". . . want to know just how is it that a black man can live in the middle of the richest country on earth and be starving like a sharecropper. Heh? Many of you want to know about that. Now, again, many of you out there . . ." and he paused to smile and point at the people, ". . . and I ought to know because I lived with a lot of you out there . . ." and there was a slight stir amongst the crowd.

Harold moved in closer. He was shaking.

"Many of you want to know what to tell your children when they ask you why you let the policeman hit you, heh? Now, I am not one to advocate anarchy, no. Brothers, I am the most law-abiding citizen. But I'm talking about conditions that require careful examination; do you hear me?" and he looked at the people for a long time, then he repeated his question, looking around the crowd. "Careful examination, a close look, a breaking of things down into component parts, eh?"

The crowd roared its approval.

"Many of you think you know a lot about the plight of our people in this racist society. You think you know, so you dont try to find out anything new. You are what we call complacent, satisfied, pacified. But you're still feeling the boot of the white man. He kicks you *up* wherever he wants you to go or sit to be his Uncle and do his Tomming for him, and when he gets tired of your weakness, he kicks you *down*. Am I right or wrong?" The crowd roared its approval. "So, you see, the white man doesnt like an Uncle Tom Negro, either. Down South he uses the Toms and lynches bad niggers. Am I right or wrong?" "Right!" the people exclaimed. "So dont think you know all things about this situation until you have done a little investigation. How many of you have done some honest investigation, eh? How many of you out there have looked into the inequities of the system? Huh?" There was a small show of hands. "Good. I can see that there are some seekers after the truth out there."

Harold did not raise his hand. He stood staring at the speaker, but his eyes seemed far away.

The speaker went on. He began a long indictment of Negro leaders, then of the white city officials, then of the rich merchants who made their living off of the Negro ghetto, then he castigated the disunity among the Negro groups, particularly the Internig factions. He called them whiteminded, brainwashed, whitewashed Toms. Then he brought his argument back to the point of knowing something more important about the trouble Negroes were having. He brought it back to unity, and the knowledge of the coming future. . . .

"Many of you out there are going to participate in Jihad, is that right or wrong?" All hands went up, except Harold's. Many turned and looked at him. Some grumbled and murmured. Harold wavered on his feet. His eyes seemed fixed on some point in the sky directly over the head of Elder Dawud.

Soon after Elder Dawud had asked for more hands on various matters, he began to concentrate a lot of attention in the direction of Harold. Not once had Harold raised his hand.

". . . and just as there are wolves amongst the sheep, there are spies and Toms among you. Why, I can spot them a mile away," and he was looking at Harold, "and you mark this, Brothers, they run as straight to the Man as if he were God Almighty, and give our precious plans away. That's why whenever we plan anything, there's the white press and police there ahead of us, waiting. Now, aint that a shame? The black man is not the master of his own destiny. I tell you, you are still slaves! Brothers, I know it as well as you do, so dont get mad at me for telling you. You've got spies amongst you. Get rid of them.

"Now, the point of this meeting, Brothers, is to tell you where you can learn something about yourselves. Without a knowledge of yourself, you cant go anywhere. Why, you cant even integrate with the white man right if you dont know anything about yourself. That's if you want to integrate. Example. Not that I am advocating the program of the Internigs! No. But just to show you that the lack of self-knowledge wont help you to even do the *wrong* thing! Here you have so-called Negroes running around Harlem wearing bleaching creams and trying to make their hair look like Marilyn Monroe's. Is that the truth? Dont deny it!" There were several women and girls in the crowd, which was growing every minute.

"Listen, Brothers and Sisters, the norm by which a people live doesnt change without some kind of action and force on that norm. The standard you have been taught all your lives is the blond, blue-eye standard. Am I right or wrong? This has been a sin and a shame to a nation of twenty million black children growing up. Children, black as night, walking around with little blond dolls! It is the joke of nations. Other countries do not look twice at an American Negro, because they know he is hooked on trying to be like his conqueror.

"I want you to tell me what is right. You have a nation of twenty million blacks who childishly think they can erase their blackness that God gave them in honor of their beauty and strength, trying to bleach it out so that they can look like Roy Rogers and Dale Evans. To me this is a shame. What is it to you! It is nothing short of criminal. I think the people responsible for this crime should be punished. . . ."

Elder Dawud had worked himself up into a sweat by now; the crowd was with him all the way. He began to point out other things he disliked. The people approved. Harold began to shudder a bit, and his face was wet with sweat and tears.

All of a sudden, a man leaped forward, his fist open and his face contorted. He glared at Elder Dawud. Quickly he was seized by the cordon.

"We hear you, we hear you, we hear you!" he shouted. "When are we going to stop hearing you and the rest? We hear you, Brother, we hear! Tell us what to do! Tell us! I want to do something! I am tired of hearing and listening, I'm tired and tired and tired," and he folded in the arms of two men. They carried him out of the crowd. Elder Dawud continued, seeming not to notice the disturbance. The man quickly stood on his feet and tried to brush the strong black hands away, but they took him inside the bookstore, sat him down, and gave him water.

"We know you," said one of the men.

Harold made his way through the crowd and stood outside the bookstore showcase. They had the man seated on a box.

A crowd began to gather inside the store. Elder Dawud's voice was driving into a high pitch. The rattle was changing into pistons, and he was fanning the hearts of the people as if he was fanning a fire that had gone out in the night.

"Forgive me, Brother," the man blurted, his eyes darting wildly from man to man, "I didnt mean to disturb the Elder, but I want . . ." He suddenly put his hands over his face and began to sob softly. The Brothers had a huddle together among themselves and then—as Harold watched from the doorway—took the man, stumbling, behind a great green curtain that hung at the end of the bookstore. A man stood beside the curtain as if he were a guard. But he opened the curtain for them. Then he resumed his pose in front.

Down the street a man had a portable swimming pool built on the back of a truck. He was charging the kids twenty-five cents for ten minutes. A loudspeaker sent carnival music out with the announcement of the swim truck. A man was loading kids on the truck. There were squeals and shouting. The man was West Indian. His heavy accent could be heard all over the block: "Y'll haf de money reddy, now. I tell you, chil'ren, haf de money in de 'and."

Elder Dawud directed his attention to the swim truck a block away. "Now, you all familiar with Tango's swim truck, eh?

If you aint, you kids is. Well, Tango is a black man from the Islands, and he is serving a need of the people. Am I right or wrong? What would you think of running that good black man out of business in order to let a few Internigs go to the white man's pool, eh?

"Let me tell you something, folks, my friends, and this is what my message is tonight to you all. There is a conspiracy going on to deprive you black people of everything you dont have. Did you get what I said? Everything that you dont have! We're strivin for something now, eh?

"Not integration. No. The poor Negro doesnt have enough knowledge of himself to integrate right with the Man. Oh, you think the Man doesnt want you to have his daughter. Ha! Wake up, men. He'll sacrifice his mother, now. He can see the writing on the wall. But this poor Negro still thinks he can be like the Man. Why, the white man would more quickly integrate with the African than the poor American Negro! Why? Why? Because the Negro is a caste man. He doesnt know his total self. He functions in a self-imposed prison, the prison of his narrow vision. He sees himself as the white man defines him. Whatever the white man calls him, the Negro agrees; witness this, Brothers: He calls you Sam, you say 'yes, sir'; he calls you nigger, you argue and fight amongst yourselves and wind up cursin each other out by calling each other nigger! Right or wrong? He tries to be respectable and calls you Nigrah or Negro, and you smile and nod. You repeat it. He rules you. He is your maker. He is your god. You are trying to be like him. Whatever you worship, you try to imitate. Negroes worship Jesus, right? They try to be like him. Now, I see Negroes trying to be like the white man, to me it means they think he is God.

"Justice, eh. But I know for a fact there's forces at work to take it away from you." The people murmured. "That's right. Let me break it down for you. Harlem is the only place on the Earth where so many black people live so close together, and yet are ruled, governed, and manipulated by somebody else, namely the white man. The only place on the planet Earth. I dont know about Mars or Venus, because I havent got there yet. They tell me that the white scientists are planning on getting a man to walk around up there soon and bring us back a piece of the land. Well, if things dont straighten out down here on Earth, then when they get up there they're going to find the place already inhabited, and the only way to get through and take the land is walk over the inhabitants of that land. I guarantee you that if the black man cant get justice on the planet Earth, he damn well aint gonna let a blue-eyed whitey run over him in his own new land, eh? What do you say about it, Brothers?" There was a round of applause. "Now what I want to say is, and mind this carefully, the conspiracy is on. But first, the Afro-American population has got to go and find out something. He has got to do some investigation. He has got to go back into his soul, Brothers, and I know you all know what that is. The black man in this country has first got to look deep into his own soul, and then he has got to travel a road back there and straighten out the mess the white man has made. Do you understand my meaning? Listen, the black man has got to clear out the funk in his own soul. Let's face the truth. The white man has maligned us so much, has stripped us so thoroughly, has whitewashed our minds and ambitions that all we know is what he tells us on his TV and on his radio and at his movie and in his newspapers (we do have a few black papers now, thank you, Brothers) and in his school system. The truth is that the journey is not so easy. It is not easy because no man knows where to start, or which way to go when he starts, or the end thereof. . . ."

And he paused, looking at Harold for a long time. Some of the men in the crowd looked Harold up and down. There was a slight movement and a rumbling. The buildings where the bookstore was located seemed to echo the sound of drums and thundering feet. The police siren came nearer, and across the street two cars collided. Elder Dawud, sweating profusely, stepped up one more peg on the ladder and seemed to wind himself up, tighter and tighter. . . .

HENRY DUMAS

"There is one who knows the way. . . ." He paused. ". . . I come in his name and bear witness that he doesnt let a black man down. He is the One. There is no other whereby you can be saved. He has told me that the white man is doomed, and he who follows the evil ways of the white man is likewise doomed. He has sent us Brothers out amongst you to bring you the message of the truth, the Black truth. So long you have heard the white truth. Now you can hear for the first time the Black truth! He who wants to find out his soul must have a map. You got to have a guide, Brothers, if you gonna travel in a region so long unin-habited. The soul of the Negro is an unexplored territory. The map. The master has the key of knowledge, and he will show us how to find out the truth. . . . Here is the . . . If you want to learn your way around Harlem, baby, you got to get to know the people. Is that right or wrong? If you want to know what the black man is like, then you got to get to know the black man's soul. If you want to know what goes on in Harlem, then you got to understand what goes on in the mind of the black people who live in Harlem. Is that right or wrong?" And the crowd applauded him.

Harold Kane continued to listen with hypnotized attention.

"Am I right or wrong! I say you would gain integration much faster if you stopped trying to imitate the white man and stand on you own feet and become a man of destiny. A *black man* of the world! The white man is intelligent, and he would respect you for being what God made you. He wouldnt love you, of course, but he would respect you. Right now he neither loves nor respects you. But the Internigs dont know this. They think if they become the exact carbon copy of their white master, then he will let them in the back door. Ha! Whoever heard of a carbon copy being of any value as long as the original is around. Why, it is a shame, running around trying to be the shadow of another man. Hell, the white man doesnt care about shadows. He cares about men. Not flunkies."

ECHO TREE

173

A Brother was circulating around the crowd, passing out a piece of paper. Harold looked anxiously at the man, and when he came near, Harold reached out and received his eagerly. But he only glanced at it, frowned, and put it away. . . .

"Why, I would be ashamed of myself if I didnt have something to be proud of. The white man boasts of his wars and his great civilization. He writes histories and books, and teaches you to bow down and worship his white Jesus on the cross, while all the time he has you working for him, and he is paying you to help make his lifestyle into law. The black man in this country has got to learn one thing: how to use the key to his soul, for the soul of the black man is an unexplored region. . . . Who has the map of Harlem? Listen, Harlem has it. Harlem has it. And I speak in the name of One who wants to see Harlem keep it."

Across the street the police were trying to break up a restless crowd that had gathered at the scene of the car accident. There was a bitter argument with several belligerent men. The cops were trying to disperse the people. But the people all stared at the white cops (politely ignoring the three Negro policemen) with a bitter hatred. They called out, "Butchers!" "Klux Klaners!" "Beasts!" "Devils!" "White dogs!" "Mad murderers!" The police retaliated by swinging billyclubs and cracking a few of the slow people on the legs. A bottle thrown from the crowd struck a policeman on the head. He drew his revolver, staggering with one hand on the ground, and fired into the crowd. A youth clutched his belly in a loud scream. The crowd roared and fell back.

A brick struck one of the police cars.

Across the street, Elder Dawud's crowd joined the melee.

Quickly, word spread that the police had killed a black youth.

The police ordered Elder Dawud to close his meeting. Bottles began to fly. The police riot-squad siren started to wail its eerie whine, and the streets around Harlem Square began to clear and alternately fill up as waves of people fell back and then

HENRY DUMAS

angrily rushed forward, moblike, pursuing the wind with anything they could get their hands on. The police arrived more and more, and soon arrests were being made. . . . Harold had moved a block away, watching the disturbance.

Soon he turned his head and headed uptown, walking close to the wall and looking in at the shops and stores of Harlem, as if he were watching the reflections that moved to and fro in the glass, fading and fleeing like ghosts.

The University of Man

Tyros, the American, looked up from his watch table one day, spitting away a speck of dust.

"Ah, phff!" he said. "Is there nothing else to do but set the flow of time?" He stared at the dismantled watch in front of him. "There is not much more to be learned about the inside of a watch than I have learned in these twenty years. I am an uneducated man," he concluded. "I am run down, tired of chasing the same speck of dust away, weary of winding myself up each morning, tired of squeezing time into metal boxes."

"What can you do?" his wife asked him that evening.

"Twenty years I have labored in my shop. What I learned years ago I know now. I can do my work in my sleep."

"You are getting senile," his wife said, not willing to admit to herself that a strange malady had affected Tyros.

"*This* I am not sure of," he said, "but now I am sure that I must find out. If I am uneducated, what is to stop me from getting an education? I rebuild old watches every day in my shop."

"An old watch can get a new spring," his wife warned, "but you cannot get another heart or a new set of bones."

"True," said Tyros, "yet even an old watch, when all the dust is removed from its parts, when good oil is lubricating the little wheels, when the worn parts have been readjusted—even an old watch will perform well for a long time," and saying this, he went out to the village to announce his decision.

After the news had spread, the whole village gathered to say farewell to Tyros. His wife begged him not to go, but the priest, seeing the light in Tyros' eyes and recalling his own years of training, said, "It is the quest for knowledge that is holy, and not the knowledge itself."

HENRY DUMAS

The villagers presented Tyros with three gifts. The old judge, who knew the history of the town and the ancestors of most of its inhabitants, handed Tyros a book. On the cover was written *Book of Our Town.* The librarian presented him with another book. It was blank. "Write down your education here," she said, "so that we will learn from it when you return." The third gift was given to him by the village musician. It was a finely wrought pen of gold filled with dark-blue ink.

"You must go to the best university," said the judge. "Go to the one farthest east, where I went."

"Go to the one in the South," said the librarian. "I graduated there myself, magna cum laude."

"The University of the North," said the musician. "It is great for every field of education. Go there, Tyros."

"The very best university is in the west," said some of the people. "We have sent our sons and daughters there."

Tyros decided to go to each university to see which one he would like.

"You are all very kind," he said, and he kissed his wife. He got into his automobile and drove away, waving back at them until they were only dots on the hill.

Soon the car began to sputter. He stopped at a gas station in a town and had the tank filled. But no sooner had he gone a half day's journey than the car again had to be filled up at a gas station. In the next three days, Tyros discovered that the car had a strange magnetic attraction for gas stations. If he were going to the University of the East, he had better stop spending money on gas. So far on his journey all he had met were gas-station attendants who wiped his windshield and took his money. The car was no companion at all. He would much rather be alone.

"I want to sell this car," he said to a used-car dealer whose lot was at a large intersection.

"Ah," said the dealer, rubbing his head and squinting at Tyros' old car. "Not worth much, not at all. I'll give you thirty dollars."

"It's worth more than that."

"Thirty-nine," the man said with finality.

Tyros took the offer and was about to leave when the man turned to him and said, "Where are you rushing to, friend?"

"To get an education," Tyros said.

"Perhaps you do need a little, but if you are going without transportation, then you need a friend."

The man began pointing to the big sign that advertised his little lot: Happy Hop, Friendly Service, Friendly Cars.

"I have just the little one-owner coupe for you, sir. See her sitting over there. Look at the rubber, go ahead, start her up."

"Why do you try to sell me a car when I just sold you one?" asked Tyros.

"Ah, my friend, you cant resist this little baby." He took out a wad of money. "Look, I'll give you twice what you gave me if that coupe doesnt run ten times better than your old car."

Tyros began walking away.

"Look, friend, dont be sore. I'll make a real deal with you. You get in that little coupe, drive it round the block, on the highway if you want, take your time, check it out good, and see if a blind man cant drive it."

"I'm not blind," said Tyros.

"Of course you're not, my friend, but you'll need a companion on your journey to get an education, true?"

"Yes."

"Then for just a few dollars more than what you got for your car, you can have that coupe."

"Why are you trying to sell me a car when I just sold you one?" Tyros asked again, walking away.

"A blind man can drive our cars," barked the man.

Tyros approached an intersection. A car came screeching around the corner and struck a bus that was stopped.

Tyros turned and asked the dealer, "Is that one of the blind men driving?"

It was only a minor incident, and Tyros got on the bus and rode to the next town.

A group of young boys was sitting in a park, watching for girls to pass. One laughed at Tyros' suit. Tyros recalled he had done similar things when he was young. He sat down on a bench a few yards from them. No girls passed, and they began to play and punch among themselves, laughing and watching Tyros out of the corners of their eyes.

"Hey," one shouted, "there she comes!" He pointed at Tyros. They all laughed.

Tyros stood up. "If I were a young girl," he said, "I'd be ashamed to be seen with a bunch of silly boys. Dont you know that by now?"

The young men dropped their heads and tried to regain their confidence and flippancy, but they could not. Soon Tyros had engaged them in conversation and was fixing the wrist watch of one of the boys. They crowded around him and asked him where he was going and other questions.

"I'm an old man, but I want to get an education. I am going to the universities." And after he fixed the watch, which had only been wound too tight, the young men said, "Maybe we will go with you!"

Tyros welcomed them, and they all walked along, very excited. But once out of the park, a group of girls passed on the other side of the street, and the boys ran off. Their confidence had suddenly returned, and it blew their chests out like wind does balloons.

The next town was much larger. A river flowed near it, and there was a bit of industry going on there. He bought a meal at a community recreation center, and after the meal went into the recreation room, where groups of men and young boys were playing pool, checkers, cards, and table tennis. He sat down at the refreshment counter and ordered a fruit drink.

"You play pool?" an unshaven young man asked him.

"No."

"Want to learn."

Tyros thought to himself, What can I lose? Maybe I stand to learn a new game. "Perhaps I'll try," he said.

Tyros did not know that there was money involved. Before he realized what had happened, he had lost half of the money he had saved for tuition fees. Tyros left the center, but a young-looking boy followed him, and when they were only a few blocks away the lad began to call after Tyros, begging him for directions.

"Sir, I am lost and hungry," he said.

Tyros looked at him. "I saw you back at the center," he said to the lad.

"Oh, yes," the boy readily admitted. "I've been staying there, but they dont want me any more. If you could buy me a sandwich, I would thank you." Tyros looked at the boy and wondered what the boy would have said if he had asked him where he was staying. He knew that he should learn to examine his own apprehensions. Often when he fixed watches, he could just tell what was wrong with it by both the person who wore it and the style and make of the watch. He had learned to follow most of his suspicions about watches; now he would have to do that with people.

"There's a place," said the boy, and led Tyros into a tavern. Before Tyros could object, the boy had ordered a sandwich and beer, was drinking the beer and talking to the bartender.

"How do you serve beer to a boy?" Tyros asked the man.

"Oh, that's little Georgie, he drinks here all the time. And besides, his father is an important man."

The boy ate the sandwich, thanked Tyros, and was about to leave. "Why did you lie to me?" Tyros asked.

"I'm not a boy, you old fart!" And the boy left the tavern, wiping his mouth.

A group of young men came into the bar. They looked like factory hands. They all sat around Tyros and ordered drinks. They were loud and talkative.

"What're you drinking?" the bartender asked Tyros, who was sitting pensively on the stool, thinking about the boy. But before he could tell the bartender that he was not drinking, one of the young men shouted, "Give 'em a drink on me. Damnit, my wife just had a baby!"

"Boy or girl?" asked Tyros.

"Girl, but the next one's gonna be a boy!" He passed out cigars, and the rest of the men gathered around him laughing and joking.

The beer sat in front of Tyros. He had had beer several times, but it was always at picnics and holidays and other special occasions. Well, he thought, the birth of a daughter is an occasion. He drank the beer slowly. The bartender watched him.

"Give 'em another," shouted the young man. "Drinks on me!"

More beer. Soon Tyros was conversing with the young men.

"We will go with you to get an education!" several of them shouted after many more rounds of beer. Tyros had five full glasses sitting untouched in front of him. They tried to make him drink, but he smiled and said he had to go.

"Wait!" they shouted to the ceiling. "Wait, and we will go with you."

But Tyros paid the bartender and left.

By now he was nearing a very large city. Its buildings leaped up to the sky, and he thought that it had been years since he had seen the city. How it had grown. Large avenues and expressways spun and twisted overhead like a maze of race tracks. The noise stung his ears, and something in the air stung his eyes. He knew this was the place described in the catalogues. The University of the East was near here.

He took a bus along the Avenue of the River. He got out and walked along the river until it broke and turned toward the outer limits of the city. He passed several factories squatting on the banks of the river. Soon the river forked, and the tributary poured into a bay and the ocean. Tyros walked along the river, content to enjoy the strange sights and the crowds of people. Soon he discovered that a canal was hugging the side of the stream, which went into the ocean. They have built a canal, he said to himself. Men have built a river. He stopped and began to watch the silent march of the green fungi floating everywhere in the canal. Much of the city used it as an alimentary canal, whereas the factories dumped much of their wastes into the river. Up ahead Tyros saw policemen and a crowd of people. He walked faster. Beyond this point, way up the river, he could make out several huge buildings nestled comfortably on a wide stretch of land between the river and the canal.

When he reached the crowd he could see that both the policemen—who seemed to be there more as a precautionary measure than anything else—and the crowd of people carrying signs were all watching the solitary figure of a man down below on the land between the river and the canal.

The man was stripped to the waist, and over his shoulders were hooked huge ropes. He bent over, pulling heavy wooden structures through the water. A thin rope was attached to both sides of the bank like some kind of a dredge. The man was moving so slowly that it looked like he was standing still, but when Tyros looked closer he could see the muscles in his legs and shoulders bulging. A small boat, picks, shovels, nets, and a pile of boards made up a tiny site, yards down the river from where the man was working.

The people buzzed and talked among themselves. Apparently some were against what the man was doing while some favored it. The policemen sat in the patrol wagon with their hats slightly cocked. They would occasionally walk to the slope, look down at the man, smile, and motion the people back. Tyros drew near and watched.

HENRY DUMAS

The sun shone bright in the afternoon.

"What is he doing?" Tyros asked a man.

"He's a fool! I represent a council for the city ordinance—"

"He's no fool!" interrupted another man. "There is no state law against fishing in the canal."

"They should lock him up. He's a nut. Dragging the canal for a body or something."

"If there was a body, the police'd know it."

"If this isn't the last month he's out there, I pity him in the winter."

"How long has he been there?"

"Since March."

"Where are the fish?"

"Nobody knows! Ha! He's a fool and we want him locked up."

"He must eat the fish raw!"

Tyros looked up the river and down the river. He saw no more figures on the long stretch of land between the river and the canal. A duck and a gull were the only signs of life. The buildings up ahead leaped high in the evening of shadows as the sun began to fall.

He asked the policeman, "What is the man doing?"

They shrugged, and said that their orders were to maintain order. As long as the man didnt break any laws, then they didnt care what he did.

"But what is he doing?" asked Tyros.

"Look, why ask us? If you want to know, go and ask him."

"What are these people doing, then?" he asked them.

"Look, mister, those people dont know what *anybody* is doing, and if I were you I'd move on."

Tyros went to the edge of the slope. The man was digging at the bank of the canal. A long hill of mud almost hid his movements.

Tyros remembered that whenever he wanted to know the truth about the ailment of a watch, he could seldom rely on the notions of the owner. Usually he had to take the watch apart, or he had to examine it very, very closely, and then he himself could tell what it was. If he wanted to know what the man was doing, perhaps he had better go down. As he went down the slope, he remembered that his wife had warned him, "An old watch can get a new spring, but you cannot get a new heart or a new set of bones."

He walked alongside the canal, watching the man mend a shovel. Tyros didnt know how he was going to introduce himself or get the man's attention, to say nothing of getting across the canal.

"Excuse me, sir," he said clutching in his hands his notebook and pen, "the people at the top of the hill could not tell me what you are doing. I came down to ask you."

The man looked over the mound of mud. For a moment Tyros thought that he was going to smile, but he didnt.

"I'm doing my work," he said in a clear voice. "You are the first person except for the children to come this far down."

Tyros looked upstream toward the buildings. He knew that the university was located near here somewhere.

"What is your work?" he asked the man.

"This river and this canal, as you can see."

"Is that the university up there?"

"What university are you looking for?"

"The University of the East."

"That one has that name."

"Are you working for the university?" asked Tyros, thinking that the man might be doing some type of excavations for the university, since he was so near their property.

"I do my work," he said and began digging in a long trench aimed toward the river. He sloshed around in the mud. The water followed him as his shovel dug away at the bank of the canal. "The university I work for has no name."

Tyros was silent for a while. He could not determine exactly what the man was doing. If he continued digging, he would eventually widen the canal until it became a part of the river. But it would take years for one man to do that.

"You are looking for the University of the East?"

"Yes. Have you been there?"

The man nodded.

"You have? Tell me, how are the instructions there? I am going there now." He took out his two books and pen as a sort of visual proof to the man and a source of confidence in himself. "Why do you say that the University of the East has no name? I do not understand?"

The man was silent. The sun was resting on the edge of the buildings, as if getting one last look at the world before it plunged into the night below the horizon.

"See how the river flows?"

"Yes," said Tyros.

"Who is it that can name the source of a river?"

Tyros thought a minute. "It is a mystery," he said.

"Then, I do my work that I might gain more understanding of that university that is a mystery."

Up above them the people began to shout and yell. Tyros felt their anger.

"Why do they dislike what you are doing?" he asked.

"People dislike what they do not understand. They do not understand anything that makes them ask questions of themselves. The children used to come and ask questions, and they would help me."

"How long will it take you to finish your work?"

"How long will you spend at the University of the East?" he asked Tyros.

"After I learn all that there is, I will go to the Universities of the West, North, and South."

"Then after going to all the universities of the world, what will you say?"

"I will say, Tyros, you are educated. Go home! Then I will go back to my town."

The man nodded, as if he understood everything Tyros was saying.

"How long did you spend at the University of the East?" Tyros asked him.

Without answering the question directly, the man said, "I learned to ask this question at the university: What have I learned here?"

Tyros reflected. "One gains an education at the university."

"What is 'education'?"

"Knowledge," said Tyros.

"Knowledge of what?"

"Need education be knowledge of a particular thing? Is it not just knowledge?"

Tyros could tell that the man was deep in thought. The people and the policemen were leaving. The evening hung over the river with a strange mixture of lights coming from the blinking neons of the city and the quiet appearance of the first stars. The luminous engagement of the sun and the moon below the sky held the shadows on the water.

"Then what need is there for a university? Can I not gain knowledge here beside the river?"

"That seems true," said Tyros, "but I have spent twenty years repairing and rebuilding watches and clocks, and my knowledge has come to an end. All there is to know, I know."

The man handed Tyros a rusted watch.

"Then you should be able to repair this watch, which was lost in the river and no longer runs. I found it when I dragged the water."

"No," Tyros said, "I would need my tools for this. But the watch is probably finished."

"You are saying that one needs tools in order to utilize knowledge?"

"I would need tools to take it apart and clean it."

"Then what is education?"

Tyros thought for a while. "Perhaps there is more to education than knowledge."

HENRY DUMAS

"Is it not true that without tools one's knowledge can become useless?"

"Perhaps it is true."

"Then what does one get at the university?"

Tyros thought again. "Knowledge and how to use it."

"And then after you have gained the knowledge from the Universities of the East, West, North, and South, what will you do?"

"I do not know."

"There is one more university. And the tools of its knowledge are learned all through the flow of one's years."

"What is the name of this university?"

"It has no name. It is a mystery."

"What happens to those who graduate from this university?"

"Very few ever finish. . . . The weight of the tool is usually too heavy."

Tyros reflected. "What is the tool? I would like to attend it someday. Where might I find it?"

"If one's own weight is not too heavy a burden, if you can bear to look into the mirror of the river, you are very close to it, then. The greatest tool of education is the soul. The truly educated man is like a giant stylus etching in the sands of the earth. As he walks, words and songs flow behind him."

"Who might be writing with the stylus?" asked Tyros.

"Who can name the source of a river?"

"It is a mystery," said Tyros.

"Who can name the source of a canal?"

"Any man with knowledge of where it begins and ends."

"With the knowledge gained at the university with no name, one does one's work and there is no end to it. Knowledge flows as time flows.

"This is my work," he said, "this canal and this river." And he went back to digging at the bank of the canal.

Tyros went up the long stretch leading toward the University of the East.

As he moved out of the line of the trees and buildings, he could see the top edge of the sun capping the horizon with an orange arc. He stood and watched.

He knew what he would do from then on. He would go to the university and get the tools of his mind and soul sharpened, and then he would come back to the place on the river and he would help the man. And if the man were gone or dead, then he would gather up all the tools of his soul and he would do the man's work.

Rope of Wind

Aint no water wave, he thought, that's a baby cat bitin my line. The cork in the water danced against the tiny waves, and the waves moved it toward the shadow of the cypress log that stretched like a cannon out from the bank. He waited. The cork began to sink, slowly. . . . He held his breath, balanced himself there on the muddy bank as if waiting for the right moment, and jerked the pole upwards. The line hung in the water for seconds, but carried upwards as the wind caught it. He slung the fish with the wind . . . breathing out . . . *got him!* Becha even Hoodoo Brown cant catch this many fish.

He got another worm, hooked it, and threw his line into the water. Overhead, clouds moved across the sun. Where you hurryin off to, Sky, he thought, and watched as the clouds seemed to dip in over the acres of September cotton, brush the land, and hurry away. We bout need some rain. Papa be glad if it do come a rain. Mr. Westland, too, with all that new land he got.

Watching the cork and the slight movement of the tall cotton and the trees that sat here and there along the road, he thought that if he were a speck of dust in the wind, he could easily sail around and see everything and everybody, and then come back even before he got another bite. Wouldnt he have a lot to tell, and besides nobody would ever know he was there, being a speck of dust on somebody's shoulder. He'd like to ride Hoodoo Brown's shoulder and one day see why Hoodoo told so many lies.

Maybe then he'd get on Jubal's father's shoulder, and Mr. Westland would show him how he made the white men sell him that land. Then he could go and tell his Pa how Mr. Westland did it, and his Pa would get some land; even though his Pa was too old now to think bout workin any land. But that wouldnt stop him. He and Jenkins and Coalnite would work that land.

While crazy Roscoe was off getting drunk; but then, with him helpin and doin Roscoe's part, and even Coalnite's sometimes, since Coalnite was married to Honeysue. And then sometimes when Jenkins was helpin round the house and all, he, just him, Johnny B, would do everybody's part, and he'd clear that land, plant it, work it, and drive off any white suckerhead that come lopin around to take what a poor nigger aint never had. Yes, he would. Johnny B do that. . . .

And he slung up another fish.

A narrow thread leaped up into the sky miles across the fields and spread out slowly, racing along the edge of the sky like a string unraveling from a rag. He watched it and noted that it was somewhere in the vicinity of Hoodoo Brown's house. Must be John Brown. He the only one got a car go that fast down here, he thought. What you hurrin for, John Brown? The sun fell, and seemed to roll along the rim of the sky like a great ball as the clouds passed . . . in black and purple, he thought, orange and red, blue and true blue, and that one looked like violet . . . and he stopped watching the sun, for the faint glow of headlites lifted over the top of the cotton. The narrow thread was a rope now, curling in the air, spinning out from the car like that car was a fat spider running along and making itself a web. Johnny B waited before rebaiting his hook. Then he climbed the bank to the levee road, and watched the approaching car.

It zoomed past him. The dust came in fast. He ran a bit to avoid it, laughing at his game. He was beating the dust too. He raced along the levee, looking over his shoulder, not letting the low loop of the dust reach his neck, and he was laughing, racing everybody, Hoodoo Brown, Jubal E, Lance, Naomi, Neppie, and even Carstairs Jackson, who could beat everybody from the churchyard to the creek, or from the Frog Dip to the Stink Place, where all the sinker-eaters lived that only came out at nite, and he was beating everybody too, and he thought that if they started to gain on him, if Carstairs started to gain first, then he would make sure he couldnt go any faster, then he would say a coupla magic words, like he heard ole man Red say that time when Jubal and him went up to see him and that ole man reach out his hand and that old dust turn into a rope in his hand, then he swing out on it and sail. . . .

The car was stopping. Johnny B stopped running and leaped down toward the river. He didnt know that car. He thought he shoulda known it, but then he didnt know the car. No tellin who was drivin in it. Especially that fast. Might be white.

He headed back to the first clump of trees just before the area where he was fishing. As he swung, panting, behind a tree, hiding, a cloud of dust fell over him. He coughed slightly, not taking his eyes off the levee.

A man appeared there suddenly. A white man. The man walked along, deliberately, coming toward Johnny B. But Johnny B knew that he didnt see him. The sun was half gone. Everything was a shadow. He wondered what the man wanted. No tellin. If there was any more white men in that car, then the devil only knew what was in their minds. Fish or no fish, he'd better set a pace that no man could follow. He took a deep breath. If he ran, it would have to be daylite or hound-dog nitetime for them to follow him.

He ran. The sun was gone. But he prayed there were no dogs before the river!

Voices! He heard voices.

"You! Boy! Wait a minute!" The man had seen him.

He could tell why. Maybe it was the way the man said wait a minute, as if he just wanted to talk about something that meant nothing between a black boy and a white man. Johnny B stopped and turned around. He wasnt afraid of the man. He tried to tell himself that he wasnt. He breathed rapidly. The man was still quite a distance away, and he began talking to Johnny F

"Wait a minute, boy," he said, pausing to see ex-
where Johnny B was located beneath the trees. "I'm loo'
somebody. . . ." The man stopped. Another man was ca'
from over the edge of the levee.

"Come here, boy," the man said softly, as if to set up some bond of communication between himself and Johnny B despite the loud calls of the other man at his back. "Come here. We want to ask you a few questions." He came toward Johnny B.

Johnny B held his breath. He saw how far away the man was, how far he had to run before reaching the river. He knew he could reach the great log before the man, and it was darker now, and it would take a bloodhound to follow him. He didnt like the man. They plannin something, he thought. Something gonna happen . . . and he started panting. . . and it aint gonna happen to me. . . .

"I'm gonna run," he said to the man. He was surprised at how calm the words sounded. Maybe he wasnt afraid. "I'm gonna run."

"Dont run, boy, I'm not going to hurt you. My name's Jackson, I'm Asa Jackson's new deputy, beside being his nephew. Now, you . . ."

The other man was coming. "Ask him if he knows 'em, and come on! We aint got all nite!"

"Looky here, boy, where bouts is the house of an old colored man by the name of Eastland? You know, boy? Now, where does he live?"

Johnny B leaped forward and was gone into the nite. It was like he was thinking, They're after somebody. . . . Eastland? Johnny B didnt know him. The man was hollering at him. Johnny B looked back. He thought he saw one of the men aiming a gun at him. . . . He dropped to the ground, still running on all fours. . . . They aint coming, he thought, they aint running after me, might send a bullet, dont hear no dogs, might send a bullet. He slanted in and out, past where his fish were strung in the water, past his pole in the water, up the log, bowing his head . . . holding his breath, letting it out, leaping along the log, feeling the fat trunk sink a bit in the water, raising arms . . . balancing, bowing down, reaching the spring-off point at the top of the fallen tree. . . . Johnny B held his breath, and leaped high, high into the sky, like

HENRY DUMAS

he had practiced time and time again, until he could clear the distance and land on the bank. . . . Only Jubal could do it now without falling in the water. . . . A good jump. . . . The men were coming down near the water. . . . He wanted to laugh out loud. Didnt they know they couldnt catch him, not him, not Johnny B. If they couldnt bring their hounds, then they neednt come at all. He stood, panting, then fell on his stomach and listened for them.

"Where'd he go? Ed? Where'd he go to?"

"Come on! Leave the nigger be. Caint you see you scared him?"

"But where'd he go, goddamnit? Where'd he go?"

Johnny B raised his head off the ground. "Here I am."

"Come on, Zack!" The other man had started to climb back toward the hill. "That nigger done swimmed the river."

The other man turned, muttering to himself. "Ed, I'll be damned if I believe a boy like that coulda stroked across . . ." and he turned and motioned to the wide dark water ". . . in such a short time."

"Did you hear 'em strokin?"

"Naw. Forget it. Come on."

They went. The car sped off into the darkening sky, and Johnny B broke into a trot, watching the spiraling rope of dust fade into the coming nite.

He wanted to laugh! He breathed hard. God! He wanted to laugh, but he didnt. He kept running. . . . Got to get home. . . . Why, they might be after Jenkins, or even crazy Roscoe, for somethin or the other. No, he thought, maybe they werent after nobody. . . . What you runnin for, he said to himself, and immediately stopped, held his breath, looked back at the sky, saw the fading spiral of dust in the air. . . . That car might of been filled with white men, might of been full, and him all alone by the river! Shucks, no tellin what was in their heads, and him just a boy. If he was as big as Jenkins he could fight 'em off, but . . . Then he let his breath go, and raced off. . . .

When he reached the road that led to the church, he began to think that he was running for nothin. Those two men just lookin for a way outa—He saw headlites far, far over the fields . . . near the old Yickson farm, and the lites were traveling fast. He knew it was them. Be here in five minutes, he thought, be here in five minutes. Got to get home. . . .

He had to pass the Westlands before he got home. He would tell them. . . . He thought about Mr. Westland, and wondered if they were after him, but what would white men want with Mr. Westland? He was a preacher now, and was probably at church right at that moment. Johnny B strained to see if he could make out the church thru trees and the dust. He raced on.

Always after somebody, all the time trying to mess with folks. Johnny B frowned and spit. Thas why I stay away from 'em, he said. Just like Papa say.

They just got thru killin Ukie Dodds, cause Ukie talked back too much. Johnny B could remember just like it was yesterday. Ukie had a store, and had to buy most of his stuff from a white man named Olsen. Lot of people say it was Olsen that put the others up to lynchin Ukie, but that didnt matter. Ukie Dodds was found shot fifteen or twenty times on his storefront veranda, and the blood ran all the way out into the yard. . . . Johnny B knew, because that's when Lance and Jubal started calling him Johnny B, because when all the people were standing around there at Ukie's place after the funeral and Mrs. Dodds was inside crying and Rev Westland was talkin, some of the kids, mainly him, Lance, Nadine, Jubal, were foolin around outside when Hoodoo Brown came up and said that Johnny was standin in the place where Ukie lay and all his blood soaked into the ground. . . . They all looked, and there was a few dark stains still there, but the rain had washed that blood right down into the ground, or maybe some of Ukie's family had come out and covered it over, out of kindness to Ukie, because nobody should die and have their blood layin around on the ground so that

HENRY DUMAS

everybody's foot could trample in it. Johnny B knew that, because that was in the Bible. And they all looked at it, and a funny feeling came over them. While the older folks were standing around, some talkin about the wrath of God falling upon them wicked white folks for killin poor Ukie, Johnny B was sitting on the porch, wondering how that blood flowed, looking at the porch, seeing those stains, and looking closer until he saw thru the cracks to the ground beneath, saw that blood upon them crossed planks, saw it black and blue, red all gone, but blood, Ukie's blood, and it was him who told Jubal and Jubal come and bent over lookin at it with his big eyes and he said it was red blood and Hoodoo Brown said it was Ukie's blood and everybody said it was Ukie's blood and Johnny B felt kinda proud and sad that he had found Ukie's blood but he didnt tell none of the old folks and Lance told Mr. Westland that Ukie Dodd's blood was under the steps. . . .

He ran on. . . . The church loomed ahead. It was lit. Prayer meeting. Mr. Westland be there. . . .

The car was still coming.

He ran up the steps of the church. "Rev Westland!" he shouted. "Some white folks comin in a car."

John Westland raised his head from the Bible. He was the only one there so far, except for Mrs. Harrison, the old lady who never missed a prayer meeting or Sunday service. Then he stood up as Johnny B stumbled down the aisle toward him. "And they up to something Rev. . . . I know."

The man and the boy faced each other. Johnny was gasping, his eyes fixed first on the older man, who seemed prepared for all this as if he were expecting the men. . . .

"Rev—"

"Son, would you do something for the Rev?"

"Yes, sir."

The older man came to Johnny B, put an arm on his shoulder briefly, and whispered, "I want you to go home to my son, and tell him his papa is gone."

A strange calm enveloped Johnny B for seconds. He had caught a strange look from Mrs. Harrison, and now he was getting the same look from the Rev. He had no time to think about it. Maybe they didnt hear me, he thought. "Them white men is after me," he said. "They was chasing me back at the creek, and I jumped it. . . ."

Johnny B saw that the Rev wasnt really looking at him. He was looking thru him, out into the churchyard, even beyond that, maybe, further, past everything. . . . And Johnny B was frightened by the look. But somehow it gave him strength. When he spoke again, he was calm and his words came easy. Yet inside he was trembling.

"But they after somebody, Mr. Westland, they after— here that car comin now!" Johnny B was surprised at the calm in his voice. He moved toward the door, still waiting for the older man to say something.

"Go on, boy, and do like I told you," the man whispered.

Then it hit Johnny B.

They was after Mr. Westland!

He was out the door, squeezing past Mrs. Harrison as she was standing up.

The old woman was silent . . . but Johnny B heard a sound of suppressed moaning and weeping such as he had never heard on the moaning bench, such as he had never heard at revival, such as he had never, never heard. And that look in her eyes before, and the look in Rev Westland's eyes . . .

The car was stopping in front of the church. . . .

Johnny B went out the back . . . running. He didnt know why, but he knew he didnt belong there, somehow.

He ran around the side of the church. Two men were walking toward the church. Johnny B ducked and hid behind the oak tree, which stood over the church like a great canopy . . . the tree where Jubal fell and broke his arm that Easter . . . and Lance got whipped by Mr. Westland for telling a lie. . . .

Now he could see them. There were two more men in the

car. One was getting out and coming around the side of the church. He was walking slow and looking around to see what he could see. Johnny B held his breath. The huge tree could hide him if he wanted it to. Better run, he thought, better run and get to Lance. Tell everybody white men gettin Mr. Westland for somethin. . . . But he didnt want to run. . . . Spose they shot him, he thought, spose they shot him.

But they wouldnt shoot him, not him, Johnny B. What had he done? He moved from behind the tree. He hadnt done anything. Or had he? He went back in his mind. But he knew it was useless. There never was any reason why a white man wanted to git a nigger. He remembered Ukie, how they had come and shot Ukie, and what had Ukie done? They say that Ukie was always having meetings. . . . Even Mr. Westland use to go to them meetings. . . . The white folks had come to the church before. . . . But Ukie had kept on having meetings, and then they just shot Ukie because Ukie was getting a store, and they say he would buy meat from this here white man that . . . Johnny B grabbed his chest!

A pain shot through him. I'm shot, he thought. They kilt me. But he was holding his breath. He was holding his breath, thinking about Ukie's blood drying up under the porch. . . .

And then he saw them. The men. Mr. Westland. They had him. They were pushing him toward the yard. They were laughing. The man who was walking around the side of the church turned around and headed toward the car. They all got in. The door slammed. And Mr. Westland was sitting between them. It was all very calm. Too calm. And Johnny B began to shiver.

He ran to the edge of the road. The red lites of the car bounced behind a film of dust that leaped up. Johnny B looked, and then he knew that something about the car had reminded him of a spider. And the spider was coming to get Mr. Westland, when all the time he thought it was after him.

Mrs. Harrison came out of the church.

She was mumbling, ". . . . The Lord will repay, He will repay. Yes, He will, yes, He will. . . ."

She looked over at Johnny B when he moved out from the shadow of the tree hanging out into the road.

"Go git Deacon Hines," she said to him. "Run tell Mrs. Westland and Deacon Hines. Go tell, boy. I'm just a poor old lady. Cant run," and she began to sing softly.

Johnny B didnt know what to do. Tears were gathering in the old lady's face, but her voice was stern and deliberate. He glanced up the road at the car and then at her again. She was leaning against the church steps. "I'll make it," she whispered. "I'll make it."

And car lites danced like two red eyes. Johnny B reached out to touch them, to bring that car back, to snatch Mr. Westland from that back seat, but he only choked on his own sob. Then it all dawned on him. They were going to do him just like they did Ukie. That was Ukie in that car. That was Ukie. And them red lites, those red balls jumping in the back of the car, they were Ukie's blood. Johnny B took a few running steps after the car. He had to see that car. Mr. Westland was going to get kilt like Ukie.

He ran some more, stopped, ran, stared after the car, ran again, and then kept on. . . .

As long as he could keep the car in sight. As long as Ukie's blood was there, he could follow that car. He could follow it. He heard somebody calling him. Sounded like Hoodoo Brown. He did not turn around. The two red eyes were growing smaller, and he had to keep them in sight. Behind him they were calling him. The people were gathering at the church and on the road. And they were calling him. He kept running, and the road dipped and headed north. The red lites were fading. And he felt his chest paining. . . . He stumbled. And when he looked again, he could not see the red lites. A strange sob gathered in his chest. He wanted to cry. He fell in the road. They got Mr. Westland and they gonna kill him. I know it, he said. I know. I can see Ukie's blood again. Them whitemen gonna kill Mr. Westland for nothing, just like they did Ukie, just like they woulda did to me if I hadnt run and got away. He held the sob deep in his chest. It rolled around like a giant ball, rolled against his sides, his heart, and his stomach, doubling him over in the road, making him stumble and moan. He held the sob deep inside him. It would not come, but the tears did. He couldnt hold them back.

So he ran and he ran and he ran, and suddenly he came to the Yickson cutoff in the road. He saw the moon ahead of him, sitting above the horizon and looking at all that was going on. He wondered if the moon knew which way that car had taken Mr. Westland. He looked at the moon. A thin cloud of dust was coming at the western edge of it. He took the fork to his left. He wished Lance and Jubal were with him. It was their father and they would never let nothing happen. He knew that. But the moon was his witness. The moon was his witness. It was up to him to follow that car. His chest was burning and his limbs felt heavy. The dust seemed to clog the air now, and a wind was blowing across the field.

How could he ever tell them how he saw them come and take Mr. Westland away? He had to follow that car. If he could just ease up on it now, and he looked thru the stream of tears and the road was dark.

But he kept on. And the moon was his witness.

Time spun in Johnny B's head as a dizziness closed in on him. He increased his pace when he thought he saw the red eyes looking back at him miles ahead, but it was only the pain of blinking and the heaviness in his chest. His heart pounded louder and louder.

He should stop and rest, he thought. Gain some strength and then go on, then maybe he could draw in closer to them. He knew they wouldnt go thru town, but town was fifteen miles, and he had only just started running.

He thought about his pockets. What did he have in them to help Mr. Westland when he caught up with the car? When he faced them, what would he do? He'd have to watch them, and if he saw that they were going to hurt Mr. Westland, then he'd have to do something. He'd . . .

He felt in his pocket, and the matches felt wet against his thigh. I got matches, he thought, I got matches! And he stumbled in a ditch, never went down, heaving and swinging himself up, and ran on. . . .

Then he saw them again, the lites, the red eyes. But they looked like tiny specks of blood far in the distance. He knew he had taken the right turn-off. The moon was his witness. The moon wasnt gonna let them get Mr. Westland.

A wave of dizziness closed in on Johnny B and lashed him to the ground. He lay there in a heap, breathing out of every opening in his body, gasping, holding his stomach. . . . Thoughts hovered over the air of confusion in his brain, hovered and then fell upon him, bringing him quickly to his feet and tracking along the rutted road in the nite. Lance aint here. Jubal aint here. It's only you, Johnny B, you and the moon is your witness. And so he ran on and on into the nite chasing a vanishing pair of red eyes. . . .

And the car appeared and reappeared like some phantom teasing him, and soon his mind lost track of time and his body became fixed, rigid, in step with some ultimate purpose that he had ordained for himself—indeed, that had been foreordained for him. Johnny B was to be the messenger of the blood. The spirit surviving in each generation and appearing in the young. He ran on, and the lites of the town shone ahead of him. He forgot about who he was. Everything passed out of his mind except the vision of the red eyes in front of him. What was he running for? He forgot, because his chest was bursting and his mind was spinning and his legs were falling off and he had no arms, no tongue, for it was beaten off by the wind, and his eyes were swollen, and every now and then a twist of wind would crash against his face and a stream of water would leap from his eyes. What were the tears for, or were they just tears of joy?

Once again the car turned off, but this time it drove to an abandoned farmhouse, parked. . . .

The men sat there for a minute. Mr. Westland, his long face poised and fixed, stared straight ahead. They had been asking him questions.

"Listen, old man, you think you're smart, dont you?"

"We know who you is. . . . Thought you could git away, eh? You black bastard!"

Somebody struck him. The blow sent his head thudding back against the rear of the car seat, and before he could straighten up, the fat man next to him was dragging him out.

"They make 'em all kinds," said one of the men.

"Yeah, but this nigger gonna talk if I have to cut each word out 'em with this here poke iron," and they led Mr. Westland to a clearing beside the barn.

"Listen, old nigger, you got five minutes to live."

Mr. Westland never opened his mouth.

"Wait, Mule, this nigger's different. Caint you see that? Let me handle him."

The moon had risen. It shone clear and round. It was rising higher. The fields and the town miles off began to sparkle under its glow.

"All we want to know is one thing, old man. Did you once live in Mississippi, in Crucible, Mississippi, and did you kill a white man? Did you? Now, aint that nice of me to ask you like that, aint that nice that I didnt call you nigger and slap your face and kick your ass, now, aint it. . . ."

Mr. Westland never said a word.

And the other man swung a fist and knocked Mr. Westland in the mouth and he fell backward. . . .

"Answer me, nigger! Aint your name Eastland? Aint you killed a white man, aint you the nigger that sneaked up behind my father and shot him, aint it the truth? Cause if it aint, you'd better start talkin."

And Johnny B fell in the grass, panting like an enraged animal. He saw it all with his eyes, thru the grass, lying on his side, holding his stomach, and feeling his chest explode. . . .

They were gonna string him up. Johnny B could see the others tying him. They were gonna kill him.

Then Johnny B saw Mr. Westland open his mouth, and his eyes had that same look they did in the church, the same look that Mrs. Harrison had. . . .

And he spoke: "Since when does it matter to white men bent on murder who they murder? It doesnt matter to you who I am. Yes, my name is Eastland, a pity I ever changed it. Yes, I am called by my father's name, John, the man from the East . . . and if—"

They didnt let him finish. His speech was too much like an attack, and no black man attacks a white man and lives.

They fell upon him like wild men. With sticks, rocks. They put him in a large white cotton sack, they tied the sack to the bumper of the car.

They shot the sack, once, twice . . .

Johnny B counted them . . . five six seven times . . . and the silence of the nite gathered in upon his sobs. The red-eyed spider rode beneath the moon . . . spinning a web of madness . . . and round his neck Johnny B felt a ring, a ring of sweat and blood. . . .

He wept beside the blood of Mr. Westland and the moon was his witness and all the days of his life swam across his mind like a legion of soldiers and he swore by the moon and by the nite to overtake that car and to cut Mr. Westland free with his knife. . . .

His heart was hurting, but he ran. . . .

The men drove the car in and thru the town, around and back, and were coming toward Johnny B again. He fell into the road and waited for them to pass. But they stopped at a house. Todd Henson used to live there. Todd Henson sent all his kids north and stayed on down in Arkansas to work and die. He worked a lot and then died and left the house to the ghost and the land. And both inhabited it.

The moon was high. It was getting late.

Johnny B was a long way from home now, maybe ten miles, maybe more. He approached the house at a slow, even trot, his head cocked to one side, his tongue laying flat against the bottom of his mouth to let in the most air, his eyes staring at the place where the headlites went off and houselites made a shadow to the car. . . .

He could hear them laughing. They were drunk. When he got to the house the windows were all barred. He saw Mr. Westland in the sack, still tied to the car. He fell down, shocked, to his knees, crawled toward the house, got up and ran to the sack, and slit it open.

The blood flowed all over him, and he could tell that Mr. Westland was dead, and his tears fell into the blood, and he wanted to be with Mr. Westland, for when he told Lance and Jubal what had happened, then they would all want to die, just like him. He filled the sack with weeds and rock, and every time he heard them laughing inside, he stumbled, fell to the ground, and stopped what he was doing. He hid the body in the weeds. He remembered the license plate . . . and just before he broke into the road again, he saw that the moon was still his witness.

He ran. As if he were making a river, he ran. As if behind him flowed a river of blood and tears, he ran, slow, like a phantom in the nite, black Johnny B, the running spirit, breaking the silence of the nite with his breathing, the only sound that kept his feet pounding the road, running, running, and running. . . .

He would tell them just where the men were. But he knew that if he did, Lance would want to kill them, and the whole town would have to either move or declare war. Lance was crazy, but what could anybody do in a case like that? It was his own father that they killed. And he, Johnny B, saw it, and they would want to kill him for not stopping them. And they should, for he could have, or how . . .

He ran.

They saw him coming at dawn.

They saw human spirit coming out of the past.

They saw their own souls age before their eyes. Johnny B came like a ghost, wavering in the road, stumbling and falling.

Lance ran from the house, leaping over the dogs in the yard. Jubal was close behind. Hoodoo Brown and Coalnite ran as far as the gate and trotted from then on. Mrs. Harrison came out of the house and managed to get into the yard. And by the time Lance had scooped Johnny B up in his arms and was bringing him down the road, the yard was filled, the house was emptied, and an electric tremor seemed to spread throughout the neighborhood as kids darted up and back with news— Johnny B was comin, Johnny B was comin!

They laid him in the spot over which Ukie's blood had flown. They laid him on the porch in the morning.

He opened his eyes, stared fixedly at them all. . . .

"Where you been, Johnny B?" asked Lance, with his lips touching the boy's ears.

Johnny B looked at Jubal, who knelt beside him. He looked at them all. They were waiting to hear him, just like they waited to hear Reverend Westland preach . . . they were waiting on him, and so he would tell them. . . .

"Mr. Westland told me to come get you . . . I . . . follow them . . . they got him . . . go to Todd's old farm . . . I follow him . . . they . . . I cut him outa that sack . . .

And the blood burst out of his mouth. . . .

And they covered him, lest the flies pollute his blood.

HENRY DUMAS

Children of the Sun

. . . . Jubal's shadow stretched across the ground where all the pine needles lay like a brown quilt. His shadow made a small cross over the cardboard box, and in the box the dead dog lay— its face covered with foam and blood. We were all waiting for Jubal to say something. But we didn't know what he was going to say. And since none of us knew what to say, we just waited.

Nathan's dog was going to die anyway. A mad dog always dies. But most of the time a mad dog has to be shot, and if Lance hadn't grabbed Nathan's gun and shot it, maybe Jubal would have, maybe I would have. I don't know. Even Hoodoo Brown might have, and I guess Nathan would have even though it was his dog. We felt more sorry for Nathan than for his dog. Lance and Hoodoo Brown were sitting behind me on the mound of dirt that had piled up in front of the cave. Pieces of the roof of the cave were still falling, now and then, as if another cave-in were coming. We knew that if we wanted to keep coming to that cave we'd have to get some logs and two-by-fours to support the entrance. I looked at Lance and Hoodoo. They weren't saying anything.

Up the hill, through the high pines, the mist from the waterfall made a rainbow in the morning sun . . . as the waves of mist hung in the stillness of the pine grove, moving like a ghost wearing a bright band of red, blue and yellow around its neck. I seemed to hear the echo of that shot which Lance had fired. It was funny trying to think about seeing that dirt tumbling down in front of us and blocking the entrance to the cave. It was funny because I was trembling still as if we all weren't free from the hole yet and Jubal was still digging us out with that stick.

Hoodoo Brown had eased himself down from the mound so that he was standing directly behind Jubal. He leaned as if he were going to say something. Knowing Hoodoo I knew he was going to try something funny to make us laugh, and while we were laughing he would make a speech or something and take the attention away from Jubal, who was standing nearer than any of us to the brown cardboard box with the dead dog in it. But he didn't say a word. Only his mouth fell open and hung when he sensed that he didn't know what to say. None of us had planned on who would say the prayer over the dead dog. Hoodoo bowed his head. His shadow merged with Jubal's in the morning sun. And a drool of saliva began to develop from the center crevice in Hoodoo's round lips, a drool that hung there in the light, building up slowly like an icicle does in the winter time from the cold rain that rolls off of our barn across from my window. I watched him. And I knew that he wanted to say something. But he couldn't.

The sun fell through upon Jubal, whose blackness seemed to reflect the light, seemed to thrust itself out at the light and shine . . . as if he were sweating—and sometimes he was—and the light and Jubal's skin seemed to grab on to each other like two forces grappling . . . and as we stood there around the box with Nathan's dead dog in it, stood there trying to pretend we were grownups having a very proper funeral, something about Jubal's manner caught us and halted us, drained us of all the horseplay and laughing and made us look at what we were really doing. We sensed vaguely that somehow he knew what he was doing, or at least felt it. I doubt now if I knew what we were really doing then. How could a group of kids know about the terror and pain of dying . . . and yet we did know, we did sense something. Jubal made us. I don't know what it was, but we sensed it. Hoodoo Brown sensed it too. His mouth hung, dropped and stayed. . . . If we had planned on mocking Reverend Flare, if we had dared plan—without any of us saying it either—if we had dared mock Nathan's dead dog because Nathan was a white boy and that made his puppy also kind of white, despite the fact that it was reddish brown—indeed, if we had dared to mock death, to ridicule a funeral, then I know we would have all felt hideously ashamed. Somehow Jubal sensed this. That's why we were all waiting for him to speak, waiting for him to save us again. And Nathan, who had not asked us to pray over his dog, sensed it too. He mumbled something about going, but bowed his head in anticipation, his blond hair flopping over into his face like a veil. I watched him and I wondered if he were going to cry.

Lance was cocking and recocking Nathan's twenty-two rifle, cocking it and aiming it here, there, and over and around. I could feel him, feel his indifference in back of me. I wanted to turn around. For some reason I thought I felt him aiming the gun at one of us, just for fun, and I was hoping it wasn't loaded. Out of the corner of my eye I saw Lance jerk sideways. I couldn't help but turn to look. I saw him aiming the rifle down the road, through the pine trees, following some target! Hoodoo looked, Nathan glanced up past Jubal who was looking at Lance, and then we were all looking at what Lance was aiming at and it was a road runner! The wingless bird was racing along, just passing by. Soon it would be out of sight behind the trees. If Lance was going to shoot . . .! It had a snake in its beak, and the snake was flopping back like hair . . . and then before we could all breathe in and out, the bird was gone, racing into the wind. Lance leaped up and ran a couple of paces, pretending to follow the target and firing, "Whuck! whuck! whuck!" As he was making the sounds with his mouth the sound seemed to fill the whole place. Why didn't he shut up? I felt like telling him something, but I knew if I did we'd be in an argument, and Lance was bigger than me and always won the fights. Then Jubal pointed with his finger. His arm jerked up toward the trees. The only one of us that didn't know what he was pointing at was Lance. We looked. And there sitting on a pine limb high in the tree over Nathan's head was a red bird, and it was watching us. We had seen it before but paid no attention. Now Jubal was pointing at it. Lance turned and saw Jubal's arm retreating and he looked into the trees, and when he did, the red bird flew away, and the sun broke through upon us more . . . and beat down upon us standing there beside the mound, and Jubal stepped upon the rock and he spoke. . . .

Devil Bird

I think it was Satan the Devil who came first. I was sitting just inside my grandfather's room, reading a comic-book story of David and Goliath. My father heard the knock at the door and let him in. My father must have been expecting someone, because he didn't ask who it was. I heard the door open, heard a scuffling, and felt a rush of hot air. When I looked up from the comic book, I looked into the eyes of a very tall man. He wore bright carnival-looking clothing that shone iridescently. He paused at the door of my grandfather's room, and a shadow fell across my knees, extending to the edge of the bed. My grandfather, who had been quiet all day and who seldom moved, suddenly sat upright, his eyes popping and his thin chest heaving. His groan filled the whole house.

Then the Devil—I am sure it was him now, because of the things that happened afterward—bowed slowly, almost imperceptibly. In his gloved hands he carried a tapering rod shaped at the smaller end like a key. As he passed by the door, his eyes rested on me, and I think I heard him chuckle. At the same time, my mother, who had heard the scream of my grandfather, rushed past the visitor and entered the room. I had stood up, unable to do or say anything. My father followed the visitor into the front room which we called the Game Room, and there they began to examine carefully our family Game Book.

My mother and I tended to my grandfather. It must have been the sudden rush of air that choked off his breath. Soon he was resting as before. His eyes were half closed and he lay still, making only little grumbling noises now and then, which I had learned—after listening to my father and mother discussing Grandfather's activities in his younger days—were fusses and fights he had had with his deacons. My grandfather was a famous Negro minister in his day, and there were many who were jealous of his closeness with God and his influence as a Christian.

My mother gave my grandfather some medicine and sent me out of the room. Then she turned out the light and tiptoed out.

We were all in the Game Room now. I sat in the corner, watching the tall visitor thumb through the Book. Every now and then he would pause and look up at my father, who would study the page and shake his head. My father called my mother to his side, and they examined the pages together. After looking through half the Book, the visitor closed it and took out a long, narrow cigarette. He touched the end of the cigarette with the key, and instantly flames sprang up. The smoke smelled like burning weeds.

Soon there was another knock at the door, and my mother got up. She asked, "Who is it?" There seemed to be no answer.

"Who is it?" she asked, louder.

There came a voice: "I am here."

My father stood up, and the visitor, laying the lighted cigarette across the Book, also stood up.

"That is my partner," said the visitor.

"Your partner?" asked my father.

"Yes, oh, yes. Didn't you know?"

"Well . . ."

"You were expecting someone else?"

"Well, according to the Game Book, we . . . are partners. . . ."

The visitor laughed. "You *are* a partner," he said. "Are you like the old man in there, who thinks a god is his partner?"

"Let him in, Grace," my father finally said.

I looked at the Devil. He was smiling. He pranced around the room now, and his footsteps shook the floor. I don't know what got into me, but I got mad at him. I could feel my comic book tearing under the pressure of my hands.

"My father doesn't want anybody to put their cigarettes on the Book," I suddenly said to the visitor.

He faced me and blew a smoke ring. I pointed at his smoking cigarette. "And besides, it stinks, and Grandfather is sick."

He looked quizzically at me and pranced about heavily. But when I fetched an ashtray from the Game Room supply closet and placed it on the table where the Book always rested, I noticed the cigarette was out and the visitor was waving the key rod around as if he were writing in the air. He then smiled at me, bowed, and continued marching around, stepping so loud I thought the walls would fall and the floor would give way.

Then entering the room was another tall man. He was dressed shabbily, as if he had been in an accident or a fight. His eyes were dreary and his head bent over. He came in, my mother following closely behind him. He sat down at the table and began looking through the Book. In the sick room my grandfather moaned. My father and mother came over to me now, and I could tell that they didn't know exactly what to do.

When the second visitor had finished looking through the Book, he looked at my father and said, "Do you have any good cards?"

"I don't know," my father said, going over to the supply closet. "What about these?"

"The Book says a game of cards," said the second visitor, "and may the good man and woman of the house accept their hands."

The Devil began to clap his hands and dance around the room. He grabbed God by the shoulders and hugged him, calling him "Partner! Partner!"

Every time Satan the Devil touched God's shoulder with his long gloved fingers there was a sizzling sound. A cool wind was blowing the smoke out of the room. Suddenly a light came on in my grandfather's room. My mother hurried to the room. I could see my grandfather's thin arms wavering across the sheet, as he was trying to reach and pull it over his frail body.

"The Book is right," said the Devil. He prepared the table for a game, ushering my father around as if he was a child. I didn't like the way he did things, but then, a person isn't supposed to like the Devil. It doesn't matter whether or not he really is the Devil, or whether he does good or bad things. If he looks like what you think the Devil is supposed to look like and if he acts like the Devil, then you are supposed to fear him and hate him.

Soon God Almighty and Satan the Devil were sitting opposite each other at the card table. They were partners. My father was sitting opposite the vacant chair. Our family played cards often. I had seen my father and uncles, aunts, and relatives play late into the night, often sending me to bed before the games were finished. There was something about the way they played that made me stand for hours, watching the plays and expressions on their faces. They played as if everything counted on the game. Sometimes I believed it did. When I played with my friends, I found myself putting on the same expressions and acting with the same intensity, whatever the game was. I went to the table. God was still studying the Book. My father had his head in his hands. When he heard me climbing into the chair, he looked up.

"Little fellow, that's not your seat."

"But who's gonna play with you?"

He looked at God, fumbled with the Book, and cleared his throat as my mother turned out the light in Grandpa's room.

"But I want to play," I said.

"I know, son, but when Mother comes you'll have to get up."

"Why?" I asked. "She's taking care of Grandpa."

The Devil, reaching out for the ashtray, looked at my father and said, "Do you want to play or forfeit?"

"Let him choose," said God. "Let him make sure he wants to do what he does." He looked at my father. "I will allow you another chance."

My father began to shiver. I wanted to help him. Here were God and Satan, playing against him. It was against everything I had learned in Sunday School. I got mad at both God and the Devil, but I felt ashamed and tried to keep quiet. I was waist high to my father then, and I wasn't supposed to know as much as he did. Yet I remember everything that happened as if it were only yesterday.

Father thumbed nervously through the Book.

"There are some mistakes," he began, "because, according to the Game Book—"

The Devil cut him off. "Is it not true that he is your father and that for twenty years he was the spiritual leader of ten thousand Negro Christians from all over this nation?"

"Moreover," added God, "you and she have played the game of cards. You know the game, and it would be unfair for us to use another method. Am I not true?"

I heard my father whisper "Yes" under his breath. He withdrew his hand from the Book and watched as my mother took the seat opposite him.

"And so," said God, suddenly seizing the deck of cards. After shuffling them deftly three times, he handed them to the Devil, who looked them over and asked, "Why are you giving them to me?" Still holding them, God reached and touched the extended edge of the key rod to the deck, and immediately there was a flash. Then God shoved the cards in front of my father and said, "You shall deal your hand."

It is the rule in whist that the opponent to the right of the dealer shall cut the cards. My father, forgetting this rule—although he was an expert whist player—began to deal out the cards. As soon as my father had given God and my mother their first cards, the Devil held up his hands. "Halt."

"What is wrong?" asked my mother.

"The Book says that I have to cut the cards."

My father looked dumbfounded. He knew the rules, and he dropped the cards on the table and prepared to reshuffle them.

"No, no," said God. "Let him cut as they stand. You will learn that you get no second chances in this game. Mistakes are costly."

The Devil cut the cards, and I am sure that the cards he got from then on were better than the ones he was going to get, for I could see his hand from where I stood and it was a very good one.

"But the Game Book doesn't say you can cut after the cards have been dealt," protested my mother. She was angry.

Then God and Satan the Devil put their heads together, whispering and thumbing on the table as if they were in deep concentration.

From Grandpa's room came a stirring about and a series of grunts.

The Devil took out his key rod and waved it. He touched the Book with it several times, pointed it around the room. When he pointed it toward my father's clothes closet, the door opened and a hat fell out. Before anyone could react to this, the Devil jumped up and seized the hat, putting in on and stomping around the room, growling and fuming as if he were the meanest Devil in hell. While he was doing this, God was thumbing through the Book, making funny marks in the Book with his right finger.

Then the game resumed, and when my mother brought up the same protest, she was allowed to examine the Book to find the rule she was quoting. While she searched, God toyed with the hat the Devil had been wearing, twirling it around and around in his right hand.

When my mother found the rule she read it:

Upon the failure of opponent to cut cards before the commencement of dealing, the opponent shall halt the dealer and perform the ritual of cutting as prescribed without the reshuffling of dealt cards.

When she finished reading she gasped, for obviously the rule was different.

"He did something to it!" I said, pointing at God. "He did something to it!"

"Now, now, young man," the Devil said to me, "when your turn comes to play a game of cards with us, I hope you have learned the rules yourself." He smiled and turned his back on me.

My father frowned at me.

Mother looked at her cards now in wonder and fear. My father dealt out the entire deck.

"Love," said God, "is the ultimate rule. If you love the game, there is no rule."

"The Book speaks in many languages," said the Devil. "A lifetime can be spent in the worthwhile pursuit of the wisdom of the Book. There are special situations with no rules, and special rules for no situations."

The game progressed. I could not tell who was winning, but the Devil and God had two private conversations. My parents looked at each other rarely and kept their heads down. On each hand they looked at their cards with less and less enthusiasm. And I guess I can say that since they had no enthusiasm in the very beginning, their faces were vacant and without hope. I was not only sad, but scared. I had never heard of folks playing a game with God and the Devil.

Then the two visitors seemed to get into some kind of an argument. They were on their third private conversation in the corner by the supply closet when their voices grew loud and vexed.

"Let the father," screamed the Devil.

"Let the son," persuaded God.

"And what about the other?"

"She will come in time."

"No."

"I want them all. Did we not make an agreement when he arose?"

"That was for their sakes. Even he knew that. How many more races do you think we can afford to let into the Promised Land?"

"Ask him if he really loves her."

"Let the son do it."

"Why should we tarry over this issue? Did not Jesus prove they cannot live without grace and there would be no grace unless he died?"

"Then we will take him?"

"It is written. He served his purpose. His love shall justify their hate. He has overstayed."

They went on like that for some time. I sat down with another comic book, because I had begun to believe that the visitors were imposters. But all that changed soon enough.

Suddenly from the sick room my grandfather appeared, standing in front of the table like a ghost. He heaved and wavered, a stack of bones held together by withered black skin. He had wrapped a sheet around himself, and under his arm he carried a replica of the Book.

"Blasphemy! The smell of blasphemy is abominable. In my own house my children curse me and Jesus."

"So," the Devil said, turning to my grandpa and smiling at him, "Uncle has arrived and can speak for himself."

"Let him speak," said God.

My grandfather seemed not to see them. He directed his whole attention to my parents and me.

"You allow this young one to learn the vocabulary of evil. For twelve years I have pastored this flock, and never have I heard anyone blaspheme against the Holy Ghost! God is no respecter of persons, and His love is free to Negroes as well as whites. When we get to heaven there won't be any racial trouble, because those risen in Christ are free of the flesh."

While he preached the Devil motioned to God. They both tiptoed out of the room and then turned shortly. At first I didn't notice anything, but when they took their regular seats I noticed something peculiar. The Devil was twirling the hat with his left hand and God, smiling wryly at my grandfather, examined the key rod. There was no mistake. They had changed clothes.

Soon my grandfather was down on his knees, witnessing and beseeching God and Jesus to save the souls of all the Negro

HENRY DUMAS

Christians who had gone astray. My mother was down on her knees, trying to get him back into bed. But he was wild. My father sat in his chair, his head in his hands, shuddering. I thought he might be crying. I hoped not.

Then the Devil cracked the key rod on the table. When he did that, a long-beaked bird that cawed like a crow flew from the hat God was twirling. It flapped around and left droppings on the Book. Finally it balanced itself on the shoulders of my grandfather and began to bow, repeatedly, at its audience. I hated that bird. It was funny, but the moment I saw it I disliked it and what it was doing. It was bad enough for Grandfather to be wallowing on the floor, but to see the bird make fun of us was too much.

"How beautiful is the dove of peace," smiled Satan.

The next thing I knew, my grandfather was sitting on the chair opposite my father, and my mother was trying to get him to rest. Then they began another game.

This time, after my father cut, God dealt. The Devil lit up a stinking weed, and the smoke began to fill the Game Room.

My grandfather tried to hold his cards, pleading with God to forgive him.

"Lord, forgive Thy servant. My daughter has just informed me that you are here. Lord, Lord . . ."

No one spoke. Several times the Devil made quick, angry motions with his hands, pointing to the center of the table for my grandfather to play his card and stop running his mouth. The game was on, and that was all there was to it. You play the game or you get out of the seat. I knew that much about it myself. My father was getting restless.

The smoke got thicker, and all that could be heard in the room was the whining of my grandfather and the cawing of the silly bird. It was flying all around the place now. Once it tried to light on me, and I slapped it all the way across the room. I watched the table. I was planning on getting a hold of the Devil's key rod, and if that bird came again, I was going to set it afire.

The game went on. "Please, forgive Thy humble black servant, Lord, for sin did lurk in the innermost parts of his soul, but Lord Jesus, with Thy cleansing power he shall be washed white as snow . . ."

Somebody's voice came through the smoke—"He is not here, Reverend."

My mother coughed and went out of the room. I couldn't see anything except that silly bird flying around the room. I looked for the key rod that God had been playing with. The bird cackled and screeched, as if it were making fun of my grandfather. And even if my grandfather did sound a little crazy then, I didn't like any silly crow making fun of him.

The smoke got really thick. My grandfather coughed every time he said two or three words. Nobody was talking except him and that bird. Every now and then I could hear the two visitors snorting. I couldn't tell whether they were laughing or emphasizing some point in the game. I could hear the cards hit the table. My father wasn't saying anything. I rolled up my comic book as tight as I could so I could hit that bird if he tried to settle on my head again, and I eased my way toward the game table.

"Lord . . . aggh . . . if I had only . . . aggh . . . known You were coming . . ." My grandfather's thin shadow showed itself through the smoke. When I eased a bit closer, I saw the craziest thing. That bird was hopping around on the table. My grandfather's head was bowed. He was on his knees, holding onto the edge of the table with his hands.

"Lord God, I have been Your servant nigh unto seventy-five years. Why are Your ways still mysterious to me, Lord? I fast. I pray, Lord. But I must still have a little sin lurking somewhere. Your will be done."

He kept on like that. And all the time he was talking, I could hear the game going on. I saw the cards hit the table, WHACK!

"What I have done, Lord? What have I done? At least I thought that my onliest son here would deserve Your blessings?"

The cards were hitting the table more now, WHACK! The smoke got thicker. And I came right up to the edge of the table.

Then I saw what was going on. My father was leaning over his hand, shaking. I got scared just looking at him. He was playing cards out of his hand. The Devil was playing cards from his own hand. God was playing cards from his own hand. But that crow bird was playing from my grandfather's hand, which was face down on the table. He was kicking the card into the center of the table with his beak and then on the next play, he'd use one of his feet. He was showing off and strutting about. I raised the comic book to knock him off.

"Boy! What you doing?" It was my father.

"Look at that bird! He's messing up Grandfather's cards! Grandfather! Grandfather!" I yelled.

Before I could say anything, one of the visitors said something to me through the smoke. I couldn't see their faces any more.

"It's all right. It's part of the game. All you have to do is to be careful when we come back again."

I didn't hear them. I was furious. I called my mother, and I could feel tears swelling up. It wasn't fair. I called to Grandfather, who was still talking. Suddenly he seemed to get angry at me, at Father, at everybody except that bird and the visitors.

"Blasphemy! In the House of God! I won't stand for it, Lord! I have told them. I have told my son and my daughter . . . these children. They have strayed, Lord. Forgive me, Lord. I waited so long for You to be my partner, Lord. We are partners, aren't we, Lord Jesus? We are partners, aren't we? Ask me, Lord. Command me. I want to be in Your name . . ."

I shook Grandfather and told him that my father was his partner, and that he should play. "Please, Grandfather." But they laughed at me.

It was funny, listening to them laugh. It sounded far away. Then I could hear my grandfather moaning. The smoke got in my eyes, and all I could hear was my grandfather asking

God to change places with my father. He tried to make everybody change places so he and God could be partners. And when this happened, I felt a hot rush of air, then a cold one. Then the smoke cleared.

I saw the Book, burnt, and the key rod lying there—which I quickly snatched—and I saw the visitors leading Grandfather away past his room. They looked over their shoulders at all of us, and just before they went out, one of them said, "I'll be back."

We sat tight, but nobody ever came back.

I think it was Satan the Devil who said it, but I'm not sure.

I had a lot of fun chasing that bird around the house, trying to set his tail afire with that key rod. Finally I caught up with him, and just before I set him afire he cawed,

> To profit by what is heard,
> You must remember that
> I am a prophet,
> And not a bird.

I didn't pay any attention to it. I jabbed him, and when I did he burst into a stinking smoke.

My father took the key rod out of my hand, and I think he was getting ready to say something to me, but we heard it again:

> To profit by what is heard,
> You must remember that
> I am a prophet,
> And not a bird.

I have been trying to figure it out since. Whose voice did that bird's sound like?

HENRY DUMAS

Invasion

The explosion made a small hole in the screen door! It seemed like a firecracker or a miniature grenade. Mr. William Jackson closed the door and stood there, panting. The noise of retreat sounded from the children outside. He backed away from the door, looking at the hole. My God, he thought, What is going on?

Grasping his chest, he slumped his huge weight into the soft couch in the living room, and shielded his ears from the noise. He needed time to think.

A few weeks ago, before his vacation, he had been in the basement with the kids, and they had acted peculiar, secretive, and cautious. They had eyed him suspiciously and talked through the drainpipe. There was a lot of talk about a General Hannibal. John, the oldest, had talked of maps and counterattacks, and his younger son, Robert, had taken a new liking to tanks. Of course, this was not out of the ordinary for growing boys, but obviously there had been somebody on the other end of the drainpipe. He knew it now, but then he had thought it was only part of the game.

He had to think. He got up and went to the window. Far in the distance a thin line of smoke split the gray sky. He could not see them, but he could hear voices outside, near the house. Now and then he heard the distant crack of what sounded like a rifle. He looked at the clock. Ten A.M. Betsy had been gone an hour to do the weekly shopping. He looked out the window at the garage door. It was closed and locked. He knew Betsy hadnt closed it. She always liked to drive the car in without getting out. Still panting, he reached for the phone.

Before he could make the call, two young soldiers burst into the house and found him. They grabbed his arms. "Mr. Jackson, if you want us to win, you have to come now! The General wants you to lead a company against them. . . ." Both carried wooden rifles, with sharpened kitchen knives as bayonets.

"What's happening now? I'm tired," he protested. Yet he did not find the strength to resist their pulling. They led him through the house and out the back door.

"You see, they're close now," one of the soldiers said. "They got your house." He looked at these kids. He knew them all. Neighborhood boys. Knew their fathers.

He heard a long-sustained scream.

"Who's close?" he demanded, jerking his arm away. "You kids are going to have to explain that scream."

The two soldiers ducked, pulling him down with them. They hid under the back steps. Mr. Jackson was so big that he scraped his back on a nail. He felt the warm blood stick to his shirt.

"Look," he said finally. "I'm not playing anymore. Tell John that his father wants to see him!"

"Nobody's playing anymore," they both said, turning to stare at him in disbelief. "They've got grown-ups on their side now too."

He wasn't going to let them trick him. He would not listen. "Besides, I dont have a uniform like the rest of the kids."

One of the soldiers took out a little metallic object, raised an antenna-like rod, and began tuning a knob. He whispered and mumbled gibberish that Mr. Jackson thought made little sense.

"Hannibal's blood, suffering from battle shock, balks duty, up against it, you move, over. . . ."

"Frank's down bad. Orders from General: Quit blood. They are coming with heavies. Wait seven seconds, will contact across town, and move to you first. Over, out."

"I said I dont have a uniform like . . ."

Mr. Jackson could see that their weapons had been fashioned to hold. One of the boys had a bloody bandage around his head.

"We have to go inside, sir," he said. The other remained standing outside the door, peeking around the corners and hiding out like a sentry.

"Where's John?" Mr. Jackson asked. "I want you to tell him—"

"To the basement!" the soldier said, prodding Mr. Jackson in the back with the bayonet.

Before he knew it, Mr. Jackson had let himself be led down into his basement. When he looked around he saw a stockpile of strange-looking equipment. Near the drainpipe was a pile of dirt. A tunnel! He scrambled down on his feet and peered into it. Then he heard the cellar door slam and the gentle *click* of the upstairs bolt.

He had to think. The phone began to ring upstairs. Oh, if he had only made his call! It must be Betsy calling, he thought. He ran up and banged on the door.

"Open this door!" he yelled. His chest ached.

When he stepped off the cellar steps, a sharp pain went along his spine. He shook his head and sat down. Outside he could hear the sounds of explosions. A great roar rumbled the ground and grew louder.

Then he saw lights coming through the tunnel.

Upstairs the phone was still ringing. He could hear footsteps running. He moved back into a corner, and sat panting like an exhausted bear. He could still make out the lights coming slowly through the tunnel, as though someone were crawling.

Suddenly a hole was cut through the floor with an electric saw. The phone was lowered through.

"For you, sir," a voice said.

Mr. Jackson snatched the phone. "Hello?"

"William, is that you?" came the voice of his wife.

"Well, who else?" he shouted, as though to blame her for all the trouble.

"Well, I didnt know. There were a lot of children talking. Listen, something's wrong in town."

"In town? Something's wrong, all right, but it's out here! These kids, why the Kennard kids, the Sims kids, the Osky's— the whole neighborhood is gone crazy—"

"Be quiet, William! They're coming. Listen."

Mr. Jackson pressed the phone to his ear. He heard sounds of marching and roaring. A loudspeaker was blasting. He could hear the voice: Mothers and fathers, be calm. We have the situation under control, but you must, I REPEAT, you *must* cooperate with us. You *must* cooperate. We have no other recourse. Our munitions have not yet arrived. You *must* cooperate. Mothers and fathers . . ."

"William, the children are having some kind of a parade. They didnt tell us about it. John is here and they're calling him Hannibal."

"Betsy, I'm locked in the cellar," he cut her off. "Hurry home—I'm locked—"

"Bobbie is here too. William, they're all marching. They passed right by me!"

Mr. Jackson saw the first light go out. A figure emerged from the tunnel.

"Betsy, hurry home. Do you have the car?"

The phone was snatched from his hand. The figure, a tiny boy, jerked it several times, his little body swinging at each jerk. Mr. Jackson saw more lights arrive and then disappear as the basement filled.

There was a roaring outside. The new soldiers began examining the basement. They tied his hands behind his back, shot the lock off the door and went up. Mr. Jackson, shaking off their efforts to handle him, began to weep and yell.

Suddenly a burst of fire exploded point-blank in front of Mr. Jackson. His eyes shot out of his face, and his body made a liquid, panting sound. He slumped over—My God, what is going on? It cant be true, it cant.

The Lake

At night he would always watch for the moon first before he went over the fence, and on the nights when there was no moon, he would travel slowly, going down on his hands and knees at intervals to feel the grass and the pathway that he made in his mind, for the pasture where the bull roamed was miles long and filled with ditches, trees, and rivulets that streamed off from the lake.

He would always wait in his shack until the moon began to rise. He thought of the moon as his eye, and when the moon was not out he would recall how it was the night before that one. Guided this way, he would go.

But the moon shone high on this night. A sheet of clouds—like a purple curtain in the sky—fanned by it, and the moon kept on rising. He moved out from the shack, making no noise as he slung the goatskin sack over his shoulder, walking with his bare feet on the grass instead of on the pebbles of the path. Tonight will be good, he thought. The water should be cool. The bull should be resting.

Coming out of the grove that ended where the long stretch of bitter weeds began, he broke into a trot, easy at first, then a bit faster. He thought of how he had known it would be when he came out tonight. All day—while the rest were laughing, patting him on the back sometimes and kidding him, telling him that he should not spend his time thinking about lakes, that there were no magic lakes at all—he was thinking of how he would break into a trot and then pick up the pace, then maintain the pace until he reached the fence . . . and then he would leap . . . *and he leaped!* A good fall, upright! He remained there, puffing silently and watching shadows down the field.

He thought he saw a shape move. He wondered why the bull was resting at this end of the meadow. There was no water here. Clouds, purple and black, unraveled. The moon was looking at him from behind the great mountain of dark clouds. He was charmed. The rhythm of his breathing slowed, and he peered into the night. His tongue was drying, and he knew that he had better get going, so he did. He felt something new in the meadow tonight, something vague but not formless. He gripped the neck of the goatskin water bag, feeling the oil ooze when he squeezed.

Going along the side of the fence for quite a distance, he suddenly broke away, and after peering into a large grove of trees, he sprinted for it.

The light of the moon struck the top of this grove like water striking long, beautiful hair, and the water flowed to the ground. . . . Beneath the grove he stopped, and his breathing came, but it was not the only sound of breathing. He knew now that it was not the bull, nor was it one of the cows. He looked where a slant of moonlight poured through the top of the grove, and there he saw her . . . stretching her arms skyward like a kitten, her bare back to him, and before he could say anything she came toward him, and he broke through the grove, striking the open air and the moonlight like a panther. What was she doing there? He had better get to the water before her. Who was she, anyway? Why was she racing across the field? The lake did not belong to her.

They were far apart now, and he increased his pace. Then he was struck with the idea that whoever she was, she had not seen him at all! She was heading for the opposite side of the lake, running and picking up speed as the reflection from the water came closer and closer. He slowed near the bank, looking around for the bull, listening for its snort and smelling the air as animals do to try to sense if the bull were near. It wasnt.

He went down on his knees, crawling the seven feet to the edge of the lake. Just before he filled the bag with the precious water, he paused and stared across to the other side. He thought he saw a figure kneeling in a half-lit clearing, but a cloud made the moon blink, and he was thanking the lake for still being there, and shaking with that great feeling that he knew would come. It always came at the lake. This was the lake that no one could ever find, no matter how many people he told about it. No matter how many people set out to find it, they always came back saying that he was lying. But he knew it was magic, and he dared not tell anyone else or speak about it or even try to discover the reason why the lake was there, lest it dry up or disappear. He remembered how he first discovered it. . . . It was somewhere in his mind, at a strange time when he was growing up, when he was thirsty and there was no water.

He smelled something in the air, a strong odor, but it passed too quickly to tell what it was, although it smelled very familiar. . . . Well, he was remembering things, thanking the lake, and wanting to know what else he could do for it besides love it, cherish it, and keep it.

The moon was out across the lake. Across the water! He saw her dipping an object into the water. The thought came to him that she was doing . . . she was praying . . . she was—No, and he pushed the thought aside . . . but it came sliding back and struck him. He stood up.

A slight wind was gathering. He hung his bag upon the limb of the tree and slowly went back to the clay bank. He cupped his hands and lifted drink to his burning mouth, and he let it go down slowly. It was cool, good water that made him drunk inside, strange water, filled with a power potion he could only trust but could not understand, and with the seventh cup he looked up—his eyes closed—and turned to the moon, his hands outstretched.

Naked, he dove deep, deep, deep, for that was the way, his way, the right way, and as he was coming up—letting the pressure of the current carry him—a thought flooded his body, a thought . . . but he was trying to remember how it would be when he came up, and the wind would suddenly grow stronger and dry him off, and he would reach for his bag hanging from the limb, and then after a meditation break, out across the grass to the first grove . . . but a thought came pushing in, a good thought, and then . . .

. . . the thought was before him, and beneath the water he saw her, and he could tell that she had not known he was there, but she must have known something, just as he did at first . . . and the light of the lake was bright, bright. They saw each other. They touched, and the current instantly wrapped them together, and the lake said,

"If you love me, if you think I am beautiful, then give thanks to me by taking that which I give you. I am happiest when I give,"

and they were a song beneath the sky, and the lake was their first note.

The Distributors

"We start at eight sharp," the foreman said to me, "but you and your friend be here at seven-thirty tomorrow so we can sign you up." We shook hands and I left.

A job at last. Kenny and I had spent the last three weeks looking. I found a phone in the corner restaurant to call him. He would be excited, even though it was only construction work. We had both wanted to spend the summer in the sun. School had drained all the blood out of us, anyway.

The line was busy, so I ordered a cup of coffee and sat down near the phone. Halfway through the cup I called again. Still busy. He must be calling ads in the paper, I thought.

A neatly dressed woman came into the restaurant. She and the waitress began talking.

". . . and it's saved me so much work. Honest, Sue, I just dont know what to do with all my time."

"Where's your father-in-law?" asked the waitress.

"It's amazing, Sue. That's taken care of too. And maybe he's better off. Even the baby rests good now." And she whispered in the waitress's ear: "They call it acceleration or something."

"Well, what's Fred think?"

"Oh, he's too crazy about the automatic memory cells to worry about that. You know it tells you everything you were thinking all day!"

"Yeah," said the waitress, "I've heard about it, but we cant pay for one right now."

"They're cheap," whispered the woman.

"How much did you pay?"

"They have a special credit plan, and you dont have to pay unless you like it."

As I dialed Kenny's again I wondered what it was they were talking about. The line was still busy. I decided to take a bus, because Kenny might be talking to Edna and on the phone a long time.

Mrs. Waspold came to the door.

"Hello, Carl," she said. "Kenneth is on the phone."

I knew he would be. I told her about the job possibility and that the foreman had said he could use two men for the summer. "Well," she said, "I dont think Kenny will like it. They just called him up for a job a little while ago."

I sat down in the living room, wondering who Kenny was talking to. From the kitchen Mrs. Waspold stirred about. A pot dropped and she became irritated. As I sat there I could hear a heavy wheezing coming from old Mr. Waspold's room. Kenny's grandfather was very sick and helpless. The chortling of his chest sounded like the dying sputters of an engine.

Just then Kenny came into the room.

"Hey, Carl, listen! Great news! How would you like to be a representative for American Dynamisms Incorporated?"

"What're you talking about?" I asked. His enthusiasm had taken me by surprise. He moved like a guy rushing to catch a train.

"Come on," he said, running to the door. "I'll tell you all about it on the way."

He got the keys to the family car. "Mother, if Edna calls tell her I'll be by to see her after the interview."

I followed Kenny out. We were halfway across town before he could settle down.

"Listen," he said. "Carl, baby, we're in!" We stopped for a red light, and among the people crossing was the same woman from the restaurant.

"I got us both interviews."

"Doing what?" I asked.

"Well, I dont know exactly . . . using our college training, he told me. I talked with a Mr. Mortishan, and he promised us jobs making over a hundred dollars a week to start. Man, oh, man!"

"How certain is this, because I've already made arrangements for us to start at the construction company down Canal Road."

"Forget it, Carl. We're in. Mr. Mortishan said for us to come down immediately, and he'd sign us up for the whole summer. With raises!"

"Sounds too good to be true," I said. "But I'd like to know a little more about it."

"Well, what's the difference what we do? If we can make that much money starting out—"

"Wait," I interrupted. "Suppose we get hooked doing something we dont want?"

"Dont be silly. This is a big outfit."

"Who was the guy you talked to, and why cant we know what kind of a job we're being considered for?"

"Listen, Carl, I talked to the guy. He sounded okay to me. I'm not going to tell them how to run their business."

"Yeah," I said, "but I'd like to know what's the job."

Kenny became defensive. Ever since taking that course called "The Sociology of Management," he seemed to be tolerating me. Once he said that the course I was taking was totally useless.

"Where'd you get the tip about this place?" I asked. I had heard of American Dynamisms, but I couldnt remember where.

"Remember the guy who came around during exam week, sending kids places for jobs?"

I did recall a well-dressed, efficient-looking guy around the campus before graduation, recruiting seniors, but for what, nobody knew.

"This is his card," and he handed me a card. "Mr. Mortishan said to see no one but him, under any circumstances."

The card was the folding kind. On each section were bold letters in the center and small ones at the bottom.

STAY UNDER CARE KINDNESS EFFICIENCY OF R
Processing Card
DISTRIBUTING AMERICAN DYNAMISMS ABROAD
Rek-cording Card
SEND THE WHOLE FAMILY TO CAMP
Human Factor Card

Mr. Mortishan's name was not on it. I handed it back. Kenny parked the car in front of a deserted store three blocks from the river, behind a factory. Closed Venetian blinds hung at the windows. We checked the address. No mistake. This was the place. The lettering on the door was plain and neat, just like the card.

We went in. Down a narrow hallway in front of us were double doors. They looked tight, but noises drifted through the place, as though coming out of the walls. A thin haze of cigarette smoke mixed with a stronger odor, possibly of cigar or burning wood or incense. Off the hallway were doors; the first one was extremely wide, as though it contained a gigantic piece of equipment that could not go through an ordinary door; the rest were shut. We didnt see anyone at the huge desk in the first room.

Strange music penetrated the walls. We heard voices, then a roar, as if people were cheering. The tempo of the music was one degree faster than any human could keep up with.

"What can I do with you?"

Standing in the hall behind us was a neatly dressed man with close-cut hair whose ready smile was wide, even, and precise.

"We have interviews with Mr. Mortishan. I just talked—"

"I'm sorry. Mr. Mortishan is very busy now. May I help you?"

"I have an interview at eleven," said Kenny.

"Fine. I'm Mr. Mortishan's assistant. Come down the hall to my office."

Kenny stood still. "I just talked to Mr. Mortishan on the phone a few minutes ago, and he warned me not to talk to anyone else, under any circumstances."

HENRY DUMAS

"Oh." The young man laughed. "I'm sorry, but you must forgive me. That was our Rek-cording. Mr. Mortishan is on an extended visit out of town. He will process in later. Wont you step into my office."

Kenny looked at me, shrugged his shoulders, and went into the room.

"Not you." The young man halted me. The door slammed. From behind the double doors down the hall came the continued rise and fall of unintelligible sounds, like some kind of a meeting.

I went up the hall into the open room and sat down. I didnt know how long Kenny's interview would be. I looked for something to read. But there were no books, magazines, or pamphlets, only a picture hanging almost to the ceiling. I looked at it. What an odd place to hang a picture, I thought. Even more, what an odd picture. I couldnt tell if the thing was a multicolored machine or an Expressionist painting of an elongated peanut.

Just as I was beginning to examine the rest of the room, the picture began to move. I was not scared at first. What kind of gag is this? I wondered. For a moment I thought the room was some kind of a psych testing lab, and if it was, Kenny and I were going through the test for hiring.

The picture moved down the wall, and as it moved, the wall opened in back of it, unzipping itself. I stood up. The noises increased, and before I could think of moving out of the room, the picture was touching the floor—flat on its face—and stepping out from behind it was a very fat man.

"Sit down, Carl," he said to me. He waddled around to the great desk. "I'm sorry to keep you gentlemen waiting."

"What kind of positions do you have open?" I asked.

"Stop," he said, lighting up a fat cigar. "Stop." He reached into his drawer and handed me a stack of forms, saying, "Fill these out first, then ask questions."

He picked up the phone and began dialing. I wondered if he were Mr. Mortishan. I didnt have a chance to say anything.

He was talking and blowing smoke. After looking at the application, I knew that it would take almost two hours to finish. I wondered if Kenny was going through the same ordeal. The questions were routine, and as I hurried through them I could hear the fat man talking in a low voice on the phone about demonstrations and appointments and camps. He was watching me out of the corner of his eye. I hadnt noticed, but the picture was back in its place and the wall was closed.

All of a sudden I heard voices in the hall.

"Stop writing," the fat man said. "Go into the hall."

I got up and went out. The double doors were open, and the hall was filled with young men dressed in shirt-sleeves and ties, milling about, drinking from cups. I saw Kenny just as the assistant was shoving a cup in his hand.

"Hey, Ken . . ." He didnt hear me. The men were moving back through the double doors. Behind me came several more, and I was swept into the room through the double doors. Inside was like an arena. I lost sight of Kenny. In the center of the floor was a large area that seemed like a threshing floor. It was sunken and worn in a circle. Around the room were hundreds of chairs. Some of them were occupied by fat-looking men sitting like dignified spectators. Their weights seemed to spread out over the seats, as though in a moment they would turn to lard and flood the floor.

"Selling is the business of every salesman! But our men distribute rather than sell. Rekcus sells himself! Rekcus Rekcus we adore! Rekcus Rekcus nothing more!" It was the assistant. He ran to the center of the floor, holding a metallic-looking suitcase in one hand and a torch in the other. He raised the torch and shouted, "Every person you meet is a potential customer. Consider him already owning a Rekcus. Never cross him off until—"

A bright light suddenly shone from the ceiling on the assistant; otherwise the place was still dim.

"—until we demonstrate and deliver him—"

A roar came up from the men, a frenzied sound, as if they were drunk.

"—Rekcus! And remember: D-A-D, Deliver American Dynamisms to your home! your job! your place of play!"

Someone shoved a cup toward my hand. I didnt want it, but rather than let it fall I received it, since the person was letting it go. I was about to taste it when the odor of some chemical hit me. I put the cup on a table and sat down in a chair, feeling a bit dizzy. The crowd was forming a circle around the speaker. I tried to spot Kenny. He was lost in the crowd, which began a mad chanting after periodic shouts by the assistant. It was crazy. I looked for the door.

Two men came over to me. A light shone in my face.

"We would like to demonstrate at your initiation ceremony," one of them said. The other one held the light steadily on my face.

I tried to dodge the light. "What're you talking about?"

"Dont you believe in the Rekcus principle of acceleration?"

"In the factors of humanoid control?"

"In simuldad?"

"Yes, distribution and demonstration simultaneously?"

"Do you have old parents?"

"Where is your appointment card?"

"Your initiation card?"

"What initiation?" I asked.

"Would you simuldad a Rekcus to your mother?"

"Your father?"

"Have you ever sold anything to a child?"

"Do you understand Rekcus dehumanization?"

"Are you ready to sell?"

"Who is your dadsponsor?"

"What?" I asked.

They looked at each other; then they jerked me off the chair and shoved me out into the room among the crowd, which seized me, spun me around, locked arms, and we all went frantically around the center of the floor. Sitting on an elongated bulletlike structure in the center of the room was the fat man. He was grinning at me. Then he pointed at Kenny: "Get him!"

They all descended on Kenny. He ran. Was he playing the game? I couldnt tell. One man tackled him waist high, bringing him down to the hard floor. The shrieks, shouts, and laughs grew louder and louder. Speeches were begun and not finished. Hot drinks were flung to the ceiling. Desperately I tried to find the door.

"Where do you think you're going?" The ready smile of the assistant greeted me. I coughed. "Well, I was looking for the other fellow. Kenneth . . ."

He began to laugh hysterically, bending over several times. Kenny came limping over to me, a big grin on his face.

"Carl, we're in! We're accepted. All we gotta do is sell—I mean, simuldad—I mean—"

"REKCUS REKCUS WE ADORE! REKCUS REKCUS WE ADORE!"

They kept it up, and Kenny, his lips hesitating at first, then catching up with the words, broke away from me and skip-hobbled back across the room with a couple of young men running on either side of him, trying to trip him up. Then Kenny suddenly turned and hollered at me: "Carl! I told him I'll be your sponsor. You have to come to my initiation tonight. Your whole family is coming. At my house!"

"What?" I asked, but he didnt hear me. Suddenly the assistant stopped laughing, came over to me, looked me over, glanced at his watch, and said:

"Get out."

He spoke softly, but his words were like two knives stabbing, one on either side of my chest. The double doors opened in front of me. I stumbled over somebody, felt for the door, and was out. I waited. The doors closed and the shouting went on.

I hurried out to the car, and sat in it, sweating. When I tried to go back in an hour later, the door was locked. I sat in the car for another hour, waiting for Kenny. Then I went to look for a phone. No one was at my house. I phoned Kenny's. No one answered. Mrs. Waspold was probably helping the old man to the bathroom. I ran back to the car. It was gone.

I phoned Edna, Kenny's girl friend, to see if he was there. "Oh, Carl," she said, "Kenny was looking for you. He's on his way here. Congratulations on the job. You're coming to the demonstration tonight, arent you?"

I held the phone away from me and stared at it briefly; finally I managed to say "Yes" and hung up.

Wandering through the park, I watched a softball game. After that I sat near the pond, watching the ducks paddling around. But even when I went home my head was ringing: *Rekcus Rekcus we adore. Rekcus Rekcus nothing more.*

After dinner I drove my folks to Kenny's house. The living room was filled with talking neighbors. Kenny rushed over to me.

"Carl, buddy, how do I look?" He had gotten a crew cut, a new suit, a manicure, had shaved so close he had nicked his chin, and he was smiling in a peculiar way.

"Sharp," I said. "But what's all this demonstration business about?"

"Ahhh," he said, looking at me with a doubtful frown, "then you didnt get *your* appointment yet?"

"I dont think I want anything from that place," I began, but Kenny wasnt paying attention. "What's the initiation for? I waited a couple of hours for you."

"I'm hired, Carl!" he said, racing off to answer the door. "I start selling tomorrow. My first contact will be your house. It has all been arranged."

Coming in and following Kenny to the center of the living room was the assistant. Kenny made a brief announcement. The excitement was high as everybody took seats and waited.

While Kenny was introducing him, Mr. Mortishan's assistant was setting up a metallic tube box.

"On behalf of American Dynamisms I want to thank you all for coming, and especially you, Mr. and Mrs. Waspold, for allowing us to use your home. Today we discovered Kenneth

Waspold. D-A-D is looking for loyal, dedicated young men with bright futures and clear minds. We think we found another one in Kenny." He smiled, executed a turn, saying, "Now to the point of the meeting."

He pointed to Mr. Hendy, sitting nearby. "Come here, sir." Mr. Hendy got up. "Put your hand here." Mr. Hendy did it. "Squeeze." A narrow tube began to rise from the strange-looking case. Mr. Mortishan's assistant seized it and put it close to Mr. Hendy's ear. "Continue squeezing." After a minute of this Mr. Hendy looked astonished, faced the audience with a look of paralysis, opened his mouth, and speechlessly turned red in the face.

"Incredible . . ." he mumbled and stumbled to his seat.

The assistant went around the room with the same procedure, next with Mr. Hendy's wife, then Kenny's father and mother, and after each person had a chance they all were gasping with amazement.

I sat in the corner. A curious fear held me there. Not once had he looked at me, and when it finally came my turn—since I was the last—a quiet fell on everybody.

"You had your chance this afternoon?" He wasnt asking me a question, as it sounded. Rather, he was telling me.

The guests began asking him questions. My only question was, What had they heard and felt? But he didnt give them a chance to overwhelm him. "We believe firmly in letting our products sell themselves. That's why we never high-pressure our customers. Ladies and gentlemen, there is no product more capable of selling itself than Rekcus! You have just met Rekcus!"

Kenny was wide-eyed, taking it all in. No doubt he thought he would use the same procedure at my house. The neighbors were awed. My folks seemed very receptive.

"Have you ever met a machine like this one?" he asked. The people shook their heads. "You have seen nothing yet!" He pressed a button, and the machine began to enlarge itself. Sections opened and closed, fitting with other parts. It stopped. It looked like a metallic peanut. When he pushed another button, the machine began to hum as a handle came out; the assistant seized it and pushed the machine around the floor for five minutes in a vacuum-cleaninglike motion.

"Examine your floor," he said to Mrs. Waspold.

"Oh!" she exclaimed, after careful examination.

The women began buzzing. The assistant went through several other miraculous demonstrations: cleaning and washing dishes without soap and water, air-conditioning and moisture control, dry-laundering without removing linen from bed, massaging, electric cooking, and more.

"Ladies and gentlemen, there is nothing Rekcus cant do in the home!"

He demonstrated for the men. The machine began ejecting tools, gadgets, and supplies. It was a workshop in itself: a radio, a TV, a phonograph, a fan, a movie projector, and more. I couldnt believe it, and I began looking for him to make mistakes, like a magician does once in a while.

But he was polished in every way, a master salesman. The machine did all the work. Both were perfect.

After an hour of breathtaking feats, the machine began to expand by itself, unfolding like a crib. I could see soft blankets inside.

"Would you like to put your baby in the crib?" he asked a woman with a newborn child. "I assure you, the child will be the better for it."

Smiling, the woman placed the baby in the machine. "He's going to cry," she frowned. Once down, the tiny baby began to whimper, then cry.

Mr. Mortishan's assistant just stood there with a ready, even smile.

The machine hummed and began a liquid motion back and forth. An arm appeared and cuddled the baby. A bottle leaped up. Music and the sound of a woman's voice—very much like the mother's—calmed the baby. It stopped crying and closed its eyes, sucking away.

"Ladies and gentlemen, you have seen nothing! I speak the truth. There is no machine like this one. You cant buy it in the stores, you cant see it in the shops, but you can own one without any money down. You have just seen it *perform*. Now see it *live*."

The machine grew again until it was about six feet, standing on wiry metal legs four feet from the floor.

"I want a volunteer. If you have been suffering from backache, heart trouble, rheumatism, hardening of the arteries, sinus, colds, flu, fevers, high and low blood pressure, gland trouble, liver infections, kidney ailments, lung trouble, overweight, under-weight, headache, ulcers, sores, boils, cavities, tumors, and old age, then come. If your spirits are deflated, no pep, no get-up-and-go, no zoom, no desire to do anything but sleep it off, if you have longed to travel to distant shores in search of a utopia and bliss, if you need a doctor, then come, I want a volunteer.

"Ladies and gentlemen, D-A-D will go even further for you. You have heard many hot-line salesmen attempt to force something on you that you dont need. If you are in what you think is good health, you might want a change of disposition. Modern psychology has taught our scientists that there are many of us normal people who desire to experience the difficult aspects of living. Rekcus and our scientists have discovered a unique method: cytoplasmic acceleration of metabolic processes. Through C-A-M-P and psychotherapy we can induce any malady known or unknown to man.

I repeat: if you're suffering from aches and pains of body and mind, youth, old age, come. I want one volunteer!"

Several people got up, but old Mr. Waspold was being led up by Kenny's father. He was so old and helpless that he had been kept in his room during the demonstration. He mumbled things to himself as Mr. Waspold and Mr. Hendy helped him into the machine. He lay down immediately as if he were back in bed.

"The Rekcus is both a dehumanizer and a humanizer, two-in-one, a truly amazing machine. Right here I hold in my

HENRY DUMAS

hand the simple program card that will set the vitalizers to charge the patient."

A lid slid over the sleeping old man. The machine looked like an overgrown bullet. He inserted the card. A humming sound filled the room, and the old man's voice could be heard chuckling. Then it grew higher and higher, as if it were going back in time. Soon it was whimpering like a baby. The people buzzed and talked to each other.

Suddenly the lid opened.

The assistant motioned them to come. From where I was I could see the old man's face. It was the same, but the inside of the machine had been dressed up with silk, and the old man's clothes had been changed to suit and tie.

"He's resting well," a voice said.

When it came my turn to look, the lid closed, and the assistant said to me out of the corner of his mouth: "You get out."

Kenny's grandfather hadnt moved. The people were poking him and exclaiming.

"This machine is not only accurate in telling the body's time, it is practical. It *does* something about the body's time. And it is very cheap if you want to get another Rekcus ..."

I left and sat in the car. Tall buildings blocked the moon. *Oh, you don't have to pay unless you like it. Fred's too crazy about it to think. Get out, get in, get out. Rekcus will help you. Get out, Rekcus will get you.* I left the keys in the car and walked home, thinking I hoped I got there before Kenny.

"Well," said the foreman the next morning, "did the other guy find a better job?"

"No," I said.

"What? Is he sick?"

"Yes," I said. "He's sick."

"Well, I cant wait. I'll have to get another guy in his place."

"Yes," I said. "He's very sick."

Thrust Counter Thrust

Long black clouds lurched across the sky, bumping into the moon. The November wind, blowing up suddenly, whispered low sounds in miniature whirlwind fits. Saul Newman, his dusty head rising slowly from the ditch where he had fallen asleep, blinked his good eye, stared, blinked, and saw two moons hovering like drunken eyes over the church steeple. The low hiss and swish of dry grasses bowing in quick jerks, mixed with the sifting of sand and dust and a dryness, a burning, converged in his throat. He stumbled out of the ditch and peered down the country road. Maybe this was how Lon got it, he thought. Dark shadows jabbed and retreated down the road like troops of soldiers running in the ditches. Maybe some of them Koreans, he thought, coming to finish me too. He stumbled to the road, raising the wine bottle to his face, feeling the wind thrust deep into his body, hearing in his mind the rumble of the bus that had let him off hours ago. Through the wine bottle he saw the eye of the moon, cold, indifferent, a single force, standing immobile on the tip of the white folk's church steeple. "Watcha lookin at me for? You goddamn . . ." and with his elbow knocking free the flap of his denim jacket, he hurled the empty bottle high, high in the sky, and a fierce grunt followed his arm like the tormented scream of a soldier in pain. When the glass was tumbling piece by piece, like frozen bits of flesh, from the roof, Saul fell to his knees whimpering, cursing, unable to bring into focus the object of his hate, unable to accept the news that his brother had been killed in action in Korea, unable to push aside the memories of him, unable to ask Jesus for forgiveness, because the pain was too much of a reality. The wine, churning in his stomach, burned and gushed through his veins, gushing *thru* him as it probably had done *from* Lon over there in that cold ditch. Who had helped Lon? Who had come? Maybe some buddy. They send you off to war to be killed, and when your own brother tries to enlist they turn him away. O Lawd! he thought, I'll show them white bastards, if I ever git my eye fixed up.

A pair of headlights loomed down the road. Saul fell away from the road. The ditch! Combat maneuvers! The dirt! Hit the dirt! The car stopped. Saul squinted at it from his position. The light was yellow, striking the ground yards ahead of the car, illuminating the dust, which moved like scampering feet.

Saul heard a voice—*sounded like Mr. Vance!*—another voice, and then he heard the skidding of a piece of glass from the church roof. It tumbled and crashed, and Saul held his breath. His head reeled while the men began calling, "Hey boy! Commere!" And Saul saw the moon, its naked oval appearing from a cloud, staring and throwing a light over the ditch ahead of him. He hid in the shadows of the church.

"Coulda sworn I saw somebody up there, Reverend," one of the men hollered into the night. The car moved on. Reverend Donaldson, thought Saul. That lying bastard. Reverend Donaldson. The men drove near the church and stopped. The service sign shook in the wind. Saul was sure the voice was that of Togart Vance, who held the land that extended from the church all the way back to his house and beyond to Hoesville Pond. He knew them both well.

Reverend Donaldson was pastor of the church. What would this holy white man do if he knew that Saul had just thrown a wine bottle and it had fallen on the church steeple and broken? Saul hugged the dirt. The men went into the church and presently lights came on, and a faint purple light filtered into the night from the stained glass.

A fear gripped him. Sweat gathered on his skin. He began to crawl toward the lighted area outside the church's long shadow, but hesitated, knowing the moon was traveling high into the night and feeling himself ready to bolt across the pathless field toward his house. He waited. A troop of clouds butted across the sky, and he knew that when they struck the moon he would be off. What was he afraid of? He had done nothing wrong. If he had just kept walking along the road when he saw the car, then they might have . . .

"Goin home, Mr. Vance."

"Where you been, boy?"

"Been to town," he would say.

"Sorry to hear about your brother, there, boy," Reverend Donaldson would say out of the corner of his mouth. "Hear your mother's takin it pretty fine, though."

"Yessir."

"He was younger'n you, wernt he?"

"No, sir, older three years."

"You drunk, Saul?" Mr. Vance might ask.

"Well, Mr. Vance, I just was feeling bad and wanted to—"

"Nigger, are you drunk?"

"No, sir."

"You been drinkin?"

"Well, I—"

"Well, dont you have no respect for the Lord? What the hell you mean passin in front white folk's church, stinkin like a damn fool! Git the hell off the road. Now, run! Run, nigger!"

And he would run, and his fear would subside and he would slow, listening, and he would hear Mr. Vance laugh, and Reverend Donaldson would be saying something in a low tone, and then Mr. Vance would probably yell, "Hey, boy! Commere back!" And then he knew he would be in for a night's trouble, cleaning off the church steps, wiping dust off their car, all for a quarter, and listening to the stern chastisement of the Reverend. The image of this man hung in his mind as the figure of the cross, reflected off the church steps, glinted in his eye.

"That's one-eyed Saul," Mr. Vance might say. "You remember coupla years ago when one nigger brother blinded 'nother in a fight? Well, this here's him."

"Yes, well, what—That's time my stained window was broke too." Mr. Vance would agree, and the cloud fell upon the moon. He bolted up, crouched, and ran the wind, bowing the grass of the field ahead of his sprinting feet. Dirt! Hit it! He lay panting.

The wine tasted sweet upon his tongue, but his head was clear. Up! Running! Across the field, back toward the road, down, leaping over the ditch, eyeing the moon over his shoulder, his jacket flapping. He stopped, turned. Panting, he looked back at the lighted church. Another car was pulling up to it. He watched. The stained-glass windows came alive with light now. He remembered the day when it had happened.

Lon was taking him over to Mr. Vance's to get the job. Lon had worked for Mr. Vance for a year, and when he had been called into the Army, Saul was going to carry on. He had liked his job, especially because Gloria was cooking part-time in the kitchen. She was Lon's woman. They had a kid, two years old, and he had always liked Gloria. She was finely shaped, small, very black, with hardly a rough spot on her skin, and her voice always had a smile, as if she was having some secret pleasure out of talking to you. But Lon had taken her; Lon was older, bigger, and Lon was good, not like him, Saul. O Lawd, he thought, when you gonna save me? When you? Then he bent forward on the road lit by the light of a cloud-winked moon, and he knew that if he went to Mr. Vance's house before he went home, Gloria would be glad to see him. He knew she wanted to see him. He knew how she felt since Lon was dead, but maybe he'd go on home and play with Lon's baby, his nephew. Mama would be looking after that little baby. Looked like Lon, too. Mama would be there, but so would that goddamn preacher, Reverend Wiggins, that gold-toothed bastard! waiting for Gloria and making eyes at his mother. If Lon would be there, that dog-eyed, grease-bellied, pig-suckin preacher—Lawd! How he despised that high-yellow sneak, a snake in the grass, layin low to jump when some woman'd pass, the . . .

The Vance estate loomed through the trees. He decided he'd go. He trotted around, out of the woods, back to the paved road. No cars. He walked briskly. "Jesus," he said out loud, "you just aint gonna help me, is you? I been askin you till I'm black and blue. Askin you, you Jesus, to let me help my brother." He stood in a clearing. The moon spilled down upon him. Across the meadow, down into a valley, up and onto a tiny rise, sat his house, the third shack in a clump of dark buildings lit with oil lamps. Him and Lon used to walk that. He remembered that day. The pain came ripping back, a memory that reeled his head down, and he fell upon his knees again, sobs lurching out of him, and the pain was so mixed with bitterness that memories became only tears, like drops of blood cutting through his eyes.

They were climbing the green meadow toward the Vance estate, and Lon was talking about Gloria. Coming up behind them, Richard, the youngest brother, was throwing sticks for the dog to get.

"'N she more'n a woman than Lucille, man. I'm tellin you," Lon was saying.

"Hell, if I ever catch Lucille's sister 'gin like I did up in Cooty's loft . . ." he was saying.

"Man, thas good stuff, but she jailbait, I'm tellin you."

They jogged along together. Lon was much taller, maybe a foot or more. Saul was stocky, and he moved in a thudding, plodding manner, as if he was still ploughing in loam clods. Richard was only a boy. They had let him come along, but Lon had told him he'd have to wait down by the road because he was sure the white folks didnt want a whole tribe of niggers coming up to get one job. Besides, Mr. Vance was known to have evil streaks. Not like Mrs. Vance, with her petite fingers and dainty voice waving and whispering music in the air. Mr. Vance was quick-tempered and hard on Negroes. He was a graduate of some military school in the North, and he always acted like he was reliving the days when he was a major in the First World War.

They never made it to the house. Richard was playing down the road. He was training that mutt that Reverend Donaldson's son gave him when some white boys, about five, began rocking him. He threw back, retreating up the road toward the white church. They chased him to this point, but always a point where Negroes were forbidden. This was enemy country for any nigger who wasnt able to account for himself. Richard hid behind the church, wondering how the dog was making out. The white boys closed in, yelling, "Hey, you black sonofabitch! Come way from there!" And Richard, trembling beside a shrub, picked up some round driveway stones, filled his pockets, ran out toward the back of the church, whirled, catching sight of them coming, and began a fierce bombardment. He struck two or three boys, but they closed in, shouting insults. A rock caught him on the shoulder. He ran. And another rock crashed into his temple. He stumbled, again, again, knees, hands, ground, up, stumbling, and shook the blow loose. Circling the field, he eluded the boys, who probably were content to have driven a nigger from their citadel.

When Lon and Saul returned, the boys were sitting on the steps. Saul remembered how he felt then. Every movement, every detail of his life up till that day often appeared like paintings or voices, clear and exact. Lon was mad. Richard's dog had come barking behind them before they reached the Vances' gates.

"Gitta way dog," Saul had yelled.

"Where's Richard?" Lon asked the dog, who was acting strangely.

Saul peered back through the few trees where the road bent. He saw no one. Lon took a few steps back, trying to see.

"Come on, man," Saul said.

"Naw. Wait, Saul," Lon said. He remembered how acute Lon's senses were for detecting something wrong. The dog had acted as if it had been hurt. Probably one of the boys had popped him with a rock. Saul watched his brother.

"I think that's Richard yelling for help."

Saul listened. "Somebody's hollerin," he decided, "but it soun' like more—Wait, man, reckon . . . ?"

Lon was off. The dog barked and bounded out ahead of him. Saul leaped behind them and gained at the road.

Goddamnit, he said to himself, I'm gonna kill me somebody today, so help me, Jesus.

They attacked the white boys, who were dressing their wounds on the side of the church. Richard saw them coming and circled to join them. Blood was clotting on his shoulder. He held his head, and when he saw his brothers coming, he held back tears. "Five of 'em," he said, trotting beside Saul.

They caught the white boys by surprise, and the fight raged for almost half an hour. The white boys had a whole driveway of stones, but after Lon was hit and driven away from the road, Saul and Richard, retreating to the field, began to run low on stones. Lon knew where an old car was rusting in a swamp pit. The white boys were attacking them now. Lon was hit hard in the neck. He kept shaking it now and then to ease the pain away. One white boy whom Saul knew, one of the Donaldson boys, was rushing them. Lon called to follow him. Richard's dog was hit again. The white boys were laughing now. "Hey! Another nigger! Get that four-legged bastard, too!"

Lon reached the car, ripped off a strip of iron and began trying to break up pieces. Rusty pieces fell away. Glass shattered. Saul remembered seeing Lon face them.

Some fear, blazing out of his eyes, seemed to color everything he said. Saul had never seen his brother act like that. "Let's go, man," he said to Lon, who was pounding away at the car. Richard held his head nearby, calling the dog.

"Not till I get me one, just one lick!" he grunted, breaking and bending rusted metal.

"Come on, Lon," Saul remembered he had said. "They coming!"

"You scared them devils?" He glared at Saul, who saw rocks begin to fall near them. One struck the car and bounced, striking Lon.

"See that!" he yelled. "They tryin to kill us!"

And the fight was on again. With the rusted car as a fortress and an arsenal, they had held off four white boys who were cursing and laughing. But before the fifth boy could return with more rocks, they had run out, and Lon, seeing this, leaped forward. When the boys saw him leap up like a jack-in-the-box and come charging across the field, two of them bolted and ran. Saul followed, hurling a piece of iron that must have struck one of the boys hiding behind a clump of bushes, for he yelled and was breaking off a stick for a club when Lon, running toward him, hurled a piece of glass, which curved, curved, and sliced off a piece of bark from a tree.

One white boy was yelling now. "Niggers, you better be careful! Watch what you—" He retreated. "Better not catch you niggers again!"

They were scattering now, amidst the careful aim of Lon, who was bearing down toward them, dodging an occasional rock, and calling for Saul and Richard to back him. Then Saul, seeing a white boy returning with more rocks from the church, charged to meet him. He hurled a large piece of iron. The boy hurled back. Both pieces fell short. They approached each other.

"Nigger, I'm gonna rock your ass in the ground."

Saul was frightened, but he answered the announcement with a mighty throw of curving glass. The boy leaned away from it, then threw. Lon was coming toward them. The white boys behind began calling retreat. The boy carrying rocks in his pockets turned and ran back, turning twice to hurl rocks to slow down the pace of Lon and Saul, who were giving hot chase.

"Not too far," warned Lon. "I got one shot left."

"Well, I got four pieces glass here, man. Take one."

"Naw."

"What's matter?"

"Richard's hurt bad. Bleedin."

"Let's get 'em fore they can get to the church and get more rocks," said Saul. He tossed Lon two pieces of glass.

Saul gave chase, but the boys were gathering in the area around the church and suddenly counterattacked with a bombardment of rocks. Lon called, "Come on back, Saul!"

"They cant reach us now," Saul screamed.

"Then les' get while we can!"

Saul fought down a torrent of fear and rage. Why was Lon retreating now when they could have overtaken them? He fired several pieces of glass and retreated safely across the field before they had time to gather more rocks. He didnt know, but he trusted Lon, and . . .

"Dammit Saul, come on, man!" Naw, he thought. He was still running, and he had two pieces of glass. They were his bullets, he thought. He'd split that dog-haired Tim Donaldson's head wide open, the sneaky bastard, always talking religion to him and Lon, always laughing at them with that silent smirk. Whenever he went to Vance's store he had to control his temper. That Tim was a teasin sonofabitch. Calling other guys niggers and fools, but always meaning something deeper, always meaning *him*. He wanted to get one good blow at Tim, but he couldnt tell—Yes! He saw him coming toward him now. Tim was yelling, "Hey, you coons, watch this!" and he hurled, another boy hurled, and Saul ducked, still moving forward, his left arm shielding his face, his right cocked to throw, and he heard Lon hollering.

"Saul! Come on, man! Get 'em tomorrow!"

But he was propelled, and rocks were striking him, one! two! three! and the white boys were yelling, the dog was yelping, and he aimed a piece of glass for Richard. It curved, missed! They closed in on him. But he knew Lon. . . . A rock thudded his head. Dizziness. Stumble. Up, down, more rocks, yelling. Up, one piece of glass left. Aiming. Running blindly. He was crying now, yelling himself and cursing, "You white trash! Bastards! Kill you!" Fear was upon him. He saw Lon coming, hurling and hurling, fiercely. The white boys retreated now.

"Hey, you all throwing glass!" Tim screamed. "You nigger bastards!" He advanced upon Saul, pommeling him with stone. Saul fell to the ground.

He recalled all this as if it were happening again. He was standing now near the spot where the road bent and went up to the Vances'. Gloria would be getting ready to come off soon. Perhaps he ought to wait for her. He sat upon a stump. Naw, he thought. I'm not sober. But Gloria wont mind. She's good. She's good. Dammit, my brother had a good woman, and now she gonna be mine, if that white bastard Vance dont rape her. I kill him and all his kids for that. Honest to God, I will. Gloria, you oughta quit that place. Plenty places, other places . . .

Other voices rang in his mind. His mother, Lon, Reverend Wiggins. "Saul, Saul, how come you cant keep a job?" "How come you aint marry Gloria? She need a man take care that child, and you always talkin bout likin her." "Saul, you better come to church. The Lord got a word to say to your soul." "Saul, you drink and you lie too much, Saul, you sawed-off nigger runt. Git your black ass stone. Dont come back to Cooty's but you pay Cooty his money! Man, what kind of friend you tryin to be . . ." Mr. Vance, Mr. Vance, Vance. The nigger-loving killer. Vance, the credit-giver, the sharecropper. Vance, advance. "Goddamnit!" he screamed, and tears came again, just like they did when he got up and fell again, only the next time he fell he never got up under his own power.

Lon was attacking, Richard following behind him. The white boys held their ground, and when Saul got up he hurled the last piece of glass blindly toward the crouching figure of Tim, but Tim leaned, the missile curved, rose, rose higher, and crashed one of the stained glass windows of the church.

Lon fired on and on.

Amidst the melee Saul turned and began to retreat as rocks fell all over and around him. He started to leap toward them, but he never finished. Something took his eye away, a slicing, curving object took his eye, crashed, ripped, dug deep into his forehead, and he fell, the pain blinding him.

Lon screamed, "Saul, Saul, git down, man! I did that! I hit you!"

Tim Donaldson and the rest retreated and watched from the front of the church. Occasionally a stone landed near Saul, but the war was over. He could tell it in Lon's voice. The dog was sniffing his face. Saul lay, his face buried in the grass, not wanting to think of the pain that was filling up his head. Lon reached him, pulling on his arm. "Saul, what happened? That last piece I chunked got you? Did it?" Saul wanted to say naw. He rolled over, holding his face with both hands. Naw, naw, naw. But Richard was upset.

"Saul, you bleedin worse'n me. Saul."

Lon was carrying him across the field, running now, running faster. "Put me down, Lon. I can walk." Faster, as the taunts of the enemy faded beneath the excited tone of Richard running beside Lon. Saul held his head, held his palms tight over his face. But the blood came on, reddening his hands. "How you feel?" he managed.

"We all right," Richard answered, but Lon said nothing and Saul knew that he might be crying. He managed to look. "Saul, your eye bleedin bad," said Richard. "Maybe we oughta make it to Mr. Vance's. Gloria be there. She fix it."

"Mr. Vance cant do nothin for this," whispered Lon. He jogged along as Saul asked again and again to be put down, and Lon would say, "Save your strength, bro, you hurt," and Saul felt his strength flowing down his arm and onto his chest and neck.

When they reached home he remembered that he lay on the bed for hours, days perhaps. He wasnt sure. His mother and Lon bandaged, then rebandaged and finally the doctor, Dr. Oaks, the colored doctor from Little Rock, came and bandaged and announced after healing set in, after weeks at the hospital and office, that he was blind in one eye. But he knew he wasnt blind because he could see faint traces of light, and he prayed someday to see with his left eye again.

Hardly before the bandages were removed Uncle Sam called Lon into the service and over to Korea, and Gloria cried, for they were set to get married. "Mama," she would say to their mother, "Lon say he marry as soon as he come home on leave."

"Child, that rusty nigger'll tell you anything. You oughta drag him up. I gotta good mind to really tell him a piece of mine tonight."

"Yessum." Gloria was sweet, and Saul felt that perhaps Lon was taking a bit of advantage of her innocent and easygoing behavior. After all, that girl in Hevysville tried to cut Lon so he would marry her. Even Lucille slapped him, but Lon had been drunk himself and had fought with her. Her sister got a baseball bat after Lon, and chased him across the field, where he turned on her, threw her, and took her right there, and Saul had heard these episodes over and over again until they were part of his memory, his view of life. He had started going with Bessie, because he had dared her to hit him with a baseball bat. They were hot, tempestuous, and wild.

Saul had lain in the bed for centuries while the fear, the dread of losing that eye, came leaping up at him out of the somber nights and the gray days of fall, out of the stuttering tones of Reverend Wiggins at church, out of the soundless days when the plough cut up the fields, the smell of cotton and the sweet potatoes and greens swirled in his mind like the north wind. The day was like a single shot, a burning picture, never consumed like the bush Moses saw, and he recalled how he never talked to Lon again as they had earlier. Gloria came to his bed after chastising him for moodiness but showing a tenderness she seldom if ever showed to Lon, a tenderness like something he imagined would have explained the feeling of the love that the preacher always lied about, trying to show forth like a light to the world.

Lon was eighteen then and in a few weeks he was gone. Gloria's baby came months later in the spring, and Lon came home for a couple of days to play and bounce it, but his eyes showed something new, something far off and distant. He wore his Army suit around, complaining about the discipline of training but boasting of his new status whenever he got the chance. Saul questioned him and ached to go with him. He dared not ask whether they would take anybody with one eye, but he prayed and begged God or—he couldnt bring himself to believe as his mother and Gloria did—Jesus or somebody to allow him to fight along with his brother.

"Naw, man," Lon said the day he was stuffing his things in a brown duffle bag. "This Army'll break a man. Damn, man, I aint had no woman cept what we pay for. But man, that aint no good."

"How they test you for aimin a gun?" asked Saul.

"Ah, man, it's tough as hell. I'm telling you. Man, nigger sergeants worse'n the white. Man, this one sucker from Oklahoma. He grab me one day, and I had been on the firin line before too, he grab me, talkin bout, 'Soldier, dont ever let me catch you aim that weapon anywhere but there!' and he hauled off and kicked me straight up the ass. Dammit, I learned."

That night, with Lon and another guy from Little Rock going away, six or seven of them all went out looking for girls at Cooty's Inn, and they all got drunk. He recalled that Gloria met him when he staggered home. She didnt say anything. Lon had gone. Mother was sleeping, the stars were out like frozen tears, he thought, a wind was coming up and the leaves, rustling across the stretches of . . .

He thought a poem:

> The universe shrank
> when you went away.
> Every time I thought your name,
> stars fell upon me.

and wondered about the sleeping sun:

> The lights gathering
> on the night lake
> sing a thousand songs
> of the sleeping sun.

HENRY DUMAS

Six Days You Shall Labor

The fumes from the solvent can were making me and Big Mo drunk. I wished HyLow would get back with the soda pops we sent him after. Big Mo coughed and went over to the window. He opened it and motioned to me. I stooped down and came around from behind that printing machine. It was a good thing Big Mo had let me come along with him, because I know he couldnt have squeezed in and out from behind that machine and cleaned it as good as I was doing. I am small and never had no trouble squeezing in and out of things.

Big Mo was coughing out the window. I took deep breaths out the window. I looked down the street, and I saw HyLow talking in front of the shoeshine parlor with some people dressed for church. He got the pops in one hand, and he takin somethin from one of the group with the other.

I say, "Here come HyLow."

Big Mo, he coughed and bring in his head. "He been gone half hour." Big Mo sneezed and his whole body shook. I see his muscles shaking, and I think I know why people called him Big Mo, but then I know why he always got mean when somebody called him fat. Big Mo was like that. He didnt mind you callin him Big Mo, but you couldnt call him anything else except his name, Morris Haynes. They tell me Big Mo almost killed a man once for calling him a fat nigger. The only one I ever hear mess with Big Mo was HyLow. HyLow was a year ahead of me in school. He was one of the craziest niggers I ever run into. Some people say he's crazy. Some people say he's not.

When he got back with them soda pops we could hear him hollering at us like he didnt know where we were. Like he was bringing back them soda pops, and they werent soda pops but something better than soda pops, and we were suppose to thank him for them.

He came in the door. "Hey! While I'm away the Ink Spots play." He put two pop bottles on the table away from the rags and solvent can, brushed himself off like he didnt want none of the dirt from us to get on him, and then sit down in a chair in the corner, drinking his pop and laughing. That guy is always laughing. No matter what happen to him, he laugh. Big Mo, he just the opposite. HyLow pulled out a pack of cigarettes and pretended he was trying to strike a match. That just about tore Big Mo up. But we kept on working. With me helping him, this job was gonna be cut in half.

"Hey hey hey?" HyLow laughed, bending over with his soda in his hand. Suddenly he laughed so hard that he spilled a little on his suit. "Whoops!" But he keep right on laughing. "Now see what you Sabbath breakers done made me do." He finished the bottle. "Now I cant put no money in church with this stuff on me. People think I been out drinkin gasoline from under trucks, stinking with that stuff you boys got over yourself." He pointed to the solvent cans. "Naw," he shook his head. "Think I gonna go into business today." He took something out of his pocket and cracked it with his jaw. Big Mo, he let the top down on the machine, and we shined it.

The church bells were ringing again, and we got ready to go. Big Mo, he went over, let the window down, and then sit down in a chair.

"We finish?" I asked him.

"You is, kiddo," he said.

"Hey hey hey, listen to the big boss," said HyLow.

"Shut up an gimme couple of them pecans," said Big Mo.

HyLow laughed and went into his pocket and then brought it out empty. He winked at me.

"Now listen, kid. I gotta wait here till she call," said Big Mo. "I dont need you no more. I'll stop by your house and pay you."

I didnt say nothin. I aint want to go. I figured it was because of HyLow. But I didnt say nothing about it. When Big Mo drove pass my house early in the morning, I was sitting on the porch doing nothing. I waved him down. I ask him could I go along with him on the job. I knew he must be going out for some job, because that's how Big Mo made his living. He had an old piece of car full of junk and tools. He would haul or do anything for a little piece of money. Everybody used to say that he was eating that money, because he didnt drink, smoke, or waste himself.

He say he going up to the Collier newspaper office to clean a machine. He ask me if I was going to church, and I told him I didnt have to if I could make some money to show Mama when I got back. About halfway through the job, right after Sunday School let out, old crazy HyLow Walker pass by and see Big Mo's car and found us in that building.

"Dont do it, kiddo," said HyLow.

It was about eleven o'clock. We could hear church bells ringing down the street.

HyLow, he sat over in the corner, cracking pecans and tossing the shells into a trash can beside him. Now and then we'd hear shells hit the inside of a barrel or trash can next to us, and then he bust out laughing again.

"Working on Sunday, same as working on Monday to some people. Yes, sir, you spots got all the money, all the—"

"Gimme some of them pecans."

"You boys know where I got these?" And he took out a handful and shook them like dice. They sounded good, and I could tell that they werent the pea-size kind that tart your mouth.

Big Mo, he raised up, cleaning his hands with the rag, and looked over at HyLow rearing back in that chair, pretending he been sitting there all his life.

He tossed me one and I caught it.

"All right, lil bits, tell your boss what you got." I looked at it, and I could see that it was a big brown nut, shaped like a watermelon. It even had a few snake lines on the ends, left by the shells. That was a sign that it was fresh off the tree. It was thin-shelled and the meat was juicy. We called them papershells. When anybody got them kind of nuts, they knew they had some good eating. The best ones came from Georgia, but there was one place around our town that had trees and that was on the Collier plantation, which had been closed off for years.

"Papershell, right?"

I cracked that pecan open. It fell perfect. I halved it, trying to keep the solvent on my hands from getting on it, and then I ate it. Big Mo, he watched me.

"Shore is," I say.

"Hey hey hey, tell my secret, then it be yours; keep my secret, you look for yours."

"He bought them things over at Yancy," Big Mo said to me.

"Now, aint that just like a jealous nigger. He cant get none from there, so he say they didnt come from there. Now, you look and taste that papershell, kiddo, and tell your boss if it aint just come off the tree last night."

I handed the other half to Big Mo.

He waved it off and went on cleaning. "Dont let 'em fool you, kid. He's tryin to be slick."

I chewed and looked. I wondered if them papershells come from the Collier place. "Where you get them?"

And just about that time the phone rang. We was standing near the door. Me and HyLow. Big Mo picked up the phone. He say, "Hello?"

Then he listen. Then he say, "Yes, Mrs. Collier."

Then he don't talk for another little bit. "All right, Mrs. Collier. I want it today. I need it today." Then he hung up.

HyLow began to laugh again. Then he looked at Big Mo. "Look at that, wont you." He punched me on the arm to make me pay attention to what he was talking about. "Just look at that. Old big boss talking to Mrs. Collier. Man, I know he gonna get him some of those papershells out there."

Big Mo was paying nobody no mind now. "Yawl git out." Then he went around the side of the machine, turned off the power, and fixed everything right. He turned out the light and came out the door behind us.

When I got out into the air, the sun was bright. Church was about ready to take in. I could see all the people along the street. Everybody in town came that way to go to the Baptist Church. Everybody in the country went to the Baptist Church too. There wasnt no other kind of church around, maybe except the Methodist Church over in Haleton.

"Big Mo, how bout let a Christian ride in your 'chine for the morning service?" said HyLow.

"Tie your tongue up, nigger, and get in."

We all got in the car, me and Big Mo in the front, and HyLow in the back.

"You know, Big Mo," said HyLow as we headed down the small street, "I thought you wanted to make some money."

"What you talkin about?"

"I thought you were smarter than that. Dont you know where these papershells come from?"

Big Mo aint say nothin. Keeps drivin.

"Out at Collier's," I say. HyLow, he wink at me.

"Kiddo, you smart."

"Where you get them papershells, boy?" Big Mo said.

We had to stop for a lot of people crossing the street. I looked away so as the people dont see me. My aunts and uncles in town, if they see me in Big Mo's car and not in church, they be tellin it before I get one dollar of my money. About that time the car is pulling near the corner where the church is. Big Mo slow down and stop. HyLow, he crack a couple more them pecans. "How much you think you gonna get from them for that job, boss."

Big Mo, he shake his head. "I dont *think*, I *know* how much I ask for. I work for my living, like anybody else."

HyLow, he laughed. "Thirty dollars?"

When I heard him say that I almost jump out of the seat. I know it aint worth that much, but I was wonderin just how

HyLow get such a notion in his big head. Thirty dollars. I know I'd be gettin about five or more.

"None of your business, boy. Now get out and go on to church like you ought to."

HyLow, he opened the door and shook some papershells on the ground. A lot of people were looking at the car. They knew Big Mo's car, and some of them were straining to see who it was with Big Mo. "Ah, I cant go in there with the smell of that stuff on me."

HyLow, he lean back and wave Big Mo on like he real mad for having that stuff on him.

"Man, aint nothin on *your* clothes," said Big Mo.

"How come I can smell it?"

"That's us you smell," I say.

HyLow, he winked at me. He slam the door and set back.

"Well, either you gettin out or you aint," said Big Mo.

"Hell, they think I'm one of you guys, working on Sundays for the white man, like you aint got no respect for Christian upbringing at all."

"Shut up and go on to church."

Just then crossing the street was old Mrs. Rankin. She was hobbling along on her cane with a couple of other women. One of the women was suppose to be some kin to Big Mo, but I never knew how. It didnt make no difference, because soon as Big Mo see them he turn his head and look at HyLow. "You gettin out or not?"

Everybody knew that beat-up old wine-colored Studebaker. It had no shocks, no springs, and would just make thirty-five miles downhill. It couldnt go uphill at all. So, they act like they aint see Big Mo at first. Then, just like that, Mrs. Rankin, she stop, turn around, and look at Big Mo.

"Morris Haynes! I want to talk to you!" She came over to the car. I was sitting there wishing I had a place to hide my head.

"Yes, mam," Big Mo says respectfullike. Big Mo is very respectful to old folks. I never heard him raise his voice to old people. But he could cuss you out in a minute if he wanted to.

"Morris Haynes, I been watching you for a long time now. Why dont you do your duty on the Lord's Day?"

Big Mo looked down at something on the steering wheel.

"Your mama and me was good friends when she was living, and when she died I promised myself I'd keep my eyes on that boy of hers. Now, Morris, you been round this town all your life . . ."

We all knew what was coming. HyLow cracked one of them papershells. I heard him chewing and fidgeting.

" . . . and you was baptized, as I recall, along with Sister Tinslow's daughter yonder . . ."

We all knew what was coming, but it didnt do no good. I guess I felt about as bad as Big Mo did. Big Mo never laughed at religion. He might curse out a preacher, but he never talked about the Church like HyLow sometimes would do.

" . . . you aint got decency and respect enough to set aside one day, the Sabbath, to thank the Lord that He let you live the rest of the week. Son, I been watching you. You know better. That's why I said to myself: 'This time I aint gonna do what others do, pass him by and turn my face. I gonna speak my mind.' Because, Morris, you raised in the Church. Your mother was a Christian woman. She raised you right. Son, you ought to think about your soul."

Big Mo was looking down, nodding his head a little, but he never turned off the engine. HyLow never stopped cracking them papershells. A few people slowed down to listen. I hoped none of my aunts or uncles came by, cause they would jump on me worse than Mrs. Rankin was getting on Big Mo. She looked in at us and called our names. "That goes for you young men too." Then she nodded her head, agreeing with herself like I seen old people do when they know nobody's listenin to them so they got to agree with themselves.

Just before she left she poured it on strong. "I'd be ashamed of myself if I was you. Takin something that dont belong . . . Six days . . . but the seventh is the Lord thy God's.

Now, I want to see every one of those young faces back in church next Sunday. And I want yawl to come to the Thanksgiving program we having this evenin."

We all said, "Yes, mam," and Big Mo drove off. The people were gathered in front of the church. It was a bad time. Big Mo couldnt turn around. He had to drive right past the church now. People started hollerin at us. It wasnt too bad, but then Mrs. Rankin was right in the middle of the crowd, and she pointed several times, and people turned.

"Man, Big Mo, your people sure make a fuss over church," said HyLow. "Last summer when I was in Memphis, niggers went only if they felt the spirit, and nobody said anything."

"Well," said Big Mo, "that's Memphis. This is Bottomsup, and Negroes like to go to church down here. I got to go back sometime too. That woman is right—"

"Now, listen to this sinner," said HyLow.

Somebody hollered at us to stop. Big Mo kept going. It was Russell Moody. He ran across the street and waved us down. Big Mo pulled over. Russell Moody had a truck. And now and then he did a little hauling and such. Russell Moody always did handyman work like Big Mo, but he had people that called him, just as there was people that called Big Mo. I guess the jobs were about split up between Big Mo and Russell Moody, but Russell had another job cleaning the jail and the law building. Plus he had six kids. He was older than Big Mo.

"Tell me you worked on Collier's press," he said to Big Mo.

"What's on your mind, Moody?" Big Mo never had no likes for Russell Moody.

"How much he pay you?"

"How come you didnt take it?"

"I woulda, I woulda," he said in a hurry.

"You scared of that machine?"

"Now, now, Mo, you know me—"

"Yeah, I know," said Big Mo. He took his arm off the door frame, away from where Russell Moody was leaning into the car. Then he did a funny thing. He turned and looked at HyLow. "Man, I see why you always laughin."

Russell Moody said, "Any time you get a job you cant—"

"Moody, what's wrong with you on Sunday morning? There aint no job Mo cant take care of."

"Well, I just want to ask you about what . . ."

Big Mo started shakin his head. I didnt figure it out until pretty soon Big Mo and HyLow were laughing. I never seen them laugh together. It looked so funny that I laughed too.

Big Mo drove on out of town. We ate up all the pecans.

HyLow said, "Looky here, kiddo, why dont you and me get out the car before Collier Road, and make it along the wet side of the levee till we come to them pecan trees other side of—"

"Boy, you gonna get us all shot," said Big Mo. He looked at me. "Kid is working with me."

"Listen to this preacher, will you, kiddo? Jack of all trades and that's about it. If you make a little money, you'd have a fit. Big boss, hey hey hey. Mo, you as good as Russell Moody."

"That nigger's a fool and a ass-kisser. He lick the white man's ass so shiny he can see how to grin in it." I had heard HyLow say that in school one day. Big Mo was pickin up things HyLow says.

"Yeah, but at least Russell'll jump at a chance to get thirty dollars' worth of pecans."

"Thirty dollars?" I said.

"That's right, kiddo. Now, if you asked Russell Moody, he would say, 'Naw, naw, they got dogs, dogs.' All I have to say to that is, 'Now, whoever heard of a nigger scared of a dog that's tied up?'

"'Naw, naw, I'm talkin about—'

"'And who's gonna let a dog aloose?'

"'We might run into one of them peckerwoods live out there.'

"'They be doin the same thing we doin.'

"'But them dogs . . .'

"Then I say to him, 'Listen, Mr. Moody, I guarantee you we'll be safe, because I guarantee you two things.'"

And then HyLow leaned over like he was really talking to Russell Moody.

"'What's them two things?' Russell Moody would ask.

"'Number one, I ain't going to go up to that Collier place and ask them white people to let me turn their dogs aloose . . .'"

Then he laugh like he knew he was gettin to Russell Moody, and it sounded just like Russell Moody, and I was laughing, and Big Mo, he had to grin.

"'And number two, I know you aint either . . .'"

And he laughed like Russell Moody, and we all laughed, and then HyLow, he said, "'Right?'

"And Russell Moody, he laughed out loud and said, 'That's right, that's right.'"

"So then, what're we waiting for?"

That's how we all got headed to the pecan trees.

At the Delta Switch we pull off the road and drive up to Gary's. Mr. Gary was fixing a flat tire on his old Buick. He was dressed for church, and all his kids were standing next to the Buick, waiting for him to fix it. His oldest boy, Clint Gary—he was in my class—was helping him.

We all got out. Big Mo, he ask Mr. Gary if he had any croackersacks. Burlap bags, as some folks call them. Mr. Gary told us to come around to the back, and we went around to the back. He went in his shed, and we go in behind him, and then he turned and say, "I hope yawl aint goin to mess with that man's trees?"

"Just what you think," say Big Mo.

Mr. Gary, he was an old man. Everybody liked him because he spoke his mind and he dont cheat you.

He say, "I'll tell you what I told Russell Moody the other evening. I told him what I know about the Colliers. Just as sure as these bags got dirt on them, they be waiting for you."

He handed the bags to Big Mo. "Mr. Collier stopped by here two weeks ago fore he go and say to me, 'Gary, I'll be glad to let anybody that wants to gather him a few pecans, but they'll have to come up to the house like a man and ask for permission.' But he say if he or his man Fane catch anybody trespassing his land, they'll shoot them."

"We aint going in daylight," said Big Mo.

"I'm just tellin you what the man said," Gary said as he closed the door to his shed and headed back to his car.

"But you know he lyin," said Big Mo.

Mr. Gary, he just looked away. "That's right."

"Well, on Sunday aint no niggers or crackers down in them fields, so we got to make it."

Mr. Gary, he aint say nothing to that. He just half nod his head and walk on. Then he turned and say to us, "That crazy fool Fane, he patrols round on a horse and couple of dogs. But he always do it around lunchtime and late at night. Sometimes the sheriff and him come out to talk with Mrs. Collier. The best time is dusk. They're eating dinner, and the dogs have to be fed. Save me a few of those papershells. I aint had any since they closed it off."

Then Mr. Gary looked at me. "Boy, you stay close to Big Mo, you hear?"

"Yes, sir."

I see him get in the car, and I could see Clint Gary in that car. I know that Clint Gary knew what we was doing.

We drive down that Collier road. Their plantation is spread out. But you can see for miles and miles in places. Over to the east was corn and tomatoes. He had a tomato factory at the edge of it. Them pecan trees run along the edge of the cotton, which was in the west, along the river. We could make out the levee pretty soon, and old HyLow, he lit up a cigarette and cursed imaginary niggers and white people out in the cotton fields. "Look at yourselves, stinking and rotten, all weighed down with the white man's cotton."

He kept it up for a long time. "Shet up," say Big Mo, "cause I saw you in that patch once or twice."

"Hey, now!" And then HyLow broke into a laugh. It was something so funny he was just doubled over laughing. He took off his sports jacket and laid it on the seat. Then he raised up. "Did you hear that, kiddo? Did you hear that?"

"Yeah," I said, but I didnt know that I was playing into HyLow's hands. He sure was a trickery nigger himself. I had picked so much cotton myself that I aint think it possible for me ever to lie and say I didnt.

"He saw me in the cotton field. Yes, he did. But Big Mo, you know me good enough to know one thing . . ."

HyLow, he looked at me. I wanted to ask what it was, but I figured this time I'd keep my mouth shut.

"One thing. And I tell you just like I told Russell Moody the other day. I know, but you dont know what I was doing there. I was in the cotton field, but I didnt pick no cotton. But I sure know what Big Mo was doing whenever I seen him in the field. Old Big Mo got a big, long, strong back, walking in the mud with a cotton sack."

"Shet up, boy. Least I work honest for what I get."

"Except when?"

"Always."

I wanted to laugh myself, cause HyLow had him again. And Big Mo didnt even see it. We drove the car onto this gravel road that was wide. It led to the pike, which we would take to the center of the plantation.

Big Mo was driving fast and the car was overheating. I looked at the heat gauge. It was broke, but I could feel the heat coming in and hitting my legs. I opened out the vent on the window. The window of the car was broken out, but Big Mo had managed to have a vent. And I guess that was about the only thing on that car that wasnt broken. We reached the plantation. Big Mo, he knew where to drive around to the back. I could just see his old raggedy car, now, parked in front of that big house. We looked over it, and HyLow, he hollered, "Nigger, nigger, in that house, come on out and look for that cat! White folks, white man, nigger sucking louse, why you treat a nigger like that?"

"Dont holler," I say.

"You scared, kiddo?"

"Naw."

HyLow knew I was scared. But I told him I wasnt. I wanted to go.

"Stay close to me, then, kiddo."

"Leave the kid to me," Big Mo said. He pulled the old Studebaker up to an old trough where they water cattle and stock. We hear dogs barkin, and across the road is two parked cars. One looked like the one Mrs. Collier drove sometimes, and the other we knew was Fane Paxton's.

"If you want to get straighten out, kid, you listen to me, hear?"

I say, "Okay."

Big Mo, he get out and walk to the house. Now, this aint the big house. It was down the road. We could see it from where we was. Big Mo, he walk to the house. And me and HyLow, we hear the dogs barking, and then Big Mo, he turn and walk around to the back of the house. We dont see much of him, as he is standing up on the steps of the house. Then we see Big Mo come back to the car. He wave at me to get out.

"Come on, kid."

"What for?"

"Just come on. You helped me, didnt you?"

I got out and went with Big Mo. HyLow, he hollered at us. "Man, you mean I didnt help none?"

Big Mo, he looked at him, and then all he could say was, "Come on."

Big Mo stood on the steps and we stood in the yard behind him. When Mrs. Collier came to the door, I aint expect to see what I see. Big Mo rang the bell about five or six times. We was gettin ready to leave.

She opened the door. "Oh, Morris! I just forgot about you." She laughed a little. Her hair was loose and all around her back, and she was wearing one of those loose see-through dresses. "You know that Mr. Collier is away, and Mr. Fane has your money."

"Yes, mam," said Big Mo. HyLow nudged me. Mrs. Collier was swaying in the doorway. "But there's something I'd like to ask you. Walker and young Neal, they gave me a little hand, and I was wonderin if we could have your permission to pick up a few pecans."

She laughed and waved her hand. Then that redneck Fane came to the door. As soon as we see him pushing her out of the way, we all stiffen. Big Mo, he dont move.

"You Morris Haynes?" He opened the door and came down the steps. He was drunk.

"That's right," said Big Mo. He didnt move none.

"Well, fore I pay you for the job you sposed to have done for me, I want to see it. Now, what you bring all these boys with you for?"

Big Mo huffed himself. Mrs. Collier was laughing. "Give them the money. Frank does business with Morris all the time, doesnt he, Morris?"

Big Mo said, "He always pay me too, Mrs. Collier."

"Well, I aint got nothing against a nigger. I just want to see the work before I pay him."

"I cleaned up the presses, the ink rollers, that's all. Here's the key."

Big Mo showed the key to Fane, and then dropped his hand. All he was doing was showing Fane that he had the key, but I felt that he had made a mistake. HyLow did too. He nudged me. Big Mo asked Mrs. Collier was there anything else she wanted him to do, and she said no, and Fane, he reached in his pocket, leaning up against the wall. He was very drunk. "I say I want to see the work."

"Frank, you cant see the work," screamed Mrs. Collier. She was not mad, but laughin. I knew she was going to let us get some pecans, then . . .

HENRY DUMAS

Fane gave Big Mo the money. "Three dollars, right?"

"No, Mr. Collier always give me five for the job."

Fane, he squint-eyed at Big Mo. That red-faced white man was so drunk, I bet he thought we all was one nigger. "Day's Sunday, and these niggers dont stop workin."

Mrs. Collier came out. "Please, yall go now."

"I come for my money, Mrs. Collier, like you said."

"Oh, Frank, this is silly. Give them the five dollars."

The drunk man, he just looked out at us, staring from one to the other, trying to make things out, I guess, then he grunt, and start mumbling something about giving us a minute to get out of his sight and letting loose them dogs. And then he took the five out, and he handed it to Big Mo. Big Mo gave him the key.

We turned and went to the car. But we could hear Fane cussing and laughin behind us. Then we heard the dogs barkin.

We got in the car. Big Mo drove fast again. He was mad. I could tell. HyLow, he was shakin his head, grinnin.

I couldnt tell what HyLow saw funny. I figure he sometimes lose part of his mind, crack his brain or something, and laugh at anything. Big Mo ask him what he laughin at, but HyLow, he dont hear. He got tears in his eyes. I dont know what made me start laughin, but pretty soon, I just laugh, and Big Mo, he gettin madder and madder. We all laugh so hard that Big Mo stop the car. Me and HyLow get out and fall on the ground. It was just too much, and I tell you that is one of the first times that I think I found out what make HyLow laugh at everything. I'm tellin you I think I looked at everything different from that day on.

We couldnt wait till dusk, like we said. No. We head for North Bend, where the river turn and straighten out and come along about one quarter of a mile in from the plantation. Cotton grew all along there. Come Monday morning, you still find a few niggers out in some of those fields, pickin the last of it. We head for the bend. Big Mo drivin fast. We meet a car. It looked like somebody going out to the Collier place. Nobody say nothin. We know we had one thing to do. Big Mo wanted to wait till dusk, but HyLow was against it.

"How we gone to frail a tree at night and no lights?"

When we heard that we didnt say nothin. I hadnt figured on frailin a tree, but just picking a few and gettin out. HyLow must know more about it than he told us. We parked the car under a row of trees and headed for the levee. The best way to keep out of sight would be to hit the levee, get on the wet side of it, and then go back downriver, keeping out of sight on the low side. HyLow said by the time we got there it would be dusk anyway. It was about three o'clock in the afternoon then, the sun was far away, but it was hot. We started out. Big Mo, he in the lead, walking with his croaker-sack over his shoulder. HyLow next, and he always looking back at me, winking. I say to myself, That nigger is crazier than a coon.

We march along for a while. If anybody come along and see Big Mo's car, they'd know. But it would take them to be doing the same thing to see the car. The river was moving along like a big snake. We could just make out the other side good. Twice we saw people on the other side. Nobody say nothing. After a while, Big Mo slow down. He way ahead of us then. He hold up his hand for us to hurry. We get to him, and we see we reach the first of the pecan groves, but it aint papershell.

We pick up a few, crack them and eat them. But Big Mo, he didnt mess with them. They were them pea-size pecans, real hard, and if you get any of the hull in your mouth, your mouth draw up like it was gettin smaller. It was a funny feeling, and we mostly used the pea-size nuts to chunk at people. Nobody would eat 'em. You couldnt sell 'em to storekeepers, and you couldnt make no money yourself. Only poor people and squirrels ate 'em. So as I was cracking one open HyLow say, "Kiddo, you know what happen to you if you mix peas with papershells, dont you?"

I spit out them shells. "Naw," I say.

HyLow, he shake his head. Every time he open his mouth, he either laugh or makin rimes. That's the way he was.

"Man, if you dont know, then I have to school you, cause I dont want nobody to fool you. There's an old saying my mother taught me. It go like this:

> Whiteman work him
> cause he cant figger.
> He run and eat pea-nims
> and turn to a nigger.

"Then there's another one:

> That's an old story
> about an African slave.
> Brought 'em to America
> but he wouldnt behave.

> White man wonder
> what's in his gut.
> They cut him open.
> They find a pecan nut.

> Black folks bury 'em
> in the middle of the night.
> African scare 'em
> and the nigger turns white."

Pretty soon we come to the clearing. HyLow, he tell us we can see the papershell trees from there, and he point. They about a quarter mile away, running along the edge of the cotton to our left. Every now and then we hear a dog bark. Big Mo, he steady watching in the direction of the big house.

"If we get spied," said HyLow, "I'm going south along the

river. I know a place down there, I can get across. Mo, you take kiddo and make it out."

Big Mo didnt say nothin. He was just ahead of us.

"We stick together," he said.

"Like hell, man," said HyLow. "If them dogs come after us, we split."

Big Mo, he think about it, then he say, "We stick together unless we hear dogs comin."

"Well, if the dogs come, you know where Nadley's cotton gin used to be? Well, I meet you there one hour after we split."

"I think about it," said Big Mo.

"Man, there aint nothin to think about. When somebody spy us, then we dont have no time for thinkin."

So we went on. I was spose to stick with Big Mo. HyLow would go downriver to draw them off us. Nobody said anything, because we hoped we wouldnt have to do anything like that.

One thing in our favor is that we knew what was going on back there at the Collier house. At the big house there probably wasnt nobody there except Mr. Collier's old grand-mother and grandfather and their nurse. Maybe one of the sons home from college, but that was all.

When we reached the papershell grove, I could tell that nobody had been picking those pecans. Sticks and limbs, leaves and nuts, were scattered on the ground. We fell into the first tree like crazy men.

For about half hour we filled the sacks, all the time we were gruntin and thankin Jesus for such beautiful nuts. We picked up under five trees, and then Big Mo said we should move on to the next ones.

"Aint no more like these," said HyLow. "That one yonder is stunted this year. Worms in every other nut. Something got them. The other ones down the line are the same. If we want any more nuts . . ."

Big Mo, he come over to us and examine our sacks.

Now, a croackersack can hold a lot of nuts, and by this

time we had filled each of them with about thirty pounds of nuts. HyLow said we ought to get as much as we each could carry. And Big Mo said he could carry two sacks, and with that we just kept on pickin them up. Now, huntin pecans is not as simple as it looks. When there's grass and brush around, you have to know how to look for them. Some people, after they have cleaned from right under the tree, think there aint no more on the ground. But most of the time if there is a little grassy spot right outside of where the tree's shadow falls and when the wind or a storm hits, as one hit the night before, then you can bet your hammer hand that you can pick up a couple of pounds of nuts from there.

So on, it was almost dusk. We looked along the edge of that cotton. HyLow started climbing a tree. He had a long stick, and leaned it against the tree.

When you get ready to frail a tree, then you pick out the one with the biggest and the sweetest nuts and then climb it with a bamboo stick or something, and then just sit out on a limb and knock that tree till all them nuts are on the ground.

Now I saw HyLow get up in that tree. "Man, we better get out of here!" said Big Mo.

"I thought you could carry two sacks," said HyLow.

"Yeah, but if you get shot up in that tree, I might have to carry you too."

"Nigger, you know if I get shot you'd run," and he was knocking down so many pecans that they were raining on us. "Listen to him, kiddo, listen to this big old ink spot, so black that aint nobody know we even out here."

"Well, I aint never seen but one dog climb a tree," said Big Mo. He was laughing himself now and filling his sack.

"Whose dog is that?" I asked, cause I aint never heard of a dog climbing a tree. Big Mo, he laughed.

"That one that's in one now," and he hollered up at HyLow, "Man, you see any possums in that tree?"

HyLow, he was grunting. Then next thing I know, Big Mo was climbing the big tree next to the one HyLow was in, and his big self was sitting out on the first branch, and he was shaking it just like a wind had hit it. I kept looking because the limb sounded like it was cracking. I dont think there was one pecan left. Then he came down and got up in the one HyLow was frailing. "When you do a job," he said to HyLow, who was climbing down, "do a good job."

"Listen to him, kiddo, will you? Braggin. You better hurry up. We cant come out here every night."

We frailed three trees so good there wasnt no pecans left except for stunted ones. Our sacks were loaded. Big Mo had two croakers on his shoulders, and HyLow had one. I carried the two twenty-pound flour sacks.

Just at dusk we heard the dogs barkin. They sounded close. We started back the way we came. We saw a car coming. Looked like the same car that had passed before.

When we reached the car, we could still hear dogs barking. They must be loose cause we was a long way from the house.

We loaded the car down. Sweat soaked our backs, but we hadnt stopped for nothing. Big Mo drove. We got back on Collier Road and headed toward town. All the way back we laughin and eatin them papershells.

If you aint never had pecan nuts right off the tree, then you ought to try some, because when you do, then you dont want no more of the ones that dry out in the store and the ends crack. Fresh pecans got all the good-tastin oil right there in the shell. The best time for papershells is right after they come down out of the tree. The shell is thinner than pea-sizes and the other kinds. If they stay around too long, they dry out.

HyLow, he say we ought to go by the church.

"Them people dont want to see us," said Big Mo. I felt he was right. HyLow, he come to shake his head. He put on his sports jacket.

"Listen, Brother kiddo," he said to me, "I aint got time to mess with thick-headedness. You want to make some money or not? What you make with Mo today? One dollar? I fix it so you can make ten dollars, what you say?"

I didnt know what to say. Big Mo, he driving the car. Pretty soon we in front of the church. The people were having some kind of Thanksgiving program.

"Well, you know damn well we aint gonna eat two hundred pounds of pecans by ourselves. Let's go to that Thanksgiving program," said HyLow.

"You crazy, man, I aint ready for—"

"You promised Mrs. Rankin you be back."

"That be next Sunday," said Big Mo.

"You make your contribution while its still in you, or you wont make none at all. I know what I'm going to do. I going in just before the services are over. I wont have to sit long, and then they'll know I'm there, and I can pass out a few papershells, and then that's it."

"You bout the lowest Negro I know, and—"

"Listen to this big old nigger." HyLow started to laugh. When HyLow laughs, his laugh just make you think, and when you hear him, you know he aint foolin. If there was one thing that never told a lie, that was the way HyLow laughed. He had a slippery tongue, but if he laugh and you listen, you find something there. He was laughin, and then I found myself grinnin. Big Mo he aint say nothin, but I could see him figurin out. Suddenly the car started making a loud noise, and then it jerked. The car suddenly stopped going and steam was popping out of it.

Big Mo jumped out. While me and Big Mo were looking under the hood, HyLow dissappeared.

Pretty soon we could hear the people turning out of the church. Big Mo and me, we get back in the car, but the hood was still up. Before we could hide, here come HyLow, bringin some people.

"The best papershells this side of the Mississippi. We sellin for not one hundred for ten pounds, like Yancy do those dried-up things he ship off up North. But we selling them for twenty-five cents a pound."

Russell Moody was there. The Gary kids crowded around the car, and before we knew it we were digging into those sacks, selling the papershells to the whole church.

While we were tryin to shorten the line of kids and people, I see Mrs. Rankin coming along. It was my job to hold onto the money in the front seat and pass out change. This time, Mrs. Rankin with some of the old ladies. I figured she wouldn't stop, but I was wrong.

She come over to the car, look at me, and watch HyLow and Big Mo sellin the pecans.

"Well, Morris, I can see you worked the whole day. You know the Lord said six days was allotted for work—"

"Yes, mam," Morris said. He was always respectful.

"And on the seventh Thou shalt steal," whispered HyLow to me.

We all knew Mrs. Rankin knew where them papershells come from, because she used to work daywork for the Colliers. She come over to the sacks. "Papershells?"

"Yes, mam."

"Here, try some," said HyLow. He gave her a free sack, but she shoved his hand away, ramblin in her purse. "Those are good pecans," she said. "I cant chew like I used to."

But she handed HyLow a coin, anyway. "I want to see you young men in church next Sunday." She looked at Morris. "Morris, you need to lose a little weight."

"Yes, mam," said Big Mo.

"And you, young man." She pointed at me. "Better stay away from these older boys, you hear?"

"Yes, mam."

Then she came over to HyLow. "And you, I bet you can smell when pecans are ripe. . . . Comin round here, acting like you from somewhere. Why, all of you ought to thank the Lord that man aint shoot you. . . . Now, save some of them papershells for your own people."

"Yes, mam," we said. Then she went down the street.

"Now, how she know where we get them papershells?" asked HyLow.

"That old lady know the day you was born," said Big Mo.

"Hey hey hey," said HyLow. But it was the first time all day I aint heard him laugh. He didnt have to laugh. The truth was the truth anyway it come.

The Man Who Could See Through Fog

The sun would soon rise over the hill ahead. Smithy still could not see his shadow. The highway disappeared until it reached the foothill. At the top of the hill he could see an Air Police gate at the entrance to the base. So far only one car had passed him since he had turned onto the road from the mesquite hills. He rubbed the sore area on his body, feeling the needles of pain take a definite shape. Hah! He wanted to laugh, but he couldn't. He had been kicked before by horses but the old mare really rocked him. He watched the flickering dawn rise like smoke on a windless mountain.

Smithy heard the jet sound long before he saw what was making it. Along the road a drying stream weaved in and out, crossing the road at the foothill. A bridge stood over some rocks and a fallen tree. The August dog days were beginning, and in spite of the unusual July rains, the parched Texas plains were still thirsty. Smithy had listened throughout the early morning to the sounds of the dawn. He knew the croak of the bullfrog, and the dry warning of the rattlesnake. He had kept an irregular pace to frustrate pursuing mosquitoes, and he would swing his arms across his face, around his head, fanning away flies and gnats. He did not have to look and see if he were being attacked anymore. He swung his arms and dipped his body by an inner timing, by his knowledge of the ways of insects and by the zigzag path of their flying. He did not tolerate bugs, but he did understand them. As he swung his arm around and around his head, the explosive machine-gun roar cracked the air.

The noise increased as he approached the bridge. On both sides of the road scrawly mesquites reached out gnarled limbs as if begging the sky for water. At the center of the hilltop he could make out the lighted command post of the Air Police gate.

HENRY DUMAS

Standing on the bridge he could feel the vibrations of the sound trembling the steel frame and sending tiny stabs of pain through the bandaged area on his backside. I'll never work with animals again, he thought.

Suddenly an arm of white smoke reached over the hill. Urged on by a slight breeze, it took two directions, sweeping down the hill along the mesquite range on the east side of the road and upward into the rising dawn light.

Smithy thought a house was on fire. But when he saw the strange vehicle crawling over the crest of the hill like a scorpion, he knew that he was dreaming. . . .

He shook his head but the little tractor crawled on, first behind the guard shack—sending out a cloud of white smoke that completely engulfed the shack—and then downward on the east side of the hill. Like a mechanical spider it crawled down, weaving a smoke-web that billowed into the sky.

Smithy paused on the foothill side of the bridge. He lifted his right hand instinctively as if to shield his ears from the *putt-putt putt-putt!* It sounded like a jet taking off in slow motion. He could make out a figure sitting upright on the small tractor.

When it reached the bridge, the driver, a gas mask strapped over his shoulder, waved to Smithy. The roar from the engine shot through the ground like a current. White smoke shot out from a jet-like tail and curved with the wind. The driver wore a bright red shirt and green fatigue pants. Smithy got a whiff of the smoke now and coughed.

Then the driver began to wave Smithy up the hill. He could see the man's lips moving, but he couldn't hear. Jamming his hands over his ears Smithy trotted up the hill, looking back every few paces.

Suddenly the driver swung the tractor around and aimed the blasts of white smoke under the bridge. He jumped off the tractor, adjusted some dials, and came running toward Smithy while the engine blasted away.

"Go on up!" Smithy could finally hear him. "I'll give you a chance to get up past the General's house! Go on up!"

Once Smithy paused and saw the tractor blasting a blanket of white smoke across the road. Far behind the tractor now, he could make out a row of cars waiting behind the smoke-screen. By the time Smithy got to the guard shack, he felt that his chest was closing and he was going to fall down and die. The two AP's in the shack moved out, one with his arm outstretched holding back two cars. Smithy heard a whistle blowing. The guard was motioning him to hurry.

Up the hill came the mechanical jet. Wisps of the white fog twisted and skittered as if happily separated from the main body of the smoke. A thin film of fog clung to the wet grass on the lawns in front of a circle of houses on the ridge at the hilltop. The acidity of the smoke hung in Smithy's throat, making him cough and spit.

After he had fogged the General's house and the circle of houses running along the top of the hill, the driver turned the machine off, and the silence struck the air like a million little bells ringing simultaneously. It was a long time before Smithy uncovered his ears. The guards had returned to their post. One had checked Smithy's identification. Soon the morning traffic rolled through the gates with the first rays of direct sunlight.

When the hum of the tractor's tiny engine sounded nearby, Smithy thought it was the jet getting ready again.

"You get used to it!" the driver shouted.

Smithy lowered his hands. "What you say?"

"You get used to it!" he said, lowering the tractor's engine speed and slowing down. He smiled at Smithy and pointed to the back seat on the little tractor. A seat for the jet engine operator was attached on the back. A huge fifty-gallon barrel was banded to the tractor's side with feed-tubes leading into the neck of the jet engine.

"Where you go?" he asked Smithy.

Tasting the bitterness of the oily smoke, Smithy said he was looking for the personnel office. He had worked on military posts before and he could almost find his way around them without any directions. But he didn't want to walk anymore. He felt nauseous. The less walking, the better. If he had not been so surprised and frightened at the dyno-fog machine he knew he would have been angry. He looked at the ugly gas mask flopping on the operator's back. The mask seemed dead. Not once had he seen the driver put it on. Perhaps you get used to it, Smithy thought, but he saw no sense in it. He could feel the soreness on his backside spreading a bit. It had been a physical necessity for him to quit the rodeo. Well, after all, he thought, I really didn't get started. It was like he thought, you either like animals or you don't. How many times had he tried to rope that calf? Eight, eighteen? By the time it was all over, he was limping from bruises.

"Come on amigo," beckoned the driver, driving the tractor right alongside of him. "I take you."

Smithy tried to convince himself that it was not the curious attraction of the machine that made him jump upon the seat, but rather his feet and his aching backside. He stood on the running board as the driver sped the tractor along the road. He introduced himself as Tito.

"What does this machine do?" asked Smithy.

"Oye! You got to sit down," waved Tito, turning into a large fenced area marked Civilian Personnel. Smithy looked at the ground racing along. He gripped the metal bars on the other side and leaned a bit into the wind. He could hear himself growling as the wind and the smell of the fumes from the hot engine blew into his face, growling as if he were tugging raw hide and bringing it to the dust. The heat rose.

Tito, the wind blowing his long black hair, his face squinting now in the sun peeking over the tops of the long rows of barracks, pointed to a building. "Civilian people," he said. "But they not open yet. Too early. Open at eight. You look for a job?"

"Yeah."

"What you do?"

"I used to be a stable hand for the rodeo in Hondo. What does this machine do?"

"This my bronco-jet," Tito laughed. He looked at Smithy. To Tito the fogging machine was the greatest thrill since his riding in a helicopter with an entomologist to survey an area infested with screw-worm flies. No one ever asked what his machine did. By the second time you heard it, you had asked enough people, and you knew.

"Sit down amigo. You no ride standing up. She throw you," he laughed.

When the tractor changed directions, the wind blew the hot fumes directly into Smithy's face, and no matter how much he held his breath or leaned his head, the wave of oily carbon fumes choked him. He turned his body, waved at Tito, and jumped off the tractor.

"Come on for a ride! Come on, come on!" Tito waved.

As soon as Smithy hit the ground, he felt his legs buckling. No more working with animals, he thought. He hitched up his pants and watched the tractor move over a concrete compound area filled with parked military trucks. He turned and headed toward the personnel office. If he had to wait a few hours it didn't matter. He would walk around the base. He coughed and spit. He would be careful what kind of job he got.

An air conditioning unit hummed and dripped from a window in the office. Smithy crossed the gravel path and stood in the shadows beside a row of soda machines. Already the racks of empty bottles were buzzed by flies. Even a colony of ants busied themselves on the ground under the racks. Smithy peered through the screened windows. It was dark inside. Any kind of job in there, he thought to himself, will tide me over. He had worked for Civil Service before, and he knew the routine on military posts. He would tell them he was sent down by Colonel Ashford or Captain Bailey or even General Hanson. He could see expressions now when he mentioned a name. "Colonel who?" And he would explain elaborately at first, and then with some reservation. After all, who were you if you hadn't heard of Colonel so and so?

He would take any kind of laborer's job, and after several weeks he would know every job on the post. He had a knack for things like that. Maybe that's why he tired so fast. There was no challenge and he became careless. But he would not let it happen now. No more working with animals. Even working with horses in Hondo had gotten boresome. A horse can tell if you don't like it or if you don't have your heart in all that you're doing, and the horse acts accordingly. It's the way with animals. They got more sense than they show at first. Even insects got that kind of sense.

"What are you qualified to do?" the neatly dressed secretary asked him. Smithy sat down, softly at first, then with pressure, relishing the feeling of comfort again. He almost did not mind the days of soreness now that he was getting back in shape.

"I mostly work with animals, stables, you know and with the vet."

The young woman frowned as she thumbed through a card file, looking alternately at Smithy and his application. "There're no openings under those qualifications, sir. What else do you do?"

"I am good at everything mostly," Smithy smiled. The young woman frowned. "I can work with my hands, I am a good mechanic and I know trees well. I did some gardening work . . ."

"You say you are good with machines?"

"Everything." He smiled.

"I think I know what you can do. We have had trouble with a second man. Will you work the night shift?"

"Yes."

"Then you go over now and talk to Mr. Knotterwing, area 3."

Smithy arrived at the maintenance area 3. He walked down the huge lot filled with trucks and tractors, trailers, pumps, lumber, pipes, bricks, barrels, and storage sheds with tarred roofs to a shed marked Insect and Pest Control.

A familiar vehicle was parked alongside the shack. Dismantled, minus the jet nozzle at the end, minus the saddle-like seats, the dyno-fog was the same.

Suddenly the door of the shed popped open and a tiny bespeckled head shot out. "Come right in, young fellow, come right in. They sent you down from CP, eh?"

Smithy did not like the old man calling him young, although, looking at his balding head and wrinkles, Smithy guessed he was in his seventies. He knew the pattern of foremen. Once you let them start off with something they continued it. He recalled the guy in Hondo calling him Shorty. He withheld his resentment because there was something funny in the old man's voice. Smithy stepped into the tiny shed.

"Good morning," the old man shouted. The smell of insecticides and oils filled Smithy's nostrils. He coughed and handed the old man his application form.

"Carlos Smith, eh? Well, well, I'm Mr. Knotterwing." They shook hands. "Glad to have you on the crew. Yes sir. We need some more good men."

The old man kept talking. Smithy watched him. He looked like a little bespeckled frog, five feet five, round, a perpetual grin on his face, a shiny bald head, and fat chubby hands. Smithy could not imagine that this old man could be a foreman.

He learned immediately that Mr. Knotterwing did all of the talking. You didn't even have to answer questions because if you asked one, Knotterwing supplied several answers, nodding at you to see which one was correct. He showed Smithy the layout and equipment. He described each spray can, each dusting gun, the gas masks, rows of shelves and locked closets with poisons and chemicals.

"Yes, sir, Smith, we need more good men like you on the crew. Now on your sheet it says you've had some experience with insects. That's fine. Fine. We don't require much here. Just satisfy the top brass, that's all." He smiled at Smithy when he said "top brass," and Smithy smiled back.

"Well, I see you volunteered for the nightshift. Now that's fine. Fine. We need more good men on the nightshift. Yes sir. More good men. I can see that you're going to handle things quite well, Smith. Just stick around here until the day crew gets in and they'll show you the ropes. Yes sir. Now, any questions?"

"Yeah," Smithy said quickly. "I'd like to know if the night crew has to operate that machine outside." He pointed out the window at the dyno-fog.

"Oh! That's our dyno-fog. Fine piece of equipment. A bit noisy, but effective. Does the job. You might notice that there aren't any flying insects on this post. No sir. Except those few brought in by the wind. Let me explain the principle to you. I can see you are inquisitive. That's fine. We need more curiosity on the crew. Stimulates ideas. Yes sir. Now, this is a dyno-fog machine. . . ." He spread out a colored photograph of the machine mounted on the back of a truck.

Smithy coughed and looked on.

"The principle is the same as a jet. Same. You see, we hire nobody that doesn't have a pilot's license." He smiled at his own joke. Smithy coughed. "Now, my boy, this is a remarkable machine. We couldn't keep mosquitoes and flies down without it. A gasoline carburetor ejects a spray into the neck of these coils here, see, and this ignition head fires the gas. You get your sound from this long cylinder head, and when the coils are red hot, then you turn on the insecticide, which hits the red hot tubes and vaporizes, burns up, and shoots out the back end. You get a heavy smoke that will kill a mosquito or anything flying in five minutes. Yes sir. It's just a matter of mixing the chemicals right, and adjusting the flow to the temperature of the head. Now that's our dyno-fog. It's the favorite of the Post Commander. Yes sir. General Hastings loves to know that we are doing the job. But I don't want you to swallow it all at once. Take your time. What did you say? Did they have anything like our machine where you worked at before?"

Smithy shook his head just as the door opened and in walked Tito, his red shirt half open at the chest and his eyes sparkling. He waved at Smithy immediately.

"Amigo! I see you again. You work with me, eh?"

"This is our new crewman," began Mr. Knotterwing gravely. He stood between the two men, and Smithy stood up. "Smith, this is Tito, our dayshift assistant to the crew leader."

They shook hands. Tito extended his hand, slowly, his eye lighting up and a grin racing across his lips. He did not speak anymore but went to the rear of the shed and began loading the pump cans.

"All right, Smith. I'm assigning you to Tito. He will show you what is to be done on the dayshift. You have to know that as well as the nightshift, because this shop is flexible. Sometimes you work with me, sometimes with others. You're a good man, so don't worry. Yes sir. If you want anything ask me." He adjusted his glasses.

Outside the shed a military jeep squeaked to a halt and Smithy could see through a window as two military men momentarily inspected the dyno-fog.

Mr. Knotterwing was still adjusting his glasses when the door swung open and in stepped a tall heavy-browed lieutenant followed by a young sergeant dressed in fatigues.

"Morning Lt. Doyle, sir," spoke Knotterwing.

The lieutenant, stooping his head rather than taking the chair which Knotterwing had pushed forward, peered around the shed critically for a moment, then swung his glance heavily at the little man.

"Mr. Knotterwing, I've been told that you did not get a work order to dyno-fog the amphitheater this evening."

"This evening? . . . Well," Knotterwing said and thumbed through a pile of papers on his desk.

"Afraid not sir," he said.

"You recall that I told you last month that we'd need the area fogged?"

"Lt. Doyle," Knotterwing said smiling, "I'm not a mind reader. I go by the work orders."

"Well, this is just routine. They're having a concert tomorrow evening and the General is expecting visitors from Headquarters. We'll need the entire area de-bugged before the concert."

"Well of course you know there's an inspection this afternoon too sir. I'll have to work two shifts. I'm only authorized one shift."

"Mr. Knotterwing, who's in charge of this shop?"

"That's not the point Lieutenant. I've been asking you to get me an authorization for more men. I need at least 6 men on duty, 4 during the day and 2 at nights and . . ."

The Lieutenant took in a deep breath, puckering his lip in annoyance. The Sergeant beside him stared at Mr. Knotterwing in bemused silence.

Smithy and Tito had busied themselves loading and checking equipment and chemicals.

"Well Mr. Knotterwing, you're showing unnecessary stubbornness."

With that he turned to the Sergeant. "Sergeant, I want you to go up to maintenance office and wait for a work order to be given you under my name right away."

"Yes sir." The sergeant hurried out and as he was leaving the Lieutenant was calling on the phone.

"Is that what you want?" he said after getting permission for an emergency work order from a Major Dempsey.

Mr. Knotterwing shook his head solemnly. "No," he said, "I have been trying for months to make you understand that if you want the dyno-fog working on a regular basis, I'll need somebody to operate it regularly."

The lieutenant, drawn by the activity of Tito and Smithy, directed his attention to them. "Mr. Knotterwing, I don't make it a habit to argue with General Hastings." And he walked outside and began a silent and disdainful appraisal of the dyno-fog. When the Sergeant returned with the work order, the Lieutenant signed it and put the piece of paper on Mr. Knotterwing's desk, got in the jeep and they drove off.

Mr. Knotterwing took a deep breath, got on the phone, repeated his gripes to another officer and eventually hung up, disgruntled. "Fog, fog, always they want fog! Tito, come in here!"

On their first assignment that day, Smithy sat in the hot cab of the pick-up truck loaded with two spray cans and chemicals.

"What's the job?" Smithy asked.

Tito laughed, whistled at a secretary passing along, and said, "Never mind the old man. He talk, but I show you. Now, first lesson. Don't pay any attention to what the people call up and say. A woman called in a little while ago screaming, 'My house is crawling with roaches.' The old man tell her to go next door and visit the neighbor until the day crew comes. And so here we come. The day crew!" He laughed.

"Ten to one, that lady don't have no cucarachas. I bet you she just come back from vacation and see a dead fly in the window. Be prepared for anything. Last month I help them deliver a baby. I'm a doctor now. Dr. Tito."

When they arrived at the complaint house, a woman, nearly hysterical, ran out of the house when the truck door slammed.

"In the kitchen! The kitchen!" She held a towel in her hands. Smithy followed Tito into the house. The woman followed closely at Smithy's elbow. "You won't hurt my philoden-drons, will you?" Smithy, shaking his head, went into the house.

In the middle of the kitchen floor, after a glance in the right places, Tito gesticulated. "Where are they madam?" The woman burst past them, shaking nervously.

"There!" She pointed high in the corner of the window. "There's one of them!"

The team of exterminators advanced. A tiny winged creature bumped helplessly against the window. Tito picked it up in a sample jar and nodded. Then he motioned to the spray can in Smithy's hand.

"Coat this entire kitchen with a point two residual lightly to keep down the smell." He faced the woman. "How long have you been away on vacation madam?"

"We just moved in. This is our second day here, and I have been seeing some strange bugs. . . ."

"Do you have any pets?"

Smithy watched Tito busily write what the lady said in his notebook.

"Oh no. Please, will this stuff hurt my plants?"

"No mam," assured Tito. "It is a special water-based chemical, harmless to plants, but deadly on insects. Let the air fumigate for an hour and then you may put your things back. If you have any more trouble call us. Thank you madam. Please sign here."

Speeding away in the truck again, Smithy looked at the tiny insect in the test jar. "Well, what do you know? A flying ant!"

"That's right. A queen ant. It's a wonder she didn't complain of mosquitoes. You got this job figured, eh?"

"Not all yet," said Smithy. "You tell me now, how you gonna be on both the night shift and the day shift. You got a twin brother or somethin?"

"Ha ha! I see you getting smart man," said Tito.

"And where is the rest of the crew? The crew leader?"

Tito began to laugh. "Come on man. Tito is your man. The old man is the crew leader, get it? He's the boss at all times, no matter who works. He takes all the credit and you get fired if anything goes wrong, get it? The night shift? That's you and me."

Smithy shook his head. He could feel all this shaping up in his bones, but now he was seeing it. "You mean to tell me . . ."

"That's right," said Tito. "If the Lieutenant wants to please the Generals, then you fog. Maybe sometimes the old man give us a couple days off in a row. But we gotta keep the dyno-machine runnin. That's the thing that keeps them all

fogged up about bugs. They swear that thing is killin the bugs.
Since I been ridin that machine I swear there're more bugs and
flies than ever. They breathe that smoke . . ."

"I don't think I'm gonna get used to it," said Smithy. He
hated to admit it, but his plans did not include riding bare back on
a machine like that. "Why don't you wear a gas mask?" he asked.

"You get used to it."

Smithy had promised himself to work this job as long as
they wanted him. You get used to it, he thought, but how long
was it going to take to get used to it?

The next night Smithy and Tito left their quarters, a
converted truck-shed at the end of the post which had been
remodeled for transient help. It was 3 A.M. and Smithy found it
hard keeping his eyes open. He trudged beside Tito now,
wondering what was so awful about working with animals. He
had to get up early, but not at 3 A.M. Cows and horses had more
sense than that. He coughed and spit.

The dawn had not yet broken the sky. They trudged
along the base road toward the maintenance compound.

"What is all this fuss about the General coming?"

"Man, Headquarters is gonna inspect this whole base."

"Yeah, and everybody'll be shook till they leave."

"Yeah. The more generals, the more we fog. Man, when a
general hears that noise he'll come out in his night shirt. First
time General Hastings hear it, he call up. They tell him what the
thing does and then he called us up and say, 'Come back!' and do
it once more around on his lawn. It best to keep them all foggy,
then they leave you alone. They scratching bug bites, but as long
as they smell that stuff and see it blowing, they think it must be
killing something. It's half killing them."

The cushioned saddle on the tractor rode a bit rough to Smithy,
but as long as he didn't have to bring the machine down by its
horns, he dismissed the rough ride. During the first few hours of
the early fogging, he concentrated on directing the flow of the

smoke. You had to anticipate the turns in the road and the shift of the wind even when there wasn't any.

His biggest trouble was adjusting the flow of the insecticide. Too much and the pipes clogged up. Too little and the residual would not be wet enough to stick or kill. By the time they had fogged the whole east post, had lunch and slept for two hours on a golf course hideout that Tito knew about, Smithy felt he knew how the machine worked. Yet he still could not get the ring of the noise from his head.

After fogging the inspection, Smithy was convinced of the invincibility of the dyno-fog. He and Tito had driven along the back row of men, following the parallel path of the inspecting general. They directed a heavy stream of smoke at the feet of 600 cadets standing tall, fearing to sneeze, let out their breath or breathe too deeply.

When Smithy had saturated the parade field until nothing could be seen but the stick-like rows of legs and the moving ensemble of the inspecting officers, he turned the stream off. He could not believe that anyone could last that long under the fog. "Turn it back on!" Tito had shouted, waving frantically back at him. "On! On!" And as Tito circled around for the last blast, he turned it back on. By this time Smithy could see a few of the cadets begin to stagger. The inspecting officers, standing off, pointed and gesticulated at the machine. General Hastings, his face beaming, seemed to be explaining the situation to the visiting general, who despite the handkerchief over his nose, seemed in extreme discomfort.

Normally, after a fog run in the afternoon, the night shift would have the rest of the day off, but on this occasion someone had to fog the amphitheater where a concert was to be held in the evening.

Smithy found that the gas mask was more bothersome than it was worth. His vision was greatly diminished. He could not turn his head back and forth as fast, nor could he anticipate the wind changes, nor could he see Tito's movements.

When he finally took off the mask, he found Tito slowing down and approaching the pick-up truck parked along the road waiting for them.

"Fine, fine," Mr. Knotterwing spoke from the cab. He wore a helmet like a fireman. He had seen the whole affair. "That's what they like. Give them what they want. Now Tito, I want you to take Smith there. . . . Well, well, Smith, I see you have mastered the gas equipment already. Fine. Tito, you have a good man with you. Now, you know about this concert tonight, eh? Well, now, the amphitheater is crawling with ants, mosquitoes. You and your crew must inspect it first. But if you don't have time, well, just fog it good."

Tito roared the engine, gave Smithy the signal to turn on, and drove off, waving his red sleeve in the air at everybody that passed. Smithy soon got the feeling and he too waved.

They arrived at the amphitheater that evening at 4 P.M. and made a brief inspection. Smithy jumped off and walked along a long plank inclined into a construction area. Walking under the scaffolding, Smithy could see the concrete roof and the head of a great underground dome coming into existence. A roadway led onto the roof where concrete trucks and supply wagons moved back and forth. Tito waved at a guard stationed at the front gate. The guard waved back.

The amphitheater was a huge sprawling stadium. The wide stage, standing under a saucer-like dome, caught the dying rays of the sun. The dome shone like a spaceship. The rear of the stage was undergoing expansion. Smithy walked down some steps into the theater. Across the field Tito waved at him and the little tractor, sounding against the acoustical side of the stage, roared. Tito's silhouetted arm looked like the threatening tail of a giant scorpion.

They fogged from the east, letting the heavy smoke drift across to the west. The guard on the west gate moved out of range of the smoke. Soon Tito decided that nobody would believe that they had fogged the amphitheater. The wind was high and the smell would all be gone by the time the top brass arrived for the concert. After circling the theater again, Tito pointed to the ramp which led to the roof of the new dome. It was ideal for resting the tractor and staying out of sight. Tito drove the tractor up the long ramp and brought it to a halt near a wall which overlooked the entire concave of the east side.

"We got too much time," Tito yawned. He sat down on some bags of sand and leaned his head back.

The hard riding had brought back Smithy's earlier pains. He tried to shake the thudding of the dyno-fog from his head, but even the memory of the vibrations seemed to drive him down. Sitting down he was convinced now that the dyno-fog was invincible. Hah! he thought, they like to stay filled up with this stuff. He had not seen one insect die yet from it, although Knotterwing had declared, "At top efficiency, the equipment will reduce 50% of the flying insects at a wind velocity of 2 miles per hour. And 30% of your crawling insects. It is 100% effective against gnats."

Tito had fallen off to sleep.

Smithy's eyes were burning. He lay on his stomach and watched a lone ant zig-zag. . . .

Neither Tito nor Smithy knew what sound it was that woke them. Insulated as they were from the gathering crowd, they had slept for an hour and a half, waking dream-like once or twice. The smell of the dyno-fog fumes had reassured them during their sleep. The evening arrived with a cooler wind. The guard had turned on all the lights. When they leaped up, it was to the roar of the crowd applauding the arrival of the conductor.

"Hey! Let's go man!" Tito leaped on the tractor.

Smithy, his eyes burning more now, stumbled onto the seat. The engine whined and wouldn't start. Tito cursed. He tried it again. No good. It was flooded. He ran and peeped at the crowd. Smithy waited for the signal to start the fogging equipment.

"Wait a minute!" shouted Tito. He pointed at the unfinished wall through the scaffolding. "Wait a minute! Why didn't we think of this before? Eh?" He slapped his hands. Smithy frowned.

Quickly they pushed the tractor to the opening. Just as the conductor was about to wave his baton the dyno-fog spoke its music and a line of white smoke leaped out toward the hundreds of people. A faint, almost choked and embarrassed roar swept over the cadets. The conductor, horrified at first by the sound, was nauseated by the smell.

Soon the space between the waves of smoke shortened. Smithy increased the flow and Tito directed a stream down the pathway on the ramp. He knew that mosquitoes loved cool dark places. The protecting scaffold was perfect. With this action they were sealed in from all sides by the smoke.

The reverberated roar of the jet-fog destroyed all sounds near it. Tito and Smithy could not hear the wheezing and coughing and screaming that soon marked the end of the audience's enforced composure. They could not hear the percussionist wildly beating on the kettle drum. They did not hear the siren of the Air Police who were finally summoned by the guard, who had to obey the tear-eyed General and the coughing Lt. Colonel and their wives. Neither did Smithy and Tito hear the final cries of the base fire engines. They didn't see the ambulance arriving.

Unable to reach the top of the dome, and fearing that the concert would be a flop if so many people were flushed out of the amphitheater, a group of strategists, joined finally by an embarrassed Knotterwing, decided to stop the fogger with water. One eager captain, holding a handkerchief to his nose, directed the fire truck into position so that hoses could be brought close to the dome. People rushed past coughing and stumbling. A few women screamed as a cloud of smoke swallowed them up. One of the musicians rushed past, "A plane must've crashed up there! It crashed!"

People who knew the smell could not figure out how the tractor had gotten up so high. The sergeant in charge of the fire truck ordered two hosemen to aim the hose at the top of the dome. But they were having a little trouble keeping out of the shifting waves of thick smoke. One general, gagging and holding a handkerchief over his mouth, tried to question Knotterwing who was shaking like a trapped insect.

" . . . . What do you mean harmless? You mean to tell me that . . ."

Suddenly the hose was in position. A group of airmen directed people out of the theater. Above the shouts and the blasting of the dyno-fog, the sergeant hollered and gave a signal with his arm, "On stream!"

At first Smithy thought the water was rain, but Tito didn't have time to think because the full stream struck him in the chest and he fell over. Soon both of them were sitting among the sand bags as a wall of water leaped over and fell upon the machine. It kept pouring over until the machine coughed, sputtered and stopped.

Tito leaped to his feet and looked over the wall into the faces of hundreds of people. He saw the fire truck and the ambulance. "Amigo," he said as Smithy stood bewildered beside him, "I think maybe we don't have no more job." And he began to laugh, but stopped. "Look at them amigo! Like ants."

And Smithy, rubbing his backside, watched as a procession of men marched toward the ramp. "I think I like working with animals," he said.

The Voice

We were kicking around down near the river, just walking off the feeling that came when Spencer died. We just walked around, silentlike, our hands stuffed in our pockets, mainly for style. It wasnt that cold. We were just kicking around down there, me, Willie, and Blake, trying not to think about Spencer, but knowing all the time that we were lost without him, knowing that we would never sing the same again, knowing that something had died within us as a group.

We named ourselves the Expressions. We sang gospel and blues all over Harlem. We had been together only a year, but our reputation was good and we were starting to make a few coins. It seemed the more we sang as a group, the better Spencer sang alone. He was a lead tenor, and his voice was like one you never heard before. The guy could sing. Girls, they fell out when he sang. But then one day he just got sick, and in a week he died.

We had been kicking around ever since the funeral. For a while we were spending a lot of time at Spencer's house. But after a couple of weeks we stopped going regularly. A lot of Spencer's kinfolks were still coming to the house. Some were coming from Virginia and Georgia, where Spencer's mother and father came from, and even though the funeral was over people were still dropping in. We felt that some of them couldnt understand why it had to be Spencer.

After a while things started to drift back to the way they were before it happened, like everybody going to work and school. This is what made us kick around a lot. We felt things would never go back to the way they were. How could they? The Expressions. We were the Expessions, not singing any more, not even wanting to harmonize or anything, just wearing our group jackets, which werent very warm. They were red, with the group's name in blue letters on the back. Our individual names were written in fancy letters over the left front. But all we could do was kick around down by the river.

Willie scraped a handful of snow from a piece of metal sticking out of the shore like it was a cross. He began to make a perfect round out of it, packing it slowly and neatly.

"Arnold wants to come in," he said.

Blake kicked at a rusted can and walked closer to the edge of the water. We all knew that Arnold just couldnt sing. Arnold was Spencer's brother, but he had no tone or color in his voice. Once or twice when we first got together he messed around with his guitar, but Spencer began to sing him out. Arnold couldnt sing, and Spencer was doing more with his voice than Arnold was with his guitar. He just faded out and never was around much when we practiced, but we knew he was getting better and better picking on that guitar.

We didnt say anything about Arnold. Willie suddenly took a quick leap and hurled the snowball far out over the river. It broke in the wind and splattered the water. We watched, then moved on down the shore. A seagull dipped in front of us, swung upwards in an arc with the wind, and faded into the haze over the city.

Blake walked a few feet ahead of us like he was looking for something in the sand. He was shorter than the rest of us, but he was wide and strong. Even Blake's mustache was fuzzier than ours. He had shaved once, but all of us—except Spencer, whose mustache had never started—were letting ours grow a bit more, at least to where it could be seen. Blake's mustache stood out well against the brownness of his skin. Since we were all darker than him, we would have to let ours grow. Blake told us that if we shaved, ours would grow back much faster, but me and Willie didnt do it. We just shaved around ours.

"You know what?" Willie said.

"What?"

"If I was God . . . if . . ."

"What you mean?" I asked. Willie and me were walking together now. Blake trudged ahead of us. I looked at Willie. I had never known him to talk about God except to curse.

"You know what I mean, man, you know."

I mumbled something and plunged my hands deeper in my pockets. Maybe I felt the same way. Why had God let it happen?

The river curved and we took to the streets, shifting along three abreast, not looking at the people, and crossing the streets without waiting for the lights. We had a silent pact. We dared anybody to hit us. The Saturday traffic was heavy too. A lot of people were getting ready for Easter, buying things and going places.

We didnt say anything for several blocks. We were nearing St. Nicholas Park, which slanted off the side of a cliff on top of which ran Convent Avenue. The park lay beneath a fluff of snow. The rocks—some buried deep in the ground—seemed to peep from peaks of ice and snow. Bird tracks on a few benches, the tracks of a dog and somebody walking, were the only signs of life in the park. A wind blew up from the spaces in between the Harlem buildings, and we began to feel cold.

The park was a big place and we liked to come there. Every time we used to come, a funny feeling would get us. Once in the fall we tried to practice, but the wind and the leaves made so much noise that we had to cool it. Spencer, though, he kept on singing by himself. He just kept on singing, making up the song as he went along. We gave a low harmony, but the wind was blowing so hard. When he finally finished, we patted him on the back and told him how boss it was and that we all had to learn it. The song was so good that we were kinda scared of him.

The wind whistled every now and then. We were kicking up a path in the snow ahead of us, walking through the park that we knew so well but that had taken on a strange quietness. All of a sudden Blake stopped in his tracks, stared at Willie, and said, "Only the Devil would do what's been done to Spencer."

HENRY DUMAS

We stopped near a bench. I brushed off the snow.

"Think maybe Spencer made it to heaven?" asked Willie. He didnt know what Blake was talking about.

"Remember that!" said Blake, pointing a finger at Willie for emphasis. "Only the Devil."

"Yeah," I said. "Ole Spence is in heaven, and he'll be singing to the angels up there and get up a group—"

"What kind of a God would let him die? Answer me that!" Blake walked off a piece and kicked at the snow.

"Maybe God didnt have nothin to do with it," said Willie.

"That's what I'm sayin, Willie. Didnt you hear me? There *aint* no God, man. There aint *nothin.*"

"Except the Devil?" I said. "You just said the Devil did it, man."

Blake was silent. Maybe he didnt believe in the Devil. We watched him.

"Well, man," said Willie. "Somebody has to be up there in the sky. I mean, God made us and everything in the world. Aint that right, Al?"

"Yeah," I said.

"You just like the other suckers," said Blake. "Man, dont believe everything some preacher spits in your face. There aint no God, no nothin. When you dead, you dead."

"Ah," said Willie. He turned to me for support. "I mean, I dont know about where I'm goin myself, but I believe Spencer's in heaven right now."

Blake frowned. We all moved on a bit.

"If there's a heaven, then there's got to be somebody in it," I said.

"Why so? Why so?" Blake shouted at me. "What kinda talk is that?" We had trapped him, and he was trying to think his way out. We got kinda scared of him. "If Spence went to heaven, then there must be a heaven, and if there's a heaven, then there's got to be a God to run it, right, Al?"

"Yeah," I said.

"Have you ever seen God?" asked Blake.

I was silent. We were going up a hill. A man walked ahead of us, and a big brown boxer loped among the shrubs and rocks.

"Man, you're crazy," said Willie, picking up a handful of snow. "You cant *see* God. Not even Moses could see him. But maybe you can see Jesus Christ. He was God too, you know."

"Well, I aint never seen Jesus Christ, God, and none of the rest of them people. Look here, Willie," Blake said, scooping up a handful of snow, "you see that dog over there," and we looked at the dog. "Well, man, I believe in what I can see and what I can feel." He patted the snow into a round ball. "I can feel this snow and I can see that dog. I believe in both of them. And he threw the ball. It thudded off the side of the dog. The dog jerked and turned around, sniffing the snow and the air, but it didnt yelp.

The man turned around. He was an old white man. We had seen him a few times. He lived somewhere over Convent Avenue near the other side of Manhattan. Once when we were practicing he stopped and listened.

We slowed, but he waited for us, the leash swinging in his hand. "He's only a pup," he said as we were still far away. "He wont try to bite."

We had prepared inside ourselves to fight. We moved on cautiously and the dog began ranging off again. The man reminded me of a rabbi. He had a funny-looking beard and he wasnt too tall. Even Spencer was a bit taller than he was. The only thing we were really afraid of then was maybe having to outrun a dog.

The man began to talk to us, very softly, as if he had known us all his life. We didnt speak to him. Blake wouldnt look at him. And then, as all four of us moved along the path, the man said that he had heard us singing several times and had enjoyed it.

We were cautious. We thought he was lying about seeing us. How could he enjoy our singing? We were singing soul. He was white. How could he even pretend to understand? We didnt say anything. Maybe we were better than we thought, if a white man liked our sound. We tried to walk ahead of him and get out of his way, but suddenly the dog loped in the middle of the path in front of us. Blake was up front, and instead of going around the dog, he slowed and let the man pass, and we all three lingered behind.

"Let's go see Arnold," said Blake. We stopped. The man was putting the leash on the dog.

"Come on, man," said Willie, "let's all go up on Convent Avenue."

"For what?" I asked.

Blake wasnt going to go up on Convent. He was always the leader of the group in things like knowing what to do and all that, but it was always Spencer who led us when it came time to sing. It was late afternoon, and pretty soon it would be getting dark. the man was passing us now. He was going back down the hill.

Then he shook us up.

"Did you fellows ever resolve your debate about whether there was a God or not?" he asked, pulling on the dog. "I heard you as I passed you below."

Willie and me looked at each other, but Blake drifted down the hill, as if he didnt hear the man.

"Where is your tenor today?" He was talking about Spencer.

Blake stopped walking down the hill and looked back. Willie and me stood near the man, staring at him. Then we stuffed our hands deeper in our pockets, kicked around a bit, and shrugged away, the only sound coming from the wind and the panting of the man's dog. What could we say to him? He didnt know us. He should have been afraid of us, but he wasnt. A lot of times guys will gang up on somebody who looks like money. Sometimes we'd stomp a guy just because we didnt like the way he looked. We had done it a few times, but usually on other guys.

"He got sick," said Willie, but he was looking at Blake. The man stopped. "And he died," said Willie, looking at me.

And before the man could finish expressing how sad he felt about it, Blake came running back up the hill.

"Hey, mister, you Jewish, right?"

The man nodded slowly.

"Then tell these stupid guys that there aint no heaven. Jews dont believe in Jesus, right?"

The man pulled in the dog. "Werent you talking about God at first? What has that got to do with whether or not there is a God?"

"I say there's no God. No *good* God gonna kill a guy like Spence." He bowed his head and kicked snow off a rock.

"Nobody killed nobody," said Willie. "It was some kind of disease."

"Spinal meningitis," I said.

"He knows what I mean!" said Blake.

"You're trying to get me to admit that there's no God," said the man to Blake. "I cant do that. I believe in God."

"Tell me this," said Blake. "If God is good, then everything he does must be good, right?"

"Wait, now," said the man. "Let me ask you some questions."

"Answer mine first! Do you believe in a Jewish God? Yeah, I guess you do!" Blake wouldnt give nobody a chance.

All of a sudden, Blake burst out laughing and he wouldnt stop. "Look, *Reverend,*" he said, "these guys here are my friends, see, and havent seen God, but they believe in Him. You're a preacher, so I guess you *seen* Him?"

Slowly but surely the man breathed and said, "Yes."

Oh, no, we thought, Blake had trapped him.

Blake cocked his head in doubt. He smirked and turned around to go down the hill, still laughing.

"Wait, man," said Willie. "Why you runnin away? He said he seen Him—"

HENRY DUMAS

"What do you mean?" I asked the man.

But he didnt answer. Instead he started walking down the hill. He unleashed the dog and it began to range all around. Suddenly Blake turned around and asked, "Where?"

And the man said, "Here." He pointed with his arms, sweeping the whole landscape.

Blake broke out into a fierce laugh. He bent over and groaned his guts out.

Then he started picking up snowballs and hurling them at the dog. One missed, but another one hit, and then he turned on the man, hitting Willie once by mistake, me twice, and the man several times. He was crazy.

We started to rush him, but we retreated, not because we were scared of getting hit, but from the same feeling that hit us since it all happened. We couldnt dig what this feeling meant. I guess I kind of envied Blake for doing something. He was letting it out, even though it was scaring the hell out of us.

We left the man in the park. He had shouted at Blake and us too. We fled him and finally caught Blake in the streets.

Something kept us from saying anything to him. We walked along abreast until he stopped and faced us. We were standing in front of a church, and a priest was coming out.

"So, did he tell you where *he* saw God?" laughed Blake. We kicked around. Snow was falling slowly from the sky.

"Ah, man," said Willie. "Stop being so messed up. I mean, nobody knows where Spence is except Spence."

Willie shouldnt have said that, because Blake turned on him all over again. The priest was listening to us.

"If you can see God, tell me what He looks like. Tell me," said Blake.

We were silent.

"What color is He, huh?"

"You cant see a spirit," said Willie.

"You stupid m.f.," said Blake. "You believe what that white man told you?"

"You cant see a spirit," said Willie.

"That rabbi was talkin about *his* God. *His* God is a white one. We're black. What color is that snow?" Blake pointed.

We tried to laugh and argue Blake down, but he pressed in on us. The priest was coming near now.

"Every time I see a picture of Jesus, he white, right?" We were silent. Willie shook his head.

"What you mean?" Blake turned on Willie.

"You're sayin there's a God now!" I pointed at Blake.

"Shut up, Al!" he shouted at me.

We were standing there as if we were going to fight. I got mad at Blake.

"Man, you didnt have to snowball us," I said.

"You a crazy fool," said Willie, but Blake cut him short.

"I aint admittin nothin. All I want Willie to do is to tell me what God looks like."

The priest was standing near the curb now, as if he was going to cross.

"Man, aint you never seen no picture of Black Jesus?" asked Willie.

Blake broke out into a laugh that even made me ashamed. "Dont be a sucker, man. Just because some white man come along with a bucket of paint and paint Jesus' picture black so he can get your money, dont make me fall for that jive. Not me, baby." Blake laughed.

"What bout Black Marcus?" asked Willie. "He said God is black."

"Black Marcus aint believe that jive," said Blake. "He only say that because he know niggers are stupid. You cats are suckers!"

"Ah, you crazy, man."

Blake grabbed Willie by the sleeve and spun him around. I thought his fist was going up beside Willie's head. "Sucker," he said. "Father Divine is your daddy of Grace." Willie shoved Blake off.

HENRY DUMAS

I guess we had never really thought about things too much. When Spence was here, all we did was sing and go to parties looking for girls. Willie felt it like I did. He looked back at the priest who was coming toward us. Blake was talking loud about everybody having their own different gods. The same difference between people was the same between gods.

"I aint got no God," he said.

The priest was near us now. We had heard kids call him by name—Father Wilson. Blake walked away slowly, stuffing his hands in his pockets. A few people passed and turned their heads toward us but kept going. Once an ambulance screamed down the avenue and drowned out what Father Wilson was saying. We thought about Spence.

". . . the Creator is invisible, like the wind," he was saying. "He cannot be compared to a man."

Blake turned. "What about Jesus Christ? Wasnt he a man?"

The father nodded and looked over at Blake. Blake walked near a garbage can and sat down on the lid after banging off the snow.

We followed the priest over. He asked us what had started the argument, and we told him that our friend had died.

"Yes," he said, nodding his head. We knew he probably knew about Spence. A woman carrying shopping bags passed between the priest and Blake. When she had passed, Blake's eyes were following the path of her feet in the snow.

We didnt say anything. The priest was waiting on Blake.

There was something funny about the way we were silent. I felt that Blake was thinking about Spencer. He was frowning. If there was no God, then Spence was dead and gone forever. If there was, then Blake was wrong. All of a sudden he turned on the priest and asked, "Okay, tell me, what color is God?"

"I once saw a painter," the priest said, "after he had labored weeks on a painting. It was a painting of a summer sunset over a lake. There was a house where a man sat playing a guitar. When I looked at the painter's hands, I saw all the colors that I saw on the painting. . . ."

Blake didnt say anything. He stuffed his hands in his pockets and drifted on up the street. We couldnt tell from his back if he was laughing or not. Willie asked the priest something, but I watched Blake.

Then we heard him yelling: "You guys comin? What's the matter, huh?"

The priest stood near us, but neither Willie or me dared look into his face. We waved at Blake to leave us alone, but there was something in his voice. We kicked off up the street behind him, leaving the priest there. We didnt worry about the priest. Religion was his business.

We thought we were mad at Blake, but deep down we sorta respected him.

"Man, what's the matter with you?" I said.

"Yeah, man," said Willie. "You scared of gettin made to look like a fool?"

Blake walked ahead of us, crossing the street against the light and telling us to shut up. But he didnt seem to be mad, only confused. We believed in something but didnt know how to say what it was. Blake believed in something and was saying it. He must have done a lot of thinking about all those things, but he still couldnt figure them out, especially since he liked Spencer as much as we did.

"I'm goin to see what Arnold's doin," he said.

We followed behind him. He knew we would come. Going through the streets toward Spencer's house was like coming back to places we knew before. Right then I thought I didnt want to hear Arnold's nowhere voice. And I didnt want to be thinking about all the good days of the Expressions. Willie was feeling the same way. He pulled me aside, and we stopped for a couple of minutes for an orange drink in the candy store a block from Spence's house.

"You goin up?" he asked.

"You?" I asked.

And neither one of us answered. We walked on down the street. When we came to the stoop where Spence lived, we just went up the steps and on up the stairs. Spencer lived on the top floor. Blake had already gone up and was almost up the last flight. We stood looking up from the first floor for a while.

We heard the bell ring and the door open. I thought I heard a few guitar chords, but it didnt last. We heard the heavy voice of Spencer's father from the back. When me and Willie got up the steps and into the house, we could hear a lot of voices. Spencer's father shook our hands like he always did. He liked to treat us like men. We went in and his mother began kissing us. She wasnt crying, but there was a strain in her voice. Several people were seated in the living room. All three of us were introduced as Spencer's friends, the singers. They made us sit down, but we didnt want to.

"You boys sit down," said Spencer's father. "Arnold be right up here—Arnold!" and he leaned his head toward the hall and the back rooms.

"Arnold! The boys are here!"

I glanced around the room. The two women and a man were looking at us. One of the women I had seen before. She was Spencer's cousin. I didnt know the others, but the man and woman on the couch had something familiar about them. Blake was moving toward the hall. He stood looking at Spencer's mother as if he was asking her permission to leave. She was a short, dark woman, with a sparkle always coming out of her eyes. She was quick to cry and quick to be glad over anything that she liked. We liked her. Sometimes she called us her children.

"If my children dont sit down," she suddenly said, "I'm going to have to ask them to sing us a blessing before dinner." And she stood up smiling and went out of the room.

"In my church," said the man, "I have a group like you boys." So he was a preacher, I thought. I knew there was something familiar about him.

"I need a drink of water," Blake said, going back toward the kitchen.

Nobody heard him, because Willie was talking about the priest.

"Well, what I really dont understand is if all the religions believe in one god, why there isnt one religion," Willie was saying.

"There *is* one religion," said the minister with a smile. "But everybody has his own private interpretation of God's word. We all have to worship God the way our conscience tells us. If you got a clean heart and you can ask a good, honest question, God will answer you. He never failed yet. Dont worry about all the confusion of religions and the babel of tongues. They're all man-made. God has one religion and He's always on time."

He was a pleasant sort of a guy. Not like a lot of the ministers we'd seen. He had a Southern accent, but it was pleasing and he wasnt too old. I kept looking at Willie every time he would ask a question. He was *really* trying to find out things. The minister was talking about the young man who came to Jesus, asking Him what he must do to get into the kingdom of heaven. I thought about Spence.

I got up and went back to the kitchen, where Spencer's grandmother was cooking. The smell of roast chicken and dressing filled the hall. Memories of those feast days at parties and church affairs filled my mind. From the kitchen came the sound of a guitar. I could hear Spencer's mother saying, "Go on, go on," and the grandmother saying, "Hum. The Lord blesses good singing," and I came into the kitchen. Blake was standing there beside Arnold, and Arnold was picking that guitar.

Soon the women went back up the hall, and we didnt say much. Some feeling was pulling us. Arnold was picking loosely at the strings of the guitar as if he was inspecting them. Blake just stood there for a while, his big chest puffing out and his eyes blazing. Then he broke off into a chorus. I couldnt help but follow, and Arnold was right there and it was a good sound. We were singing "The Hills of Love," the song that Spence got that day in the park.

Then, coming in from behind us, was Willie.

We sang from our souls, and before long everybody was standing round listening. Spencer's mother was trying not to cry. And then all of a sudden Blake caught a note, and we all heard it and we came to his aid. We got to feeling good, and the people backed us up with some hand-clapping. Spence should have been there then, because we were all singing and making one voice.

Thalia

The mind knows only what lies near the heart.
—Paraphrase of an old Norse saying.

Somehow I heard the snow begin to fall even before it began its slow feathery descent. I thought of the sweater of wool you made for me. I was sitting upon the damp tree where we always sit, the tree with the notches carved from the first limb down to the roots. You know the tree, the tree where I wrote to you and you cried. And afterwards the tree broke the silence of winter that year, and shook away the fist of ice that paralyzed it. Remember how my knife bit into the bark and the tree bled, and you sang warm verses? The same tree I sat beneath, and I heard the wind, hoarse from barking all winter, but cold and ruthless. Maybe it was the wind that told me that the snow was going to fall. I cannot say, for I was listening for your voice. Everywhere I turned I saw you, and whenever I reached to touch you the touch of passion told me the truth, that you were gone and I must bring you back. Thalia, every moment you were gone has been like time racing backwards into a darkness I care not to try to remember.

As soon as I felt the snow I rose up and crossed the field to your house. And there I stood for an hour looking in at the empty house, recalling how you always looked inside, and how you came from it to greet me and how you departed from my vision and my arms to the warmth of the house. Soon your father discovered me standing outside. I looked like a pillar of snow, a snowman sprung up out of the yard, I imagine, and he hurried me inside, chastising me for inviting a chill. Inside you embraced me, and I never heard a word your parents said until your brother came downstairs putting on his coat.

"Let's go over to the Club."

I asked him what was over there because I didn't want anything or anyone to take your closeness away, but he begged

HENRY DUMAS

me to come, if not for my sake for his, because he anticipated being bored by the discussion and wanted to have some reason to leave. You know your little brother, and for you I rose up and we went out together.

"I am writing Thalia a book of songs tonight," I said, "and just as soon as you are bored I want to leave."

As we drove along the streets the snow increased. "Take me quickly to my house, only for a second."

He didnt ask any questions but drove to the house and I went upstairs into my study and shook the snow away from me. How close you felt to me then. I closed my eyes and searched around the room like a blind man. I had not forgotten where I kept the sweater, but I wanted to discover you. Thalia, how I miss you, and I touched blind fingers against the window. (Oh, if your brother saw me I know he would confirm his suspicions of my lunacy, and yours for loving me, but he never said anything, caring only to observe us, as you well know, with his impartial botanical eye. Sometimes I think he believes that we are plants, trees entangled, I hope.) And my fingers found you, warm! I discovered you. And I put the sweater that you made with your hands, I put it on and pressed it so hard that the woolen sparks went into my flesh and burned my skin. I covered you with a warm coat and went out into the snow.

There was a crowd at the club. I looked at the great face of my watch. It said 1:00. But I remembered that the club never opened until 12:30, so all the people standing out must be gathering for something special or my watch was fast.

We went in and found several friends at the Lounge, waiting for the activities to begin.

I watched them all in the great mirror that hung over the blue ceiling. I began to feel cold and distant. I wanted to leave, but I had promised your brother, so I ordered something hot to drink and drew you closer around me. The big clock on the wall showed the time to be exactly 12:30. I looked at my watch. It was very fast. I was about to set it when a group of girls came into the Lounge and, after briefly talking to several others who were all drifting off to the activities, they came over to me.

There were eight of them and they asked about you.

I closed my watch and watched them through the mirror. The warm drink slid down inside of me and drove out the cold, and the sweater pressed in close locking out the cold forever, and I looked at them waiting there and I felt you tickling me, and I opened my eyes very wide and they looked into them. Suddenly they were gone and I saw you in the mirror briefly, and I took out my pen and wrote a song to you.

Your brother was delivering a speech to some group, and while he spoke I listened to you sing beneath the tree. I am so peculiar sometimes that I don't hear people unless they speak of you or quote your verse to my ear. I think perhaps this is unfair to other people, Thalia, but I do not care. If I could not find you somewhere then I would depart outside the universe and search for you everywhere.

With all the songs I am making for you I will make one great song and sing so loud and so sweet that you will come back to me, for the world of reflections is hard to bear sometimes. I do not know how long my mind can deceive my spirit, nor how long my body can remain warm. Thalia, my beloved, when I sing my song, time will stop to listen and his racing feet will bend to the ground. The sea will blush and turn a thousand colors and breathe glass spheres that hold your image. Thalia, my beloved, and I will come down to the sea singing you up out of broken glass.

The eight girls suddenly entered the room and sat down together in the back. Your brother seemed not to notice them, but others in the room turned to glance at them. A discussion period began after your brother finished speaking and soon people began to leave, but the girls stayed. I dared to listen to the discussion.

"We live in a world which has made love a beast that stalks the mountains and valleys of earth seeking whom he might destroy."

But this is only a phase which is a part of the dissolution, the evil which affects us.

"What evil?"

In my speech I spoke of the transformation of power, from the gods of power to the god of power, that power is none other than the obsession to creation. Man is obsessed, not toward creating but toward creation. The gods of power were worshiped in early times and man was inspired toward creating. He created everything to the gods of power, not because he loved, but because he feared. Then the god of power, the force which united the strivings of man, began to breathe upon man, and he became obsessed toward creation. By this unity man began to see himself and love himself, and love God and respect God.

(Thalia, if he was saying that since that time God has loved us, then I will make a song to God also.)

The discussion went on.

". . . . The evil that has returned to the earth is the evil of the death of the god of power. What will follow, no one can say, but I am sure it will be a terrible time. Man will be obsesssed again to create, and there will be chaos and destruction. Instead of another transformation, there will be a dethroning. The force that drives man to discover creation will no longer exist, and man will be driven by the evil powers of imitation.

"How is this evil?"

The beast which stalks us now is not driven by a desire to understand himself, but to satisfy his hunger, which is not one hunger but many. He has no respect for the diversity of creation. His end will come when he devours that which is poison to him.

"Love?"

I did not hear the answer to that question for I was leaving the room. When I got outside I saw that the eight girls had also grown bored and were filing out. They mingled with several young men at the Lounge. I watched them through the mirror.

Then I went outside and sat in your brother's car. "We live in a world which has made love a beast that stalks the mountains and valleys of earth seeking whom he might destroy." The voice echoed in my mind and I wondered what your brother was thinking about this. When he came out I asked him, but as hard as I tried, I could not bring myself to listen to him. Every time the snow struck the windshield I watched it cling, thaw and melt into spring water. A warm sensation hurried from the arms of your sweater and churned inside of me, and while we rode I sang song upon song to you, upon the dead explanation of his treatise.

I looked at my watch. It was 2:00.

"I'll buy you a drink," he said.

"Only if I pick the place."

"Okay, where?"

I guided him to the little place outside of town where they play music that haunts you in your sleep. Remember? That place where we discovered a book of songs in the one solo of the bassist?

After your brother had had one small drink he wanted to go. I tried to persuade him to stay until we heard the song you liked, but he insisted. The atmosphere was too wet and loose, too slimy and incoherent. I felt cold suddenly and told him I would go.

Thalia, how impossible it is for even those who are close to us to know how it was with us. Forgive me for that thought of wondering if they are supposed to know. My watch was running fast again, how fast I do not know. Again I was watching the snow melt into rivers that flowed down like your hair spreading in front of my face, and I breathed, you came, I was warm.

I took my watch to a watchmaker.

"You have broken it," he said.

"I know," and I saw your face in the crystal.

"You will need another watch," he said.

I looked at it. "Yes, this one runs too fast or too slow."

"No," he said, "it does not run at all."

All day long I wrapped myself in the sweater you made for me. I began to study the design in it and the red trimming traveled around me like a river of blood. There was fire in you, and when I looked at my broken watch again I knew that the wool shaped by the touch of your fingers was turning into my skin. I lay upon a bed of tears and sang a song that Thalia might know wherever she was that I loved her only, that I was obsessed by the creation of love, that none would ever touch me if I climbed outside the cell of time and slew the beasts with every song that you gave me. All the day long and the night through I sleep in the shell of your kindness, and I could hear the armies of the sea roaring up out of the mist of time and my eyes were opening in the dream that brought you close to my bosom, where I made you as warm as you made me.

There was a crowd gathering on the shore, a crowd of shapes like children running. They paid no mind to me as I approached them. The games engrossed them so that when the mist began to creep in from the sea they did not notice.

First they made war against the sea, leaping and charging naked into the green waves. Then they dragged a great fish from the sea and up onto the sands and danced around it. When they saw me they hailed me to join in. I went to look at the dead fish. They built a fire. But they sang no songs and their voices were like the croak of dying frogs. Soon they began to play in the sand. One muscular boy carried eight great stones; from off the land they all built a fortress. They hailed me and invited me to join in. The mist hung over our heads like a curtain about to fall. I went to the edge of the sea and listened, but I could not tell them that I heard you singing out there. My heart leaped, for as naked as they were, so was I; but on me there was the touch of fingers designed upon my skin.

They looked at me and began a discussion and I could not bear to listen to their croaking. My ears were tuned to the sea, and whenever I stooped down I could peep through a line of separation between the sea and the mist of the sky, and along the line was a bright light dancing into shapes and colors. How beautiful was the specter out there. No one noticed it but me, and while the children played their games of life and death, I scanned the horizon with my eyes and leaned my ears out to sea.

Beneath the rumble and the roar of the vast blue expanse I thought I heard what I was trying to hear, and what I was trying to hear was what I wanted to hear. Then I could not hear anything but the croaking, and no song grew louder in my ears until I went to the edge of the yellow sands and waded out into the water. The waves roared in under wings of foam, and Thalia, I knew your ship was coming over the line in the sky, but the children were calling me and their voices were angry.

I watched them build a fortress and make war. I watched them tear it down and dance around it. All the time I leaned my head out to you.

Up the beach the children ran. They passed me by and locked my arms to theirs, dragging me for a mile. They laughed and squealed and their voices began to cut my ears away. I heard a sound of breaking glass inside my mind. They were drowning out the rumble and the roar of the vast sea, and driving you further and further away from me.

When I could not stand it any longer I took my watch and flung it at them and stood to watch. But their games engrossed them more than me, and they played on and on, up and down the shore, and the mist hung lower and lower.

The Metagenesis of Sunra

Rain God

Cud and me are running so fast that the two birds over Ned's head are slowing down in the sky and now they are passing behind the low cloud, which must be the one sprinkling these few raindrops on us, but we are still running faster than the drops, me and Cud. They know where the Devil is at.

Cud is ahead because he aint afraid of the Devil, but I am, and we are running along the fence and Cud is leaping over. I am sliding on the little slope beside the fence, catching myself on the leaning old fence post, pulling up, and then I am standing high on the fat fence post, looking at Cud as the big hole in the seat of his overalls shows his black skin and his legs roll away over the field. Ned is standing near the stump waving at us like he found the greatest secret in the world, and I am standing higher on the post, puffing, stretching out my arms like a bird so that I can see if I can *see* the Devil beating his wife. If I can see from here, I am staying here.

I am a waterfall flying off that post and I must be a river because the fence is shaking like the dead trees did in the stream when we were fishing. A waterfall can put out the Devil in a hot Hell, so I am running faster, and then the sun stands on top of me and then hides his head again and you should see my shadow leap away from the side of myself, just like when I was swinging from the oak limb on Cud's rope yesterday, and higher and higher! and I'm gone. . . .

Look at Ned. But I am looking only at Cud when he slows down. What's he slowing for? He must see something. Ned stops waving me on. If I really see this Devil I'm gonna be scared of *everything* for the rest of my life.

But Cud he sees something and he keeps seeing it and now he's waving and it is my turn to see but I am slowing. Then I am running faster and faster as the sun comes out over the center of the field, like a fat pillar of golden air and the rain is catching up with me and I can see it on the grass and feel it climbing over my muddy bare feet, cleaning the stink off. . . .

"Hurry, Blue!"

"You missin it, man!"

What they yelling me on for? They see I'm coming, and while I'm coming I strain to see what they see, but I don't see nothing but the sun shining down from the sky and the dark field all around shaking in the wind and the rain striking across the light. And on the grass I slide and I am there!

"Look!" Ned is crazy.

"They dancin!" Cud, he crazy too. He leans in on the stump, squinting at two figures, like little carved dolls, on top of that old stump. It's an old stump, rotten, and a hole is right in the center. The rings for age are around that hole, which is a rot hole, and the rings are like little ditches. Splinters and twigs stick out of that stump, but not like the two figures dancing in the light around the center hole, and when I see it I close my mouth shut. Then my mouth drops open on its own, and I feel the rain spirits soaking into me.

Ned is whispering:

> If in the rain you find a snake,
> The Devil's will you sure can break.
>
> But if in the rain you find the sun,
> The beating of the Devil's wife's begun.
>
> Turn the snake on its back,
> Lay the snake out on a fence.
>
> The Devil sure to lose your track,
> And you bound to keep your sense.

HENRY DUMAS

And Cud is whispering a little, and I am shivering because the sun *was* hot, but now it is rain-cold, and the little dolls on the stump are dancing faster.

I see the Devil dressed in red, swinging a whip around his head, snorting smoke when a rain drop strikes, striking the other on the back. The Devil's wife is dressed in white, and the Devil's wife is falling, and she falls. . .

into the hole. But she catches the edges of the stump and the Devil pulls her up, and gets on top of her and I am watching him straddle her, and then I hear a scream and the wind is slashing me with rain. Sun is gone, just like that! and in the field I am alone. Cud and Ned are racing away, yelling, and when I look at the stump, only the twigs dance in the wind, slow, back and forth, growing bigger and bigger as the sun flicks off and on, off and on, clouds running, and both of them are getting taller and taller, giants with hands so big that the fingers are reaching for me now, and then I am stumbling over my legs, leaping with my heart which I can feel driving a river all over my body and I fly.

They are way ahead of me and I don't know what's in back of me and don't see anything but the Devil chasing me, and at home I am puffing out everything, watching Cud's eyes and Ned's eyes when we all climb on the back of Papa's wagon, which Papa is driving into the yard, and I know it's my turn to feed the mule, but I still am puffing when Papa gets down and that's my papa, he knows everything.

". . . . Yall git your chores did 'fore it start lightnin."

I am puffing and Cud and Ned climb down, but I cannot stop puffing and Papa hears me puffing and I can't talk because the Devil is still chasing the road, and I point into the sky where the sun is setting and where the rain is still coming and going.

My papa don't care nothing about it and he is saying, "Boy, that ain't lightnin!" and I am still puffing and then I have to get off the wagon, and they all looking at me.

"Rainin and sunshinin at the same time," says Ned, and he whispers something to Cud, who don't say nothing except work his mouth. And Papa says, "Rain under the sun, you stick a pin in the ground, and put your ear to it and you can hear the Devil beating his wife."

"We know it," says Ned. I tell my papa I know it, and my head is nodding up and down, up and down, dizzy, and I have to say it.

I have to say we didnt hear the Devil beating his wife this time because we see him do it and my papa is looking at all of us. He is going to holler at us but he dont because he sees something . . . maybe over our heads he sees him coming . . . and maybe out of my eyes too, raining, and I have to tell him, but I dont right then. . . .

"How come he beating her?" I ask. My papa is unhitching them mules and we all around him, and he tells us the truth, and the truth is because it is raining and sunshining at the same time.

The rain spirits are coming strong now, and my papa, he says, "All you got to do is stick a pin in the ground or a stump and put your ear to it and you can hear the whole thing. Now y'all git and do them chores!"

But we are standing there, dripping, which is a lot of rain by now, and I feel a river rising up in me and I see Cud's eye and Cud, he looks at Ned, and Ned, he looks at me, and I am licking my bottom lip with my tongue, tasting the sunny salt in the rain, and I am going to be the first to tell him. . . . I'm going to tell my papa we see the Devil.

The Bewitching Bag

or

How the Man Escaped from Hell

(An Afro-American Folk Tale)

This is the story of the Devil's bewitching bag.

A man died and because during his lifetime he had prayed mostly to the Holy Ghost, neglecting God and Jesus Christ, he went to Hell. On his way to hell, he prayed, as was his habit, to the Holy Ghost. While he was praying to the Holy Ghost, for it is always the Holy Ghost which comforts the distressed and those condemned, the Spirit breathed upon his soul. Nevertheless the man had to continue his journey to Hell, for to deny the Godhead in life is to deny one's holy ancestors.

When the man arrived at the edge of the great valley of Hell (for Hell is down and the Heavens are up), he was weary from travel. All along he had heard the voices of spirits going and coming. The road to and from Hell is always filled with moanful sounds. In the center of the valley was the city of Satan and soon the man found himself compelled to travel toward its great shining steeple, which was the castle of Satan the Devil, ruler of the whole kingdom of Hell.

Well now, it came to pass that he arrived at the castle, and since it is the business of the Devil and his servants to know such things, they were expecting the man. The gates of Hell opened and the man went inside.

At this time, however, the Devil was not in Hell, but had left instructions to all his servants and demons to care and guard the city while he was out on his routine journeys. For those who do not know where Satan was, then I must tell you again. He was tending to matters on earth, going to and fro seeking whom he might recruit for his service. Indeed, Satan had long been known to spend more time on earth than in Hell. So by this time things ran smoothly and Hell was ruled as if the Devil were actually there.

All his servants and demons feared him and obeyed him, for if they were disobedient the Devil had warned them:

> He who raises the master's ire
> Will suffer in the Lake of Fire.

On the morning before the man arrived Satan had left for a tour of the world. On this brief stay in Hell he saw to it that all souls were suffering properly and none of his servants were planning escape.

Now the Devil had a beautiful daughter. And because she had once visited earth as a little girl, and had seen the Holy City, she was filled with a Godly love for it. Of all the cities that are great upon the earth, none can compare with the Holy City of God.

Now it happened that Satan detected a change in his daughter. One day he had said, "Why is it that you sit and weep? You do not inflict pains upon those condemned to the Lake of Fire anymore."

"I am unhappy and I do not know why," she replied.

The Devil looked at her and said, "You have a fever! Then I will find out why," he shouted and stomped off to his secret chamber.

He returned with a magic bag, called a bewitching bag. Now the Devil took the bag out into the courts of Hell and there he spoke to the bag. This bag is like any kind of bag except that when you command it to do a thing it will fly up on a golden string, and it will do that thing. So the Devil commanded:

> Jump up my 'witchin bag,
> Jump down my 'witchin bag.
> What's east, my 'witchin bag?
> What's west, my 'witchin bag?
> Name the fever in my daughter's chest

The 'witchin bag sang:

> I see three castles in her eyes,
> One is the other and three in the skies.
> The fever burning in her soul
> Is what she saw in the . . .

"Don't say it!" shouted the Devil, for he knew it. He clasped his hands over the 'witchin bag's mouth and locked it back in his secret chambers.

"You are sick with a God-fever!" he condemned his daughter and ordered his servants to bind her up.

With this he stormed off to his chambers of sorcery and magic.

Now the Devil had a secret stable where he kept three special horses. The first horse, named Lightning, was the fastest, being able to travel 100 miles per hour. It is on Lightning that the Devil toured the world and other realms in space, seeking souls and hiding in dark places. Now the stable was located deep inside the castle and the only one who knew where it was, besides the Devil and his faithful servant, was the Devil's daughter. But the key to this stable he gave to his most trusted servant.

Having instilled the fear of fire and brimstone in the city, the Devil departed in a gleaming invisible chariot, leaving behind a long trail of black smoke.

The man was confined to a room to await judgment when the Devil returned from his journey. Now this room was right next to another room where the Devil's daughter was locked. By and by the man could hear sobs through the wall. Thinking that the noise he heard was the souls of people condemned to Hell, the man prayed to the Holy Ghost, and the Holy Ghost, being in fear of neither the Devil nor Hell, came unto the man and breathed Comforting Grace. When a man is condemned in Hell, he is not lost until God Himself declares his soul lost.

Now there was a door between the two rooms, but it was shut tight. The Devil had condemned an evil spirit to guard the passage between the doors. Anyone passing through the doorway without saying a certain password would immediately be condemned to the Lake of Fire.

Now all this crying that the Devil's daughter was doing became louder and louder, and the man, because his soul was not yet lost, felt sorry that he could not help. Thus he began to sing a song which he knew from his mother. It was a song that her mother had sung and her mother before that and so on back into the holy generations. The song goes like this:

> Majesty of Majesties, come as
> The tidal seas.
> Bear me up as a high cloud
> In the sky.
> Protect my children in
> Their greatest needs.
> Forgive this sinner never
> To know the seas.

Now the Devil's daughter, even though she was weeping, could hear the man singing in the next room and it took her no time to figure out that it was the man who had just arrived from earth, for she had seen him from her window which opened toward the road that goes to and from Hell.

Now the Devil's daughter put her head to the door and spoke the man's name, for she, being the Devil's daughter, knew such things. No sooner than she did this the man began to sing louder, for he thought her voice was a spirit, which in many ways it was. Now the evil spirit which protected the door from passage had power over the Devil's daughter as well, but the louder and more beautiful the man sang, the more the singing made the spirit become drowsy. The Devil's daughter spoke the man's name louder and the man sang louder. So beautiful was the song which his mother had sung to him that it put the evil spirit to sleep. As soon as the Devil's daughter saw that the invisible spirit had fallen asleep, she tiptoed up to the door and tried to open it. But it wouldn't open. So she whispered the man's name and asked him to push it from his side. The man, thinking the voice he heard was an angel, pushed against the door with his shoulder and lo and behold the door opened and he was inside the room of the Devil's daughter.

The spell over the spirit was broken when the man stopped singing but once you pass through a door in Hell, no one can bring you back, because you have seen the other side and no guardians can come after you. You have broken their rule.

Thus the Devil's daughter and the man got together and made a plan to get free of their predicament. Their plan was to escape before the Devil returned, but they had no way of doing this.

Now the Devil's daughter was as smart as she was beautiful, and knowing that the guardian spirit at the door would be listening to them, she and the man laid a plan.

Now here is the way Hell was set up in those days. Nowadays Hell is so full of people that none of this is so, but in those days Hell was made up of places called "chambers." Now the place where the Devil kept all his secrets and his sorcery was in his chambers. For you remember in the beginning he went off to his chambers before he left. In these chambers he kept every kind of magic in the world and out of the world. Some were made by him and some he stole. Being the Devil, we should understand that he stole most.

The two prisoners, as that is what they were, thus began to sing aloud:

> Happy shall be all the souls of ire
> When the Heavens shall fill desire.
>
> Freed from perdition, both saints and sinners,
> When the end begins beginners.

Happy shall be all Lucifer's servants
Bearing the lights of holy savants.

No more days in burning Hell.
All earth shall hear the bell.

Rung by the angels flying high
Nevermore to suffer or cry.

Happy shall be all the souls of ire
When the Heavens shall fill desire.

Now when the evil guardian spirit heard this message, he was happy and flew off to spread the news, for this is the interpretation of what the song meant: That the Holy Gods and angels were going to free every saint and sinner in Hell and the great war of good and evil would be declared, and as all of the ancient oracles had said, the war would be won by the forces of good.

Now of course all of this was a trick. And when all the servants in Hell got the news, they were surprised. All of them believed it except the one who was the faithful servant of the Devil.

Not only did he disbelieve, but while the others were rejoicing and creating a loud noise all over the dark city, the faithful servant of the Devil, an especially ugly demon named Uggomugo Wilson, went to the Devil's stables and got on the second of the Devil's horses.

Of all the horses in the world, this horse, whose name was Thunder, could go faster than any other except, of course, Lightning, and the Devil was at that moment riding Lightning over the earth seeking whom he might capture or whom he might devour or whom he might entice, for this is the business of the Devil.

Now in his haste Uggo forgot to lock the stable, leaving the third horse, named Fourwinds, alone.

Now Fourwinds was known for his speed and his ability to leap. Of all the horses in the world none could go as fast as

Fourwinds, except, of course, Lightning and Thunder. Now here are the speeds of these great horses which the Devil held in his stables: Lightning, 100 miles an hour as I have told you, Thunder 80 miles an hour and Fourwinds 70 miles an hour.

By and by the servant of the Devil and his followers arrived at the chamber where the man and the Devil's daughter were locked up and he asked her what she would give them if they unlocked the door with a key, for being the Devil's daughter she still knew many secrets. Now the servants of the Devil did not know that the man was with her, nor did they suspect them of plotting to escape.

"You have not earned a whole reward, but only a half one," she replied. "What is it you wish?"

Then the faithful servant of the Devil made his offer. "You must become my wife while the master is gone."

Now the Devil's daughter had known all along that the faithful servant of the Devil was planning to usurp all authority, and now this was the perfect time. She had to be careful.

"I'm flattered," she said, "but you do not give me time to think it over."

"I will give you seven minutes," said the 'faithful' servant of the Devil, "and while you are deciding I will sit outside this door."

"But you cannot marry half of me, since you have not gained a whole reward," said the Devil's daughter.

"Well, I will marry half of you now and the other half after we are married," said the 'faithful' servant of the Devil.

By this time the man, who had been trying to figure a way to help out, spoke up. "Tell him that you must consult the spirit of the Oracle in order to get the blessing. Tell him you must sing to the Oracle and that he might stay and listen. And that whatever the Oracle says, he must do."

The 'faithful' servant of the Devil was so eager to marry the Devil's daughter that he consented, whereupon she and the man began to sing this song, which the man whispered in her ear:

Masters of the tidal seas
Sailing under a bridal breeze,
Begin the beginning with beginners
Bringing all the saints as sinners.

Now the Devil's daughter could sing as well as use her brain, as you already know, and her voice was so beautiful that soon the 'faithful' servant of the Devil was asleep, and while he was asleep, she changed the lyrics so as to trick him.

Masters sleeping on their knees
Under the door push the keys.

Even in his sleep the 'faithful' servant of the Devil knew he was being tricked, but the spell of the song was too much. While his left hand was pushing the key under the door, his right was grabbing his left elbow and pulling it back, but the prisoners sang louder. Soon the key was under the door and immediately the man snatched it up.

Thus they made their escape from the two chambers. They locked all doors behind them and found their way through an underground passageway which the Devil's daughter had known since she was a girl. The passage headed toward the stables. "We must hurry!" she said, "for my father's servant has taken the second horse, Thunder, and is riding at this moment to warn him of our escape."

"How do you know this?" asked the man.

"If you listen you can hear his hoofbeats galloping far, far away," she said.

Even as they were hurrying along the dark passageway, the man could hear the walls shaking as the great horse, Thunder, traveled on his mission with the faithful servant of the Devil riding his back.

Now when the Devil's daughter came to a chamber hidden away in the walls of the tunnel, she recognized it as the

HENRY DUMAS

one which contained many important magic things. With the special golden key she unlocked the chamber and looked around for something to aid her escape.

"What will we need on earth?" she asked the man.

"We'll need feet to run with and eyes to see with," said the man.

"What else?" she asked.

"We'll need good memories to remember the words of songs."

And so now here is what they did. The Devil's daughter found inside the chamber the bewitching bag and a little purse with three seeds inside. She gave the bewitching bag to the man and hurried out the tunnel to the stable.

As I have said, the great horse, Fourwinds, was left unguarded and the two prisoners were able to get on their way. But it was not a minute too soon.

No sooner had they both climbed on the back of Fourwinds than the faithful servant of the Devil woke from the spell and set the whole of Hell loose after them. But do not underestimate the power of Fourwinds, for there was never a horse like him. Just as the man and the Devil's daughter reached the edge of the Lake of Fire, the demons and souls from Hell poured out behind them in pursuit. By the sound of their roaring, like a pack of mad dogs, you knew that vengeance was on their minds, for not only had they been tricked, but they would have to face the wrath of the Devil when he returned.

Now here is something that you must always remember about this story. Traveling as fast as he could (and who really knows how fast that is when a good horse is in a hurry) Fourwinds leaped, and when he leaped it was over the Lake of Fire.

Now you get this picture, which is the sight of Fourwinds leaping out of Hell and leaving behind a horde of demons who were bent on casting them all into the Lake of Damnation.

"We must hurry," said the Devil's daughter, and she urged the man on. For she knew that in a very short time her father would return, and would do everything possible to get them back, even if he had to destroy Hell doing it.

Sure enough, when the Devil heard the news from his servant, he flew into such a rage that bad weather sprung up all over the earth, causing hurricanes, tidal waves and every kind of trouble. The Devil was so angry that when he got back he not only flung all his servants into the Lake of Fire, but his faithful servant too.

"Why do you condemn me master, when it was I who was faithful to you and brought you the message?"

"Because you did not stay here and put down the rebellion, and because I am tired of your ugly face." And with that, he flung his last servant into the Lake of Fire. And when he had done it, a silence reigned over Hell such as had never been heard before. "I will capture the man and my daughter and make their children my slaves," he said, and rode off in hot pursuit.

Before he left he went to his chambers and found his most important one opened and missing were the purse with the magic seeds and, above all, his bewitching bag. And this made the Devil sorely angry.

Now all this time the man and the Devil's daughter were riding on the road which is called the road of Grace and it is this road which the Holy Ghost had whispered in his heart that he should take.

But the Devil is not unknown to travel on this road too, and he found it soon enough and began to gain on them, pushing Lightning to travel as fast as he could, and whenever Lightning got tired, he would jump off and run back and ride Thunder, who was close behind, and when Thunder was tired he would jump off Thunder directly onto the back of Lightning, who had caught up by this time. In this way the Devil steady gained on the two being chased.

By and by they knew their danger. They could hear the hoofbeats and the lightning flashes coming closer and closer. It was at this time that the man felt his dread coming back, and he would pray and sing his song, and the Devil's daughter would sing with him.

But their singing did not stay the Devil, for his anger was hotter than any fire in hell, and he wanted them back in Hell lest he be without servants. If this happened, he knew that he would have to stay in Hell himself and not be able to seek over the earth.

"Now is the time to use the bewitching bag," said the Devil's daughter, "and here is what you must do." And she told the man.

So the man held out the bewitching bag in his right hand and held the top of Fourwinds with his left, and he sang this song:

> Jump up my 'witchin bag,
> Stay up my 'witchin bag.
> Make me eyes my 'witchin bag,
> Over skies my 'witchin bag.
> Jump down my 'witchin bag.
> You see him?

And the "witchin bag said, "Yeah, I see him."
And the man said, "Well, how far is he?"

> Along the road passin a toad,
> Comin fast, bringin storms.
> Along the road passin a shack
> Hurry, hurry and don't look back.

Now when she heard this, the Devil's daughter opened the purse and dropped one of the magic seeds. And it turned into a great patch of briars and thorns so thick that not even Lightning could leap over or pass through.

And the Devil he cursed and he lurched, fumed and stomped, but on magic seeds he could do no magic deeds. That's when you got the Devil tromped.

So the Devil had to turn around and ride all the way back to Hell and get an axe out of his chamber. Then he rode back to the briars and cut a path for Lightning. And it took him a year to do it. By this time the Devil's daughter and the man were passing into another road, called the Road of Hope.

But as you know, the Road of Hope has known its Devils too, and so when the Devil passed through the obstacles they had sown for him, he began to gain on them.

Pretty soon they could hear the hoofbeats and they could feel the weather becoming evil, and they knew that any minute they would be captured.

"Now is the time to use the bewitching bag," cried the Devil's daughter.

So the man held out the bewitching bag and he sang:

> Jump up my 'witchin bag.
> Stay up my 'witchin bag.
> Make me eyes my 'witchin bag,
> Over the skies my 'witchin bag.
> Jump down my 'witchin bag.
> You see him?

And the 'witchin bag said, "Yeah, I see him."
And the man said, "Well, how far is he?"

> In the desert blowing dust,
> Your 'witchin bag 'bout to bust.
> In his hand he got a hook,
> Keep on goin and do not look.

But before he could stop the Devil's daughter had dropped the second seed, and it turned into a great sea, so wide and deep that it was impossible for even the Devil to cross.

So the Devil had to ride back to Hell, and he returned with one burning cinder from the Lake of Fire. Now as you all know, the Lake of Fire is the hottest thing burning anywhere, and just that one cinder was enough to set the seas to boiling until they had evaporated.

So the Devil had defeated two of their obstacles and resumed his pursuit, more determined than ever now to capture them. He drove his spike-spurs into the sides of his horses when he was riding them, and under this goading it is no telling how fast they traveled. It is certain that they ran far over what they were used to doing, but each time the Devil spiked the beautiful horses the spike went nearer their hearts.

Now the man and the Devil's daughter had entered the Road of Illuminations, and of course it, too, was no obstacle for the Devil, for out of much evil sometimes comes illuminations. And the Devil's great shadow gained on them, sending a shiver across the whole earth.

The man knew the time by now, and he said:

> Jump up my 'witchin bag,
> Stay up my 'witchin bag.
> Make me eyes my 'witchin bag,
> Over the skies my 'witchin bag.
> Jump down my 'witchin bag.
> You see him?

And the 'witchin bag said, "Yeah, I see him."
And the man said, "Well, how far is he?"

> In the desert blowing dust,
> Your 'witchin bag 'bout to bust.
> In his hand he got a hook,
> Hurry, hurry and do not look.

So the Devil's daughter knew then that this was their last chance. The last seed she dropped, and the man said to her that they would say a special prayer over it. So they both got down from the horse and sang a song. It was the same song they had sung before.

And that seed turned into a great mountain, such as there never was before on the earth. It was so high and so wide that nothing could jump over it, nothing could go around it, nothing could go under it. Now this time the Devil knew he was stomped, and so did the man and the girl, but it takes more than magic to stop a Devil from accomplishing what he sets out to do. Many of you know that a Devil can be a most obstinate person when he wants to, and there ain't nothin you can do about it but let him alone.

Now the Devil had to go back to Hell and he went into all his chambers hunting for something that would take him over, around or under the mountain. But he found nothing. While he was sitting concentrating on the situation in his chamber room, he saw a hole in the ground. Now in this hole there lived a little worm called the Slander Worm. And the Devil had a plan. He dug into the ground, captured the Slander Worm, and then leaped onto his horse and the chase was on again.

When he reached the mountain it had grown bigger. But as you know, a little worm can eat his way into the tightest of places and cause all kinds of trouble, especially if it's a Slander Worm. Now the Devil commanded the Slander Worm to bore through and eat a hole in the mountain.

And sure enough, this tiny worm, boring night and day for two years, finally made a passage large enough for the Devil to ride through. By this time though, he was raging, for he had lost much time.

Both the man and the Devil's daughter were now very tired. They had gone through Grace, Hope, Illuminations, and they were about to give up when they came upon the Road of Love and Respect, a wide road with a golden pavement. For a long time they rode upon it, but when they heard the sound of thunder and hooves beating behind them, shadows fell over their faces. Closer and closer the Devil came.

And the man took out the bewitching bag and rubbed it and held it out:

> Jump up my 'witchin bag,
> Stay up my 'witchin bag.
> Make me eyes my 'witchin bag.
> Over skies my 'witchin bag.
> Jump down my 'witchin bag.
> You see him?

And the 'witchin bag said, "Yeah, I see him."
And the man said, "Well, how far is he?"

> In the shadows coming fast,
> Blowing dust and cinders past.
> In the middle, in the top,
> He'll be here when I stop.

Then the Devil's daughter said, "We should be near the place I told you about now."

She made the 'witchin bag jump again, and it reported that up ahead there were three large castles, one at the end of the road and two on opposite sides of the road.

"Who lives in them houses? Will they give us protection?" asked the man.

But the Devil's daughter said, "Hurry!" For coming down the mountain now was the Devil, and his anger had swollen him so large that the hook he was swinging at them was as close as an inch is to a ruler.

They jumped off Fourwinds and ran up to the first house. They knocked on the door. "Who lives here?" asked the man.

"God, the Father," said a voice. "What do you want?"

"The Devil is after us and we want you to save us."

"Go across the street and tell my son."

They ran across the street and knocked. "Who lives here?"

"Jesus Christ," said a voice. "What do you want?"

"The Devil is after us and we want you to save us."

"Hurry down to the house at the end of the road."

When they knocked no one answered, but the door opened and they went in. When they got inside they knew that it was the house of the Holy Ghost.

No sooner had they left the first house than the Devil was right there. But when he heard the answer, he fell backwards because the name of God is too much for the Devil, and just the thought of His name drives the Devil mad.

He went across the road and knocked. But when he heard the answer there, it drove him backwards onto the road, for just the name of Jesus Christ is too much for the Devil.

But he was still determined. So he went to the last house. This time he said, "Good master of the house, I am on a mission from the Father and the Son. I bear messages for the two you hold inside. I am Lucifer, the bringer of Light and News."

But there was no answer from behind the door. The Devil knocked again, shouting that he had news and that he was a messenger. But still no answer.

Then he asked in furious anger, "Who lives here?"

And three voices sang from inside:

> The Holy Ghost,
> The Spirit of Truth,
> In the name of the Father
> And the Son and the Holy Ghost.

At that, the Devil fell backwards, for the name of the Holy Ghost is too much for him. He could not stand it.

When he fell backwards, he fell into a great abyss, dark and deep, so deep that it has no bottom, and the Devil kept falling, and when he hits bottom one day the whole earth will hear him moan, and there will be a day of celebration, for if a person can escape evil, it is a time for rejoicing.

HENRY DUMAS

My Brother, My Brother!

Mtaka is my brother. What he feels I feel. I do not have to look at his back to know that the sun is baking him too, nor do I have to look in his eyes to know what they are saying. We have reached the impala's trail. I can smell the sweat from their hides. They have left dung and urine. Mtaka is marching along at my side as he has done since they turned us aloose. I do not want to kill Mtaka, nor do I want to kill any of them even though I would say that if there were any who deserved to be killed, it would be the invaders. They have sported with us since they arrived, and now they have a new game. We are the chosen pair. Mtaka and me, who have the love of brothers.

Over that way I can see a herd of oryx. Now they are running. Mtaka sees them but we cannot stop to watch. Behind us is the strange invisible wall which the invaders call a force field and it chases us so that we must travel without stopping to the river and then to the center of the island. If either of us should die or be injured before the game, the invaders will throw our family from the ships in the sky and they will fall and die. So we must go on and stay ahead of the force field. It is useless to resist. They will reward one of us with Grazaza, who is the most beautiful of women.

We have crossed the trail and are heading down the long slope of ilsa grass and bak shrubs. This is the way toward the river. Mtaka and I will have to swim the river. But we will use a log. One of the strange things about the invaders is that they seem infinitely smart and infinitely stupid at the same time. The dangers of swimming the river do not seem to be apparent to them, for they have never saved any of our people from the crocodiles or the snakes in the river. They have not allowed for the time it takes to make a raft. Many times our trackers have been caught by the force field and suffered severe burns from it. That is why Mtaka and I are moving along at a steady pace. If we were to resist, the invaders would kill us both and our family too. There should be a way for somebody to resist and escape into the forest, but there seems to be no way of hiding from the lights and eyes of the invaders. They are everywhere. At night they are like the stars used to be.

Mtaka and I are naked. We see the green gleam of the river now. We hear nuksabird and the wa beetle. The nuksabird sings oheeeeeeeeeg! oheeeeeeeeeeg! and stops. When it flies to another tree, it will sing again. The wa beetle guards the dung of the impala and the oryx and the others that eat grass. The wa beetle makes a clicking noise like this, *tik!* and that is all. Mtaka is slightly taller than I, but we are equal in strength. Our skins are baked well by the sun. We are dark brown, and our family marks almost the same size. No one can tell the difference except that Mtaka's first tattoo on his right arm is wide because it did not heal well. The iron tongue on my thigh spoke too deep. It did not heal well either. I could not lay with my woman for several days, and this was an unfortunate thing.

We are walking along the river's edge toward the narrow gap. We look for logs.

"My brother Yetubwa, I have a plan," says Mtaka.

"If it is a good one, my ears will cherish it."

"Is it not true that the invisible hand which they send behind us never slaps backwards?"

"That could be true," I say, "but we have no proof."

"But this force field never returns. It goes always forward."

"Then how do the invaders control it?"

"They bend it when it goes so far."

"But what is your plan, my brother?"

"Let us begin to build a raft, as others have done to deceive the watching eye. But when we feel the force field upon us, let us not leap into the water as others have done, but rather withstand the heat until it reaches its end, and just before the

HENRY DUMAS

field passes over us and kills us, let us dive with rocks to the bottom of the river."

Mtaka's plan sounds workable but I have a question. "Mtaka, which of our ancestors revealed this plan to you?"

Mtaka does not speak to me. He is silent. We hear the roar of a lion and our hands reach for our spears, but we hold only air. I am walking ahead of Mtaka now, along the narrow path made by animals who drink from the river. This plan of Mtaka's is dangerous because we cannot be sure the force field does not slap backwards. If it does we will both die as well as those in our clan.

Finally Mtaka reveals where this plan comes from.

"While we were marching across the trail of the impala beasts, a voice spoke to me in the ear on which the sun shines in and said, 'I am the mouth of your great father Uhagjumono. Obey and save us all from destruction.' And his voice told me of this plan."

"My brother, do you know that Uhagjumono is the evil one who once led our people to worship the invaders?"

"I have heard this. But was this not the trickery of the invaders and their machines?"

"Uhagjumono did an evil thing my brother, for many of our clan died from his treachery. Do you not recall what they said at the council of elders?"

"I recall. But no one knows the ways of the invaders so that we can determine their weakness. My brother, I feel that this is a trick. Uhagjumono seeks revenge on our people. All the spirits who follow him are enemies of our people."

"It is not a trick. I listened to his voice. It did not waver. No voice contradicted him. It is true, Yetubwa."

We do not argue. It is forbidden for two brothers to argue over the ancestors. We must put it to the test. But we are at the narrow part of the river. We can see the island, sitting like a boat in the center. On that island are the flat plains where the invaders focus their great lights at night and watch the games. We do not have much time. By the sun the force field is not far away. Mtaka pretends to look for logs. It is absolutely necessary that we stay together in whatever we do before we reach the island. But now Mtaka is doing this thing. If we delay, the force field will kill us.

We find a log. I am silent. Mtaka is bringing vines from the side of the river. We hear the nuksabird above the sounds of the jungle. We know that we must hurry now. I push the log out into the river and let the cool water climb slowly up my body to my waist. My arm is around the log and I wonder what weapons are waiting on the flat stone of the island.

"My plan is a good one," whispers Mtaka. He is dragging a pole for the raft. "We must try it. The invaders do not suspect us."

But one thing Mtaka is forgetting. Even though the invaders might be ignorant of how we receive help from the spirits, they know that the spirits speak to us. They have talked with those who have grievances and seek revenge. It is known that the invaders used the spirits against us. Mtaka knows this and I am not sure why he trusts the voice. I do not trust the voice of Uhagjumono. I do not know what to say, for the terror of the world is upon me. There is my brother and in him, I see myself and all that is great with our people. Here we are. Both of us, and the hand of the invaders is tightening around our throats. How does the jungle manage to laugh at a time like this? The time of the sun says that we are only minutes away from the invisible wall creeping behind us like a forest fire.

I push out into the river. I hope that Mtaka follows me. That is all we can do. One of us must live.

"My brother." That is Mtaka calling me. "If we can escape, we can break the spell of the invaders."

"I do not trust the voice of the evil one, Mtaka. It is a bad omen."

We have delayed too long. A stinging heat strikes us. Mtaka falls, and wraps the vines around his body. He whispers and evokes the sacred name of our fathers. From his mouth he issues the sound of a trance and he calls his spirit guide and I see a spirit riding Mtaka. He rocks Mtaka, moaning back and forth. The hand of fire is coming. I am holding the log. Mtaka, Mtaka. Come with me. Trust me, Mtaka Mtaka, but he is testing the power of the invisible hand which slaps so hard it kills, and I am kicking the log back to shore, wading out, begging for the sun, which is below the trees now, and the pressure of the force is getting greater. In a few minutes we will be dead, and I am calling on the spirits to aid me, and I fall in the vines, which begin to steam, and the wa beetles are clicking louder and louder and when they stop, we will have only a few seconds to live.

I am talking to Mtaka, pleading with him. I am blowing in his ears, and touching his tattoo marks on his face to break the spell he is under, but I cannot, and now I am doing a terrible thing. I am dragging Mtaka to the river. I am breaking the tribal custom which does not allow you to touch a person who is under the trance, but to me this is an evil spirit and soon I am pushing Mtaka in the water and I am pushing off into the river as the death fire of the invaders stops the song of the wa beetles. We are in the middle of the river, and I am thrashing with my legs, driving Mtaka on the log ahead of me, and I know that he has been burned.

The beasts in the river do not like the heat which is so close upon us. I become dizzy and my head forgets which way I am going. I am calling on the spirit of the water in my mouth to help our people. I am cooling off and the island reaches out and pulls both Mtaka and me onto its lap, like a hunter does the impala beast he has just slain and is skinning.

I am weeping for Mtaka. His is weak. His arm is around my shoulder and I am dragging him to the flat stone. What else can we do? The sun has fled and left the sky filled with the eyes of the invaders, and as I drag my brother over the soft sand, I can hear the weird sounds of the invaders' flying ships as they hum. Their lights, like stars, are increasing as they turn on eyes to watch.

They have given us spears. I am weeping the river. Mtaka is my brother. He is weak and cannot fight. He will die soon.

And they will kill me because they have not seen a fight. They will throw all of them from the flying ships. I cannot let this happen, and I am breathing into Mtaka's face that we must fight, we must fight, but he is . . .

Mtaka is not dead. He is watching me. His eyes are open. Now they are shut. His skin is hot. I step away from him. He grunts. Mtaka is pretending. He is not as weak as he seems. More lights come on.

Then the invaders signal with their shrill pipe that the contest is begun. I am standing. But Mtaka is crawling to the flat rock where the two spears lay. He is crawling. . . . Now he is up, and grabs a spear. . . . He aims it at me and holds it . . . but he doesn't throw. I do not move. My eye fixes on Mtaka's eye. You will not throw at your brother, and he throws!

He is weak. I see the spear and evade it. Mtaka grabs the other spear and aims it. I run to get the one he has thrown. It is stuck in the sand. I pull it and see my brother coming toward me with his spear. The invaders are making noises which hum, and this means they like the fight, and my brother Mtaka has fallen on the ground, and he is moaning, and I raise my spear and I approach him, and he looks up at me, and I am thinking of her when she comes and I will tell her of my brother and she will cry and I will go to sleep between her legs and I will cry, and the sprits will say to me, *Take This Woman and Make Children*, and Mtaka tries to get up and I am standing over him with the spear and he sees it coming and I watch the blood leap out at me from his chest and when I scream it is like the loud, loud, cry of the nuksabird.

The Metagenesis of Sunra
(to Sun Ra and His ARKestra)

No man has yet been able to dig the exact time of Sunra's birth. Scholars have pondered and measured documents and sounds created by the instruments forged by his fire. Some people sing a song which says that Sunra was the sperm cell which the Creator gave primeforce to in the beginning and after his union with his other half, Sunra grew up out of the earth among the sun-burnt, among the people of ashes, among the despised and wicked, among the people so black that they were blue. And it is among the Bluepeople that Sunra gained his early impressions of the world he was to reshape.

Then there are those people who sing in their songs that Sunra was not born but was made, not as one makes an object, not as the earth makes a tree out of a seed, not this way, but in the way which sound becomes energy and energy becomes sound. That is, by metagenesis. And the metagenesis of Sunra is said to have come about through the intercourse of the sun with the comet X, which has been seen traveling through the universe only three times. No one knows where this strange visitor comes from nor where it goes. It travels at impossible speeds so that when it is near, time goes backwards. All things become new. The first time it entered into our dimension, it collided with the sun, many thought by accident of course, but when no explosion followed, when a great shadow fell over the planets—as a curtain is drawn over a place of love—it was known that the Creator was giving breath to a womb and the time-studiers predicted that new music would someday come from another dimension.

The second time comet X visited our dimension, it left a luminous vapor around the planet Venus. The vibrations from Venus since that time have grown stronger and stronger; yet, since they are only tiny electric pulses, the scientists and time-studiers cannot determine much. Among the Bluepeople there is a song which says the metagenesis of Sunra is related directly to the third visit of the comet X when it came as close to earth as the moon. Every human witnessed this great purple force above the moon spinning with such a velocity that it made the moon shine brighter, so bright that the moon shone during the day. This period lasted for 40 days and is known as the Time of the Two Suns.

So you can see that the birth of Sunra is a tradition. It is not a mystery in the sense that its nature is completely unknown, for all people who can radiate wavelengths of variable lengths and distances understand that Sunra's music is his birth and his birth is our music. To know one thing is to know all things. To hear is to feel. To taste is to speak. To exist is to swing as a child from a long umbilical rope on a tree, and from that height the child knows that he is a bird, because he is. The birth of Sunra is like that.

For the notes we are going to sing here, we will play Sunra's birth and his message this way:

The white Wof, Nyck, used to rage up and down the coastline. He was a great wicked beast who survived the traps and the resistance of the Redpeople who he had decimated. In the winter the wild Wof was fiercest, lapping the blood of his victims off the snow and the ice, tracking the wounded for miles, and often hunting them in packs. So thorough was the Wof in winter that a fear spread amongst all the painted people that it must be slain at all costs. And so this is what they did. The Redpeople, who had come from the land of the sun by way of the north, made music from skin and smoke and sent brave warriors to the land of the spirits beseeching the ancestors for help. The Bluepeople spun songs from their own blood and their own bones, and asked the wisemen who sat upon the silent drums when would be the time of the skinning of the great white Wof. But no answer came from all the spirits save this one:

When the acorn wears a crown,
The evil oak must not come down
A child into-its blue-black night
A people intuits sonic light

For centuries no one would sing this song except the priests and drummers. The Wofpack believed that their power over the painted people was absolute and endless, that their god, who dwelled in the Kingdom of Ice, had ordained that the flesh of the painted people should be the food of the Wofpack. And so the Time of Endurance set upon the Blue and Red people, a time in which many rivers of blood and trails of tears were etched among their low lands. And the people toiled on and on, humming the wavelengths of songs remembered from their mothers' wombs, for when a child is born amongst the Bluepeople it is a holy time; priests chant over seed and the drummers ease the child's passage. But the prophesy remained buried, safe inside the bowels of the people. It trembled on the lips of babes, but ventured no further. It hovered in the air when death struck his cymbals but retreated back inside the people. It transposed and altered itself and all the white scientists (children of the Wofpack) mimicked the cries, believing that their ears were nets and that their tongues were whiplashes, believing that their howls were songs.

And then one day a woman, Panta, who was descended from the Redpeople, labored in her bluesong with child. She sang the memory of her husband, descendant from Bluepeople, who had been devoured by the Wof Nyck. As she rested beneath the arms of the oak tree Rak, she could feel the child inside her, hear the child's lips making sounds and she knew that soon would be her time for deliverance. And she sent out prayers for the message of the drum. But she was a long way from her people. Her flight away from the city of Nittok in the south (where great flesh camps and icefactories thrived) had brought her north. The northways all led to the Kingdom of the Ice King, so that the woman's weariness was not her enemy but her friend, for if she had continued on, perhaps, this story would be different. Who knows but that it was the wise singing of her son in her womb which warned her body and bade it slow? Even the oak tree Rak, knowing by way of sonic law that certain vibrations coming from the woman were voices from the spirits, spread out his arms and shook down a blanket of leaves for the woman's deliverance. As the bluesong of her labor increased, the earth trembled, and everything living and non-living was *into-it.* All would bear witness to this birth.

And Nyck, looking more like a man than a Wof, heard by his instruments that the Bluepeople were being blessed by the ancient spirits, and being ever anxious to devour and maintain his authority, he measured the distance to the great tree Rak, and traveled to it. He arrived to hear the final chorus of the woman's bluesong, and when he looked upon her essence and upon the miracle of her body and the homage of the trees and land, he grew cold with anger and jealousy. He descended upon the woman in her helplessness and swallowed her whole, so anxious was he to destroy her music. But inside of her womb, the child had already made his plans. For this child was Sunra.

Heeding the bluesong of his mother, Sunra hastened from her womb, and she, dying in the mouth of Nyck, gave her last rhythm to her son. And Sunra felt it was a song of his father. See this sign. It is the sign of a babe in the fanged mouth of a beast, and what did the babe do? And what did the babe sing? Having heard with his blueears the summons to come forth from his imprisonment in Time, Sunra reached back into the belly of the beast with a blue-arm, and touched a bone, and brought forth the bone, and it was a thigh bone, and he reached again and brought forth a bone and it was a blue-bone and he propped them both in the mouth of the beast. Nyck roared and tried to close his mouth, but the strength of the bones was too much. Sunra, naked, crawled from the mouth of destruction, and the earth sang a song for his coming: one verse for the memory of his father and mother and one verse for the fulfillment of the prophesy:

HENRY DUMAS

When the acorn wears a crown
The evil oak must not come down
A child into-its the blue-black night
A people intuits the sonic light.

And Sunra stood in the light of day and sang louder than the death whimpers of the beast. He took the blue-bone and pierced Nyck through the vacuum where his heart should be, and in rushed the breath of life and killed Nyck and all his corruption spilled out and his hide lay waiting in the sun.

A child and a babe, a learned sage, a hunter, he took the other bone from the mouth of Nyck and the beast's fangs fell shut and cut off Sunra's umbilical string which had stretched from his mother to his own belly. And there was Sunra, a prince and a priest, *the music who makes the musician.*

Now these are the days of Sunra during this time, for he became known as the Terrible Child, feared by the enemies of the painted people, loved by their friends. Of course chief among the enemies of the people were the children of Nyck, for it must be remembered that the Wofpack was numerous, and they believed that their king had given them a divine right to rule over all the peoples of the earth. So it is during this time that Sunra began his ministry telling his people that there was to come a time in the near future when the Wofpeople would feed upon the Blue and Red people no longer. It was written in a prophesy. Whenever he spoke this, he would take out his long bluehorn and his bonelute and he would attach the bronze cord from his belly to the end of the long bone and he would anchor the bone against his thigh, and when the pressure was just right, he would pluck the cord and the people would hear the music and it taught them. When he had another thing to tell them, he would take the bone that he saved from his mother and he would place it across the cord and stroke it, and a sound would spring up such as the people had never heard, except in their womb memories, and Sunra would spend days teaching the people thus, and then he would take the omega of the cord, attach it to the alpha of the otherbone and he would shoot himself away like a marksman shooting an arrow. When he was gone to another city, the sun would come out. During these days the people awaited the visits of the child Sunra, for he brought them hope and restored their perceptions for he taught them to believe in the impossible thing. He taught them to believe in death as a dimension of sound.

Once Sunra was in the midst of his own people and they were toiling in the icefields of Berg, a great northern city which employed Bluepeople from the south on the pretext of sending them to a happy land to work among their ancestors. The trick was this: When the Bluepeople arrived in trainloads from the great city of Nittok in the southern deltaland, they were given a test on paper, a test which confounded their sense of sound and tone, and as you know, few Bluepeople or Redpeople ever passed this evil test and so they were hired as day laborers, to cut slabs of ice six feet by three feet wide from a mountain of ice. All who failed the test soon found themselves in debt to the Wof owners and hirers, and soon were locked behind a series of ice walls, reinforced with the metal alloy called steel, and these large camps were called factories. Sunra found himself among his people one day in the city of Berg. Now let me tell you a bit about this city of Berg, for of all the cities in the Kingdom of the Ice King, this city could not be surpassed in wickedness against Sunra's people.

A decree had been issued that all those entering the city for the first time must show their willingness to obey the divine rulership of the king by a 6-day "freeze." Most Bluepeople and Redpeople were used to "fasting," and so they thought that "freezing" meant the same as "fasting," but great was their horror when the truth struck them down.

Here is what is meant by "freezing" in the icefields of the Wofland. A soul comes into the city in one of the iron trains or labor cars and at the edge of the city, he is ordered to strip. Every single soul must go through this ritual. If you can survive the better for you. Of course many wisemen have questioned the validity of

HENRY DUMAS

what one should do in such a case. Anyway, a Wof-guard drives you with an ice lance to the freeze line, which is a frozen ridge of water about six inches wide and thick enough to support the weight of one person if that person is not too large. Below these lines of ice are great metal jaws that move like a beast chewing. Now the people on the freeze line do not see this. There is no light and the movement is silent. Those who enter the freeze line must cross to the other side in six hours. If they can manage to stay on the slippery freeze line over six hours, without reaching the other side, then they are automatically frozen there. They eventually fall slowly to hang bottomsup, like bats in a cave. The whole Ice Mountain is filled with thousands of caverns with victims like this and whenever there is a famine in Wofland, there is always plenty to eat. The scientists have measured and studied the prevailing patterns of "freezing." Only one third of those entering the "freeze" reach the other side to become laborers in the icefields. Half of those who do not make it fall off and become gristmeat in the vast underground machinery. Some women and children make up the larger portion of those who do not make it across. Of those who "freeze" the majority are women as well. So this is the kind of city that Sunra, the Terrible Child, arrived in.

On the journey to the icefields Sunra had sailed the spirit of the people with song. He created a song which only the people could understand and the wavelengths struck their ears and their blue souls caught fire and this is the flint of the song:

> The lives into it are evils through it
> All the pain shall turn to rain
> Tears shall flow, wind shall blow
> Into it we make mouths that eat into it
> All the pain shall melt to rain
> Into it the evil lives
> Tears shall flow from ice and snow
> The lives into it are evils through it

And the people ate this song, but there were no real words to it. The transcription that you have read or heard is only an attempt to allow you a bit of the feeling of how and what the sounds were saying, for they meant far more than the words, being as you know, *meta-music.*

The sound which Sunra generates from his bonebow so astonished the guards at the gates that they were paralyzed themselves. And when all the people began to dwell upon the electric energy of their own consciousness, then a great force was added. And this is what Sunra could do.

Now there was one great child of Nyck, a direct son of the old Wof, who had devoured Sunra's mother, Panta (May the spirits handle her soul in blue). He resisted the power of the song. When the force of the Bluepeople had melted all the ice lances of the guards and left them wandering around in a zombix (a state of temporary insensitiveness wherein many wofguards fell into their own gristmills), this Wof, whose name was Nykson because he was the son of Nyck, retreated out of range of the power of Sunra the Terrible Child and spread a general warning that the city was under attack by the Bluepeople led by a Demon Child. . . .

This is the time called "The Time of the Fast" and it is remembered because not one soul was lost, but all crossed over and survived the ordeal of the fast. Needless to say, Sunra, hiding in their midst then, began to teach them. He was forced to move from village to village, from forest to forest, constantly fleeing the alarms set off when the Wofguards caught up with him. Nykson was now the appointed guardian of the icelances and a special decree from the king had given him the power to hunt down this terrible child and slay it before it upset the world. At this time Sunra was busily trying to prepare the people, and since he knew that his days were numbered in the flesh, he taught and fasted and communed with the spirits of his ancestors. He went among the people at night, even disguising himself and working in fields with them.

Once he disguised himself and hid in the great storage chamber where all the slabs of ice are stacked. He wanted to see

HENRY DUMAS

what was the purpose of these ice slabs, so he got inside the hollow portion which a blueworker had carefully chiseled out. Sunra closed the lid and waited. Soon many slabs were on top of him. He fasted and kept himself warm by gently stroking his cord and by humming from his insides. Soon he felt the ice slab moving and when he peered through it from a little hole he had made, he found that he was under a great dome with lights and all around were Wof scientists and they were examining and codifying each slab as it passed one conveyor belt and at the end of the belt was another belt, which met at the point where a third went off and this is what Sunra saw: The bodies of Bluepeople, Redpeople and Yellowpeople were being stuffed inside the slabs of ice and shipped on to the third belt which took them up a long height which Sunra could tell went into the belly of the mountain. No doubt the Tomb of Preservation.

From this point on Sunra began to burn with a blue anger, for this was his time. This was the time spoken of by the ancient prophets:

> A child into-its the blue-black night
> A people intuits with sonic sight.

And he knew that his growth was upon him. No longer was he the size of a child, but now took on the dimensions of a great youth and he struck terror in the eyes of any that saw him, including his own people. It was then that he knew it was time for his great journey. He knew that if his people were to ever be saved, then it would have to be by the power of his bonelute, and he went upon his journey which fulfills the prophesy.

The Journey of Sunra

Now there have been many things said about the journey of Sunra, and no doubt as you all know, there are many versions of what happened. But what concerns us here is the fact that

Sunra had to make the journey to obtain the blessing of his ancestors and to plant the seal of the prophesy.

When he took leave of his own people, the Wofpeople had issued alarms and decrees, and there was a price on the head of the Terrible Child, but of course Sunra had grown, and he could walk among the people with less of a disguise than before. The Wofpeople wanted him at all costs because he had caused them so much mischief, disturbing the peace and timidness of the Bluepeople and the Redpeople with his bonesongs which were vibrations from the ancient times.

His music was such that the Wofpeople became drugged by it and in time it permeated all the provinces and any person walking in the day or night could feel and often smell the music. For the Wofpack it was an unpleasant feeling and an alien smell which they went to great lengths to destroy, even employing Bluepeople themselves to detect and to counterattack it with special chemicals and wofmusic. But nothing could eradicate the power of Sunra, for each day he grew in strength, wisdom and insight. When he took leave and began his journey, all the people sang a song. They did not know where he was going or if he would ever return. All they knew was what the songs had said, and that the prophesy had to be fulfilled.

With his two blue-bones Sunra set out. No longer was he a child, but a great warrior, and he had learned better how to use his two weapons. Not only that, he had also learned to use the natural weapons all around him and so most of the time the bone of his father and the bone of his mother remained strapped to his side and slung over his shoulder. Many times, instead of using his bones to escape or defeat a pursuing Wofguard or Nykson himself, Sunra would concentrate his energy on one thing and call upon the spirits to witness and assist, and they would, and often one note or chorus from his instruments would be enough to seal the intensity of the wavelengths.

Pretty soon the pursuers would find themselves surrounded by an ocean of water. Many would drown. Once

HENRY DUMAS

Nykson himself barely escaped this method of Sunra's, and he vowed that he would pursue Sunra to the ends of the earth. He even vowed that he would pursue Sunra outside of the earth. So it was not to Sunra's surprise when after two days on his journey, he found that he was being pursued by a fierce Wof patrol.

Now at this time Sunra was passing through a region called the Land of Haasabird. Now a Haasabird is one of those high flying birds which have no larynx, and no chords in their throat. They are silent birds, who fly high in the sky, searching eternally for the opening in the heavens. A legend has it that when the Haasabird finds the opening in the heavens, a voice will descend and teach them how to sing again.

Now Sunra was traveling through this cold green land. It was filled with rivers and forests, but it was a silent land, for neither beast nor fowl dared disturb the silence, so great was the unhappiness of the Haasabirds who ruled this region. Now when Sunra entered the land, the silence was oppressive and he swore that he would find the reason for this and he did.

He found an old hermit who lived on a mountain and the hermit told Sunra the story of the Haasabird. And it was after this story that Sunra took out his weapons and began to make music. His sorrow for the Haasabird was almost equal to his sorrow for his own people. There are no creatures on earth who can exist very long without the sound of their own souls. And so Sunra played. He played for three days and three nights and each day the music grew louder and louder until it went into-it, that is, until it reached the dimension of the Haasabird and then all the Haasabirds trembled, fluttered on the ground in great ecstasy, sailed up into the sky, and just as Sunra stopped playing a great sound filled the heavens. It was the soul of the Haasabirds, enraptured by the searching sounds.

From that day on the Haasabirds began to sing, and nowhere on earth can you find a song as beautiful and as lofty as that of the Haasabird. When the enemies of Sunra passed through the region, the music they heard was so alien to them and so powerful that it confounded them. They all became crazed, and fell into the state called zombix. When they came out of this trance, they knew the power of Sunra, for he had escaped them and was on his way to his destination.

The destination of Sunra was the great Msippi Valley in the region called Nittok. Many adventures did he have on this journey, but that is another story. The thing that we must understand in this story is that a prophesy had to be fulfilled and so that is what I must tell you about.

Now when he reached the great valley, he went by instinct to the place where his mother was born and there he made a song and communed with her spirit, for her spirit left the body of Nyck and land of the north and returned to its origins, and Panta spoke with her son and warned him of all the dangers around him. Sunra communed likewise with his father and other ancestors and they warned him of the danger. In the city of Nittok at that time there were traitor Bluepeople who were being paid as spies for the Wofpeople, and so Sunra had to be extra careful to see that he did not meet these treacherous folk.

When Sunra reached the place called the Delta, he heard the spirits in the trees, who were following him for protection, whisper that he must stop and rest. While he was asleep, he dreamed, and in his dream he was told what he must do to save his people.

He must take the acorn, which he carried with him always, and he must bite off the tiniest of pieces from both of his bones. He must put these little invisible pieces inside the cap of the acorn and he must put the cap of the acorn back on very tightly. Then he must dig a great sowing place in the black earth and he must plant that acorn.

When Sunra awoke, the light of the sun was bright and he sang his accustomed hymn to the dawn and the dawn approved and then Sunra knew he was ready to fulfill his mission. He dug in the earth and he planted the acorn, and then according to the rest of what was told in the dream, he went toward the city of Nittok.

HENRY DUMAS

Now many things happened to him in this wicked city, for he lived there for three years, but that again is another story. When the time was ripe the spirits told him to return to the place of sowing and he found that where he had planted the acorn there was a giant oak tree greater even than the one in the north called Rak, and so he named the tree Kra, which means son of Rak. So great was Kra that its trunk and limbs were hollow.

Inside this great tree were pathways and little rooms. There was only one entrance, however, and it was a secret to all except the spirits who themselves dwelled inside the tree. Now in the center, high up, near the heavens, imbedded deep inside the flesh of the tree, there was a great ebony horn, which had grown from the boneseeds left in the acorn. This ebony horn had a red bell omega, green valves, and streaks of orange and yellow along the side. It shone in the dark and emitted a chameleon light and there was also a fragrance. Its alpha reed was black.

Now there are many adventures which befell Sunra inside the tree of his ancestors; for he was still being pursued by his enemies and traitors. But it is not the purpose here to tell that story, but rather to show you just what the ebony horn was supposed to do, and so we might well hold back the delicious details of Sunra's struggle to get to the ebony horn, his fight with the invaders and his escape back to the city of Nittok, and, finally, the long journey back to Wofland where the majority of his people were held in bondage. When he returned he found that conditions had grown worse.

Instead of trains to bring people back to the icefields, the Wofpack had made them build a special road by hand, and it is upon this road that all the people began their fated trek to the northern factories and ultimately to the Tombs of Preservation and the dungeons of the Ice King.

And so now here is how Sunra saved his people. When he arrived he carried with him under his clothing all his instruments. People did not recognize him. Many thought he was just another trekker, for he toiled and ate among the people. He tested the people. He asked them about their songs and he asked them to sing some, but alas not many of his wretched people could recall their own songs and none could recall that there was a prophesy. So ruthless and evil had been the Wofpeople that they had beaten and blotted-out the memories of the Red and the Blue and the Yellow. Very little remained.

Sunra found great cities of stone and steel. Machines flew in the air. The whole system of destroying the painted people themselves agreed with the follies and deceits, the traps and the evils. Daily the people entered the freezelines and lost their souls.

No doubt you can see that the condition was terrible. Far be it for me here to paint a full picture. Being of such a patient and alert mind, you have already heard and understood the fullness of this thing. So all those details and items of horror which I leave out for the sake of relating what happened with the ebony horn, I leave to you, and your own song making; and this is as it should be, since even the gods are reluctant to think of what was done to the painted people.

Sunra unfolded his arms in the daylight and let the spirit of the years console him. He reached back into his soul and this is the beginning of the first note he played upon the ebony horn. And the note grew and it said:

> I am the spittle of Brahnogum. I am the movement of waves at sea and the invisible children who dress in the sound of the sun. I am the spittle and the blood of Brahnogum. I make rain from nothing and the rain I turn to tears and the tears to blood and the blood to sweat and when I am through with you I spew you out to be made again, for I am Brahnogum, maker and remaker. My music returns to me as an old song and I send it out again as a child.

And when this note came from Sunra's horn, there sprang up from the skin of Nyck and the tree of Rak a great drum. And this drum grew and grew. It grew higher than any of the Wof skyscrapers that leaned up from all the cities, and its sides were inaccessible. Even planes flying over it were driven away by the gentle vibrations emanating from it when the hand of the wind blew upon the skins. And when Sunra changed notes, the drum stopped growing.

And this is his second note:

I am Vishango. Out of me will you get all your words, for I neither destroy nor create. And this is the echo of my sound, that it is an echo of the inner door, and from behind that door comes the one true light and this light I reflect as a mirror and I am not false nor am I ever late. Whatever you sing, I sing and I sing it again and again, even into the generations waiting in heaven and hell.

And when Sunra played this note, a pulse flowed and the people were quickened and their memories leaped, and vibrated inside. It is a fact that when vibrations coalesce and travel in the same direction, then anything can happen. This is what you call the dimension of the unpredictable. Only the essence, the soul of this life knows what can happen, because it is the soul, the bluesoul making it happen.

Now when he stopped playing this note, all the painted people were aglow like pieces of coal.

Now Sunra took his beautiful horn and aimed it toward the great mountain where dwelled the King of Ice and all his Woflords. And when the ebony horn grew into the third note this is what happened.

All over the land, from north to south, the painted people—too hot to get near now—began to march. They did not follow any outward road or way, but did the things according to where they were located. They all began to march toward the direction of the drum. For some time now, the Wofpeople had been trying to destroy the drum, but nothing they did seemed to touch it. It was indestructible. They bombed it, tried to set it afire, shot great guns at it. They even tried to round up all the painted people now, because they knew there was a connection between them and the drum's power. But the people were too hot to handle. The Kingdom of Ice began to thaw. And the heat was on. A helio heat.

Suddenly the horn broke into full chorus and light came from it; and sweet sounds, deadly to the untrained ear; and the sounds penetrated and traveled and worked miracles.

After many others had failed, a Blue youth climbed up the side of the drum, and finally reached the top. Songs and prayers from the wretched below helped him. When he reached the top he fell across the great skin exhausted and the sound reached up to heaven and cracked the clouds, and then struck the earth like thunder, and the youth got up and began to stroke the drum; and his mighty fist struck. And while Sunra played louder and louder upon the ebony horn, the boy stroked louder and louder and then something happened. The windows in the city buildings in the Wof regions exploded. Some of the smaller buildings had bricks which shook and tumbled aloose. Wooden horses rocked and several burst into flames.

Machines died in the air. An electric power plant reversed its power and the plant electrocuted and melted everything in range of it for ten miles. The ice mountain melted and the freezelines dissolved. Icelances faded, and panic went through the Wofpack. But it was too late. Sunra took panic itself and drove it into them.

The drum beat a steady rhythm. Its message traveled farther and farther. Out into the universe it went and right along side was the intuitive sonic notes of Sunra; and, finally, when the message had reached 7 suns in distant areas of the universe, a great chorus grew up, creating a dimension called the Bluesol. And never had it been invented before and when it reached the earth, it fell like a mighty spear upon the icefields and as the rhythms increased and the ebony horn blasted, the sun itself could not stand the ecstasy, could not stand the beauty, could not stand it and so the sun gyrated into its own dimension and burst forth with a song and all who heard it, *into-it.*

And all who sing like the sun are children of the sun.

Riot or Revolt?

The police barricades squatted on the sidewalk surrounding each place where the mobs had struck.

Harold stood on the ramp in the middle of Seventh Avenue and 125th Street and surveyed the area which the night before had swarmed with police and angry Harlemites. A youth had been slain by the police in Brooklyn.

The traffic on the avenue moved slowly. Some of the barricades had been posted around the burned remains of stores and looted shops. The police were getting ready to block off to traffic the entire area around 125th Street. A city truck had parked across the street and some men were unloading more barricades. A policeman directed the last of the cars through the narrow section in the middle of the avenue, and blew his whistle, waving a group of people—mostly guys in their teens—to stay away from the area. Harold stood surveying the area beneath one of the sycamore trees which had been scorched during the night by a gasoline bomb. He recognized many of the guys. He touched the burned bark with his stickball stick. The smell of burnt wood and gasoline filled his nostrils. Looking across at the LeMoor Brothers' Bookstore, he saw that it really had not been touched by the crowds. He recalled someone shouting "Don't touch LeMoor Leave LeMoor Leave Lemoor!" And the crowd had swept by, smashing the jewelry store next to LeMoor's and setting it afire before the riot squad and the fire department arrived and drove them back.

A hot August sun pressed in on the Harlem streets, examining, Harold thought, every niche and corner for looted relics and lost wallets. He recalled the frenzied cries of the Hasans, a group of guys—some of whom he knew—from 129th Street, who had protected LeMoor's against the attack of the rioters. But this all was done in proper style, just to let everybody know what was really going on. Harold had never been in LeMoor's, but he knew that he would have never tossed a brick or a bomb or anything to destroy the face of the store. LeMoor's store had the face of a museum. That's why a lot of people called it a museum, and there were few black folk in Harlem who would not protect the store in times such as last night. It was a custom to let your brother live. If more black men owned the property and rented out the buildings, then just like Harold had heard the Harlem Square speakers say, there would be less need for white policemen to protect the interest of white merchants and less need for Negroes to get mad. Everybody knew that.

The heat rose out of the streets and pavements like aroused snakes, and as Harold stood under the shade of the tree, he could not help but wonder what it was that made people protect and honor LeMoor's store. And although he had obeyed the wild yells to save LeMoor's, he knew that he would not have dared, and it was this feeling which stirred him and urged him. There must be something there for all the black brothers to stand around it shouting to the mobs, "LeMoor is a brother. We are brothers!"

A neatly dressed man in a blue suit and a red fez came out of the store with a flag. As many times as he and his friends had passed by LeMoor's, they had never thought of visiting. Once Harold recalled he had looked in the window at all the books, pamphlets, statues, flags, and placards, but his curiosity had been quickly smothered by his desire to get back uptown to a stickball game against the Lenox Avenue guys. They were playing for money.

Harold watched as the man placed the flag neatly in a little hole in the pavement. The flag began to flop and wave in the wind, as if it were announcing the arrival of some great dignitary to Harlem.

Harold wondered why the man had put out the flag. Although he recalled that he had seen it before, right there where it was during the speeches of the street speakers, Harold suddenly began to wonder what was the reason why you always had to have the flag out when you got ready to do something. Maybe, he thought, if he copped him a flag for the guys, an American flag just like the minute men and all the rest of the guys in the history book had when they got ready to kill the Indians, then maybe nobody would say anything about what they did. The thought amused him. Hell, if a flag made what you did right, then he figured he would cop a flag. The man went back into the store. Harold looked inside. There were several people inside.

He rubbed his stick clean of ashes and leaped from the ramp, flopping his sneakers on the street, plop plop plop plop!

As he was crossing the street, the scene of the smashed jewelry store window caught his eye and instead of running toward LeMoor's, he ran directly toward the barricade, and ducked his head, under. He heard the sound of scattering glass beneath his foot, and he wondered who last night had got to the store first. It might have been the Hasans since they had stood in front of LeMoor's. It might have been the Lenox Avenue guys . . . or it might have been some of the older people. They were mad too about that kid getting killed in Brooklyn. Hell, thought Harold, every nigger was mad, because if you shot one Negro, you shot them all. That's the way he and his friends felt. He stood there and peered in at the broken window. A huge piece of glass, resting like a guillotine, remained at the top of the showcase. Harold started to reach his stick up and make it fall, but if he did that he would have to get on the inside of the other barricade, and if the glass fell he would not be able to get out of the way in time. . . . He just stood there.

"Hey you kid! Get the hell away from there!" It was a cop. Harold saw him coming, ducked under the barricade to the open side and stood up to face him.

"Scram! Dammit you . . . Kid!" The cop was racing along the barricade now, coming toward Harold. Harold looked. The man had drawn his revolver.

HENRY DUMAS

"I was just crossin . . ." Harold attempted.

The cop had him now by the neck collar, dragging him toward an approaching patrol car. "You goddam hoodlum! I saw you. Don't lie to me. Who do you think you're tryin to kid? What you think you gonna do? Finish what you started last night?"

"I was just crossin . . ." Harold choked. He struggled and gripped his stick. The cop quickly seized him, stood him up and glared at him. Harold stepped back and went to pick up his stick. . . .

The cop, enraged, put his revolver away, and drew back his billyclub. . . .

"Hey! Don't you hit that boy!"

Harold turned and saw the man who had put out the flag running toward them. The squad car pulled to a stop and a couple of officers leaped out and tried to stop the old man. But he dodged them agilely.

"Are you cops crazy?" he asked. "You just had a taste last night and now you want more! If you hit that boy, don't you know what'll happen?"

The cop had put away his club and had begun to frisk Harold, who stood with his hands above his head as the officer had ordered.

But the old man, one of the LeMoor brothers who ran the museum, suddenly ran up to the officer, leaned over into the officer's face, and growled indignantly, "This boy didn't do nothing. I saw the whole thing. Now let him be."

He looped his arm under Harold's arm and pulled Harold toward the entrance of the store. The policemen, standing in a huddle, watched.

"Pick up your stick son!" the old man said roughly as he led Harold away from the policemen. Harold picked up his stickball stick, and they entered the LeMoor bookstore moving through a crowd of people which had gathered to watch. Some of them followed Micheval LeMoor and Harold into the store. "What happened Mr. LeMoor?" somebody asked. The old man was leading Harold to the rear of the store. The other old man,

Carib LeMoor was quietly looking out into the street from behind the books counter.

"Brother Miche," he called quietly, "the police are coming to the store."

"Now look here boy, don't you ever let me catch you do a thing like that again, do you hear?"

Harold looked into the old man's fiery eyes. His eyes were on fire, but Harold couldn't feel the fire burning him. He could feel the heat and the anger, but that was the way it was supposed to be. The old man must have seen everything he had done. But had he seen his thoughts?

"All I did was go under the barricade," he said, not as a defense but just as a statement to see how much the old man knew.

"Yeah," repeated Mr. LeMoor, "And don't do it again. Didn't you see me save you from that damn fool cop? Don't you know those crackers'll crack your head! If he bothered you any more, don't you know what would happen to Harlem?" He pushed Harold to the crack in the door and told him to look through to the outside. Harold did. There was a noisy crowd gathering. The policemen were arguing and yelling right in front of the store. One policeman was talking to the other brother, Carib, who was standing among a group of brothers who were in the store all morning. "Niggers are mad, son. Don't forget that. Don't do anything foolish. You knew that barricade meant keep out. You knew them cops were around this area like flies. You shoulda stayed out. Now keep yourself calm. . . ." And he rushed out to the front to talk to the policemen.

At the front of the store several angry men were demanding to know why the policemen had tried to arrest a black youth for crossing the street. The crowd led by these two men and one woman followed the cops around until they all were driven back behind, near barricades that were going up in front of the store. More policemen arrived. No shots were fired. But several officers had to draw their revolvers to force back the gathering crowd. A police loudspeaker sounded now, telling the

HENRY DUMAS

people to get off the streets. It began to circle around all the blocks around 125th Street.

Harold stood in the back of the store looking at all the books, his eyes widened, holding on to his stick. The men and the two women in the store were talking about him, but he knew he hadn't done anything really wrong. Maybe going under the barricade was dangerous, but he didn't think it would have started another riot as Mr. LeMoor seemed to believe. But on second thought, he knew if the people had got to the cop snatching on him like he did, anything might have happened. When niggers get mad, anything was liable to happen. Harold bit his tongue and felt the sweat soaking up his tee shirt.

Outside the crowd was growing. Voices and shouts. A few more people had managed to make it to the store before the barricade was put up.

"Brother Micheval, what you let them put that barricade in front of your store for? You gotta go under it now to get in or out."

The older man came and squinted out at the activities on the street. "That's for that goddam Governor and the Mayor," he mused.

Somebody laughed as if they had heard a joke.

"What you laughin at?" the old man turned still in his indignant pose. "You think the white man don't know where it is at? Hah! You're foolish then, foolish!"

There were several people there among this crowd who deserve identifying. First there was the quieter LeMoor brother, Carib, who had taken up a position beside Harold and was talking to the boy from time to time. Behind them, sitting in a corner which could not be seen from the door, was the well known Harlem leader, Brother X. He sat with two people, one known as Al-Haji Zadik bin Talafa, and a representative from the city council, Edward James Hawkins. Although the men frequently gathered at LeMoor's, seldom were they there together. Brother X, a dark brooding man, whose silent pose and attentiveness was deceiving. He could electrify a crowd. It was said that he belonged to the Brotherhood. He never denied it. He was very popular in Harlem, and if the people had known he were inside the store, they would have demanded his appearance. Zadik, one of the top leaders of the Brotherhood, often spoke for the Brotherhood on official matters. He was a brown man, goateed and bearded, wearing a fez and stroking his beard. Both he and X were listening to the councilman, Hawkins, who was bemoaning the results of the recent city council meeting. He was a light man, with narrow eyes and nervous hands. He kept beating a rhythm out on the table with a pencil as he talked.

The older LeMoor came at intervals and stood by their table. He would say something in the councilman's ear and then return to the front of the store.

The others in the store were customers and neighborhood people who hung out there all the time. About five.

Harold noticed the difference in the LeMoor brothers right away.

"Well, son," Carib LeMoor said to Harold, "are you ready for your picture?"

"What picture?" asked Harold, looking at the older man quizzically.

The other laughed a bit. But he wasn't laughing at Harold's innocence. Just at the situation. "You didn't start another riot, but by nightfall all Harlem will know about you. You will be a hero."

"What for?"

"Son, that's human nature."

"But I didn't do anything. . . ."

"Well, we'll see about that son. My brother and I want you to pose for a picture." Harold felt a wave of pride, but it was swept away when he heard a police car whining the riot siren. Both he and the old man turned and looked out the window. "You better stay away from the crowd for a while. They know you alright."

Then Carib LeMoor got on the phone and called a man who, he told Harold, would come immediately and paint his picture. Every Negro who came into the LeMoor bookstore got his picture painted, he said. It was a tradition. When the painter came, he told Harold that he would show him the inner chambers where all the paintings were. There was no collection of black faces assembled in one spot like this on earth. Harold felt a hidden rush of pride and he wondered why it was that Negroes didn't know about LeMoor's, and why all the guys he knew didn't know about the place. He never heard anybody talking about it, and it gave him a sense of pride to know that when he left, he would spread the word in Harlem about the greatest place for black men in the world. "Knowledge is power," said a sign.

Micheval LeMoor was arguing bitterly with one of his steady customers, a man with a clean shaven head and smoking a pipe. The man's aged look was deceiving, but he was about fifty and he wore a brightly colored sport shirt. While this group carried on a heated conversation, the group in the back room sat quietly, tensely, examining a set of papers passed between them, and alternately listening to the councilman point out some point about the papers, tap his fingers, smoke a cigarette, and begin talking again. Brother X and Zadik listened without a word.

In the front of the store Micheval LeMoor, squinting his tired bespectacled eyes outside now and then, waved his hands in the air.

"I've been here thirty years. Thirty years! And the only time this store get crowded is when there's trouble in Harlem. The only time!"

"Hell," grunted a man sitting near the window on a box, "it ought to stay full then. Cause ain't nothing in Harlem or any other black ghetto but trouble!" He was a well dressed man, in a dark suit with wrinkled black skin. His lips were large and full and his eyes were steely black and piercing.

"The colored man is on the move," said the man with

the clean head. "You got to have trouble and riots for us to get what rightly belong to us."

"Who told you that?" asked Micheval. "Who told you that brother?" And when the other man was about to answer, Micheval waved him off.

"Listen, I know niggers. I can talk about 'em because I come from among them! Now listen. Thirty years ago I moved into this goddam store; we moved in and a Jew moved in next door. We went into business on the same goddam day! Mind you! Now here I come like a dam fool selling niggers a little knowledge. Do you know what that Jew was selling?" He laughed. Then paused, spun around in the floor, and pointed high into the air, as if pointing off in some infinite direction. "Today that man has got a million niggers' dollars in his pocket. He wines and dines on the French Riviera, goes off on long vacations. I haven't seen him in Harlem in fifteen years, but he still owns the place. He got a factory downtown and one in Chicago . . . That Jew was smart. He went into business selling hair grease, pomades, and conk juice. Eh? He was putting something ON the niggers' head, and I was trying to put a little something IN their heads. You see the difference? That man is a millionaire, flying all over the world, and my little money ain't even good enuf to get me a cup of coffee. Don't you let nobody tell that lie. Niggers is on the move, brother, but they need a goddam direction."

"Micheval Mr. LeMoor," his wife interrupted from behind the counter where she and the other Mrs. LeMoor were sitting at a table, marking books. "An angry mob sure isn't going to bring that boy's life back. I think you men will have to do more than tear down."

"That's only part of it. Now woman, listen," he said gently, "When this black man really wakes up to what is going on, look out! Right now he's mad. He knows somebody's been holdin back the meat for years and givin him bones. What do you think would have happened if that damn fool cop woulda hit that boy back there?"

HENRY DUMAS

There was a brief silence, as if a sudden rush of wind had blown through and sealed off everybody's lips.

Suddenly a short light man, with a whine in his voice, and a habit of scratching his head, spoke up: "Brother LeMoor, why you so hard on colored folks. The white man is hard enough on us. He the cause of our condition, and he the one that's got to suffer for it. The Negro is waking up and you ought to give him that much credit."

Among the several people there were a few halfhearted attempts to agree with the speaker, but nobody ventured to say anything. It was LeMoor's move.

"All right Brother." He walked near to the man, a smile in his voice but not on his lips. "If you were a foreigner, and you come to a country and you saw an orchard of apples and you wanted to buy some apples, and the sign said: 'JONES' Farm,' then you saw a group of men clearing the trees of that fruit, what would you do? Eh? Why you would ask for Mr. Jones and if he wasn't there, then you would buy from his representative, right? Well you tell me how many farms does the Negro own in this country? I'll give him credit when other nations and people collectively or individually deal with him as such, as a man who has something to offer. The Negro ain't got nothin, because to be a Negro is to be nothing!" And he clapped his hands together for emphasis.

"Ah now Brother LeMoor," whined the man, grinning and turning his back.

LeMoor leaned in further, looking from face to face now to get their attention.

"I want to tell you a little story. Any man let himself be called a Negro is letting himself be called a nigger. They are the same words, like father like son."

There was a silent approval of Micheval's words. The short man nodded, as if to point out that he understood.

"Don't think that I'm hard on niggers for no good reason," Micheval said. "I got plenty reason. If you want your horse to move, you can't whisper soft words in his ear. They do that in the movies.

"If you go up to the average white man and ask him, 'Sir what is a nigger,' why, he would say, well . . . er . . . He might think a bit, but then he would say, very properly (unless he was from down south or from up south) 'You don't mean Negro do you?'

"It's the same. To the white man, a Negro is a nigger. And that's his name all the way. If another man can give you a name and you go by it, then that man owns you. It's a simple law of nature that most people have forgotten. You go up to the average black man and ask him what is a nigger and he'll hem and haw, but he'll probably say it's an offensive term for Negro, if he don't misunderstand you first and go up beside your head."

Harold was listening intently to all that was going on. He had heard such talk before, but this time he felt that it was especially for him. The painter arrived and Harold watched him as he set up an easel and canvas in the opposite corner. He motioned to Harold and told him to stand naturally. Harold held on to the stick, and the painter positioned it in Harold's hands as if it were a rifle.

Then he told Harold to stand. And he began furious strokes, looking up, cocking his head, and sketching away. Harold heard the sirens outside again and felt the sweat jamming up on his skin. He wondered if the painter knew how to paint sweat.

" . . . and that ain't all," Micheval was talking over a sudden burst of laughter at something else he had said about the Negro. He was taking the word and saying that any black man who allowed himself to be called a Negro was a nigger.

Then as if to forestall any attempt to beat Micheval at this word battle, the whining man asked him a question.

"So you think niggers want to go back to Africa?"

"I never said that, I never said that Brother. But if anybody ask me, me, Micheval LeMoor, I'll tell them: I been here for 400 years and I'm still catching hell. If it gets any worse,

I might as well go some where, and I don't want to go to Iceland!"

"You think all white people are like a few that have made it hard for us. They ain't all like that," protested the short fellow. "As soon as integration comes, the American dream will be the truth and not a dream. . . ."

"What are you talking about integration? The Negro preachers have been spitting that brainwashing powder out to baptize niggers' heads since 1954. What integration? You can't legislate and regiment this thing. If you want to be swallowed up by the majority in this country, then go ahead with your integration. I wouldn't want it if it could work. It's only a trick my friend, a trick. The Man knows he's on the downgrade and he's letting everything go into the war now. He'll even stoop down and let a few niggers into the melting pot. But it's all a trick. The whole concept of democracy ain't integration. It is brotherhood, and the rule of the majority, and the right of each individual to his own. Now where is the Negro got anything to offer the white man but his muscles and his black skin?"

There was a motor brigade pulling up outside. The barricades were being opened, making a pathway to the store. Harold could see clear to the front of the store, and he saw both the LeMoor brothers in a huddle now as motorcycles roared to a halt outside and a ring of policemen made a great circle all around Harlem Square to hold back the crowds. In the distance the loudspeaker steadily urged the people to be calm and in the interest of safety and respect not to linger on the streets unnecessarily.

"Here they come," said Carib to Micheval. A photographer rushed through the policemen outside and began asking questions about the incident with Harold. Micheval was reticent. Everybody shook him off and did not answer questions, except the one little man who had whined and argued with Micheval. He had seen most of what had happened and after he told him, he pointed to the back of the store and said that Harold was being painted back there as part of his fame. The photographer was writing all this down, and got ready to go to the back, when the motorcade pulled directly in front of the store and a chauffeur, policemen standing behind him, opened the door, and out stepped the Governor, followed by the Mayor and the Negro Mayor of Harlem.

Photographers outside flashed pictures, running around like bees after honey. One of the aides was talking to Micheval now, and trying to get a statement.

The official party walked quickly toward the bookstore after an examination of the damage of the jewelry store. The owner of the store accompanied them. There were people from several insurance companies there, and all over the square there were detectives and FBI men.

When the Governor's party stepped inside the threshold of the bookstore, flashbulbs went off and he paused. He was a tall graying man, heavyset and forward looking. If the occasion had been less grave, it is certain that the Governor, used to showing his amiable personality with a ready smile, would have swung off his hat and waved at the solemn crowds behind the barricade. But he moved inside quickly, his aide telling him the name of the bookstore and introducing him to the two brothers, who stood solemnly, Micheval with his arms folded. In the rear of the store, the painter stroked away on the image he was making of Harold. "You're going to be famous," he mused absently at Harold.

"Would you paint all the guys' pictures if they came in here?" he asked.

"That's my job," said the painter.

"What about the Governor and the Mayor?"

He laughed. "Naw, their image would fade. I'm painting black young brothers. Black. Now hold still."

After the Governor and the Mayor had been introduced, the Governor directed his words to both of the brothers.

"I understand that you have operated this bookstore for many years, Mr. LeMoor. No doubt you have been in a unique position to sense the opinions of the average resident. . . ."

Micheval shifted his arms. He was waiting for the Governor to make a false move. He hoped he wouldn't, but he had never seen it fail that a white man didn't step in a hornet's nest when he called himself coming out looking for what stirred up the niggers.

"That's right, your honor," said Carib.

A few flashbulbs blinded the scene.

"You're fortunate that the rioters didn't touch your store. . . ."

"Well," said Micheval, "I don't think it was luck."

"Yes, you've been in business for a long time," said the Mayor, a blondish man younger than the Governor, but with less of an amiable front. The Mayor looked hard and brutal, as if he were preparing himself for some great task ahead of him. "You men, have been the focal point of many situations over the years."

"Well, Mr. Mayor," said Micheval, "we live in Harlem. The people know this store. A lot of these folks on the street are my friends."

"Of course, of course, but there is an investigation going on about the cause of the rioting. . . . And if it happens again, nobody's store will be safe. . . . You gentlemen living in the area must have some theories about why the people are so easily aroused. . . . We apprehend criminals everyday, and we don't have riots because of it. All kinds of criminals, colored and white. I for one want to get to the bottom of this thing. Our citizens are aroused now. . . . and," he coughed nervously as Micheval shifted his folded arms and looked at the men solemnly. "If there's going to be trouble like this just because . . . the police department is doing its duty, then more measures will have to be taken. . . ."

"Mr. LeMoor," the Governor said, after a careful look around the store, "what is it that you hope to create with this store?"

"Pride dressed in knowledge!" said Micheval emphatically.

The Mayor of Harlem, who had visited the store himself years back, stepped forward and excused himself to the Mayor and the Governor. "This is a part of the program I was telling you about. The people are in need of some outlet for their energies."

The Councilman, James Hawkins, made his way through the crowd in the back of the store and came forward. He shook hands with the officials amidst flashbulbs.

"Excuse me Mr. Mayor," he said, talking to the Governor, "but these are the kinds of things that arouse the people—committees and meetings, investigations and the like. Do you know that half the black men on the street are out of work?"

"Mr Mayor, asked Carib quietly, "what other measures were you thinking of for Harlem. . . . ?"

He had spoken softly just as the Governor was about to say something, and the Governor's words broke through.

"Well, gentlemen, I am impressed by your achievement here. I have heard a lot about you. . . ."

" . . . But," interrupted Micheval, "this is the first time that any state or city official has visited my store. . . ."

"That is a pity," said the Governor calmly.

The Mayor whispered something in the Governor's ear. Then he turned to Micheval and asked, "Mr. LeMoor, I understand that you have some kind of statement to make to the press about the riots."

Micheval did not blink his eyes, but coolly unfolded his arms, and walked near the book counter. He picked up a book. He was in the spotlight. The white power structure would have to listen to him now.

"Why is it that you think that the proprietors of a bookstore have the last word on the riots?"

"Well, it is obvious," said the Mayor, "that the rioting is spontaneous, and the mobs have no organized leadership. You men talk to a lot of people in Harlem. . . ."

"I must say," added the Governor, "all of the damage

seems to be done to targets that seem to be patterned. But the white merchants are bearing the brunt of the attacks. . . . "

"Mr. Mayor, your honor," Micheval said to them, ignoring the colored Mayor of Harlem, "I must say that no amount of persuasion is going to convince me that the city and state officials don't know what's going on. When a Negro boy is shot and killed by policemen who do not check the situation before pulling their guns, the people get angry. It is simple. I have no special message from God about the thing. I'm not a preacher. It is a simple law of nature. The people get tired of dying. Just because you have other problems, doesn't mean they die less. The people don't have to be investigated, interviewed, questioned, grafted for a group of social workers or white college students to know what they're suffering. That's a smoke screen to let you know that ain't nothing going to be done. The people know that. When the baby cries and you give him a pacifier, then when he discovers he's been tricked, he cries louder."

The Mayor was getting nervous. He tried to interrupt LeMoor, waving him to be quiet and nodding as if to say he understood, but that he couldn't listen right then, but LeMoor went on. The Governor, frowning, but listening, blinked as the photographers began snapping pictures of LeMoor.

Harold, standing in his pose, facing the whole scene, hearing every word, sweated. He wondered if the painter could paint sweat.

". . . Your Honor," Micheval continued as Hawkins and the Mayor of Harlem tried to get a word in. Carib moved next to his brother as if to back up everything he was saying. Several of the customers, who were standing back, began to move forward.

". . . don't think the last two nights were riots. You are welcome in my store, anytime. But I don't appreciate being thought of as a good nigger. You want to come visit here and get the notions about things being better, while right now some disrespectful guardian of the citizens beats a black man's head in. It doesn't matter if he's guilty or not anymore. Can't you see? Your honor, what you are facing is the full anger of a man who has been under attack for years. Unless you can call off the attackers, be they merchants, disrespectful policemen, or the American majority, then the black minority is going to tear your house down...."

"Well," said the Governor, "I had heard that you were outspoken...."

"Yes, because I want to tell the truth, like it is!"

His brother was nodding. The Mayor was motioning several officers back, and one of the aides flanked by several cops. He moved away from the Governor slightly, and began talking to the Mayor of Harlem.

"Mr. LeMoor," the Governor asked gravely, his finger resting on his chin, his neat suit wrinkled under his arm. "Perhaps you would like to tell what you just did to a committee. I'd like to see you. How about coming to the Mayor's office tomorrow...?"

He motioned the mayor to his side.

"Sir, I think you have misunderstood what I've been saying or someone has led you wrong," said Micheval. "I am not a Negro leader. Do you think that the people know me as a Negro leader? I speak as a private citizen, who comes in contact with the people. There are others, and some are among you, who are Negro leaders. If you want to talk to leaders, then you must find them among the people."

"That is one of the reasons we are here today," said the Governor sternly, visibly upset now and trying to recapture his poise.

"Here?" asked Micheval.

"Well," said the Mayor suddenly, with a smile. "Are you gentlemen trying to tell me that none of the leaders are known to come here?"

"If you know who they are, call them up or send couriers with a message," said Micheval. "I am here in my store 12 hours a day and I can be reached on matters about books and education at my home. About the goings on in Harlem, all I can do is speak my mind as a private citizen."

HENRY DUMAS

The Governor and the Mayor had a brief huddle and amid the flashing of bulbs, all the men shook hands and began to leave. Micheval walked them to the door. The Governor, turning, looking far in the rear, said:

"Do you have an art studio also? I see . . ."

Micheval smiled also. "Sir," he said, "that is my pride shop. When you come on more important business, I will show you around."

The Governor turned to Carib, "Is your brother always this hard to bargain with?" Everybody laughed in the store. The tension subsided.

"Oh yes," said Carib, "he's the Pride I'm the Knowledge. We work as a team." The Governor smiled.

"Well," he said, "I can see how you have built a success-ful business. It was a pleasure." He extended his hand and shook hands with both the brothers.

"Good luck with your store gentlemen, and I believe you have something that the youth of Harlem will be proud of."

They left, the reporters and photographers shooting pictures and running about, in and outside of the store, as if trees were sprouting money and blowing it all over Harlem.

The crowd of people outside had grown. The official party left, the motorcycle brigade roaring off ahead. There were a few boos, and the policemen who had pushed the crowd prac-tically a block away now, began to wave their arms madly getting the cars out of the place in a hurry.

Some people got through the barricades and streaked toward the store. The loudspeaker still barked away around the corners. One cop, dressed for riot duty, halted a barricade breaker and ordered him back. The man reluctantly back-tracked. It was afternoon now, and the August heat seemed to gather in the center of Harlem Square and simmer there. And the sun was examining everything, closely.

"There! Young Brother," said the painter. "You are ready. I hope you are ready."

"Ready for what," said Harold.

The painter smiled and turned to Micheval, and they began talking. Harold wondered if he had painted his sweat.

"Did you get the sweat?" he asked, falling loose from the pose and examining the portrait.

"Boy," said Micheval, "that's *all* he got." Harold didn't understand that, but he smiled because he felt that it sounded good. It meant something.

Then something began happening outside. Sirens wailed and there were shots. Everybody rushed to the front of the store, except Carib, who grabbed Harold and led him through the back room.

Brother X, talking on the phone now, looked at Harold knowingly and seemed to nod. He lifted his chin in the familiar greeting. Harold greeted him back. He knew Brother X from the street speakers. El Jai was reading the papers again. He did not look at Harold, but looked through the door before Brother Carib closed it. "They gone?" he asked. Brother Carib nodded and led Harold down a flight of steps.

It was the basement. He took out a set of keys, fumbled for the right one, motioning Harold to follow him, reached the bottom, flicked on a light and walked slowly along a narrow passageway whose sides bulged with books and boxes. Harold saw the dust of ages rise up before him, and the chill of the basement took away his sweat.

"Are they rioting outside, Mr. LeMoor?" he asked.

The older man went on, deliberately. He did not answer. When he got to a large door, he inserted the key, fumbled it a bit, opened the door and stood waiting for Harold to pass. A light came on.

Harold walked up, looked into the great room, looked again, and dropped his mouth. . . .

"Every Afro-American boy or man who comes to LeMoor for the knowledge and the truth, comes here," said Carib.

HENRY DUMAS

Harold looked upon the room, speechless. . . .

When he walked up the steps again, Carib LeMoor followed quietly behind. Harold heard the sounds from outside, but saw all the paintings, all the photographs of the famous Negroes, Africans and Asians, all the various black people who had visited LeMoor's since the store was opened, saw them all swirling in the masses of people yelling loud under the August sun. . . . All the black voices shouting in blood and sweat, lifting their souls up in a mighty wave, a mighty fervor, all syncopated. All joined in time, (like the time of his swing when he struck that rubber ball perfectly with his stick *whop!* and sent that ball sailing. . . .)

all the black voices speaking one thing . . .
all the buried seeds in the soil breaking the soil,
lifting their heads high, high into the sun, and
brushing off the soot when the sun scorched,
brushing off the hurt and rising,

And Harold walked. . . . They gathered around him, and when he shouted, "Freedom!," they did too.

Acknowledgments

People's commitment to the art and memory of Henry Dumas has assumed various forms, from praise-song gatherings to read his work aloud, to stage adaptations of his writings, to serious scholarly study, to the persistent laborings over his ideas and language in classrooms across the nation and world. Among the many persons who have participated in this vital support system—'Soular System'—over the past two decades are: Maya Angelou, Keith Aytch, (Imamu) Amiri Baraka, Julie Blattler, Avery Brooks, Marie Brown, Hale Chatfield, Jayne Cortez, Edward Crosby, Tommy Ellis, Sherman Fowler, Hoyt Fuller, T. Michael Gates, William Halsey, Joseph Harrison, Donald Henderson, Vernon T. Hornback, Oliver Jackson, George A. Jones/Ahaji Umbudi, Walter Lowenfels, John S. Rendleman, Ronald Tibbs, Sons/Ancestors Players, Toni Morrison, Larry Neal, Raymond Patterson, Sterling Plumpp, Anthony Sloan (WBAI-FM Radio), Quincy Troupe, Val Grey Ward (Kuumba Theater), H. Mark Williams (Culture Messengers) Jay Wright and members of the Eugene B. Redmond Writers Club (of East St. Louis) who have been an enduring sounding board for the genius of HD. And, finally, there has been the ever-present support, input, and faith of the brave Loretta Dumas. (From the acknowledgments of *Goodbye, Sweetwater*, 1988.)

Since the late 1980s, his writings have appeared in scores of new publications including *African-American Literature, African Voices, Ain't But a Place: African American Writings About St. Louis, A Rock Against the Wind: African-American Poems and Letters of Love and Passion, Brilliant Corners, Dark Matter, Drumvoices Revue, Essence, Fences, Literati Chicago, Literati Internazionale, Literature of the Southern United States, Original Chicago Blues Annual, People's Poetry Gathering, The New Cavalcade, The Oxford Anthology of African American Poetry, The Soul of Success: Quotations for Entrepreneurs* and *Trouble the Water: 250 Years of African-American Poetry*. Bio-critical essays on him appear in *The Dictionary of Literary Biography* and *The Oxford Companion to African American Literature*. Dumas was celebrated worldwide during the 30th anniversary of his death in 1998.

Since publication of *Goodbye, Sweetwater* (1988), the Dumas "cult"/"movement" has been lengthened by a caravan of additional cultural workers, visionaries and institutions. The Dumas estate esteems them for helping to perpetuate the legacy that HD heralded and extended. The caravan includes Jenoyne Adams, Michael Datcher, and Kamau Daa'ood of the Los Angeles World Stage; Alvin Aubert and Melba Joyce Boyd of Wayne State University's Africana Studies and English Departments; Keith Adkins and the "Natural Knees" project; Jabari Asim; Lincoln T. "Chicago Beau" Beauchamp of *Literati Chicago, Literati Internazionale,* and *The Original Chicago Blues Annual;* John Watusi Branch and African Poetry Theatre, Inc.; Wesley Brown; Kenneth Carroll; Michael Castro and the River Styx Association; Olivia Costellano, David Covin, Jose Montoya, Otis Scott, and Hortense Simmons of the English, Pan African and Ethnic Studies Departments at California State University-Sacramento; Nia Damali and First World/Medu Bookstores in Atlanta; Detroit's Cotillion Club; Amina Dickerson and the Margaret Burroughs-founded DuSable Museum; East Saint Louis (Illinois) Public Schools; Vernon February and the Afrika Studi Centrum at Leiden University-Netherlands; Will Halsey; Malkia M'Buzi Moore, Robert Earl Price, T.V. Iverson of First World Writers and the Atlanta Writing Resource Center; the late June Jordan who reviewed and read HD's scrolls at public celebrations; Shirley LeFlore a.k.a. "St. Louis's Mother of the Word"; Haki R. Madhubuti and the Gwendolyn Brooks Center for Black Literature and Creative Writing (which inducted HD posthumously into its National Literary Hall of Fame for Writers of African Descent; Nubia Kai, Naomi Long Madgett and the Detroit Museum of African American History; S.E. Anderson and Tony Medina; Dahveed Nelson of The Last Poets; Itabari Njeri who wrote superbly about HD in the *Los Angeles Times;* Kevin Powell; Rohan B. Preston; Remi Raji and colleagues at University of Ibadan-Nigeria; Arnold Rampersad; Wanjiku A.H. Reynolds; Darlene Roy and members of the Eugene B. Redmond Writers Club of East Saint Louis, Illinois; Anthony Sloan of WBAI-FM Radio—and the World; Barbara Ann Teer and National Black Theatre of Harlem; Chezia Thompson-Cager and Reggie Timpson of the Pratt Library in Baltimore; Cheryl Wall and colleagues in the English Department at Rutgers-New Brunswick; Michael Warr and the Chicago Guild Complex; the late Otis Williams and Nyumburu Cultural Center at U of Maryland-College Park; Hollis Wormsby, Jr. (2003)

E.B.R.

Funder Acknowledgments

Coffee House Press is an independent nonprofit literary publisher. Our books are made possible through the generous support of grants and gifts from many foundations, corporate giving programs, individuals, and through state and federal support. The Black Arts Movement Series began with a major grant from the Lila Wallace-Reader's Digest Fund. This project received major funding from the Bush Foundation, and was published with cooperation from the Givens Foundation for African American Literature. Coffee House Press also receives support from the Minnesota State Arts Board, through an appropriation by the Minnesota State Legislature; and from grants from the Buuck Family Foundation; the Patrick and Aimee Butler Family Foundation; Lerner Family Foundation; the McKnight Foundation; the Outagamie Foundation; the Jay and Rose Phillips Family Foundation; the law firm of Schwegman, Lundberg, Woessner & Kluth, P.A.; Target, Marshall Field's, and Mervyn's with support from the Target Foundation; James R. Thorpe Foundation; The Walker Foundation; West Group; the Woessner Freeman Foundation; and many individual donors.

This activity is made possible in part by a grant from the Minnesota State Arts Board, through an appropriation by the Minnesota State Legislature and a grant from the National Endowment for the Arts. MINNESOTA STATE ARTS BOARD

To you and our many readers across the country, we send our thanks for your continuing support.

Good books are brewing at coffeehousepress.org

COFFEE HOUSE PRESS
Black Arts Movement Series

THE POSTWAR 1920S was the decade of the "New Negro" and the Jazz Age "Harlem Renaissance," or first Black Renaissance of literary, visual, and performing arts. In the 1960s and 70s Vietnam War era, a self-proclaimed "New Breed" generation of black artists and intellectuals orchestrated what they called the Black Arts Movement.

This energetic and highly self-conscious movement accompanied an explosion of urban black popular culture. The Coffee House Press Black Arts Movement Series is devoted to reprinting unavailable works of this period. We have tried to choose work that is masterful, that deserves another chance and other audiences, and that will help us keep the windows to the future open.

Captain Blackman, JOHN A. WILLIAMS

FOREWORD BY ALEXS D. PATE

ISBN: 1-56689-096-9 | TRADE PAPER | $15.95

Named "among the most important works of fiction of the decade" by *The New York Times Book Review* when first published in 1972, this novel revisits the contributions and experiences of African American soldiers in each of America's wars.

    ALSO AVAILABLE: *Clifford's Blues*

    ISBN: 1-56689-080-2 | TRADE PAPER | $14.95

dem, WILLIAM MELVIN KELLEY

FOREWORD BY JOHN S. WRIGHT

ISBN : 1-56689-102-7 | TRADE PAPER | $14.95

Originally published in 1967, this surrealistic satire lays bare the convoluted and symbiotic relationship between whites and blacks. "One of the outstanding comic novels of the [sixties]." —*The Boston Globe*

Bird at My Window, ROSA GUY

FOREWORD BY SANDRA ADELL

ISBN : 1-56689-111-6 | TRADE PAPER | $14.95

"This book was welcomed when it was first published in 1966. Its brave examination of a loving, yet painful, relationship between a Black mother and her son is even more important today."—Maya Angelou

    ALSO AVAILABLE: *My Love, My Love* or *The Peasant Girl*

    ISBN: 1-56689-131-0 | TRADE PAPER | $11.95

The Cotillion *or* One Good Bull Is Half the Herd, JOHN OLIVER KILLENS

FOREWORD BY ALEXS D. PATE

ISBN: 1-56689-119-1 | TRADE PAPER | $14.95

"The current crop of young readers will be amazed to discover Lumumba's rapping prowess that precedes hip-hop culture by some ten years. In this way, and in so many others, Killens forged an alternative style, a new way of distilling black culture, and making it resonate with fresh vigor and integrity."

—*Black Issues Book Review*

The Lakestown Rebellion, KRISTIN LATTANY

FOREWORD BY SANDRA ADELL

ISBN : 1-56689-125-6 | TRADE PAPER | $15.00

When plans for a highway threaten the heart of a black community, its citizens draw upon the tradition of the trickster to save their town. Extraordinarily relevant today, this 1978 novel takes a hard but humorous look at the politics behind "urban renewal."

Reading group guides available at coffeehousepress.org

~

Eugene B. Redmond, Poet Laureate of East St. Louis, Illinois, and Executor of the Dumas Estate, has authored or edited two dozen works of poetry, fiction, drama and literary criticism including Drumvoices: *The Mission of Afro-American Poetry* (1976). He received a National Endowment for the Arts Creative Writing Fellowship, a Pushcart Prize and an American Book Award (for *The Eye in the Ceiling: New and Selected Poems)*. Currently Redmond is Professor of English and Founding Editor of *Drumvoices Revue* at Southern Illinois University Edwardsville. In 1986 a group of East St. Louis authors established the Eugene B. Redmond Writers Club in his honor.

~